THE INSTITUTE

ALSO BY KATHERINE BRADLEY

The Sisterhood

WRITING AS KATE BRADLEY

To Keep You Safe
What I Did

KATHERINE BRADLEY
THE INSTITUTE

**SIMON &
SCHUSTER**

London · New York · Amsterdam/Antwerp · Sydney/Melbourne · Toronto · New Delhi

First published in Great Britain by Simon & Schuster UK Ltd, 2026

Copyright © Katherine Bradley, 2026

The right of Katherine Bradley to be identified as author of this work
has been asserted in accordance with the Copyright, Designs and Patents Act, 1988.

1 3 5 7 9 10 8 6 4 2

Simon & Schuster UK Ltd, 1st Floor
222 Gray's Inn Road, London WC1X 8HB

For more than 100 years, Simon & Schuster has championed authors and the stories they create. By respecting the copyright of an author's intellectual property, you enable Simon & Schuster and the author to continue publishing exceptional books for years to come. We thank you for supporting the author's copyright by purchasing an authorised edition of this book.

No amount of this book may be reproduced or stored in any format, nor may it be uploaded to any website, database, language-learning model, or other repository, retrieval, or artificial intelligence system without express permission. All rights reserved. Enquiries may be directed to Simon & Schuster, 222 Gray's Inn Road, London WC1X 8HB or RightsMailbox@simonandschuster.co.uk

Simon & Schuster Australia, Sydney
Simon & Schuster India, New Delhi

www.simonandschuster.co.uk
www.simonandschuster.com.au
www.simonandschuster.co.in

The authorised representative in the EEA is Simon & Schuster Netherlands BV, Herculesplein 96, 3584 AA Utrecht, Netherlands. info@simonandschuster.nl

Simon & Schuster strongly believes in freedom of expression and stands against censorship in all its forms. For more information, visit BooksBelong.com

A CIP catalogue record for this book is available from the British Library

Hardback ISBN: 978-1-3985-1430-0
Trade Paperback ISBN: 978-1-3985-4448-2
eBook ISBN: 978-1-3985-1431-7
Audio ISBN: 978-1-3985-2989-2

This book is a work of fiction. Names, characters, places and incidents are either a product of the author's imagination or are used fictitiously. Any resemblance to actual people living or dead, events or locales is entirely coincidental.

Typeset in Sabon by M Rules

Printed and Bound in the UK using 100% Renewable Electricity at CPI Group (UK) Ltd

For my dear dad, John.

A man defined by belief

Phase 1: egg

ONE

Will Becker scrutinized the group of twenty-somethings through the train window. Six of them stood on the station platform, waiting to board his carriage. Watching their unchecked energy, the last of his strength dimmed and his sigh steamed the glass to fog, blurring them briefly. After leaving work early with a thumping headache, he'd been looking forward to beating the commuter rush home. The carriage was near-empty and, after another row with Sales this morning about next year's projections, he wanted – no, *needed* – it to stay quiet. But as soon as the door slid open, the group's noise slammed into the silence and the brief peace he'd salvaged was gone. He shifted in his seat, jaw tightened; he pretended to stare at the data charts open on his laptop, but instead checked the group's every move.

Laughing at some continued joke, they filled the seats around him. Two of the three men-boys – one with frosted tips and another with an overgrown mullet – dumped paper bags of takeout on the tables and passed out bags of chips and packages of burgers. The smell of cooked meat plunged Will's mood to pissy.

The group were all dressed in baggy jeans or tracksuits; some had piercings and tattoos. They were all just too cool, too loud and too confident for Will's tastes. His irk continued as he watched the men-boys throw chips into their friends' mouths, yelping like sea lions, and he wondered if he shouldn't just get up and move. The train lurched out of East Croydon Station.

They reached past him with a bag of chips. They don't even see me, he thought. Was he old enough to be invisible? He looked at the young women – they wore short-cut tops and, before they'd sat down, he'd noticed slim waists above low-slung tracksuit bottoms. He might be forty-nine, but it wasn't so long ago that he knew how it felt to rest his hands on waists like theirs. Feeling sick – not just from the burger smell and the lurchy carriage as the train picked up pace – but because he knew he would never hold a waist like that again.

Chips were now on the floor. One of the three girls – The Cure T-shirt – was now jumping up and shrieking, making the boys laugh. Another, with long, wavy red hair, sat diagonally across from him. Cream skin; freckles, just a little too thin – but even so . . . she was beautiful. He tried not to watch as she plaited her hair. She listened to her friends and obediently opened her mouth so her friend could post a chip in. He didn't want to stare – goodness no, he wasn't *that* sort of man – but it was interesting to see how she sectioned her hair then flicked it into a quick weave with expert, fast fingers. Her control was mesmerizing.

The train accelerated then juddered as it almost immediately cut to half speed. An announcement over the system informed them: 'Dear passengers, we regret that, due to a technical fault, customers will be asked to disembark at the next station. This will be Gatwick Station. Customers will be able to take the next available train to continue their journey. We apologize for the inconvenience.' He liked the group a little better when Frosted Tips complained with expletives. Did nothing work properly these days? That's it, he decided, I *am* getting old.

The doors opened and this time he followed the group out onto the Gatwick Station platform. Although it was May, stormy clouds threatened rain and the wind felt bitingly brutish. Today was supposed to be hot, he thought, angry that he'd left his jacket at home. Everything seemed to be going wrong. Fiddling with his phone to open the travel app, he moved only when an announcement told the platform crowds that the next train would not be stopping at the station, warning *fast train approaching*. He shuffled obediently back from the platform's edge along with the other passengers.

And then it happened.

Afterwards, with the weak, police-issue sweet tea gripped in his cold, shaking hands, he recalled what happened. Distracted by his phone travel app, he only half-noticed the group. 'But I did notice it – notice them – and how strange they were,' he said, describing their sudden switch from noise to silence. 'They just stopped moving. Stopped speaking. They all started acting the same, not there, as if they'd had a crucial circuit severed.'

He cried, hunched over the interview-room table, the

machine recording his distress. The police were kind. But what then could be done?

They were already dead.

He wept as he described what the police already knew. How the train had raced towards the platform. How a lady had spilled the contents of her bag everywhere just as one of the group – Frosted Tips – broke away from the crowd. How Frosted Tips walked firmly towards the edge of platform. How the girl with The Cure T-shirt was already following him. How she didn't react as he'd stepped – without pause – off the platform edge and onto the track. How she'd continued to follow him and also dropped out of sight. How she'd made a noise (*humph*) as she hit the rails below. How the rest of their group had followed in the same focused way. 'Like dead-eyed lemmings,' he'd said later in his statement, 'one jumped and then they all did. All jumped in less than five seconds, *bam-bam-bam-bam* – they just kept jumping.' He remembered the shove of people around him as they realized what was happening – someone screaming, someone else repeatedly saying *fuck, fuck, fuck.*

How the not-stopping train continued to approach with alarming speed. How the train driver had sounded the horn. Hearing the screeching of brakes, seeing the driver – eyes and mouth echoing Munch's *The Scream*. How Will's statis had finally broken: there was still one of the teenagers left on the platform.

One.

He ran for the girl with the long wavy red hair, reaching her just centimetres from the platform's edge. The plait he'd seen her twist together hung behind her like a rope.

He grabbed it and held on. Her neck snapped back. He held on. She tugged against it, and he grabbed her shoulder, as she pulled her hair free. She pulled again against his grip ('Strong!' he told the police. 'She was so strong!') and he knew in that moment he couldn't hold her. The idea of her slipping from him was so clear it was as if he could see it happen. But then he had help – another man came and held her too. Still, she fought them – not in a violent way, he told the police, more like a train that keeps moving with a steady tenacity. Then he'd understood the ridiculousness of his comparison and had been sick in the police station loo.

After the other man had joined them, the train guard had arrived and the three of them had held the girl as the train ploughed through the station in a squeal of brakes, the sound of metal on metal – and then another noise that he didn't want to think about. No one had cried out. No hand had reached for help.

The police had asked if he knew who the other man was who helped him save the girl's life – they wanted to contact him for their inquiries. 'No,' Will confirmed. 'He was right there, moving to save her at the same time as me, but he was slowed down by a woman who spilled her bag, so I reached her first.'

'He didn't give you his name?'

Will had shaken his head. 'And by the time you guys arrived, he was gone. But I'd know him anywhere – he had the bluest eyes I've ever seen. He deserves a medal – without him I wouldn't have been able to save the girl with red hair.'

Sarah D. Ford@FordonTour
19 Mar 202—

Freaky footage! Watch these adults jumping from the #GrandCanyon rim. All now dead. I saw this happen. Massive cover-up. Not in mainstream media or news. Why not? This is not faked!!! Retweet to raise awareness #GovermentCover-up #AlienTechnology #GermWarfare #AmericanHorror #RealZombies.

Disturbing content advised.
The following media includes potentially sensitive content   **Change** | **Settings** | **View**

Phase 2: embryo

TWO

Billie twisted her long red hair, before pressing her palms flat against the worn leather chair. She struggled to breathe. *Keep calm*, she urged herself against her raw-edged panic. Knowing this doctor was about to explain why she was here – on a hospital ward which she had no memory of arriving at – meant he had her full attention. She watched Dr Singh ease into his seat opposite her, then smooth his crumpled open-necked shirt.

He saw her watching him. 'My wife, Prisha, always complains I'm so scruffy,' he said, his smile deepening the lines around his eyes.

She didn't care, but feigned a brief smile, muscle-memory politeness. Billie's headache was back. She'd woken with it, not unlike the worst hangover she'd ever had, as if her whole brain was on fire. Her head hurt – a deep, whole-brain, raging ache – but she shut her eyes momentarily against it now. She wouldn't mention it. She didn't want to admit any weakness, any illness: she wanted to appear in perfect health – she just wanted to get out. 'Where am I? Where's my phone? And my mum?'

'Your phone, I don't know. Your mum has been in, left you some things and will be back later for visiting. Where you are is Eastleigh Psychiatric Hospital.'

Billie looked at his kind, unwavering eyes. She repeated it back to him, shocked, and he confirmed it.

'A psychiatric hospital?' she checked again. She had no idea. She had been woken by a nurse with breakfast, who answered her questions with a repeated 'You need to speak to the doctor', showered in the ensuite bathroom before being escorted straight to this office. 'That can't be ... true.'

He nodded gently and told her that she'd suffered a psychotic episode, had been sedated and admitted overnight.

She shook her head and for a long minute didn't say anything. Then: 'There's been a mistake. You see, I've stayed on a mental health unit before, and so I know I have no mental health problems now – haven't for eight long years. Hopefully you can see I am fine?'

He opened a notepad and took out his pen. 'In your own words, why were you hospitalized before?'

She decided it was better to co-operate. 'When I was sixteen, my dad died suddenly in a car accident. I suffered depression, then paranoia, and I needed some help to sort that out.' She lifted her chin a little. 'I shouldn't be here – I know how to take care of myself. I eat well, sleep well, don't do drugs, and I use the techniques I was taught. I'm well. Perhaps I was spiked?'

'All of you?'

She shrugged. 'Perhaps it was in our takeaway.'

He wrote in his notebook. 'Could you tell me what sort of techniques?'

'CBT for anxiety. I've learned not to listen to fear if I'm safe.' She glanced at him writing, then at the door, wondering if she was free to leave. A glass window looked out onto the corridor – could she just go? She wanted to ask, but didn't want to hear the answer in case... She bit her lip, knowing the possibilities. 'There's been a mistake.'

He sighed and put down his pen. 'Do you remember what happened to you?'

'Yes, I ...' What *was* the last thing she remembered? She found she didn't know – couldn't even remember this morning, yesterday – nothing. It was a blank.

'Do you remember being at Gatwick train station?'

She could remember the smell of Gez's raspberry vape and Ella's perfume. Chips. A grumpy passenger with a laptop. The sound of an announcement: *fast train approaching...*

When she didn't reply, Dr Singh took a deep breath. 'Billie, I'm sorry to tell you, but you've been part of a disturbing event,' he started. 'I'd like you to brace yourself for, sadly, I must give you some very tragic news about your friends.' And then, Veer Singh, as gently as he could, told her what had happened.

'Please, Wilhelmina – Billie – please sit down.' Dr Veer Singh stayed seated, opening his palms in a gesture that asked her to be reasonable.

Billie decided she had no intention of being reasonable. She refused to stay in his office, or on Warwick ward, or in any part of Eastleigh Psychiatric Hospital. Instead of listening to his lies, she stormed out. The corridor stank of pine disinfectant and gravy, a combination that rolled her stomach, as she followed the sign to the exit.

Gotta get out; gotta get out. Billie almost ran.

'We think you were part of a group suicide event,' he'd said.

No. Not true. Not true. Gez and everyone ... They just wouldn't – we wouldn't – do that. I wouldn't. She thrust her hands into the pockets of her tracksuit bottoms (she'd had to remove the tags this morning – an emergency purchase by her mother?) and followed the turning towards the exit. Her heart smashed against her ribs. Had Dr Singh hit an emergency button? Would they try and stop her?

Another turn and she was there. Directly in front of her were the double doors, clearly marked EXIT. Next to the exit was the obstacle she'd feared would be there: the nurses' station. A high desk, with four nurses working on computers behind it. And adjacent to that, an open-plan residents' lounge.

Billie didn't falter. I'm free to leave, she thought, digging deep. I have rights. She kept going, hand ready to push against the door (it'll be locked – what if it's locked?). She saw the black CCTV bulb.

NO TAILGATING.

VISITORS MUST SIGN OUT.

THIS DOOR IS SECURE – SEE STAFF AT RECEPTION BEFORE EXIT.

She swallowed against the dryness of her throat and pushed against the door anyway. It didn't move and a nurse looked up from behind the desk. 'Are you okay, Billie?'

They know who I am, she thought, telling them she needed to leave. 'Buzz me out, please,' she added.

The nurse shook her head, 'I'm sorry. I'm afraid the doctor needs to agree.'

Billie shook her head, feeling the burn of her headache again. She shook against it, feeling a tug of something – some desire to ... to ... she reached to understand, but she wasn't sure. It was a peculiar feeling – new, different. *Strange.*

But then the moment passed; she needed to get out and needed to focus. She pushed against the door again. 'There's nothing wrong with me. You can't keep me here against my will.'

The nurse came round the desk, hands held open just like Dr Singh's. She spoke in calming tones but nothing she said suggested Billie could walk free.

Billie felt panic seize her: the nurse's kind words washed over her, trite and meaningless. She was locked in, and they had no intention of letting her out. They wanted her to calm down, but how could she when she couldn't think straight – *because her head blazed with Mars's raging fires* – because they'd locked her up and lied to her about her friends? There was no way they were dead – just *no way.* 'I need to contact my friends. My mum. I've done nothing wrong – there's been a mistake. I want my phone back.' When the words started again, with assurances they did not have her phone, they could not give her her freedom but could give her *tea and biscuits*, her breathing increased to short, shallow breaths. 'Please, *open* it, or – or I'll call the police.' She heard the desperation and fear in her voice.

The nurse continued talking, saying soothing things that meant they wouldn't listen.

She couldn't think past the heat, past the confusion, past the very wrongness of everything around her. 'Let me leave!'

A scream came from Billie's right, then someone shouting, 'They won't let you leave! It doesn't matter what you say, you're stuck in here, just like us!'

She turned towards the direction of the shriek. The resident's lounge. There were high-backed chairs and a thick Perspex cover across the TV screen. A few people sat there, some dressed in pyjamas, some tracksuits. Some stared blankly ahead or dozed, but an older woman leaned forward, eyes locked on Billie. 'You'll never get out!' she repeated, jabbing a finger at her. 'You'll never convince them!'

Billie's panic rose higher; crows rising at the sound of gunshot. She rattled the door and kicked it. 'You can't keep me here. I've done nothing wrong. I've—'

'None of us have done anything wrong! But we're still locked in! You'll never get out!' the old woman screamed at her.

A nurse crossed to the woman and spoke with her.

Billie's mind became blurred. She started kicking at the door, frightened and furious. Not being able to think clearly because of her headache. Someone else started shouting, but she didn't care. 'Throw the chair! Throw the chair!' the woman screamed again.

The nurses didn't try and stop her from kicking the door, instead they offered her a cup of tea; their reasonableness, keenness to de-escalate, just made her feel more trapped – they expected this. She thought of Ella: she had to get to her. She had to see her and Gez and the others to make sure it wasn't just some horrible lie. She thought of the train …

the sound of train wheels on metal and then not on metal but on ... but on ...

You could smell the blood, smell the blood ...

All dead; all dead; all dead. The tattoo beat in her head like train wheels on a track. Billie picked up a chair and threw it at the door. Dr Singh had appeared, telling her to breathe, offering her a sedative. Then because they were all just so reasonable and relaxed, she picked up another one and threw it at the nurses' station.

Then things changed. Against the backdrop of the old woman clapping and cheering, the staff seem to multiply, and she was held, by many in blue uniforms with gloved hands – not rough, but strong – holding her down.

Dr Singh asked for 'Midazolam 5mg' and then Billie felt a cold incision of fear: they were going to drug her too. She swore and screamed, telling them they were not going to drug her – not that as well as lie to her that all her friends were dead, which was not true, not true (but she could smell the blood) – and even as she struggled, she was held even tighter while they put a needle in her backside.

And then everything did feel better. The crows circled and returned to the tree, their chatter calmed.

And Billie breathed out.

THREE

From: Kay.Newton@soundnews.org.uk
to: Dan.Downes@soundnews.org.uk
15 May
re: Gatwick Airport train station deaths (May) URGENT

Dan, I'm just not going to say this again, but I heard from Jerry you still want to run the story on the dead kids at GA, despite my direct instruction. Just to reiterate: you *do not* have editorial agreement.
Sorry to be hard-arsed on this but I've heard your points and they're not enough. The guidance needs to be followed, and you cannot report on the location, nor the ages, nor the fact they were a group. We've been refused access to the CCTV footage. We cannot give 'undue prominence' to this lest it's deemed as sensationalist. Therefore, you have *no* story.
    I'm refusing to sign this off to protect you and the paper. This is clearly either a dare gone wrong, drugs or a group suicide and it doesn't matter which way you turn it, reporting on this could lead to more

THE INSTITUTE

vulnerable young people killing themselves. You know if another kid jumps off a platform, we'll get the blame. I suggest you get your head out of the online murk and get back into the real world – pronto.

Kay

FOUR

Billie woke to the sound of tapping on glass. For a moment, she lay in the dark, knowing something was incredibly – horrifyingly – wrong. The light was wrong (falling under the door from an overbright corridor), the smell was wrong (pine disinfectant), but she knew there was something worse – so much worse.

Then Billie remembered.

For a moment, she just lay, trying to catch her breath under the weight of sorrow that lay like a heavy pall. Could it be true that Ella and Fin and Vena and Gez and Leo *were all dead*? As she worked her lungs against what felt like constriction, she even forgot the noise that had woken her. It seemed impossible.

Impossible.

Billie inhaled a shaky deep breath. Blinking into the dark, she tried to make sense of it. She loved them all. Leo with his crazy giggle. Gez with his bad jokes. Fin with his love of trainers and comics – knowing everything about the world of superheroes. Vena – forgetful, funny Vena. But it was Ella, her best friend, that hurt the most. How could Ella be so alive and now just be ... gone? Everything about her friend was too vivid, too vibrant to be extinguished. Billie remembered the way she'd press the bridge of her nose when she was thinking hard, how she never stopped moving or thinking or talking or singing – even writing poetry in the margins of her notebook during boring lectures. It couldn't be true. There had to be some other—

Tap. Tap. Tap-tap. The noise again that she realized had woken her. Her eyes focused in the dark.

Now fully awake.

Aware.

She held her breath, ears straining to hear it again. The bar of light visible under the door was undisturbed – no one was outside in the corridor.

Tap. Tap. Tap-tap – it came from behind her head, from the window. For a moment, Billie lay unsure, moving from half-awake to careful.

Someone was at the window. Someone wanted to be let in.

Billie slid her legs out of bed, bare feet pressed against the cool lino, waking her fully. She pulled back the curtain. A man stood ten metres back, up-lit by the low lighting outside. His face was all angles and shadows in the light, but he had a smile that suggested he wanted to show he was friendly and he held a white cardboard sign.

She gasped and dropped the curtain. A beat passed, and then, curious, she lifted it again. He mouthed *sorry* at her and pointed at the words on the sign:

MY NAME IS DAN DOWNES. I AM A JOURNALIST. I HAVE <u>INFORMATION ABOUT THE GATWICK TRAIN DEATHS</u>. CAN WE TALK?

Biting her lip, she paused. A journalist. What did he know? She needed someone to give her the answers everyone thought she had. She lifted the modern sash window – it stopped after opening two inches. She whispered through the gap, 'Who are you?'

In the glow of the light, she could see he was in his early forties, attractive, with stubble and a deep chin cleft. Too old for her but Ella would love— The memory that Ella was dead was a punch to the sternum.

'Hi, Billie, I'm Dan. I'm an investigative journalist. I've spoken to someone who saw what happened at Gatwick Station. Can I step closer to the window? Can I talk through the gap? I can show you some ID first, so you know I'm not some weirdo.' After she nodded, he pressed an identity card up against the glass. 'Do you remember what happened to you?'

She shook her head. 'But they told me ... I don't know if it's true.' And then she told him what Dr Singh had told her. She wanted him to say that it was wrong. That her friends were alive. That she was the victim of an elaborate prank. But he didn't.

'I think the truth is that something bad has happened to you and your friends; I've seen footage of similar things. You are not the first to group self-destroy.'

'Self-destroy? You mean kill ourselves?'

He nodded. For a moment they just looked at each other, faces cast in white light and shadows. The outside air felt fresh, clean; the sound of rain falling made her want to leave the ward with its synthetic smells and strange noises even more. Billie inhaled a deep, drowning breath at the night air and had never felt more like a prisoner.

THE INSTITUTE

'I think you and your friends deserve for people to know the truth. List me as a visitor for tomorrow morning – say I'm your cousin to make sure I get in. My name and number are on this card.' He passed it through the gap. 'There is something I think you need to see. Something that will help you understand the truth.'

FIVE

It was visiting time; Billie sat in the patient lounge waiting for the journalist to arrive. She grieved the absence of her phone – she wanted to message her friends; check their socials for evidence that there had been a terrible mistake; even just look at photos of them. Her hands felt empty, her head too; she needed the diversion of TikTok, Instagram and the ability to interrogate ChatGPT about her rights. And she also longed for her AirPods; she would kill for music to help block out her surroundings. From under the shelter of her trackie hood, she gazed around and wondered how her life had so quickly changed. In one corner stood the TV; even the sofas, she noticed, were screwed to the floor. A man in pyjamas rocked on a dining chair in an agitated state, rubbing his grey, unshaven chin, intermittently shouting blurred imperatives. Three elderly women sat in high-backed chairs against the wall, all mute and seemingly staring into nothing. In the far corner, a very thin and pale young woman sat reading a book.

Everything about life on the ward reminded her how much her life had changed in the space of ten minutes. The smells – always gravy; disinfectant; urine – and the sounds – screaming; crying and then silence – felt overwhelming and repellent. The staff were lovely, she thought, all friendly, professional and unfailingly kind. But there was a tinfoil centre to that kindness – to test it might be unpleasant.

At visiting time, Dan was buzzed onto the ward. He sat opposite her. 'How are you, Billie?' He reached in his bag and put on the table a six-pack of Pepsi and a family bar of chocolate. 'I also got you these,' he said, passing her a bunch of yellow roses. 'I should have asked you what you wanted, I'm sorry.'

Billie took the flowers and inhaled, eyes shut. 'I like all of these, thank you. I appreciate you coming to see me.'

'You obviously didn't have any trouble adding me as your visitor?'

'They probably didn't want me to flip out again. How did you find me?'

'After the incident at Gatwick Station, you were taken to the nearest mental health emergency unit – easy to find. Then, I waited by the bins – all glamour, this job – and eventually, a cleaner came to throw rubbish out; for two hundred quid he agreed to point out your room.'

'You make it sound easy.'

He shrugged as if it were straightforward. 'It's my job.'

'You said you knew of others that ... did you say self-destroy?'

'I did.' He studied her face. 'Billie, are you *sure* you want to hear what I know? Because, after hearing what I've got to say, you might have found it easier to think you and your friends just had a funny five minutes and made a bad decision.'

She felt the heat of her cheeks and put the flowers down.

'We did not have a "funny five minutes". I think we were spiked. It's the only explanation.'

He put out a placatory hand, resting it briefly on her arm. 'Trust me, I am not making light of your situation – it's just if I tell you, it goes from inexplicable tragedy to a very weird, complex and definitely sinister situation. I wouldn't judge you if inexplicable tragedy was difficult enough. But what about your mother – is she coming to see you today?'

'I asked her to come this evening instead; I didn't want her walking in and saying I don't have a cousin.'

He nodded. 'Good. Ask her to tell them to give you a tox screen – you're right to want being poisoned ruled out.'

'But you don't think that's it?' She thought of Ella and met his gaze head on. 'Whatever it is, I want to know the truth.'

He checked over his shoulder, then pulled out his phone. 'What happened to you and your friends wasn't the first time. I have footage of similar incidences happening elsewhere in the world. I want you to know what happened to you wasn't unique.'

'Do you have any footage of what happened to me and my friends? Did anyone film it?'

'There's CCTV. I've seen it – I bribed my way to having a quick view of it, but I don't have a copy to show you.'

Billie was silent for a moment, thinking. 'Is it similar to the footage you've got?'

'Yes, in that it's very upsetting, sudden and strange. I can tell you I saw enough to know that there are real similarities. I didn't come here to add to your trauma, but to lessen it – to let you know that you're not alone.'

'Can I see footage of what you do have? Where was it taken?' She glanced around for staff.

'I have two. The first was taken in India, six months ago. *If* you watch it you see a group of both men and women jumping off the Bhupen Hazarika bridge. You'll see them walking down a busy pedestrian-edged bridge and then suddenly a group of them jump into the river. You *don't* have to watch it. You'll learn nothing extra than what I've just told you.'

'Do they die?'

'Yes. After they jump, a car stops and then another car hits the car, and that's when it's cut. But it's not how it was reported in the media. They said the group jumped into the river to escape the car pile-up – but the truth is that the traffic accident happened *after* they jumped. In other words, the group's actions *caused* the accident, not the other way round. The drivers saw them jump and that's what caused them to crash. But the weird thing is that there was no discernible reason for them to jump. Their family and friends were interviewed: none of them had ever presented as or said they were suicidal. And even weirder, the people involved had no relationship with each other. One minute they're just pedestrians, then – all, in unison – they take a sharp detour from real life and self-destroy. Seven jumped. All died. And a further three people were killed in the resulting car crash.'

She covered her face with her hands. 'My friends – and me – we didn't want to die either.' Then, with a deep breath, she looked up. 'Where did you get the footage?'

'It started on social media and then got taken down. I got a copy before it was removed and then tracked the source. It was an Italian woman, about your age, who was travelling with a friend. I've spoken to her directly. Significantly, this video, and what she says, contradicts the official account of the pedestrian deaths.'

'Why?'

'Because they couldn't make sense of it? Because it made more sense that people jumped into the river to get *away* from a dangerous situation? Because people don't kill themselves in the same way, at the same time, without communication and for no apparent reason?' He shook his head a little. 'Sometimes,' he sighed, 'people would rather opt for the version of events that makes easier sense than the facts.'

She looked at him and blinked. 'I want to see the video now.'

He nodded, found the footage and passed the phone to her.

Wordlessly, she watched, and it was just as he described. Her throat closed as she struggled to choke back tears, but staff were ever-present at the desk or moving around the ward and she was determined not to give anything away.

She replayed the video again and again, watching each person, how they moved, how something suddenly changed, how one minute they were individuals and then, the next, as if someone had flipped a switch, they became united, moving in a strange, exact way – like choreographed zombies, turning as a group towards the side of the bridge, walking as a pack towards it, then one by one jumping from the edge.

After she'd watched it five times, Dan reached out and closed his hand gently over his phone. 'I think that's enough.'

She let him take it. 'Thank you. It helped me to understand.' She wanted to cry, but lifted her chin instead, remembering that everywhere there were eyes. Eyes and judgement. 'You said this had happened elsewhere. Is there a video of that, too?'

'Yes, but I don't think you should watch it. It's a ... tougher view.'

'Why?'

'The footage is taken from the bottom of the valley looking up to the Grand Canyon Southern Rim. You can see the faces of one of the five jumpers. It's eerie because of what you *don't* see. No emotion. No reaction. It's like a switch has been flicked and he's already gone.'

'Why wasn't there an investigation?'

'There was, but not much of one. The coroner ruled the edge must have collapsed. People die falling into the canyon every year. Fifteen died there last year. The formation is nearly three hundred miles long – that's a big area for people to miss their footing.'

'So that's it? Lots of people fall and no one thinks anything other than,' she shrugged, 'there's no fence?'

'Apart from a few very distant witnesses, there was a man who tried to save a woman – put up quite a fight to save her, apparently – but he couldn't. He gave a statement to the police at the time, but I'm still trying to trace him. I picked up the report from the adult daughter of one of the couples – she was angry and said that her parents were experienced hikers, would've never gone near the edge. She's adamant they weren't suicidal, and states that they had never been happier having just started a lifelong ambition of touring the country in a motorhome. She acquired the video from the person who took it and then posted the video under a hashtag of "cover-up". That's how she felt their deaths were treated.'

'Cover-up? By whom?'

'I don't know – yet. Billie, I don't want you to see the next video. You're an adult, you deserve to know the truth, but my advice is not to see it.'

'I want to.'

Somewhere, a clock ticked audibly. The conversation behind her became heated and then cooled. Shared laughter could be heard between a visitor and a patient to her right. A clatter echoed up the ward and elsewhere a door slammed shut six, seven, eight times.

Somewhere on the ward, screaming started again, and shouting this time too. An alarm sounded, flashing a light above the nurses' station and the staff suddenly ran in the direction of the noise.

'Now,' she said. 'They're distracted. Quick. Please – I have to see. To understand.' When he didn't react, 'Look at where I am? Being here is another death.'

He glanced around, decision made. He pulled out AirPods. 'Quick, then. For this you'll need these.'

Shot from below, the rim of the Grand Canyon could be seen. Off screen was the sound of loud shouting from several people. Someone said: 'I don't believe it! Someone just fucking jumped off the top of the canyon!' The camera moved down and then at the sound of more shouting and screaming, it abruptly moved back up again: 'There's another one! Someone else has jumped! Fuck! *Fuck!* And another one!' (Screaming.) 'And another one! Why are they all jumping? What's happening? What the fuck is happening?'

The image zoomed in on the face of a man as he fell. His face was blank. His features were disturbed by the pressure of the wind on his face, but for a brief moment, the focus was clear: his eyes were empty.

Billie rewound and watched again; in the emptiness of his eyes lay the answer to what had happened to her.

When the nurse appeared next to her, clearing his throat, she barely even registered him.

Dan reached for the phone – but just too slow. Instead, the nurse grabbed the phone from her before either she or Dan had the chance to react. 'Can I ask you what you're watching here?' he asked them both. The nurse's name badge said: *Hassan*.

Hassan continued. 'I'll be honest, it doesn't look suitable for Warwick ward.' Before either Billie or Dan spoke, he pressed go on the phone and saw only a few seconds of footage before he pressed stop.

He spoke to Dan first. 'Did you know we don't allow this sort of thing on the ward? This is a secure environment dedicated to the mental safety of our patients.'

'Sorry, sorry,' said Dan, reaching for his phone.

Hassan hesitated.

'It's my phone. You don't have jurisdiction over me.'

'Coming onto *our* secure psych ward as a *guest* and showing suicide videos to vulnerable patients who have suicidal ideation? And you want to argue *jurisdiction*?'

He called over to the nurses' station. 'Isabella, can we get some help over here, please, with this visitor?'

'Please!' interjected Billie, standing up. 'Dan is trying to help me. He's trying to find out what happened to me.'

A young woman with kind, dark eyes joined them.

She spoke, holding out her hand to Dan and Billie. Her handshake was firm, her gaze direct. 'My name is Isabella Hamilton and I'm the junior psychiatrist on duty. How can I help?'

Billie spoke to her. She liked her smile, the intent way she had of listening. 'Please, Doctor, my friend is trying to help me.'

Hassan showed her Dan's phone. 'This is not help.'

'Do you mind if I see what the issue is?' Isabella asked.

Dan shrugged; he minded, but the doctor had pressed go anyway and was watching it. After less than a minute, she paused it and sighed. 'You can see why we are concerned?'

Dan tried his best to explain, but he could see in her face that he was going to have to leave. He'd started to explain it to Billie when Veer Singh joined them.

'Can I help at all?' asked Veer Singh.

'Nothing to help, thank you,' Dan said.

'We need him to leave,' said Hassan.

'I am leaving. I just want my phone.'

Isabella handed it back to Dan and Hassan placed his hand behind Dan's back. 'Come on, mate, please do the right thing.' He started to lead Dan out.

Dan broke away and pressed his cheek almost to Billie's as he whispered, 'I'm sorry. You have my number – call me if you need to.'

And then he turned and left, and Billie was alone in the psych ward, with its smells of gravy and disinfectant, and the staff who now turned their attention to her.

THE INSTITUTE

EXTRACT OF REPORT MARCH 202—

... with two distinct stages or 'waves'. The two waves of contamination are summarized below. For full medical analysis, for first-wave contamination, refer to Appendix 4. For full medical analysis, for second-wave contamination, refer to Appendix 5.

First-Wave Contamination summary:
The first wave follows once contact occurs between the primary human(s) and the contaminant. Once it enters into the respiratory tract, it is absorbed into the bloodstream and is distributed throughout the body, resulting in neurodevelopmental changes within the brain. Presentation once contact has been made shows observable changes within 19–73 seconds. Typicality includes catatonic behaviour (lay observations commonly report as 'zombified actions'). Once absorption is complete, the neurological change is currently considered permanent. This is based on four cases observed to date. Further study is required, but an extremely high level of caution is urged (please see Appendix 17 for risk management information).

The first wave presents an acute change that, without exception, appears to provoke self-termination in the primary recipients. Reason is unknown. Current considerations are cognitive overload caused by the abrupt and significant neurogenesis within the primary brain. Further analysis is required to understand structural changes at the point of contamination, the extent of the resultant neuro plasticity, if it's an equi-experience or if there is dux gregis during the first wave. This consideration is considered a priority and requires MRI and further structural and biochemical change analysis. Moreover ...

SIX

'I don't want to ask difficult questions, Billie,' Jo Cathey said, smoothing the part of her daughter's hair she could reach despite the trackie hood. 'So, I won't. I will just gently say that the ward manager asked to speak with me. She said your cousin came in and upset you by showing you suicide videos on his phone. I didn't tell them you don't have a cousin.'

Jo Cathey was a small, neat woman, who after years of being a primary school teacher had retired when her husband had died. She wore her dark curly hair to shoulder-length, and unlike her daughter, was always calm and patient. 'So, I won't interfere, but forgive me this one question: are you in some sort of trouble?'

'He's a journalist. But I don't want to talk about it.' Billie's headache was so bad, she could barely focus. She'd asked for and been given some paracetamol but if they had worked at all, she couldn't tell. It had got worse after a furious row with the staff about her friends' funerals. She wanted to know the details, wanted to attend. 'No,' Dr Singh had told her gently, 'you cannot leave Warwick ward. Not even for a funeral.'

That was the worst moment of her life, she knew.

To feel that powerless, that amount of uncontrolled grief and anger and shock, was so overwhelming, so shitty, she just wanted to sleep or die.

And now her mother was here, wringing her hands, trying not to say the wrong thing about Billie sitting unwashed in her hoodie pulled over pyjamas. 'A journalist? Oh! That's terrible, that's—'

'Please: just leave it.'

Jo bit her lip and thought for a few moments. 'Okay, maybe another time then. Do you want to hear about something else? I'm not sure I should mention it ... but I think, darling, you would want to know. I've had a rather ... strange request.'

When Billie continued to keep her head in her hands, Jo tried again. 'The ward manager here, told me she'd had a request for contact from a private facility. This institute wanted to speak to me about you – about your care.'

'I don't know what you're talking about.'

'Billie, please try to focus. This is important. I've been contacted by a private medical company about *you*. The ward manager forwarded me their enquiry email, which said little, but when I replied, they sent me back lots of details about their clinic. They are offering you a free place at their institute. They've put it all in writing, and said I should show you their offer, and see what you think. It seems a lovely place.' She looked around the ward, her eyes seeming to linger on the elderly woman sitting in a wingback, with her fixed stare and slack, wet mouth, after her early-morning ECT.

'I spoke with a nice doctor,' Jo continued. 'She said they

were a private brain research facility, primarily concerned with finding a cure for dementia, but yours was a special case they think they can help with.'

'How do they know about me? It's not in the news, is it?'

'No darling. I asked them and they were very vague. It seemed to be a case of knowing someone, who knows someone else, who knows someone else.'

'Who is talking about me?'

'We could ask them that. That would be a good question. They're prepared to cover all costs. She says because they're licensed, you'll be able to transfer even though you have been sectioned. I suppose if they take a few – no offence, darling – charity cases then they can write it off against their taxes. The pictures certainly look very nice. Anyway, I said I'd ask you.' Jo took her daughter's hands. 'It's up to you, darling. It's in Scotland. Pretty area, the West Coast. I went there with your dad before you were born.'

Billie could barely think against the grey wall of pain. 'Can I have a look?' The screamer had started up again and the sound felt like it was flaying her brain tissue with a rusty spoon. Billie read the email three times on her mother's phone. The last time, she looked up at her mother: 'This is amazing – but surely it's too good to be true?'

If Jo answered, she didn't hear her, because she'd started flicking through the images on the website. With each slide to the left, the pain in her head seemed to ease. An indoor pool with jacuzzi and sauna; an outdoors wild swimming pond with a second sauna – and an outdoors infinity swimming pool. Then the library, the gym and gorgeous grounds surrounded by woodland – it was like a spa-dream come true.

Within fifteen minutes, headache eased, Billie had taken her hood down and had used Jo's phone to reply to the email and together they went to speak with the ward manager.

Phase 3: hatchling

SEVEN

'It's very, *very* weird, isn't it? I was right to show you before I went home, wasn't I?' asked staff nurse Nick Lewes, as he stared at the CCTV screen with Dr Veer Singh. He'd grabbed Veer as he arrived for the morning shift, taking him to one side before he'd even taken his coat off. Nick had just finished his night shift and whispered there was something he *had* to show him before the handover meeting at 8 a.m., and '*it has to be just you – on your own,*' and it had to be '*now*'.

Veer had followed him into the ward's security room and watched the footage in silence.

'Yes, you're right to show me,' Veer said afterwards. He patted his colleague's arm. 'And yes, weird it certainly is.'

'It's just the strangest thing ...' muttered Nick, this time to himself. He rubbed his sweaty hands on his loose blue uniform again. 'I'm a big Black guy; handy too, and after working on a locked psych ward for thirty years, I can tell you not much scares me.' He wiped his top lip. 'But this though – *this*! I don't like it – not one bit.'

Although it was early and Veer had just started work, he now felt so tired he just wanted to go home. He ran his hand over his face before admitting, 'I can't make head nor tail of it. Run the footage again, will you, Nick?'

Nick, rewound the ward CCTV to the middle of the night.

'They were so strange,' Nick said, repeating himself again. 'All of them were like some kind of slow-moving zombies. That sounds stupid, I know, but you've seen it now.'

Veer didn't disagree with him – but it was more than that. Hadn't he seen something identical when watching the train station CCTV footage of Billie's suicide attempt? He'd been allowed on request, to view it, as Billie's psychiatrist. Hadn't she and her friends all acted with the same shared, strangely co-ordinated group psychosis? Then, he'd dismissed what his own eyes had told him. He thought perhaps it was some kind of tech glitch, or it was a staged joke between the group – one that went wrong; or even a visual misinterpretation enabled by the camera angle and the crowds around them. Deciding then that he didn't have all the facts, he'd returned to the ward and moved on, the melee of life on a demanding and under-resourced psych ward always so absorbing.

I made the mistake, he thought, of allowing preconceptions of known behaviour to impair my critical thinking.

But now the same thing seemed to have happened again – *no, not quite*, he corrected himself – not *quite* the same. No one here had tried to kill themselves. In that respect, it was very different. The figures on screen stood in the ward's dark, empty corridor in the dead of night and there were no rushed actions, no attempt to self-harm.

But many things *were* similar. Billie was involved with both groups. Both groups moved as one – in unified movements. Needing to understand, Veer opened the small notebook he always carried in his breast pocket of his white coat; he found it easier to think when he recorded facts. The clock and date showed the CCTV footage was from last night at 1.01 a.m. The lights were low; the black-and-white image of the empty corridor might have seemed eerie to some – but not to Veer, who had worked on Warwick ward for twenty years and thought he'd seen it all.

But perhaps he was wrong. He'd received a follow-up email from Dan Downes, the man who'd visited Billie on the ward. It said little, other than admitting he wasn't Billie's cousin and instead reintroducing himself as an award-winning investigative journalist who was looking at the issue that had affected Billie. From a personal email address, Dan asked that Veer reach out if he wanted further information about similar events globally – which suggested the phenomenon had been seen in other countries. Veer had ignored it, thinking the journalist was being sensationalist and not to be trusted, but now he wasn't sure.

Now, he could feel the weight of Nick's stare; Veer was always the person with the final clinical say and he knew Nick wanted to know what his judgement was. 'Run it in slo-mo this time, Nick. And can we get another camera on screen too?'

Nick hit a few buttons, and the screen split into two, showing the corridor from both directions. 'Sorry, should have done it like this first time. You'll see everything much clearly now.'

At 1.01 the first door opened: Billie stepped out of her bedroom. She stood in the middle of the corridor, not moving, just standing still. Her eyes were open, Veer noted.

Then, at 1.04 the door nearest Billie opened and a man instantly recognizable to Veer as Raymond Tate, six foot five and fifty-eight years old, with a long history of paranoid schizophrenia, appeared. Although completely naked, Billie didn't turn to look at him, nor, Veer noted, did Raymond try to speak to her. Instead, he stood directly behind her with a gap of two metres between them, mirroring her stance: arms down, legs together – not with a military smartness, but with a relaxed casualness.

Veer knew from having just seen it that other patients would continue to come out and join this strange group.

Wanting to make sense of it, Veer continued to write down the times and sequence of events when the next door opens. At 1.06, the third patient left their room and joined the silent line. An elderly woman, Marjorie Briggs, was a regular to the ward, admitted every two years when her chronic depression became so acute she needed a dose of bilateral ECT. Normally frail, Veer watched her walk easily out of her door and take her place in the bizarre line. Seemingly not noticing the people standing one in front of the other or that the one in front of her is a naked man, Marjorie didn't show a flicker of emotion.

'She normally uses a frame,' Nick said, 'but look at her there. She stands upright. She walks confidently. Why the change?'

'It's odd, I agree.'

Then at 1.08, another patient, Marjorie's card-playing friend, Elsie Burham, came out of her room. Elsie, eighty-one, with a borderline personality disorder, also stood in line. Normally, she presented with a stoop, but in the footage, she was straight spine and shoulders back. Disturbingly, her nightgown was caught in her pants, exposing both them and the back of her legs, but this wasn't noticed by anyone other than those watching the CCTV.

These patients occupy the rooms to either side of Billie's and directly opposite hers. A coincidence? Veer decided that he didn't believe in coincidences.

'Now you'll see me,' muttered Nick. He walked into view, stopping abruptly, to face the patients. The camera showed his mouth moving, but the words used were not detectable.

'What did you say to them?'

'I asked them what they were doing and then when they didn't answer, I asked them again, but then I realized they had that vague dreamlike appearance like someone sleepwalking. You ever seen that? My son used to sleepwalk when he was a kid and we found him standing in an empty bath; one time he took out the rubbish. Used to freak my wife out and I don't blame her. He was there ... but not there. Zombie-sleeper, we called him. But ... here, this bit's the weird shit.' He dragged his hand across his top lip to clear it of sweat. 'This I don't want to see again.' He stopped talking and they both watched the recording in silence.

In unison, they all took a step forward with their right foot and then – still in perfect formation – took a step forward with their left. It wasn't like soldiers marching – the gait was easy and relaxed. It was as if Billie was just walking, and they were copying her. But it was the perfectness:

as if choreographed down to each muscle movement. They advanced on Nick. 'That scared me – all coming at me like that. And since when do people sleepwalk like they have one mind?'

It was clear what Nick-last-night said next as he mouthed the words: *Get back to your rooms*. He then repeated it again. Veer noticed what he'd missed previously: Nick had taken a step back. Nick never walked away from conflict – never. He was the solid, immoveable wall that could be relied on.

'I was freaked out, I don't mind admitting.' Nick grabbed a tissue and wiped his face. 'Wait . . . this is where I yell it. I'd decided if they didn't stop, I was going to run for help.'

Get back to your rooms.

They stopped abruptly. They all did a 180-degree turn and Billie peeled away from the line first, and re-entered her room.

'This bit too,' murmured Nick, more to himself, Veer thought, than to him. Then as soon as Billie shut the door, they were like puppets with their strings cut. Each patient's physical demeanour altered – some more perceptibly than others. Marjorie Briggs bent forward and reached for the wall as if unsteady. 'You can't see it from this angle, but I can tell you she shouted for help as soon as Billie went back into her room. Yelled like a banshee.' On the CCTV, Nick moved to take her arm and led her into her room.

Elsie's posture dropped, her hand patting around her backside, and then, clearly agitated, plucked her nightgown free, looking around to see who had seen her exposed.

'She starts screaming then. She was frightened. Then you'll see Chanice come and help.'

THE INSTITUTE

'But you didn't tell her what you'd seen?' Veer asks.

'No, I should have. I trust Chanice, she's a good colleague, but I was still shocked. You can see there that she's telling Raymond Tate to get back to his room because his wang-wang is swinging in the breeze for everyone to see, and he does straightaway. Look, he's gone in now and has shut the door – she then helps Elsie and later she asks me what was going on. I just said I got to the corridor and they were in it. Said I thought maybe they were confused or sleepwalking. She didn't even know about Billie and Marjorie, and thought it was just Raymond and Elsie. I didn't correct her. She didn't think anything of it, and I felt stupid as I was ... scared, you know? Didn't want to admit that. Not with my being in charge on shift. I just wanted time to think. Then when the breakfasts were out, I had a bit of time and watched it back.'

'How many times have you watched it?' Veer asked him, moving his head as if to address Nick but never actually taking his eyes off the CCTV.

'More than I'll admit.'

'Have you seen any of the patients this morning – have you seen Billie?'

'I went there at seven a.m. on the dot; took her breakfast. Had a full conversation with her; she didn't seem to remember the incident. The others too – all just the same as they always are.'

'Did you refer to it directly to any of them? Were you explicit about what you saw?'

'No, but only because I thought you would prefer it if I left it to you.'

Veer nodded and patted the arm of his colleague. Many years working together made life easier. 'Play it back again?'

This time, they both watched it in silence.

It was almost like they were witnessing a weaker, scaled-down version of the events at Gatwick Station, Veer thought. It was clear that Billie was the connection – so was she contagious? Could she have this influence on anyone she now met? Had she been the instigator of the Gatwick group's suicide, or – as the only survivor – was she left with some ability or influence she didn't have before? Could she do it again? Would this spread now via Raymond, Elsie and Marjorie? Or because they were sleeping close to Billie, did they somehow just pick up on her like she was some kind of radio transmitter? Or was it viral? Bacterial? Some sort of contagious brain disorder? And if so, what was the pathogenesis? Respiratory secretions? Close contact? And was he witnessing some contagion that he should now report and isolate the ward?

He felt a hand on his shoulder.

'Veer? Where did you go there?'

Veer sighed, took off his glasses and rubbed his eyes. He felt every one of his sixty years and some. 'I'm not going to discuss it with her.'

'You're not? What about telling the other staff at the handover meeting?' Nick checked his watch. 'Which is in a minute.'

'She's not our patient anymore.'

'You're discharging her? Don't you think—'

'It's not about what I think anymore. I'm due to tell everyone at handover. We've had a request from a private hospital to transfer her to their care. The request came in yesterday, and as soon as I queried it, I got an email from a lawyer that had so much teeth in it, that once I'd forwarded it to our legal team, they almost cried and told me to have her out ready for the private car that's coming for her at nine o'clock with a bow wrapped round her.'

'Really? Where is she going?'

'Some private institute I've not heard of before. The Arbor Institute. They've got a website that make it looks so luxurious I might quit and go and work there myself.'

Nick joined in Veer's chuckle, and as it became almost too excessive Veer wondered if there was fear and relief mixed into their laughter. Veer hadn't argued with the hospital's legal department. Journalists on the ward, talk of global phenomena and now *this* – possibly the most disturbing thing he'd seen. He'd had enough.

He asked Nick to run it one more time.

Veer finally felt he had seen sufficient. He stood to go but stopped. 'Do me a favour, Nick – we've known each other a long time, right? – I'd like you to delete all this footage from the system.'

'I've never done that before.'

'Stuff like this ... if it got out ...' He thought of the journalist offering to show him a video. 'It could create drama and attention our other patients don't need. We've got to think of Elsie and the others – how they'd feel if it was splashed all over YouTube. Agreed?'

'Agreed, Doctor. Watch me do it now so you know it's done.'

And Veer did. As he clicked the relevant buttons, Nick muttered, 'I'm glad she's going. You know I'm not scared of no one – but this. *Her* ... it was like they were under her spell. She was in charge. It struck me that she could be ...' He paused again, shook his head a little, the words dying with it. Clicked a final button and stood back. 'It's done. Deleted, no trace. Management better not ask for those missing minutes ever.'

'If they do, I'll tell them it was my command. Promise.' Veer sighed. 'Maybe I shouldn't ask, but tell me what you were just going to say. When you said Billie was in charge, it felt like to you that she could be – what exactly? What did you nearly say? Just because I think this is what I'll think about late at night, staring at the ceiling, for many years to come, and I won't want to guess.'

Nick started turning his wedding ring. 'I was going to say that it felt like she could put a spell on me too. That I could end up in her line following her to goodness knows where. It struck me that she could be dangerous.'

Veer met his eyes, and despite his own career of working on an understaffed, under-resourced locked psychiatric ward for more years than he cared to think about, he felt the tingle of his own fear.

Veer then did something he'd never done before and leaned in to give the man a brief hug before he left to tell the staff at the handover meeting that Billie was free to go to her new hospital. He knew he'd never feel gladder to let someone go.

EIGHT

FURTHER EXTRACT OF THE REPORT:

Second-Wave neural (non-contact contamination) summary:
NB: This *must* be noted for risk management: *exposure to the contaminant is not required for second-wave dux gregis*; contrastingly, it is in response to a first-wave primary brain. Appropriate cautions must be applied. Note the containment summary and risk assessment 3 Appendix 9. Second-wave contamination describes a definitive dux gregis with the primary first-wave host. Presentation is also noted as catatonia or 'zombie' status. Once the dux gregis has been established between the primary first wave and the secondary person (or persons), the connection duration is currently unknown. Span/closeness in location to establish connection is currently unknown. Span/closeness in location for continued connection

is currently unknown. Prohibitive factors are currently unknown. It is the opinion of this board, therefore, until further information is established, it should be considered that this second wave presents a danger to existing human life. Second-wave dux gregis has been assessed as level 5 × level 5 using the Existential Risk Calculator to Global Human Life (Appendix 18). The modelling on potential second-wave dux gregis ratios and the potential for weaponization, recognizes the global existential risk regarding potential unrecoverable civilizational collapse.

Containment summary:
Due to the unknown reach and range of a human primary who has survived first wave, it is recommended that they are detained away from towns and cities. They should be held with extreme caution. This caution should reduce contact with others and therefore subsequential second-wave dux gregis. Potential consideration of high doses of haloperidol (by subcutaneous injection, 1.5–5 mg every hour as required, usual max. 30 mg per day, under 24-hour monitoring) which have shown some evidential management success for the primary first-wave patient.
(For further treatment suggestions, please see Appendix 5.) Furthermore, consideration when containing first-wave contaminated hosts must be given to . . .

THE INSTITUTE

If this is the hospital transport car, Billie thought as her fingertips trailed over the grain of the black leather seats, then I've made the right move. She hunkered lower in the Mercedes S-Class back seat, feeling both relief and hope in equal measures. Her mother sat next to her, staring out of the window. A glass partition separated them from the driver and Arbor's psychiatric nurse, here to support the transfer; all she had to do, it seemed, was to sit back, miss her AirPods and phone, and snooze the eight hours from Redhill to Scotland.

Leaving Warwick ward had felt like receiving an early reprieve on a prison sentence. Dr Singh had been kind when Billie had apologized for her behaviour when she first arrived – even now, she could feel the heat of her blush as she remembered throwing the chair at the staff desk.

After her paranoia episode years ago, she'd been aware enough to know that it was good for her to be hospitalized – it was what she'd needed. Now, she knew there was nothing Warwick ward could do for her – and to have missed the funerals of Ella and her other friends still made her feel explosive. She had tried again to explain to Dr Singh how she felt, but he'd patted her on the shoulder and cut her short by saying he understood. He'd even suggested that, if she was ever 'worried about anything – anything at all', she'd be very welcome to come and see him. Her mother, who was hovering in the background, had then asked if Billie could return to Warwick ward if the institute wasn't 'appropriate', but if Dr Singh heard the question, he didn't show it. Instead, he just deepened his smile and looked at Billie intently with his kind eyes, as though he might find her interesting.

Then it was simple – Dr Singh spoke with the nurse who had been sent from Arbor, Billie and her mother signed some paperwork and Dr Singh explained her care was now transferred. The nurse, Callie, suggested to Jo that she stay and say goodbye at the hospital, which Billie flat-out refused, before the door buzzed her release and she left without looking back.

It felt amazing to be free of the smells of gravy and pine disinfectant. Almost immediately after leaving, partly to escape the foul headache she'd woken with again and the crystal-bright conversation from Callie, Billie shut her eyes. Billie felt the warmth of gratitude that her mother took over the small talk for her – particularly as she knew Jo was worried. It was just the two of them now, and Billie had always checked in with her at least weekly while at university, the unspoken understanding between them that her mother needed to know that Billie's mental health was strong. It hurt to see the searching confusion in Jo's grey eyes, unable to correlate the evidential suicidal desires of her daughter with Billie's weekly buoyant updates.

And despite raising the invitation of Arbor, Jo had reversed her viewpoint on it before they left the hospital.

'Why tell me about the email if you think I shouldn't go?' Billie had argued.

'Darling, you're an adult, I can't hide things from you. They asked me to show you their invite and I did. I'm just suggesting that you might be better off staying close to me. I won't be able to visit as often if you're up in Scotland and we don't really know anything about the institute. You might feel cut off. You might not like it – that's all I'm saying.'

Billie had pointed at the website photos of outside and

inside pools, extensive lawns, tennis courts and a yoga studio.

'Yes, it does look lovely, but don't you agree, there's just something terribly trustworthy about staying with the NHS, darling? It might not be glamorous here' – she'd paused as the screamer had started up again, howling for her children that Billie had been reassured were now thirty years old – 'but you know where you are with these sorts of hospitals. They're *reliable*. And please don't take offence, darling, but your generation is very interested in how things *look*. I'm just suggesting that's not always the best way to tell what something is really *like*.'

Billie didn't agree, but what had woken her at three this morning on Warwick ward, and then held her tight until dawn was a new terror: what if it happened a second time? What if she zoned out and tried to kill herself again? She remembered the blankness in the man's expression as he fell from the Grand Canyon's edge: there was *nothing* there. He'd already gone. What if that nothingness came for her again? Being in a place of observation would keep her safe.

Billie fretted as she dozed, hood up and face towards the window, glad to be heading to the Arbor Institute. It said it modelled itself on a place of retreat – she needed the privacy, peace and escape to grieve.

Eventually she must have fallen asleep because it was the sound of the engine slowing that woke her; they were in deep countryside when she opened her eyes. Billie turned towards her mother, grateful again to have her there. 'How long have I been asleep?' she asked her, feeling foggy.

'Just about for ever. You've missed some amazing scenery – forests, Yorkshire Dales, we skirted the Lake District.

I thought about waking you, but thought you've probably not been sleeping well.' Jo patted her daughter's hand. 'You must be tired. Would you like something to eat?'

Billie took the offered sandwich. 'I'm sorry about all this – you've been amazing.'

Jo smiled. 'I'm going to have to say goodbye to you before you get to the institute. Apparently, it's on an island.'

'An island? Really? Where?'

'Just off the coast in the Firth of Clyde.' Jo's brow furrowed. 'I'm glad it wasn't just me who didn't notice,' she whispered, watching the chauffeur and the nurse. 'It seems that Callie isn't from Arbor after all, but a private nurse who is accompanying us because of your mental health section. The driver says he has to take her back immediately and that means I have to fit in with her schedule and go with them. We are to turn around at a small marina near Wemyss Bay where you'll take a private boat to the island.'

Billie blinked, not prepared for the idea of her mother not at least coming to the institute. 'I'm surprised the website didn't say it's on an island – in fact it must do. Can I use the phone?'

Jo passed it over. 'But you might not get access – I've been trying but the connection must be slow.'

Billie tried and brought it straight up, selecting the location page again. There it was clear: the institute was situated on a private island accessible only by boat. 'It *is* there! Look – right under information on location. But I swear it didn't say that before. I read it twice.' She showed her mother.

They must have missed it, Billie decided. It must have been in all the busyness of leaving the ward. She looked out of the window at the coast and could see the rise of islands out to sea. Had she known about being separated from the mainland, she might've hesitated to go. She felt vulnerable and uncertain about everything in her life, and the stretch of water just felt like an uncomfortable stretch too far. She looked out across the Atlantic knowing that soon she'd be on one of those islands that stared back from the choppy grey sea.

'We've just passed Wemyss Bay,' her mother said, as they drove past a pretty small port. 'The driver said that means we're only a couple of miles away now from the marina.'

They both sat in silence for the two remaining miles; her mother placed her hand over her daughter's. Billie forced steady breathing, fighting the suffocating feeling that it was a last goodbye.

The car stopped at a small marina. Across to their right, pontoons reached into the water, the yachts' masts swaying with the swell. The *chung-chung* of metal on metal rang from the boats. 'I love you, darling.' Her mother gave a smile, but Billie noticed it didn't reach her eyes.

'Oh, Mum, I'm so sorry. All this way and then straight back without a break.'

'It's a very comfortable car and I've enjoyed the scenery. I can nap on the way home.'

'Yes, but—'

'Yes, but nothing. I'm just pleased you feel you'll be better looked after. Warwick, I understand, was challenging.' She touched her daughter's cheek. 'I can see you need some peace and rest and really, your well-being is all I need.'

The chauffeur opened Billie's door. He wore aviator sunglasses and Billie wished she could see his eyes; his voice was empty. 'Billie, this is us now. The ferry doesn't stop on our island, so the institute uses its own transport. You see the black speedboat over there?' he said, pointing to a boat hitched at a nearby mooring. 'You'll take that over to Arbor. The driver is also a nurse, so we've kept our promise to Warwick ward. I'll be taking your mother and Callie home.'

Jo got out and folded Billie into a hug. She told her how much she loved her and said they would be in touch. She asked the driver for Arbor's number. He pulled out a black card embossed only with a bronze oak design and on the back wrote a number. Jo examined it, before zipping it carefully in her bag. She started to turn away, but then grabbed Billie into another hug. 'Are you sure, Billie?' she whispered into her ear. 'No decision can't be reversed. It's just you'll be very remote – very cut off. You didn't know the institute was on an island – we could say that's why we want to return to Warwick ward. If that's what you want.' She pulled back and examined her daughter's face.

Billie felt she owed it to her mother to be brave. She managed a smile. 'I'll be fine. Go now. Don't miss your car.' Another hug and then her mother and the car were gone.

She was finally unescorted, unobserved and alone. No locked doors and screaming patients, and no confinement of the car.

For a moment, at least, it was just her. Looking across the grey sea water of the Firth, she could see islands rise like the dark smooth forms of humpback whales. She watched the waves; not swimmable, she thought, and then corrected herself: why think of escape? Wasn't she going exactly where she wanted?

No.

The only place she wanted to be going was home. Back to her uni house she shared with Ella and the others. A place now packed up and emptied in her absence.

And now she was here. The salt-tang smell lay heavy on the wind; the raw keening of the gulls above her. The city and town life she was used to was behind her. Everyone she knew behind her. She thought of her father, an old pain now suddenly meatily raw. She knew enough about grief to understand that it came and went – nothing, then everything all at once – but this press in her chest was not the old pain of a dull bruise, but something new. He'd been dead eight years but standing here looking out across the marina arm to the sea, it felt as if it had just happened.

Her lips dried in the cold wind. She glanced behind her, at the exit where the car had disappeared. Alone, the wind seemed crueller. Looking back across the water, she bit her lip and wondered what her dad would say about her being here. Checking again the exit, there seemed a possibility of something else. Her headache drummed; thinking through fog, she wasn't sure.

But then above her, she saw something that stopped her breath: the gulls were gone and, in their place, was a sea eagle.

Falcons were their shared love and high above her was the biggest of them all. It was a silhouette with a flash of white rounded tail, the reaching fingers of its broad wings. She and her father had been planning a trip to Mull to see the sea eagles when he'd died.

And now one was here.

Gazing at it, she held her breath: it felt like a sign. She felt reframed: she was supposed to be here. Her father said eagles were a sign of God's protection, freedom and strength. She saw the width of its wings and felt safe – he would watch over her. He would protect her. And I need, she decided, to accept that this is what freedom looks like for me, right now. To be out here, not locked in a ward.

She watched the bird rise and lift on the wind; then it was gone. She exhaled a long breath: she was ready now for the next step.

She looked over to the boat and could see someone waving at her. It was time to go.

NINE

'Hey, I'm Stan,' said a very good-looking man of about thirty. He was tall, a little on the skinny side, wearing a grin, a tan, a baseball cap and a pair of Ray-Bans. He reached for her hand and helped her step onto the fantastic speedboat that would've been at home in Monaco – although Billie thought it looked pretty good in this marina. Around them, the masts swayed back and forth and the *chung-chung* of the metal on metal from the dozens of moored boats already felt a million miles from Warwick ward. She sat on yet more black leather and looked around at the black and chrome craft. If Ella were here, she felt with a tug of grief, she would've wanted to sit in the driver's seat and take selfies for Insta.

'If you're Billie, move to the front here – safer.' Stan indicated the seat next to the driver's. 'And if you're not, get the fuck off my boat, you weirdo.' He laughed at his own joke. He pulled off his hat and scraped back a shock of dirty blond surfer-style hair, before pulling it firmly back on. He noticed her watching. 'You'll want me to be able to see. You okay if I go fast?' Without waiting for an answer, he fired up the engine.

Billie raised her voice above the engine noise as he reversed away from the pontoon. 'Are you my nurse?'

'Baby, I'll be your nurse if you want.' He laughed as he negotiated the boat out of the marina. 'But no – the uniforms are not my shade of blue. Is that what you were told? That I was your nurse?' he shouted back. 'That lie must have been for somebody's benefit. Who were you with, your mother or your shrink?'

But he didn't seem to care because, clear of the marina now, he opened up the throttle and the boat took off at such speed Billie was forced to grab the handrail and hang on, questions dissipating in the thrust of cold air like sea mist. Heading to an unknown place with an unknown man – who was the complete opposite of what she'd expected – made her catch her breath. But she just tightened her grip against the metal rail and stayed in the moment – like her therapist years ago had taught her. All her anxiety – which flared to paranoia – was about the past and the future. Peace was in the present, so Billie took in the boat's bounce against the water, looked out for the eagle in the beauty of the emerging blue sky, and the sunlight now throwing diamonds across the water, and determined to enjoy the boat ride. The marina, then the line of brick villas lining Wemyss Bay disappeared behind them, and she knew there was no turning back.

Stan shouted out the names of the islands as they passed: 'Bute. Great Cumbrae. Little Cumbrae. Castle Island.' He pointed straight ahead: 'That's ours – it's called Dorcha.' Finally, the engine slowed.

She watched the approach to Dorcha with a mixture of excitement and anticipation. A small stretch of beach and a jetty wall was all that could be seen, except for the determined fortress of woods that seemed to circle the island.

Stan skilfully moored and turned off the engine. 'Did you enjoy that?'

Billie, still reeling from the blast of oxygen and sea salt, told him it was great.

He tied the boat up and then helped her jump off. He grabbed her bag. 'Don't be daft, let me,' he said, when she tried to take it from him. 'It's uphill to start with and a little steep. You've had a rough time and a long journey. Anyway, it's not far until we get to the institute – just ten minutes' walk.'

'What's the institute like?'

'You'll find out.' He pointed ahead: 'There, we take the path through the trees.'

The trees rose up, a green fortress of native oak, beech and silver birch, interspersed with leylandii. There was only one chink in the wall, where the path ahead cut through the trees. With shale underfoot, she followed Stan as he walked into the woods, leaving the beach, the boat and the Firth's water behind them.

Stan strode ahead as if in a hurry. 'Dorcha is just over a mile in length and half a mile wide. It hasn't been inhabited since the seventeenth century. The Arbor's corporate backers bought it about fifteen years ago and developed it about five years back.'

'Who are the corporate backers?' she asked, but he was always just ahead of her and didn't seem to hear her question. Under the now-dense canopy of trees, the sky was nearly lost; thick boughs of the wood reached overhead, the light was strangled to almost nothing, and the beach behind them was already gone.

She jogged to keep up with his long strides. 'So, if you're not my nurse . . . ?'

He called back over his shoulder. 'Hurry; I don't want to miss the afternoon cake. Philippe bakes on a Tuesday and he promised me my fave. The others are complete scavs and we'll be left with just crumbs.'

Cake? Crumbs? Who was this man-child? It was bewildering. She struggled to keep up. But she kept moving; the wood – dense and dark – was already opening up ahead to blue sky. Who Stan meant by the 'others' was just another of her unanswered questions, which stacked up like stones in a cairn.

She eventually followed him out of the trees. At the edge of the woods, she paused, taking in the view. Seeing the institute for the first time, she inhaled a long, low breath and held it for a longer beat; her exhale was audible.

He was further ahead now, the ground dropping away. He turned, waved her on and shouted: 'Keep going, Billie, nearly there!'

And they were. There was a huge oval ring of trees – which, judging by its size and how the island looked like from the water, must encircle the island like a perimeter wall. At the centre were the lawns on all sides dropping to a dip, and sitting like a pearl in the middle, a huge oak tree, and built around it, crouched what must be the Arbor Institute.

TEN

The Arbor Institute's beauty was straight from the front cover of an architectural coffee-table book. It was without question the most beautiful building Billie had ever seen – the website hadn't done it justice. There was a central building, with interconnected ones leading from it. Each was a long, low, single-storey box constructed of huge panes of smoked glass, juxtaposed with pale stone and silvered wood. The roofs were planted with wildflowers, and bronze glinted in the sunshine. Behind it, she could make out a pool, and a little further back, what looked like a long pond. She could see tennis courts and Stan paused long enough to point out, behind a group of trees, there was a lake.

If only her mother had been able to see it – Billie knew she would be reassured by the quiet luxury of the place.

Thank goodness it's amazing, she thought as she followed Stan down the wide path, because if it was terrible, it would be a tricky place to leave. The concern chased again: *I don't have my wallet. Nor a phone. Without them, it would be really,* really *difficult to leave. No – I'm not worrying about the future again*, she thought, glancing at the sky. *This is where I'm supposed to be.*

Her optimism and the downwards gradient of the path carried her forward. And it became easier: Arbor only seemed more lovely the closer she got. The knowledge that if she left, she'd be locked up again on Warwick ward for some indeterminate amount of time, helped. She remembered being forcibly restrained and the shock and shame of being injected in her buttock and knew that anything – *anything* – had to be better than that.

There would be no screamers here, she thought. And no cloying smell of pine disinfectant and gravy.

Here, she thought, glimpsing the pool again, she could start a new life. Something far from where she'd just been. Her right hand closed over nothing but she imagined Ella's hand in hers: *stay with me.* She wasn't ready to let her go yet.

They arrived, stopping outside the largest building. The path circled the huge oak tree which stood at the centre of the drive. Billie recognized it from the card the driver had used – it was the Arbor symbol. It was quieter than she had expected. She'd been expecting the Arbor to be like the private Bupa hospital she'd visited with Ella when supporting her with a procedure; although quiet, it had still had a busy car park, with lots of staff and many patients. In contrast, this place was silent. The grounds were empty, save for birdsong. The black double-fronted doors were shut. There were no cars parked out the front. No industrial bins. No signage. Nothing to suggest that it was a clinic of any kind.

'Is it what you imagined?'

Billie gazed at the lavender and alliums, the planted roof, the peaceful parkland pressing into the woods. 'It's better than the photos – I think it's perfect.'

'Good.' Stan seemed to study her momentarily, then reached out and passed her her bag.

'Well, this is it – for now!' he smiled and briefly clasped her shoulder. 'Now you've got to meet Jenna, who's your link buddy. She can't drive the speedboat, hence me getting you, but she's waiting for you in reception. She'll get you checked in and will orientate you better than me – I can never remember what I'm supposed to say and when, so Jenna's now in charge.'

'Is Jenna a doctor?'

He gave a lop-sided grin. 'That'll keep me laughing for hours. No, she is definitely *not* a doctor, any more than I'm your nurse. She's one of us, Billie. Just another strange brain who's survived the ride – so far,' he added with a wink. He turned and headed left round the building, then stopped and called back over his shoulder, 'It's good to have you here, Billie. You're just what we need to stop it from getting dull.'

Billie stood on the gravel drive and knew she was supposed to go into reception. But before finding Jenna, she decided to get a sense of the place on her own. Although her feet were noisy against the gravel of the drive, the sound seemed deadened. She walked to the edge of the building and from there, she could see the lawns continued to stretch behind Arbor. She gazed at the encircling line of woods and looked forward to exploring, wondering if she'd see the sea eagle again. She wished again for her phone – she wanted to check what other hawks were native to the area. From when she was six, her father had kept a goshawk called Firkin; a beautiful bird. By the time she was ten, she knew more about birds of prey than about any Disney character.

I'll ask if my mother could arrange a replacement phone, she determined. Then she'd feel safer, more connected, and she could read up on the local birdlife. Here, she thought, surrounded by the wildlife, the woodland and the water, she could find the healing she knew she needed, amid the wild beauty of Scotland.

Then, just as she turned to go, the angle of sun meant she saw it. Hidden in a dense clump of black-stemmed bamboo edging the building, Billie saw the small onyx eye of a discreet camera. Most people wouldn't have spotted it, she knew. But she'd always been sharp-sighted; eagle-eyed, her dad had joked. She reached into the greenery and smoothed her thumb over it: glass-smooth snake eye. Security to watch people.

Not sure how she felt about that, Billie picked up her bag and walked up the stone steps of the Arbor Institute. She didn't know what she expected, but as she stepped inside, she knew it wasn't this.

Opening the heavy black door, she found herself in a reception room. Facing out, beyond a wall of glass, lay a terrace leading to a large pool. The room was furnished with three scarlet low-slung sofas, grouped around an oriental-style rug to face the pool. Many ferns in pots and bold abstracts on the walls finished the room. Billie loved it. It even smelt like a spa.

On the nearest sofa, with her back to Billie, sat a woman, reading a magazine. No one else was in the room – to her left even the small reception desk was empty.

'Hello?' said Billie, putting down her bag. 'Excuse me, are you Jenna?'

The woman didn't move.

'Hello? Jenna?' she tried more loudly, and this time the young woman threw down the magazine and jumped up.

'Oh, you're here, finally! I thought Stan had capsized the boat again and you'd both died in the drink! Billie, isn't it?' she said, pulling out an AirPod and extending a hand. 'Sorry, couldn't hear you. I've got "Karma Police" on repeat. The words feel important to me but our therapist, Celine, says it's bad to dwell – she reckons the lyrics are depressing.' She grinned a slightly gap-toothed smile. 'But fuck it, who'd take advice about music from a Gen Xer, right?'

Billie smiled, disarmed. Ella had loved Radiohead more than anything. She'd also listened to 'Karma Police' constantly. 'I think Radiohead *are* Gen Xers,' she said, feeling the nearest she had to amusement in what seemed like a hundred years.

'Good fucking point. I don't know what I'm talking about – they have all the best music.' She laughed, rubbed her short, dark hair and shook Billie's hand again. She was tall – over six foot and very slim, her V-neck shirt showing high, arched clavicles, while her wrists were thinner than a child's. She wore denim shorts and beaten Vans, and a sleeve of tattoos. 'I'm so nervous to meet you,' she said with a faint Australian accent. 'It's the most responsibility I've had since I got here. I don't even decide what to eat – I'm a bloody prison inmate!' She laughed. 'Anyway, I'm your Arbor greeter, so welcome to Arbor!'

Jenna's handshake was warm and enthusiastic. Billie felt any tension she had left ease. This was not a hospital, but in that case, what about her section? 'Do I have to talk to any staff? I'm—' *under section*, she nearly added.

Jenna just smiled. 'Philippe is a darling. He suggested I show you around – he said it's better to hear it from a resident, because who knows better, right? They're amazing people. Last year, I was involved in … something … that led to … well, it's hard to talk about. I couldn't get over what had happened, but I came here and I can honestly say it saved my life.'

Just a strange brain who's survived the ride – so far.

Billie thought of the people stepping off the Bhupen Hazarika bridge. Could it be that Jenna and Stan had been involved in something similar?

A beat passed between them, then the smile lit Jenna's face again. 'Come on, I've over-shared again – I always do it when I'm under pressure. You must have had enough, so grab your bag. I'll take you to your room and show you around. First, we go that-a-way,' she said, pointing to the door on Billie's right. 'Let's go discover all that is Arbor.'

ELEVEN

Billie followed Jenna into a hallway. 'The bedrooms are down here,' Jenna told her, indicating the single staircase leading down. 'I thought we could dump your bag first.'

Downstairs was subterranean, but despite the lack of windows, Billie liked the polished concrete walls and paintings. Feet silent on the sisal flooring, they passed several doors, stopping at the last one. Jenna swiped the card reader and passed Billie the card: 'Your room. Mine's this one,' she said, pointing to another.

Inside, the room was small but comfortable. Jenna walked her through all the free tech – laptop; tablet; AirPods – all hers. 'Nice Arbor gifts, right? You won't get used to their generosity – they're obsessed with making us happy. You'll be the happiest lab rat in the world.'

Lab rat.

Was Jenna trying to tell her something, Billie thought, touching the boxes. 'I feel overwhelmed; super kind of them.' She decided to test the water. Pulling an embarrassed face, she said, 'What I really need, though, is a phone – mine was destroyed. I'm sure my mother would be happy to front any costs, if that's a problem.'

Jenna blinked, smiled and moved with such smooth disregard, instead showing her where the bathroom was without comment, that Billie thought she either hadn't heard or Jenna thought her ungrateful.

Abashed, Billie concentrated on Jenna's explanation of the air-con controls. Both rooms had no windows, which might have made it claustrophobic, but a large panel sat on the far wall of the bedroom and emitted a low-level light. 'What's that?' Billie asked. She thought of the camera eye and wondered if this hid one too.

'It's a light panel; it looks after our vit D levels – they're always pushing vits here. I like my panel – except they glow it up if they want us to wake up, and down too if we should sleep.' She picked up a remote control, and started flicking. 'But you can change it to something more entertaining.' The screen displayed a sunlit forest, then an underwater seascape of seaweed and fish. 'Both of these are local and real time; or this, just north of here, you can enjoy watching eagles in the Cairngorm mountains. This one's not live though: it's the YouTube classic.' She pressed a button and then it was a roaring fire with popping logs.

Eagles in the Cairngorm mountains? Was this place made for her? She thought of the eagle she'd seen that persuaded her to stay and not make a run for it. Perhaps she just needed to lean into the rightness of this place for her. 'Can you get YouTube?'

'Nah – no internet here. Every cloud has a lead lining, right? This is my favourite – just out in the woods.' The camera pointed up at the sky through the trees. The sky showed a pink sky at night. 'If you want music, no problem. You can access your iPod here – just give your list to Philippe.'

'Philippe who makes cake?'

'Baker slash handler,' she sniggered. 'Sorry, an old in-joke with the rest of the gang. Don't call him that – he'll get upset. Stan calls him Ol' Nanny – and definitely don't call him that! He only fusses because he cares.' She adjusted the screen. 'I slam on the Pixies super loud sometimes and' – she knocked her knuckles on the polished concrete walls – 'with these bad boys between you and the next room, no one can hear you scream.'

She held up her hands palm out in response to Billie's expression. 'Hey, relax, Billie. Maybe a bad joke, I just love my classic movies.'

'No, it wasn't that. It's just you remind me of someone.' *Ella.*

Jenna just looked blank before she turned and opened the wardrobe. 'Free clothes too. If it's not to your taste or size, they'll swap it.'

Billie had a brief look, fingers trailing over the hanging clothes. All were her size and items she would have picked. If she didn't know better, she'd have thought they'd hacked her shopping accounts for inspiration.

'The bed,' Billie said, pointing at the birch-panelled arch over the pillow area. 'That's unusual.'

'It's some sort of scanner.'

Billie blinked, waiting for Jenna to laugh and say she was joking. After a long pause, Billie asked if she was.

'No. They might scan you when you're asleep – the latest device apparently. It's a research clinic after all.' She shrugged. 'But if they've ever turned mine on, I've never heard it. I think they're usually noisy, aren't they? *Clunk, clunk, clunk.*'

This was very different to being on a ward – now she would be studied (while she slept?).

Perhaps she pulled a face, because Jenna said: 'Hey, don't obsess, it's not that deep. It's just study stuff; they study us – that's why we're here. Really, I love living at Arbor – I'm properly institutionalized. I get up at the same time every day, eat the breakfast that's cooked for me, go for a run at the same time – you get the picture. But it's cool; the people are cool and where else would I get to live where I can swim in a pond and then kick back in the jacuzzi every day?'

She left the room and went into the corridor, telling Billie to keep up, as she took the stairs two at a time before opening a door into a long dining room.

Against the back wall, there was a counter with heat lamps. 'This is where they serve food. It's really good – there's always a choice. The only trouble is that there's no meat – it's mostly vegan with some sustainably sourced fish. They even use recycled leather for the chairs – Arbor has got a thing about being environmentally responsible. Outside they've got their own solar generator and we are all off-grid here. They are always banging on about how they have a zero-carbon footprint. But I would kill for a kebab. *Kill*,' she said with narrowed eyes and a wolfish grin. Something about the way she said it made Billie believe that there might be more to Jenna than she'd initially thought.

Jenna then bounced on to the next room – a stunning gym with views across the lawns and pool.

Next was a sitting room with dark green walls and

toffee leather sofas, complete with sheepskins and folded blankets. 'Worth noting – there's a drinks machine in here. Unlike meat, coffee is not considered a nuclear-level toxin here. Apparently, it blocks adenosine, which boosts our dopamine. It's the nicest coffee I've had anywhere, but don't expect to get too much or have it too late though – I've realized that after you've had three cups they switch it to decaf. Clever little buggers.'

'How do they know?'

'You'll get one of these.' Jenna held out her wrist to show a plain black smart watch. 'It'll replace your keycard and will monitor your health stats.'

The last door on the corridor revealed a library. Apart from the obligatory wall of glass, the other three walls were top to toe with bookshelves. 'These shelves are fiction,' she said, pointing at the largest. 'Bit of Dostoevsky if you fancy it. That's Maddy's, but I think she reads it just to intimidate the guys. She's too beautiful for this world and there's nothing like angry women and Russian dissidents to keep flaky men away, is there?' She pointed her thumb towards a different shelf. 'We all keep ourselves busy with study. I'm doing a psychology degree and those are my reference books.'

'I'm reading psychology too!'

'Awesome. It's the main reason I refuse to leave Arbor. They pay for all my university costs, and because Arbor is free accommodation, I'm doing my degree for zilch. No debt and basically I live in a utopia. Sounds too good to be true, doesn't it?'

Billie thought it all seemed perfect. It even smelt perfect: spicy and warm. 'Is it my imagination or are all the rooms scented differently?'

'Yes, different smells for different rooms. They get weird about it too – I've noticed they pump a different smell into your room in the morning to the one they pump in in the evening. Sensory stuff is big here.' She tapped her forehead. 'Well, it is a brain place, right?'

'Can I ask you something – about it being a brain place?' Billie thought Jenna looked nervous but she pushed on anyway. 'Stan implied that we were all the same – that we were all strange brains. Now you've confirmed being is here is about our heads, can you tell me a bit more? Not about what he might have meant – I don't want to be nosey – but just about the institute if nothing else. I know I should have checked it out properly before I came, but I've been in a bad place. I've just come from a dreadful psych ward. Don't judge, but my friends had just died suddenly, and I was on tranqs.' She threw her hands up a little, 'I barely read the info properly. I didn't even know it was on an island.'

'Just looked at the pretty pictures, right?'

Billie felt her cheeks heat a little. 'Embarrassingly, I saw it was private, free, in nature with two pools and I just got my mother to sign me up straightaway. Don't think I'm shallow, I was just really, *really* unhappy where I was. But this is different – very, very different to what I was expecting. It's so nice; so quiet. So … unmedical.'

'You want to know if it's a proper clinic?'

'No, I'm sure it is. I was going to ask about you. If … well … if anything weird had happened to you before you came here. Is it rude to ask? I don't want to pry but … I'm trying to get a sense of everything.'

Jenna nodded slowly, her face angled and now empty of humour. 'Yes. I'm here for treatment – same as you, if that's what you're asking. Twelve months ago, I was with a friend and we both stepped in front of a car. She died instantly. This was my party bag.' She turned her arm so Billie could see the long scar. 'My leg too – I needed surgery and now I set the airport scanners off.' She smiled but there was only sadness in her eyes. 'I know what it is to lose dear friends, like you lost Ella.'

Billie caught her breath at her friend's name being used by someone who'd never met her. 'How did you know that?'

'There are no secrets here; we share everything. We are more than a community: we are a family.' Jenna laid a heavy hand on Billie's shoulder. 'That's why we're so excited – you coming here is like gaining another best friend. Or even better ...' she said, her grip tightening a little against her arm.

Talons tightening on a rabbit, Billie thought.

'You being here is more like gaining a sister.'

TWELVE

'Arbor's director wants to meet you – let's wait here.' Jenna dropped onto a lounger by the pool and Billie sat next to her. Stretching out, with the smell of sea salt heavy on the breeze and the early June sun on their faces, Billie could almost imagine she was on holiday. Jenna seemed to fall promptly asleep, so Billie was left to her thoughts. Tired from a week of broken sleep and horror and travel, she wished she could rest, but there was too much to process.

Overwhelmingly, she felt relieved to be at the institute, delighted that Arbor seemed so incredibly peaceful, with the added bonus of a quiet luxury she hadn't experienced before. The pale porcelain terrace, facing the light-marbled azure water, made her wish she had a swimming costume so she could dive right in – but she did, she remembered, she had a brand-new one hanging in the wardrobe of a room that was now hers!

She reflected on the last few hours of her journey: saying goodbye to her mum; meeting Stan and Jenna; but most of all she thought about what it would be like to live here. It felt like a lifetime since she'd been in the countryside, enjoying long days walking with her father, flying their goshawk. But sitting here, listening to the soothing coo-*coo-coo* of a nearby wood pigeon, made her feel connected to that past self – to him. He'd been gone from her life so long, but here she could feel a closeness with her dad.

She'd accepted his absence from her life a long time ago. But now she had another long road of grief ahead of her, she knew. The reality that her friends were dead and she'd never see them again was starting to sink in. How could she return to university without Fin and Ella and Vena and Gez and Leo in her life? She couldn't. And under the mental health section, would she even be allowed? Her choice was of only two places: Warwick ward or here. She listened to the birdsong and knew she already felt desperate to stay here.

But would it be possible?

How could the offer for her to be here free not be one huge mistake?

After twenty minutes, Jenna suddenly stirred and checked her watch. 'I've just been messaged. The boss is five minutes away. Make sure you give me a good write-up, won't you?' She laughed again and turned to search the sky. 'I can't see . . . ?'

'What are you looking for?'

Jenna grinned. 'You'll see.'

Billie heard the low purr of a helicopter before she saw it. The sound became louder and louder and then the helicopter slowly descended.

'That's the director,' Jenna said, getting up.

What would the boss of Arbor look like? Billie thought. She imagined him in a suit, perhaps an older person, and felt – again – the prickle of anticipation. What if he said she wasn't what they thought and sent her back to the ward?

The helicopter rested against the lawn, the huge blades slowing down, and the enormous noise lessening.

The door opened and a figure jumped down, casually dressed in a black T-shirt and black linen trousers, staying low until clear of the rotor blades before striding across the lawns towards Billie. Billie hated herself a little for being surprised it was a woman. The figure smiled and waved. Assuming she was waving at Jenna, Billie turned, only to find, in the noise of the landing helicopter, Jenna had disappeared.

With an enthusiastic bound up the terraced steps, the woman beamed at Billie, her palm open for a handshake. 'Great to meet you, Billie, so pleased you're here.' She shook her hand, clasping it tight with the other. 'I'm Dr Nathalie Bruthendale, Director of Arbor. We're thrilled you could join us at our little institute. You might think we are small, but let me assure you, we are mighty!' Nathalie was slight, with dark, loose curls cut shortish, and tanned skin. She laughed a little, showing an easy grin with neat white teeth. The wrinkles around her eyes suggested she smiled easily. About mid-fifties, she had an irreverent, messy appearance that if Billie didn't know otherwise, would have made her think that she was an artistic genius or musician rather than a doctor. But Billie was mostly taken by the Nike high-tops in yellow and orange – she thought of her friends with a pang. They all loved their trainers and Vena and Fin would've vied to see who could identify them first.

Nathalie sat down at the patio table and ushered Billie

to take the seat next to her. As soon as they sat, a man appeared with a pot of tea and two cups.

'Billie, have you met Philippe? This is Philippe Bouchard, your key staff contact.'

Philippe – the handler. He was middle-aged with a shaved head to mitigate possible balding, and a deep tan. He smiled at Billie as he set the tea tray on the table. He was very good-looking in the traditional, strong-jawed way of movie actors. Like Nathalie, he was also casually dressed in a black T-shirt and black chinos, but his were pressed and neat. 'It's really good to meet you, Billie,' he said shaking her hand. She noticed that both Nathalie and Philippe, like the residents, also wore the same black smart watches.

'I saw you out exploring with Jenna and I didn't want to interrupt,' he said, as he sat at the table with them. 'And I'll not stay now either, other than to say hi.' He grinned at Nathalie. 'Let's just say, I hope you'll be more of a fan of my interference than Jenna.'

'Philippe is being modest. Jenna is a big Philippe fan – all the residents love him. He's a highly qualified mental health nurse with a master's in psychology and, more importantly, has been part of the Arbor project since its inception. While you're with us, he'll be your first point of call for anything you need.'

'What Nathalie isn't saying – but is indeed true – is that you can consider me to be your glamorous assistant for all your needs while you stay with us. Lock's broken? Call Philippe. Out of toothpaste? Call Philippe. Can't sleep? Call Philippe.' He laughed heartily. 'Seriously, I love my job. I love Arbor and I hope you stay with us, Billie. I worry about the residents getting lonely as it's so quiet here, so another face is very exciting. Now if you'll excuse me,' he said, getting up, 'I'm going to stop intruding and let you both get on.'

Nathalie thanked him and poured the green tea from the pot. 'It's matcha, and yes, I know I should do the thing with the whisk, but Philippe gives it a little whirl first. I know it's rule-breaking, but I'm a practical woman who values results over procedure.' She passed Billie a cup. 'I'm sorry I wasn't here to greet you in person, but I'm sure Jenna did a great job. I think it's better for a new resident to hear from an established resident, rather than someone like me or Philippe, in case it seems we're trying to do a sales job on you.'

Billie seized the moment. 'Dr Bruthendale—'

'Nathalie, please.'

'Thank you. Nathalie, talking of sales, I need to check – my mother said my place here was offered for free? Sorry to be blunt, but I don't have funds to stay somewhere like this ...' Billie gestured around her. 'Please forgive me for checking. I don't want to waste anyone's time.'

Nathalie rested a hand on her arm. 'I'm glad you brought that up – and you're not blunt, but clear. I like that in people. And let me reassure you, it's completely free. The pharmaceutical company that owns Arbor is called NorGline and I've just returned from our head office in Chicago. NorGline is very, very wealthy, so Billie, we don't need your money, we just need *you* – what *you* have to offer.'

Nathalie's smile was so warm, her eyes so kind, that Billie decided she liked this woman.

'Let me tell you a little more. But first, you should understand that we are *not* a hospital. We are a clinical set-up, but not a mental health facility, and if you'd feel better being on a psychiatric ward, then I can have someone drive you back to the hospital you've left or I can recommend an excellent clinic in London. I'm emphasizing this because I wasn't sure if your mother really understood the difference when we were talking; in the end, I thought it easier to have you come up and decide for yourself.

'The reason why you're in such capable hands here at Arbor is because we are a specialist brain-research unit; as part of one of the largest and most established pharmaceutical companies in the world, we have both extensive knowledge and extensive resources. I will go into more detail to explain how, but we do believe we can help you. We are not wasting your time any more than you are not wasting ours.'

'Jenna said we were lab rats.'

Nathalie roared with laughter, slapping her thigh. 'Jenna is very naughty to make such comparisons, but,' she added, wiping her eyes, 'she is right, of course. Lab rats don't have to pay for their bed and board.' She smiled and continued, 'Seriously though, we are an exploratory clinical environment and think this is the perfect place for you, given what's happened to you.'

'I ...' Billie paused, thinking of the videos Dan had shown her, remembering what he'd said about groups self-destroying. 'I'm beginning to think I know what might have happened to me. I'm just not sure why – or what went on inside my brain. And what caused it.'

Nathalie nodded. 'Would you like to know? It's what we call flocking. That's our colloquial term for what is both a brain disorder and – as we see it – a brain strength.'

Billie nodded.

'Okay, well, we think you've experienced something that is now an emerging global phenomenon. We don't know why it happens, but what we think is this: you have experienced an evolutionary jump. You are a homo sapiens *with extra*.'

Billie blinked, sharply inhaled and tried to look like she'd understood what Nathalie had said.

Nathalie's eyes blazed with excitement. 'It's amazing, isn't it. You're amazing, Billie!' She leaned in again, her voice conspiratorial. 'You are beyond the rest of us. You have abilities that others can only dream of. You are head and shoulders above the rest of mankind. And that is why we want to study you.'

'I don't ... understand.'

Nathalie squeezed her arm. 'You – and a few others – have changed and now, we think, you have a greater ability. We believe there are two stages to flocking – or what is known medically as dux gregis.'

'Dux gregis? What is that?'

'*Dux* is Latin for leader and *gregis* means crowd or, more literally, flock. And it is as it sounds. You are leader of the flock. You – we think – can control the thinking of other humans around you. Quite the power, no?'

Billie fell silent, then her eyes narrowed. 'So, if I'm the leader of the flock, are you saying I led my friends to their death?'

Nathalie's face stilled and she put down her teacup. She took each of Billie's hands and met her eyes levelly. 'Absolutely not. I need to be clear: no. *No*. Dux gregis, where we think you might be now, is second stage. Some diseases have primary and secondary stages – tuberculosis and Lyme disease, for example. Some viruses also, such as chicken pox and shingles.

'We think that this also has two stages. The first stage that you experienced with your friends is called homogeneus gregis. *Homogeneus* is the Latin word for same, so your first-stage experience was an *equal* experience. It's not quite literal as gregis is genitive, 'of a flock'. But the meaning of homogeneus gregis is clear: no leader. *None* of you made the decision to step off the train platform. Your brains were undergoing such a transformative episode as a flock, a neural remapping, they couldn't cope. We don't know why this first stage causes – *always* – self-termination. Perhaps it's overload, a way of stopping whatever is happening. We don't know.

'But you were fortunate. You were in a busy place and bystanders saved you.' She squeezed Billie's hands. 'We've discovered that if someone is saved by third-party intervention, then you survive the brain rewire. The brain copes. But what it is left with is an ability to communicate telepathically with others.' Nathalie released her and waited for a beat, before she added: 'Have you experienced anything since the accident? Any shared actions, hearing of others' thoughts – anything unusual?'

Billie shook her head, struggling to comprehend what she was being told. She remembered the strange tugging sensation on Warwick ward when she was angry with the nurses for not letting her leave – the feeling she could ... could what? Reach into them? Pull them to her will? Hurt them? She wasn't sure. And if she didn't even know what that feeling was, then how could she articulate it? 'No, I've had nothing. But who would I communicate with now, when . . . ?' She bit her lip, unable to say *when Ella and the others are dead.*

'What we think is, you might have the ability to establish a telepathic control over others – potentially anyone. Second stage is not about a group, but about you and your abilities as an individual. But we are not sure. Perhaps we will study you and find this is not the case.' She shrugged. 'But this is why we want to have you at Arbor.'

'I still don't understand – you think I can control others? What kind of control?'

'We are not sure. But what we are considering currently is that it works very much like a radio transmitter. We think this second stage means that others can respond to you – receive your commands like a radio receiving a radio programme – but the power is yours alone.'

'And the others could be anyone . . . anyone at all?'

'We are not sure. This is why we would love you to stay with us.' Nathalie smiled.

'Can others read my thoughts?'

'I can see the confusion in your face – so understandable. No – it's more that you might be empowered to read theirs. Try another metaphor that explains the potential beauty. Think of the benefit you have to give to others – think of starlings in a murmuration, following your lead, not leading you ever, but you guiding them, shifting them, turning them.'

'I sound – *it* sounds dangerous.'

Nathalie cocked her head to one side, smiled and seemed to study Billie closely. 'Interesting viewpoint. Myself, I see the potential for beauty.'

'Murmurations are beautiful, but that's not how

murmurations work. Each individual bird copies the ones around it – there's no lead bird.' For a second, Nathalie's smile dropped a little. 'Sorry.' Billie found herself apologizing. 'It's just that I know a lot about birds, my father's passion—'

'Falconry. Of course.'

'How did you know about that?'

'We invest a lot in you,' said Nathalie, offering Billie more tea, before pouring herself another cup. 'We value and feel very protective about our small community here, so it would not be enough for someone to have dux gregis, they also need to be a good fit for us. So, we do our research before offering someone a place at Arbor,' she said, pressing smoothly on. 'And don't be too sure about the murmuration – I've seen studies that suggest otherwise. Did you know that even trees communicate with each other? It's thought now that when a tree becomes sick, the others around it support it through their root systems. None of us should be quick to claim they truly understand communication of other species. This is why I love science so much: we think one thing until we learn something new and then we rethink.' She smiled. 'Now, it is lovely sitting here with you, Billie, but I'd like to know if there's anything else you need to know before you commit to us?'

Billie's gaze returned to the swimming pool. 'How long do I stay here?'

'As long as you need to.'

'Am I still under section here?'

'Technically, yes. But if you want to leave, we're not prepared to wrestle you to the floor. But we would notify your original hospital.'

'Would they try and put me back on Warwick ward?'

Nathalie sipped her tea, then poured herself some more after offering some to Billie. 'I don't know. As an NHS hospital, perhaps they are too resource-thin to chase you back into their care. But they might fear a future inquest and would therefore consider it worth doing.'

'An inquest? For investigating deaths?'

'Yes.'

Billie blinked. 'You mean an inquest for ... *me*?'

Nathalie laughed. 'Okay, let's just dial it down a bit, shall we? These are the risks mental health professionals have to consider when someone leaves their care. But we hope you will stay. Will you?'

Billie scrutinized the surroundings: the terrace; the endless lawns; she could see tennis courts in the distance. 'Arbor seems too good to be true.'

Nathalie laughed. 'Oh, healthily cynical! Good, good! Does it make you feel better that Arbor will write your treatment off through tax breaks? We declare the health treatment as philanthropic. But it's not – I'll confess that now. There's nothing selfless here. Until recently, Arbor was a dementia study clinic – and just to be thoroughly transparent, of course if we can find a reversal or cure for all of the dementias, then financially, that's the golden-ticket win. The World Health Organization states fifty-five million people globally have dementia and while we at Arbor are doughty in our desire to help, we have now paused and redirected our expertise. I'll be straight with you, I could talk about good ethics and earnest intentions, but I won't patronize you. Instead, I offer you a truth: pharmaceutical companies are the real goldmines these days. People talk about data wealth, but really, finding a cure to a worldwide concern is worth a *lot* of money. There are some really very rich organizations, governments and individuals that simply want cures for depression, dementia, cancers and damage to the brain. We hope to find root and branch cures.'

'So, the Institute is just about making money?'

Nathalie laughed, a loose, throaty laugh. When she spoke, the smile still lit her eyes. 'Yes, of course. Everything is about making money. But nice to do a little good at the same time, no?'

Billie felt relieved at Nathalie's steel-faced honesty – it suggested integrity. 'I was wondering,' Billie said, 'have Stan and Jenna been flocked? Dux gregis-ed?'

'Flocked is the easier term. Informal but clear,' Nathalie smiled. 'I need you to sign an NDA before I discuss the people who live here. Their comfort and privacy are my utmost consideration. So that is the question, are you going to stay with us, Billie, and join us in our research?'

'How does it work while I'm here? Can I go home every now and then? And my phone got damaged in the accident; can I arrange for another one to be sent here?'

'All good questions, thank you. But before you sign on the dotted line, there are a few rules I want to be clear about. Access to the outside world – phones, visits, emails etcetera – is not how we choose to operate. We offer free bed, board, food and treatment. We hope you agree our offer and facilities are generous. We will offer you everything you need in terms of wellness: connection to nature; spa and sports facilities; free therapy on tap. We encourage exercise as it's amazing at spurring neurogenesis and the growth of new brain cells. Nutrition is key here: for example your diet will include Lion's Mane for its ability to generate the protein known as brain-derived neurotrophic factor, and Omega-3 and hesperidin too. At no cost to you, we'll encourage you to study because it's so powerful to help promote cell growth. Anything you need – there is no financial limit if it's for your development and well-being – is provided free of charge. But we do ask for total commitment from you, without outside distractions, fully present and centred.'

'I can't speak to anyone?'

Nathalie shook her head. 'And this commitment is of utmost importance to us, Billie. It's what you offer us ...' she paused and smiled again '... in return for everything we give you. We don't need money – we just need you. The whole you. But none of your external networks or connections.'

Billie blinked, understanding from the heavy tone in Nathalie's voice – despite the deep smile held by her eyes – that this was a non-negotiable fact. 'Why?'

'Because we are doing serious work here and serious work is always better done when it's not interrupted.'

'By saying no access to the outside world, are you implying I can't even ring my mother?'

Nathalie laughed. 'But why would you want to? You are an adult. Your mother knows you are here; she came with you. And she knows our expectations. But it's worth it for her, I think, to know that you are being treated at a place of your choosing. And at no financial cost – and if you stay here for a few months, really, how much are you missing in terms of calls? Why not reframe your stay here as a retreat? You are here for wellness, and a break from the expectations and obligations of life can be a lovely thing – if you allow it.' She paused, finished her cup of tea. 'If you can commit to us today, your life begins anew, and we will give you everything you need. We will become your home – and effectively your family – while you are here. But that's not for ever. You can check out any time you want.'

'But I have to decide now?'

'What else do you need to know?'

Philippe appeared with a tray. On it was a black Arbor watch, a pen and some paperwork, with a plate of crumpets. 'The contract. And I included some just-baked crumpets in case either of you are hungry.'

Nathalie laughed. 'Perfect timing! So, Billie, do you stay or go back to Warwick ward?'

Billie didn't need to think anymore and picked up the pen.

THIRTEEN

in the woods.

Without realizing, she's stepped into marshy ground. Marshy and dangerous. No, this is wrong, it doesn't get this boggy under the trees – this happens by the river. But she's not by the river, she's under the thick canopy of trees, so she feels confused. And she's not got the right footwear on – in fact, she notices, she's barefoot. Her feet are cold and wet and she's sinking. Somehow, she knows she could die in here. She could keep sinking and maybe she'll not see what's happening until it'll be too late to escape.

   She can hear Firkin's bell. Her heart leaps – her beloved goshawk! She can hear the beat of his huge wings coming up behind her and relief breaks like the sun at dawn: her father will be with him. They are always together. She wants to turn around to wave so he'll definitely see her, but she can't for reasons that aren't clear. Then her father is near: she can hear his feet on the woodland path. His are on dry ground, she knows. He can help me.

She calls out to him to help her get out of the bog; he answers straightaway, his voice deep and warm, just behind her. *You're not stuck, Wilhelmina, you just think you are. You can be like Firkin if you try.*

And then there's the familiar, extraordinary beat of wings, the rush of air and the sound of his bell and Firkin is behind and then in front and then rising free.

And then she is. I have to remember the bird, she thinks.

Remember the bird.

And then she wakes up.

FOURTEEN

'We want to welcome Billie,' Philippe said to the circle of six seated people. 'And introduce her to Arbor's therapist, Professor Celine Davis.'

'Hi, Billie.' Celine waved, six inches of thin bangles clanking together, percussion to her enthusiasm. Mid-fifties, Celine was plump and very pretty, and dressed in hot pink cigarette trousers and white trainers. She had blonde-grey streaked hair that she kept long on top with an undercut, showing bold earrings. 'So lovely to meet you, Billie. I'd like to welcome you to our daily therapy. Through enriched conversation and managed disclosure, led by me, your therapist, we seek to nurture your relationships with each other.

'We feel that's important for many reasons. As you can see, there's only five residents, so you have to be essential company to each other; this group can be a way for you to manage your relationships with each other. Secondly, although we know that the first-stage homogeneus gregis can happen equally among strangers or loved ones, we hope to improve the opportunities for dux gregis or flocking among you by developing deep trust between you. And lastly, most importantly, you have all had a very unique and tragic experience. Our meetings together are to help you reflect, nourish each other and ultimately heal.'

She pressed her fingertips together and continued. 'How do we attempt to flock? We walk through different scenarios to attempt to stimulate the response. Sometimes this has been successful. If this happens and you are concerned, just alert us and we will take instant corrective action. But mostly we only aim to flock during a session where your brain is being monitored. Part of understanding a phenomenon is knowing not just what causes a reaction, but also what doesn't. This time together is a real central point of all the different activities – we always have this to come back to, to unpack in, to decompress and reflect.' Her eyes twinkled as she looked maternally around the group. 'We meet every day to support your mental well-being here in what Stan insists on calling "circle time", like they have in primary school.' She giggled, smiling at Stan like a proud teacher. 'I run these sessions, sometimes with Philippe, often without. We meet at different times depending on your research schedules, and we use this time in any way you want. We can debrief the day, talk about our worries or discuss our hopes for the future. I don't mind if you sing! Sometimes we just sit and be with each other in peace. Doesn't that sound lovely?

'And this is our space.' She gestured around the yoga studio, which overlooked the swimming pond. 'And these are our people. And now we should introduce ourselves.'

Billie looked around the group in front of her, trying her best to look relaxed and alert. She didn't feel it; her mental exhaustion felt like rusty gears were grinding in her head. Although she'd had an early night and her room was extremely quiet, she'd had nightmares she couldn't remember and had woken at three to stare at the strange arch over her head, wondering if it was scanning her as she slept. She'd been given her watch too – she touched it now, cuffed against her right wrist. It felt tight enough to bother her. Apparently, it could even measure her blood composition and blood pressure, all from a sensor against her skin. She just couldn't work out how to take it off – she'd tried last night, but it had no discernible clasp in the black bracelet. She wished she hadn't been distracted by Nathalie as Philippe had fitted it on her wrist – to see it go on would help her understand how to take it off.

Philippe sat opposite her; he smiled as if he knew what she was thinking.

They'd spent the entire day together. He'd woken her this morning, with a breakfast of cinnamon rolls he claimed to have baked himself, and then taken her, after her shower, for a range of ridiculously detailed measurements, after getting her to sign even more paperwork. 'Consents.' He'd airily waved his hand.

Billie had felt she should read the paperwork more closely, but when she'd asked what it was, he'd said, 'It's just you giving us the permission to treat you. That you're happy for us to have you as our patient. And really, Billie, if you're not, is there any point in being here?'

Because he had a point, and because he was checking his watch, and because she didn't want to go back to Warwick ward (and, fuck it, how much could they really make her do against her will?), she'd signed in the various places marked by little yellow sticky arrows, all helpfully indicating where they wanted her signature.

Then he'd taken her to the gym's changing room where new sportswear and trainers were laid out for her – again, all in her size, all exactly what she would've chosen for herself, some she swore she'd put in a basket and nearly bought online before. She'd checked herself against the paranoia: how different really were sportswear choices for women her age? She was typical in her tastes. Billie was determined to be positive and embrace this opportunity. They were investing in her and she wanted them to feel glad they had.

With that in mind, she allowed herself to be hooked up to brain, heart and breathing monitors, and ran for the designated three miles before finishing with a sprint.

Philippe proved to be relaxed company. He had a kind, friendly nature – nurturing, even. His voice was smooth and deep. She liked the way he was easy with details about himself – she already knew he was French Canadian, loved Bach, baking and yoga. His parents had died in a car crash when he was ten and it was that that sparked an interest in medicine. He told her that once he'd found Arbor, there was nowhere else for him. 'Here, if a resident needs something, Nathalie just gets it – no questions asked. It's a special place – a place of hope – and Nathalie is a special person.'

Now he addressed the group. 'Perhaps we could say our names and something about our lives before and why we are here.' He turned to Billie. 'They've been waiting for you.'

Billie wondered where Nathalie was now, as she looked round the circle. Perhaps she didn't come to these sessions. Aside from Philippe and Celine, there were only four other people – and since she'd met Jenna and Stan, there were only two she didn't recognize.

The man to Billie's right spoke first. He looked the youngest – about thirty, Black, with short dreads and intelligent brown eyes. 'Hey, Billie, good to meet you. I'm Ash and I'm a telepath like you. I've been at Arbor nearly six months. I'm from Manchester, but now I'm here,' he shrugged and grinned, 'I don't think I'll ever leave – not until they make me.'

Philippe smiled and tapped his leather notebook which sat closed on his lap. 'I'm glad you feel we've been spoiling you, Ash. Perhaps you could tell Billie what you most like about being at the institute?'

Ash laughed. 'Apart from the food and the access to the gym? Seriously, I've finally got my act together, had some headspace and am now doing an economics degree. But not just that – it's got to be the nature. The way the pine trees smell as the sun catches them. Being able to breathe.' He shut his eyes briefly. 'I jumped from the top of a building – landing in a skip full of old curtains and mattresses saved my life. Arbor put me back together and here, there's no floor above the ground floor, right?' He opened his eyes and smiled at Billie. 'I feel safe here flocking, 'cause at least someone's here to catch me.' He gestured at the discreet cameras at each end of the large room. 'So here, I can't do anything stupid – and they'll see me if I do.'

'Ash, it's not stupid to have a brain disturbance,' said Celine gently. 'It's just a health disruption.'

'Sure,' he said. 'I like that: a "health disruption".' He laughed and then sat back, kicking out his long legs and settled, clearly done with talking.

'Thank you, Ash. Jenna, could we ask you next?' Philippe encouraged.

Billie suddenly felt overwhelming relief to be at Arbor, to be among people who might understand her situation.

'Billie, you've already met me,' said Jenna, wide-eyed and deer-nervous to be talking in a group, 'but I know Philippe will want me to say, "Hi, I'm Jenna and it's really nice to see you again".' She rubbed her spiky hair, suddenly shy. 'I don't think I've got anything to add right now, other than you know I'm a telepath and I'm here to get,' she laughed a little, 'my health disruption fixed too.'

Philippe smiled as if he was her father. 'Thank you, Ash and Jenna, now over to you, Stan.'

Stan gave a thumbs-up. No cap now, he forked his fingers through the dark blond hair. 'Yeah, so you've met me already. I'm Stan and I've lived in the UK since I was fourteen. My mum was British and my dad is American. I love most sports. I'm pretty chilled here, and no need to move on, but now I'm thirty I've been starting to think I'd like to—'

'Is this what we are going to do?' said the other young woman, the only person not to have spoken yet. She had dark hair, wild with curls, and a pierced nose. Her white skin was covered in copper-coloured freckles. 'Go back over this old shit? Where would Stan love to travel in his imaginary camper van?'

She turned to Billie. 'He wants to travel east to west across America. Niagara Falls, Route Sixty-six, Grand Canyon, all the clichés.'

'Hey, Maddy! Leave him alone!' cried Jenna.

'It's not a cliché if you grew up in America. I am *actually* American so don't tell me it's shit,' said Stan, cheeks pinking.

'Maddy,' said Philippe, 'we know you're upset because—'

'You know *shit*,' she answered and got up and walked out, letting the door fall behind her.

Celine smiled, hands open. 'Maddy is right to address the anger that she naturally feels.'

Jenna huffed. 'Celine, just be straight, will you? She's angry because we are back to five. Again. She thought that four was enough. Nathalie promised her four was enough – it's not personal,' Jenna added to Billie.

'There were no promises,' Ash said.

'Ash,' Jenna asked, 'have you talked with Maddy?'

'She's just hurt. Because of' – he cut a glance at Billie – 'because of Tama.'

'Who's Tama?'

'I'll tell you . . . if you like,' said a voice from the doorway. Maddy had noiselessly returned. The slight figure stood against the door frame, hands rammed into cargo pockets, at once angular, awkward and defiant. 'Sorry I was so rude everyone. I was just upset.'

Ash got up and gave Maddy a hug. He towered above her and for a moment Maddy disappeared behind the wall of Ash. 'We're all upset,' he told her, dropping a kiss on her head.

Maddy shook him off. 'Yes, that's what I'm trying to say to Billie, so she knows. Otherwise, she won't know how we feel.' She turned to her. 'You're new. I want you to know Arbor is a place of hurting and we are like you. We have grief and pain.'

'And we have healing, too,' said Celine with a contented expression.

'Do you want to take a walk, Billie?' Maddy turned and left without waiting for an answer.

THE INSTITUTE

Everyone turned to look at Philippe, who merely smiled and said: 'Everyone is free to do what they will. Billie, if you want to follow Maddy, we can do group work another time.'

Billie looked at the faces in the circle and got up to go after Maddy, following her out of the door, into the dusk.

FIFTEEN

Maddy stood there, eyes shut, slight and unmoving by the swimming pond, and for a moment she seemed to Billie to not even be real, as if she were cast from stone.

But then Maddy moved, and with it, her face seemed to lose the tension. 'Sorry about just now,' Maddy said. 'It's all so overwhelming. Even with Celine's help, sometimes I get too fiery when I can't process what's happened to me.' She pointed up to the woods. 'There's a path that runs through the trees; it rings the Arbor site. It takes nearly an hour to walk the complete circle. We could follow it now and talk.'

They both crossed the lawn to beneath the tall pines. It was noticeably cooler under the mossy boughs, the air rich with the smells of pine and damp earth. There was a tarmacked path snaking through the trees, edged with small, low lamps, lighting their way.

This was the perfect place to observe Arbor without being seen, Billie thought. She could see the institute through the gaps in the trees and saw now that the others were all leaving the barn. Circle time must have finished. Jenna and Ash left together, walking towards the lake. Stan left separately, following Philippe and Celine in the direction of the main building.

Maddy stood next to Billie watching them silently. 'They're a good group,' she finally said. 'They've been everything to me since I met them. It's such an intense experience here – you'll understand soon. It quickly feels like your old life isn't real – never was – and the only reality you know *is* Arbor.'

Billie narrowed her eyes. 'Sounds a bit cultish.'

Maddy laughed, a tinny nervous sound. 'That's funny. When I left school, they gave out joke awards in our last assembly. I got voted "most likely to join a cult".' She smiled at the memory. 'Maybe what you say is right – I've not thought about it like that. We all worship Nathalie a bit, that's true. The first time she arrived in her helicopter, I thought she was a rock star.'

Billie laughed out of politeness. 'You don't worry about being cut off from your families and friends? Also a bit cultish.'

Maddy turned her face so the lamps lining the path illuminated it, white as the moon. 'I don't worry about that. I don't really have anybody and I think this is difficult enough without other people's visitors trekking in and out. I would not want to be this vulnerable and live in a fishbowl. And you know someone would leak it, and then what? You and me in the *Daily Hate* saying how we're a danger to everyone?'

Billie thought about Dan and wondered how he would counter Maddy's point. She might be right, she conceded. But she knew she would miss speaking to her mother. She'd been thinking about their goodbye, the way Jo had held her close and whispered that she didn't have to go. She wished she could contact her now and tell her not to worry – that now she was here, it felt like the right decision to be among people that had suffered the same as her. But it would be a difficult conversation given she'd also have to explain what that 'same' meant. Perhaps Maddy was right; perhaps explaining to everyone's family and friends about dux gregis would be too much. She reminded herself to check against negative thoughts: there was wisdom in the way things were planned; even if she couldn't see it immediately didn't mean it wasn't there.

'I've never been anywhere like Arbor.' Billie looked back at it from the trees, the stretching lawns, the low-slung buildings, the swimming pond beyond, and to the right, the outdoor swimming pool. 'It doesn't seem very ... sciency. What do they do? Experiments?'

Maddy looked at Billie as if she were confused. 'There are labs but no experiments. It's more like a sleep clinic, where they hook you up to examine your brain activity. It's totally passive, sometimes they measure in the day, sometimes at night, and it's just to gather data. Arbor's methodology is simple: protect; observe; measure; cure. But it turns out that there's a long wait between the measure and the cure. It's the wait that Tama couldn't take.'

'Tama is who you're upset about?'

'Yes ...' She pressed her hand against her chest and made a sad face at Billie. 'I had a friend here, before you came, Tama – but he left three weeks ago. It's all still so raw.'

'Where did he go?'

'He wanted to go back to his old life.'

'Why? Because of Arbor?'

'No.' She pinched the bridge of her nose, eyes shut. 'Nothing like that. He liked it here – liked us. He just missed his family. Philippe tried to tell him – we all did – that if he left, he'd be in danger, but he wouldn't listen. Tama said he was cured; we had flocked successfully several times. Because we were all okay each time and he felt in control of it, he said it was time to go home.'

Maddy shook her head and started to walk. 'Arbor is right to look into dux gregis; if Arbor doesn't understand what it is, what's causing it and why it's so dangerous, then what hope have we got? And what if it spreads?' She looked at Billie. 'There were no recorded cases ten years ago. Now they're detecting it in every continent.' She grabbed Billie's hands and gripped them too hard. 'And it always kills.' Then she breathed out, and shook her head a little. 'Except us. Except here. We're the lucky ones. Do you ever think' – she stared into Billie's eyes with an intensity that Billie found both overwhelming and compelling – 'that we owe it to the lost to help find the answer? That we owe it to those who died? We need to know why it is that Tama left here and was no longer in control of flocking. There are more questions – so many more – than answers, but here we stand a better chance of finding them than anywhere.' She let go of Billie's hands as if frustrated and walked off, shaking her head and muttering: 'My friends. Just like yours. All dead.' She yanked her hood up and dug her hands deep into her pockets.

Even in the gloom, as Billie followed, she could see the shudder of Maddy's shoulders that suggested she was crying. Her own mind buzzed with questions that sparred and jabbed for answers she needed to know. But Maddy seemed separate and fragile, and Billie decided to give her space.

For a few minutes, Maddy's pace kept Billie at polite distance, but then she slowed. Finally, she pulled back her hood. 'Sorry. Dramatic again, I know.' She dragged her small, pale hand across her face. 'The truth is, I'm not doing so well – Celine knows that. We've stopped flocking since Tama left – no one knows why. But Celine's great at hearing our frustrations. Talk to her; use her – she's probably the best resource the institute has.' With the shadows cast across her face, she now had a ghoulish appearance, as if she might suddenly draw Billie into a deadly vampiric embrace. 'I just wonder ... whether the pain will ever truly go.' She pressed her hands against her eyes. 'I know you understand, too. That's why I was so excited you were coming. Nathalie told us that your story is the most similar to mine. She said you were saved in a similar way to me. My episode was on a motorway. Apparently, my brother CJ pulled over and we all got out. It caused a huge pile-up further down the road, as everyone swerved to get out of our way. A driver died.

'But I don't remember; I don't remember anything. The four of us walked up the motorway and then three jumped over the gantry bridge. CJ was one of them. A woman who'd braked to avoid the pile-up we'd caused stopped me before I could jump too, she kicked my legs out from under me and sat on me. Emily Granger is her name. She saved me. And I've never even met her. They had me in a psychiatric unit before I even knew what was going on. I was there until Arbor tracked me down and, well.' She shrugged. 'Same as you, I'm here, and CJ and my friends are dead, and I know I can't trust my own mind anymore.'

How did they track you down, Billie wondered. *How did the institute know about you – and me?* She took a deep breath. Keep it real and present, she reminded herself. If flocking was dangerous, so was managing her paranoia. Just as she'd been taught, she focused her attention on the sounds and sights around her, concentrating on the light coming through the trees, the rustle of the wind among the leaves, the hoot of what she thought was probably a tawny owl. She thought of her father again, the smell of him: leather and bird, the mud from his boots, the whistle that called both her and Firkin. He'd never known her ill – her anxiety had started after he died. But the thought of him helped centre her. 'Allow yourself to trust,' her therapist had once told her. 'Trust in what is fact.' The fact was, everyone who was a resident loved being at Arbor; felt safe here, felt supported. It was that support she needed to believe in.

They started walking again. 'What happened to Tama? Your friend who left?'

Maddy's sigh slid into a shudder. 'Within a week of leaving, he and a stranger stepped into a road in front of a lorry. He died instantly. So I've decided, I'm not going to leave until I can be sure I'm not a telepath anymore. It's going to be a long journey, but with the stakes so high ...' She reached again for Billie's hand. Her eyes were wide and deep and filled with a fervour that unnerved Billie. 'Then what choice do we have?'

SIXTEEN

After nearly three weeks, Billie felt relieved that she'd taken the risk to stay; life at the institute was so calm – nourishing even – and unlike in the chaos of ward life, she felt able to breathe out and grieve. Her bad headaches had eased and there was joy too. The group – Stan, Maddy, Jenna, Ash and herself – had been encouraged to do nothing but relax. 'Unwind and get to know each other!' Philippe had said. He'd assured her that her mother was not expecting to hear from her and that she understood the seclusion required by the clinic. Unburdened from worry, Billie felt glad to spend her time hanging out by the pool, using the gym and reading.

The first day it'd rained, Philippe had come to her and suggested she continue her studies. 'We pay, don't forget – and upfront for the whole degree, so if you want to leave Arbor after six months, you can still finish it on us.' He'd put her in front of a computer in the library and started her on the most comprehensive psychological profiling software she'd ever undertaken. 'Just to check you still want to do psychology – or now might be the time to switch course.

The profiling is detailed, yes,' he said, 'but if you're going to commit to hundreds of hours of work, why not spend a little time answering questions on what should be your favourite topic – you!' He'd winked. 'The world according to Philippe is Philippe's favourite subject by far.'

He didn't even seem to feel bad when she was still clicking through the questions after a ridiculous five hours. He brought her a continuous array of food and drink, kept the others away, and set himself up on the adjacent computer 'to work' but to Billie, his presence felt supervisory.

At the end of it, it told her she should do a degree in psychology or sociology, so it irked her a little. Philippe didn't seem to think she'd wasted her time. 'At least you have surety now. Nothing wrong with that. And as a reward, why don't I ask the kitchen to make your favourite food tonight. What is it? Wait!' he laughed, holding up a hand. 'I'll know, won't I, from the program! I'll get it organized now,' he said, seeming to find the whole thing funny.

She watched him vacate the library and started gathering her things together, desperate to get out and breathe some fresh coastal air. Then it occurred to her – if the profiling was for careers, why would it want to know what her favourite food was and when she'd first had it and what it meant emotionally to her? At the time, she'd become so numb to clicking through hours of questions, it had barely resonated, but now it rang church-bell loud. And why would Philippe be able to access – and presumably be able to analyse – what should have been just a program called *Careers-Think-Now!*?

Careful, Billie, she was quick to remind herself. Everyone here is happy and healthy – proof there's nothing to worry about or question. You're under section still, of course they should keep a close eye on your psyche. Keep your end goal in mind, she'd been taught by her post-breakdown counsellor.

What is my goal now? she thought, picking up her cardigan, and heading for the door. Simple. To know that I am cured. Then I can start again somewhere at another university doing ... she smiled wryly, psychology again.

Phase 4: nestling

SEVENTEEN

in the woods again.

She can hear Firkin's bell up above, coming from the large beech tree. He's got a rabbit and now she's worried – how will they get him down if he's hunted and eaten?

Then her father stands behind her: she hears his boots scuff against the dirt; smells the leather of his glove, his damp wax jacket and the citrus of his aftershave. Feeling better for his presence, she wants to turn and ask him about Firkin but can't. There's lots she wants to ask him – and she can't.

'Wilhelmina, don't fret about what you can't control. Instead, think about what you can. She's out of reach. She loves you very much. Close the distance between you.'

She's about to correct him, and tell him that Firkin

is a boy, but then realizes her dad isn't talking about Firkin, but her mother.

'Home!' her father commands; she doesn't turn to look at him because he sounds so cross. Is he talking to her? Firkin? 'Home!' he bellows again, but now she knows he is just talking to her.

I am at home, she puzzles, and she tells him, 'I live in the woods now.' Then, without knowing why, she bursts into tears. Her cheeks are cold with tears. She cries and cries and cries. Eventually, she turns around to ask him why she is crying so much. But he isn't there now; she is alone except for Firkin.

But he's still watching over me, she thought. I'm supposed to remember the bird, she thinks, knowing he came to see her in the woods before and that's what he asked. She feels pleased with herself to recall what he taught her: I'm supposed to fly away if I want to live.

Go home, Wilhelmina, that's what you've got to do if you want to live. Fly, Billie, fly!

And then she wakes up.

EIGHTEEN

Billie – until this morning – had felt that she was healing and thriving at Arbor. But today, as she sat waiting for the group therapy to start in front of the smiling Celine, she struggled to hide just how homesick she'd felt since waking. She was used to living away from home, but because she didn't understand it, it only made it worse.

And it wasn't just a desire to be at home, she also, confusingly, felt anxious about her father. She'd woken in the night feeling upset: *my dad never calls me Billie* was her first thought, and then it was gone. She only knew she'd dreamed of him. Disturbingly, both her face and pillow were wet with tears. She was cold too, but because her pyjamas were dry, she couldn't convince herself it was sweat. Even after her father had died, she'd never sobbed in her sleep. Why would she cry about him now? Yes, she felt a deep grief for her friends' deaths – but how could such an extensive amount of night-weeping be normal?

To conceal her feelings, she'd smiled through breakfast, then followed the others to the yoga studio, taking their usual seats in the circle.

She looked at Celine and Phillipe as they organized themselves, and wondered if they knew she'd had a bad night. Perhaps the arch above her bed caught every tear shed. Perhaps it could read her dreams. Just because she didn't believe the tech existed, didn't mean it didn't — and if anywhere had the money for the latest tech developments such as dream readers, it was Arbor.

Billie felt watched. Previously, she'd looked for CCTV in her room and although she hadn't found it, she still suspected it was there. Even her watch felt too tight — any tighter and she'd feel her pulse in her wrist. She pulled at it to try to loosen it but, eventually, she'd gone back to sleep, before waking again with a strong urge to leave the institute and go home.

I'm getting paranoid again, she thought. No, *no I'm not*. She could tell the difference. I just ... don't want to live in the woods anymore. She winced: what was that thought? It didn't sound like something she would even think. She wasn't living in woods — and if she ever did, it would be her dream location.

Perhaps it was now because she had a strange brain. The flocking, the headaches. Perhaps now she was changed, it just meant that her dreams were more ... she rubbed her fingernail against the pad of her thumb, as she tried to find the word. *Powerful.*

That made sense — if her brain was more powerful, why wouldn't her dreams be more powerful too?

'Are you okay, Billie?' asked Celine with concern.

Billie realized Celine had been talking, but she'd missed it.

'Sorry — just lost in my thoughts. May I ask the group a question?' said Billie.

Celine smiled, throwing up jiggling bangles in a gesture of openness. 'We would all welcome your contributions.'

'Has anyone had any disturbing dreams recently?'

As soon as she asked it, she knew from the lack of connection in their faces, they hadn't. Celine however, leaned forward, eagle-eyed, her intensity unnerving. She *does* know about last night, she *does*. 'Tell us, Billie darling, what have you been dreaming? To share it, here, in this loving circle, can only help you grow and heal.'

Suddenly, she didn't want to tell Celine anything. Suddenly, she – for the most fleeting of moments – even wished to be back on Warwick ward. Yes, it had been chaotic and noisy and smelly – but if she wasn't throwing chairs, they had left her alone. She'd had the privacy of her room and if she wanted to lie in bed all day, they'd let her. The doctor too embodied NHS trustworthiness. There had been no glamour there, but Dr Singh had possessed a transparent integrity, and there, her dreams had been her own.

And I never had a bad dream there.

That struck her as significant in a way she didn't understand.

Billie bluffed with a vague suggestion about her dream being about missing her cat and Celine eventually lost interest. She changed the subject. 'Today is going to be different,' Celine started, clapping her hands together, bangles jangling, 'We are going to do a series of games where we interact with each other. But Nathalie has asked that we measure the results, so we'll need to move from here, down into one of the study centres on minus two.'

'Minus two?' asked Billie.

'Your bedrooms are on minus one and the labs are on

minus two. Exciting for you to see them! We will use hyperscanning to measure interactions,' Celine said.

'Hyperscanning,' Philippe added, 'is a technique that involves simultaneously recording brain activity. It allows us to study synchronized brain activity between two or more people.'

'Yes, and to do so,' Celine continued, 'we do very straightforward tasks like pass a ball to each other, play rock paper scissors and mirroring exercises. All very fun, all very easy. We did it before ... with Tama. Just before your first dux gregis together,' she said, looking at Ash, Maddy, Stan and Jenna. 'Perhaps,' she cut a quick look at Billie, 'it'll have the same provoking effect again.'

They blame me, Billie understood. People had been talking about why they had stopped flocking since Tama left. She'd listened in, thinking it was to do with Tama – but now she wondered if the talk had been aimed at her. Paranoia itched again.

Oblivious, Philippe beamed at them. 'Dux gregis doesn't happen inside a brain on its own, so we are looking at how social interaction changes your brain activity, obviously, but also creates inter-brain synchronization. What we are studying today is how you interact with each other. By gathering data, we'll then have information on your low-alpha and high-alpha frequency bands, which are associated with brain activity relating to attention, focus and cognitive processing. We will be able to ascertain to what extent your brain waves synchronize through different activities. And all measured in the very low-impact way of an EEG. Billie, you've never had an EEG, I know, but it's completely painless, and just records your electrical brain activity.'

They were bright, too positive, and the emphasis on fun felt forced. Billie stopped plaiting her long red hair. 'Sorry, Phillipe, might I just ask, how do you know I've never had an EEG?'

Philippe's smile slipped for a moment. 'How do I know? Because we requested your NHS health records.'

'Can you do that without asking me?' She didn't mean to sound annoyed, it was just the lack of privacy really pressed on the raw nerve, to think of Philippe accessing her private information. Perhaps the others could hear her tone too, because everyone in the circle turned to look at her.

'Would it be safe to treat you if we didn't have your health records?' he countered. 'If you went into any hospital, you'd expect them to look through your health notes, I hope. And you did sign your consent.'

Careful, Billie, she told herself. He was right of course. *Am I losing my grip?* She pressed her hands against her face – even that thought was paranoid. She reminded herself to apologize – even if she didn't feel it. *Particularly* if she didn't feel it. 'Sorry. Yes, you're right of course. It's just my bad sleep making me grumpy.'

'Never a problem! You're naturally ambivalent about something new. You'll be reassured to experience just how straightforward it is.'

'Let me lead the ducklings out then!' said Celine, standing up. Stan, Ash, Maddy, Jenna and Billie all trooped out after her, leaving the yoga studio and heading back into the main building. In the corridor of minus one, what she'd thought was a door to another bedroom actually concealed a small lift. Once in the lift, Philippe held his watch against a square black pad next to the control panel and the lift moved smoothly downwards. How much was there about the institute that she didn't know? Surely there couldn't be another floor below her bedroom? But as the door opened, she understood how wrong she was.

As the lift doors slid open onto a long stretch of corridor, the air felt immediately different to the levels above, cooler, and the scent was different too: heavier, artificial pine and masking something more ... medical.

Perhaps Philippe noticed her apprehension, because he said: 'Sorry, it's a little more clinical down here – we're all used to it so don't notice it. It's still just Arbor, though, and very exciting. You'll see we are the best people to treat you.'

It wasn't just that it felt more lab-like. There was a weight, a substantialness to the space that made it feel to Billie as if she were in a nuclear bunker: the doorways were two foot thick, every sound muffled by deep polished concrete walls, giving a solidity and permanence to the building that she hadn't felt on the upper levels. Behind smoked-glass doors she could make out people working; some rooms were like offices, others like laboratories. The palpable power of the place shouted that Arbor was indeed massive and mighty.

Philippe stopped in front of a glass door. 'We're here,' he said, using his watch again to swipe for access. The thick glass door opened with a sound like something being unsealed. It clamped shut again behind them and then the light above the door turned from green to red. With something that sounded like pride, Philippe said: 'Welcome to the large observation lab. Next door is the study lab. That's where the doctors work, but in here is where you will do today's experiment.'

The room was huge: bigger than all their bedrooms, the

library and gym put together. It was white and square; in the centre, arranged in a circle, were five reclining chairs, and next to each was a desk and chair. On the desk was a large monitor, a computer and keyboard, and something that looked like a small printer.

Billie looked at the set-up and took a step back. She suddenly – badly – wanted to go home. Just fly away, she thought – rather than be here having yet more tests. She didn't even know why she objected so much; it was like innocuous drips of water had suddenly just made her glass overflow. She thought of her soaking wet pillow: being here was making her unhappy.

Stan seemed to sense her unhappiness because he smiled and said: 'We do this stuff all the time. It's no biggie.' His smile deepened and he gave her a small wink. 'If you want, I'll hold your hand.'

'Pack it in,' Jenna said, sitting down in one of the padded chairs. 'It's actually pretty fun,' she added to Billie.

Stan mouthed *I would like to hold your hand* behind Jenna's back and Billie nearly managed a smile. She reminded herself that, unlike Warwick ward, no one here had ever forcibly restrained her and injected her with sedatives. She would be fine. She settled herself in a chair next to Stan.

Celine stepped forward. 'Most of you know the drill – we will fit electrodes against your scalp using a cap. There's a little contact gel to improve conductivity, Billie, so your hair will be a bit sticky afterwards. This session will only take an hour and afterwards you're all discharged for the rest of the day, so hopefully that makes up for it. Philippe, is there anything you wanted to add?'

'We provide you with the very best caps – so everyone,

please remember not to throw them around this time because we had to replace two last time and they're worth twenty thousand pounds a pop.'

Stan winked at Billie and mouthed: *Fun though.*

Celine waved to the large mirrored window and several people in loose-fitting uniforms came out. 'The medical team will help fit your caps. Billie, because you've not used one before, they're going to measure you and try a couple on you. Say if it's too tight, but if it's too loose, then the connectivity won't be strong and we'll lose data.'

Stan and the others obviously seemed to know them judging by the conversations that started up around her as they all became busy with fitting caps, logging onto computer systems, adjusting chairs and trailing wires.

Then Billie saw her. *Callie.*

Her hair was different: now a short, dark elfin crop rather than the rather swishy blonde curls and glasses she remembered from the day the woman had accompanied her from Warwick ward. But as Billie angled her head to watch as the nurse took Ash's blood pressure, she was sure she wasn't mistaken, even though Billie couldn't see her face properly. Surprised she looked so transformed, she tried to catch her attention to say hi – but starting to feel that Callie was actively trying *not* to notice her, Billie called out. 'It is you! Excuse me – hello!' The more Callie kept her back to her, the more determined Billie was for acknowledgement. 'Callie?'

The nurse continued to engage with Ash and the computer.

'Callie, is that you?' Billie repeated.

The nurse didn't turn but started checking the wiring to

the cap Ash was holding. Watching Billie's persistence, Ash eventually said something to the nurse who finally turned. She gave Billie a small smile that didn't reach her eyes – eyes that now were brown rather than the blue they had been. 'Can I help you?'

Billie hesitated. Now she could see the woman's face square on, she knew it was definitely the same person, but she felt confused – this woman now spoke with a Scottish accent, and, from the blank expression and polite enquiry, she also clearly didn't recognize her.

She pressed her fingers against her chest. 'It's me, Billie.'

The nurse bobbed her head, her fixed smile giving way to a deeper blankness in her eyes. 'Lovely to meet you, Billie. I hope you are enjoying your stay with us?'

Billie hesitated. She was good with faces, and felt certain – accent, hair and glasses aside – that it was the nurse who'd been in the car with them. 'We met before ... you accompanied my mother and me up from Redhill. Your hair was different.'

The nurse shook her head slowly and raised an eyebrow. 'Sorry, I think you're mistaken. That wasn't me.' She touched the crop. 'I always wear my hair like this.'

'And you don't have a sister?'

The nurse shook her head again, something about her expression suggesting a touch of disdain at the suggestion.

Confused, Billie looked from the nurse to Ash, watching the exchange from his own chair. He shrugged at her.

The nurse started to turn back, but Billie felt sure. 'Sorry, what's your name?

'Lia. My name is Lia,' she said.

Billie could see she wanted to wave her away, and the

medical assistant holding the cap next to Billie clearly wanted to crack on with getting it fitted, but Billie didn't want to be brushed off. 'Callie?'

For a split second the woman seemed to respond to her name being used. But then she paused. She turned and this time the smile was gone. 'I'm Lia,' she repeated, a touch of steel in her voice. 'You obviously have me confused with someone else.'

Billie felt her cheeks burn. She knew she was being lied to. She knew she should let it go but it mattered, because Callie, as an alleged agency nurse, had needed to go home, which had forced her mother to return prematurely. It mattered, because a member of staff from Arbor had looked her directly in the eyes and lied to her – so what did that mean?

Billie lifted her chin. 'I'm really good with remembering people, and we were in the same car for eight hours – so I know you're Callie.'

'But for most of it, you were—' The woman stopped, jaw tightening.

Asleep? Was she about to admit her presence in the car by revealing her knowledge that for most of it Billie had indeed slept?

Just then Philippe came over. 'Lia, if you wouldn't mind fitting Ash with his cap, and George,' he said to the man waiting to fit Billie with her cap, 'if you wouldn't mind assisting Billie, we're just about ready to go.'

'Of course, Philippe.' But before she carried out his orders, the nurse turned back to Billie. 'But for most of it,' she carefully repeated, 'you were a patient under ... great mental strain. I'm certain you'll see you were mistaken.' She smiled again. The correction made, she turned away. 'But it was great to finally meet you, Billie.'

The moment passed. Philippe checked the machines, noting things down on a clipboard. Celine opened a cupboard and busied herself with various bits of equipment: foam balls and colourful signs and blindfolds. The medical assistant leaned over to adjust her cap but Billie felt too distracted to engage with him. She would reason with herself later; practise her CBT-taught rationalization techniques to ensure she didn't whip herself up (*careful, Billie*) but for now, she sat with the irritation of feeling like she'd caught someone in a lie.

But if she had, it wasn't just the nurse who was lying, but Philippe too.

And then it was a question of not just who had lied, but why.

NINETEEN

'Okay, thanks for the update, Philippe; interesting data,' said Nathalie. They sat alone in the Arbor conference room, drinking coffee, looking at their laptops and studying spreadsheets. It was early in the morning; Nathalie had just returned from another trip from Chicago, where she'd been visiting Arbor's owners at the NorGline head office, and as usual after Nathalie's absences, they met first for a private briefing, before the senior leadership team meeting when their colleagues would join them. It was Nathalie's job to share information with NorGline's board, and she was adept at managing messages with the right blend of *omit* and *emphasize* which enabled NorGline's culture of risk.

And the risk culture remained high because the profits were high. High profits resulted in high dividends. High dividends meant trust in the medics' activity went sufficiently unchecked. Compliance teams were weakened by the reality of financial outcomes. *Trust the vision* became NorGline's unofficial motto. And Nathalie was a great medic with an outstanding vision.

Nathalie finished her coffee. 'It's great to have five active well-responding subjects again – that's enough to get the full understanding. Each one of the lovelies showing the same neuro plasticity post-event. But we're not seeing anything from Billie yet in terms of real outcomes?'

'No,' said Philippe. 'And more concerning, I think she's contemplating leaving.'

Nathalie looked up from her data sheet, surprised. 'Really? Already? What makes you think that?'

'We know already that the data around Billie's dreams is interesting – definitely atypical. Her amygdala does appear a little enlarged – and very active. She's obviously been suffering nightmares, possibly night terrors – she woke at three in the morning the night you left last week and we detected that she spoke in her sleep.'

'Did you hear what she said?'

Philippe opened his notebook. 'It was Stefana who caught it actually. The single word: "*home*". Followed again by the word: "*home*". Then she muttered something the mics couldn't catch, then just before she woke up, we could just make out "remember, will you?"' He snapped his book shut. 'Stefana proved her worth – *not* – by making too much of the fact Billie's voice was gravelly and, in her words, sounded "creepy".'

'But was Stefana right? Was Billie's voice creepy, Philippe?'

Philippe shrugged and blew air out of his mouth, frustrated. 'Really? How does creepy exist as a line of enquiry in science?'

Nathalie wrinkled her forehead. 'Come on, everything is a line of enquiry. The problem with you is that you don't find anything creepy. Okay, I'll take Stefana's word for it; I'll ask her about it. Anything else?'

'Billie cried in her sleep too.'

'So further REM behaviour disorder – nothing we haven't seen before in any of the subjects. In fact, I'd be concerned if she didn't have it.'

'It was seeing Lia that I think has really unsettled her,' he said and recounted the event. 'When I watched the CCTV back after, Billie's body language made it evident that she was *very* unhappy with the explanation given. Her heart rate and blood pressure were up; we used the eye-tracker software and the activity and pupil dilation confirmed she was stressed. Then after, during the actual synchronicity tasks, she literally did not speak a single word.'

'And since then?'

'In the last week, better, and she seems more settled, but still more reserved in comparison to when she arrived last month. Her cortisol levels remained elevated for twenty-seven hours which demonstrates her chronic stress. I can tell she's wavering about her commitment to Arbor.'

'Obviously, she can't leave. Obviously. We need her.' Nathalie looked at the existing data again, remembering the assurances she'd given to her boss, Jude Dennison, CEO of NorGline. 'Jude is expecting data and outcomes on *five actual real people* – not AI modelling – before we have agreement for next steps.' Nathalie clenched her fist, contemplated it and then released it. When she spoke, she sounded calmer. 'Jude will not accept any deviation this close to the project delivery. If Billie gets away from us, we will be back to four and the entire schedule will be delayed. Four is *not* enough.'

Philippe shut his eyes and rubbed his forehead. 'I agree four is not enough. The project initiation agreement was always for five. But – and I don't say this lightly – we could always move to the next phase?'

Nathalie shook her head. 'NorGline is tense enough about this entire project without us not following the agreed sequencing. No to that.'

'Okay, good, I do agree. But I do have an alternative idea,' said Philippe. 'When you were in Chicago, I used some AI modelling to run through a number of possible options. Let me tell you my favoured suggestion to retain the lovely Billie.'

Nathalie got up, helped herself to another coffee and then told him: 'Okay. I'm ready. Tell me what we need to do. And I really hope we like it.'

TWENTY

Dan Downes stood on the doorstep of a pretty terraced house in a village just outside of Crowthorne. The garden was neatly kept, with lavender overspilling onto the path and a fat tabby cat curled up on the doorstep, asleep in the sun.

When he heard no sounds of life, he pressed the bell again. He had to be in Reading in an hour, but didn't want to leave without an answer.

Then he heard the sound of feet in the hall; a woman in her early sixties answered the door. Billie's mother.

Jo Cathey dried her hands on a tea towel. 'Sorry, I was tidying up in the kitchen. May I help?'

'I'm sorry to bother you, but I'm looking for Billie. I know she's at the Arbor Institute, but I'm here because I would welcome speaking with you, primarily as a way of locating its address, if you have it.' He passed her his business card. 'I'll introduce myself. My name is Dan Downes and I'm a journalist. I've met your daughter – I visited Billie when she was on the Warwick ward. I know . . .' he lowered his voice and checked over his shoulder '. . . what happened to her; I thought I would follow up with her and check she was okay.'

Jo's mouth pressed into a line and she slung the tea towel she held over her shoulder with force, as she took the card. 'I remember being told about you. We haven't met, but wouldn't it be more accurate if you addressed me as *aunt*?'

Dan twigged. 'Ah, yes, I signed onto the ward as Billie's cousin. Apologies – she and I had thought that was the best way to ensure that I could be an agreed visitor.'

Jo paused, studying him, before giving a long exhale. 'Okay. Would you like to come in off the doorstep, Mr Downes? You're obviously here to talk about Billie and I'd actually welcome the chance to speak with you.'

He followed her through to the rear of the house and she gestured to him to sit at the kitchen table. 'I'm going to make tea and then perhaps we could swap what we know. I can be honest with you – on the proviso that I have your assurance this won't go in an article.'

'It won't, I promise. Everything is off the record. Really, I just want to check that Billie is okay.'

Jo leaned against the kitchen worktop with a sigh. 'The truth is, I don't know if she is all right. I haven't seen or heard from her in six weeks. She normally stays in regular contact but not now. Normally it wouldn't matter; she's a grown-up and six weeks is not a long time if your daughter is busy. But there are a couple of niggles about Arbor itself that make me feel a little ... uneasy. Firstly, because I wasn't allowed to actually visit the institute, despite the long journey to Wemyss Bay, in Scotland. I was forced to leave her and return home the same day. They said the nurse who had accompanied us had to be elsewhere, but it felt like an excuse. I offered to catch the train back, but – Billie doesn't know this because she was asleep – the chauffer told me that I wasn't welcome to visit the island. He was cold and even a little intimidating.'

'You didn't let Billie know?'

She shrugged. 'Part of me had to accept that it's a good thing that a psychiatric facility is careful who they let in, don't you think, nephew?'

Dan felt his cheeks pink a little in response.

Jo gave him a smile that told him it was forgotten. 'Besides, Billie was so desperately unhappy on the ward. She was declining at an alarming rate rather than getting better. With her friends dead, I was scared where her rock bottom might be. So, why would I insist on her returning to that place just because the chauffeur was rude?'

'I take the point.'

'But another concern is there's so little information about Arbor and what details are available are very vague.'

'I can find no reference to it – that's why I'm here.'

'Yes, and that's unusual, isn't it? When they first contacted me, the website said the institute was on the West Coast of Scotland, there was no suggestion it was on the island. It's called Dorcha and in the middle of the Firth of Clyde. Totally isolated. But when I looked again, the website had changed and gave the location on the island, which was strange. It made Billie a little nervous to know she would be staying somewhere so inaccessible, but then we were en route and it was too late to turn round.'

'It's odd that it would change.'

'And that's not all.' Jo retrieved a business card from the windowsill and handed it to him. 'Before the chauffeur left, I asked for a contact number. You can see the number he wrote out on the back – well, it's wrong. I've tried it a hundred times and it doesn't work, so I have no way of contacting her.'

'What about the initial contact email?'

'Now deleted from my account. I've tried to remember the email address, but they all bounce back.'

She sat down, face tight with tension. 'I have to remember she's an adult and she made her choice to go there. It's not like she's missing; I know where she is. And to be fair to them, after I got the initial invite, when Billie was still on Warwick, I spoke with the director on the phone, and she was clear contact would only be in emergencies. Apparently, their patients are offered privacy, seclusion and peace from the outside world. I don't even disagree with that in principle – given what Billie's been through – but that number I spoke with the director on doesn't work anymore, and it's the wrong number on the card and then there's the changing information and the missing email.' She shrugged. 'That and I'm her mother. I trust my gut and I'm becoming worried. I don't want to crowd her or embarrass her, but I'm thinking of going up there.'

'I can check in on her if you want. I've got to be in Glasgow in ten days.' He'd pulled up his phone and located Dorcha on Google maps. 'It's only an hour from there. Have you got a greeting card you can write out and I can use it as an excuse to see her?'

Jo's eyes lit up. 'Really? Oh, Dan, I would find that very reassuring, thank you.' She found one and wrote out a note to Billie, wishing her good health and asking her to be in touch so she didn't worry about her.

Dan watched, deliberating if he should tell her about the phenomenon he suspected Billie had experienced. But as he left, after exchanging numbers, he reflected that he was right not to bring it up – it was not his news to tell. Not yet.

But, he thought, he would visit the institute, deliver the card and speak to Billie. Then he'd be able to give Jo good news before the end of next week.

He pulled the garden gate shut behind him and unlocked his car, feeling happy that he now at least knew where to find Billie.

TWENTY-ONE

After Googling directions from Glasgow to the West Coast islands in the Firth of Clyde, Dan headed to Wemyss Bay. It was a small town with the charm of the coast, and he'd parked in the car park by the ferry port. He'd paused briefly to look out across the Firth, the cool sea air making him draw his breath, before heading towards the ferry office. But after standing in line, he was told: 'No ferry goes to Dorcha. You need to try a private tour from the marina up the road.' Parking at the marina, he asked again and was told, 'You want Josh Andain', and was thumbed in the direction of a sign proclaiming *Island Tours*.

A man of medium build with a dark beard, sat in a boat reading a manual. Dan asked him about solo island tours and Andain stood, keen to welcome him aboard. But when he heard the destination, he shook his head. 'You can't land on Dorcha. I'll take you to the other islands though. Lots to see, charming little places. Isle of Arran, Little Cumbrae, Bute—'

'It has to be Dorcha.' Then Dan named a price he couldn't turn down.

But Andain was reluctant, viewing him with suspicious eyes. 'Why'd you want to go out there? There's nothing on it but money, and money like that brings trouble.'

Dan smiled and added another hundred and the questions stopped.

He accepted the life jacket and looked forward to getting closer to whatever it was he was trying to find. He'd spent several evenings chasing facts down metaphorical black holes. He'd found out that Arbor was owned by NorGline Pharmaceuticals. But what he'd then discovered was that NorGline was owned by Magnus Inc. Magnus Inc was currently the fourth largest multinational investment company, with a specialist lens in managing portfolios with interests in environmental, social and governance initiatives. Currently twenty-third on the Fortune 500 list, it was a big player, and growing bigger. To Magnus, money was no object. To Magnus, money *was* the object.

So, what did Magnus want with Billie? Certainly not to heal her: there was no money in curing the niche and the rare. He just couldn't get the link. Whatever had happened to her and her friends meant – without intervention – certain death. How could Magnus Inc monetize something that caused almost certain death?

Like his thoughts, the waves brewed dark. The wind whipped yeasty heads, spraying sharp salt against his skin. Keening gulls rose and fell above the boat, following their wake, hoping for potential fishing spoils. The marina, then the row of houses fronting Wemyss Bay, disappeared behind him.

Eventually, after what felt like much longer than half an hour, with the earlier grey mizzle behind them, the skipper pointed out the wooded island they were approaching as Dorcha.

'What does Dorcha mean?' Dan asked.

'Dark. Take note, son. Places get names for a reason.'

As if to dispute the point, as they drew closer, the grey clouds dissipated to blue sky. The sun came out, and even out on the water, he could feel the July heat on his face. They pulled up to the jetty, where Andain repeated his prices. 'Three hundred pounds for every hour you keep me waiting. You can have your car keys back when you've paid.'

Dan surveyed the surroundings. There was a pretty stretch of pebbled beach backed by a green wall of thick pine trees breached by a narrow path. Someone had planted for privacy, he noted.

The path it is then, Dan decided, glancing over his shoulder, glad for the skipper watching.

He walked up the incline and stepped under the trees. He'd not gone far before boat and beach disappeared from view and he was engulfed in the darkness of the woods. Perhaps I shouldn't have come alone, he thought.

A figure stepped out from behind a tree, making Dan start with alarm.

'Can I help you?'

'Hi!' Dan smiled – it was always better to be friendly, particularly when you were the uninvited guest. 'My name is Dan Downes and I'm here to see a friend.'

The man pulled his cap down a little and then pushed his hands into his jeans. 'That's not going to happen, mate,' he said from behind Ray-Bans. 'Nice idea, but you can't come any further. You see this is private land and you're trespassing.'

Dan held both hands up. 'Sorry, I get that. It's just that my friend Billie is staying here, and her mother was given a number for the Arbor Institute and it doesn't work. I was in Glasgow and I thought I'd visit while I was in Scotland.'

'Sorry to waste your journey.'

It was dark under the thickness of the canopy, everything cast into shadow. But Dan could make out that the man who had appeared out of nowhere was tall, around six foot four with broad shoulders, but it was the shotgun slung casually over his shoulder that suggested he was the island's muscle. Or the visible part of it, anyway. He didn't doubt that there would also be lawyers, and CCTV – and very possibly some less-legitimate means of security. But being persistent, even in the face of such granite, was part of Dan's job. He knew that the skipper had thought him a naïve Londoner to pay so much to wait for him; but his safe passage home was well worth the money. And others knew that Andain had taken him to Dorcha – and locals couldn't easily go missing.

'You're right, it has been a journey. It would be fantastic to just get Billie on the phone to her mother for a—'

'You need to leave.'

'Look, sorry to be a pain, but if I leave here without some sort of reassurance that Billie is alive and doing well, then her mother's going to call the police. Not me: *her*. So, I'm not your enemy here, I'm just in the area, looking to help a mother worry less about her child. What say you help me with that?'

'You're refusing to go.'

Dan wished he could see the other man's eyes – who wore sunglasses in such deep shade? But Dan could see the way the man took a step forward, noted the flex and stretch of his back into his shoulders and he knew he was squaring up to him. That always made him want to dig in. His own temerity in the face of conflict was what he liked most about himself. It was also what made him good at his job. Dan smiled and leaned into the argument. He thumbed over his shoulder. 'I've got my man on the boat back there. He's waiting for me. I'm paying him three hundred pounds an hour to wait for me and I gave him my car keys as a bond. He thinks I'm a soft touch. I think not. I think I've made sure he won't leave without me. He also knows what shape I was in when I got off the boat, so if I go back anything less than perfect, I've got myself a witness for a police complaint.'

He let a beat pass before he held his hands palms out, in a gesture of openness. 'Come on, let's start again. I just need to see that Billie is safe and well so I can go back and reassure her mother. That's got to be achievable, hasn't it?'

The man turned away from him and spoke into his phone. Dan couldn't hear what he said but decided to underline his stubbornness by sitting on a log. He got out his phone and pretended to start making notes, except he had nothing to say other than *arsehole* at this stage.

'Put your phone away,' the security guard said when he got off his phone, 'or I'll break it.'

Dan's hands went up again in a back-off gesture and he slid the phone back into his inside jacket pocket. They were obviously waiting for something or someone. Deciding to get comfortable, and obviously so, he positioned himself so he benefited from a single shard of sunlight that had broken through the trees above. He shut his eyes and enjoyed the feeling of sun on his face. Man, there is *nowhere* better than Scotland in the sunshine, he thought. 'Beautiful spot you have here,' he said, not expecting a reply and not getting one.

Then he could hear a quad bike approaching, and knew whatever they were waiting for was about to happen. At three hundred pounds a pop, he hoped they would hurry up so one hour didn't tick over into two.

The quad bike pulled up on the path in front of them. A man dressed in black, tanned, got off, greeting him with a smile. 'Mr Downes, I assume? Philippe Bouchard, the institute's director of operations.'

Dan got up and held out his hand, surprised when it was taken. The arm was lean and the grip was strong.

'I'm sorry we can't let you see Billie, but I understand you're needing reassurance that she is well and happy. She is. Will you take my word?'

Dan shook his head. 'I'm afraid – no offence – I'm going to need more than that.'

'Let me get you something more concrete then.' He fetched an iPad from the quad bike and pressed a few buttons. 'I'm logging into our security system. It's pretty good – it picked up the noise of your boat as soon as you pulled up to the pontoon. The cameras were tracking you on the path.' He looked up, still smiling, but his blue eyes, Dan thought, were so cold they were dead.

'Here, Mr Downes,' he said, passing him the iPad. 'This is what Billie is doing right now.'

Dan took it. Billie was lying on a sun lounger by an outdoor pool in a green bikini. There was a young man stretched out on the one next to her – square shoulders, a shock of blond tousled hair, very tanned. There was no audio, but he said something to Billie and she laughed and threw a coaster at him. It looked flirty and fun. Watching them, seeing Billie's youth, suddenly made Dan feel middle-aged. 'How do I know that's happening right now? It could be a recording,' he said. 'You'll forgive the suspicion, it's just as an investigative journalist, you learn not to trust the slick PR.'

'This is not slick PR, Mr Downes, this is simply the truth. Perhaps you've learned not to see it.'

Dan nodded. 'Philippe, is it? You might have a point. But I'm still going to need more to reassure her mother. Me saying, well, Arbor showed me a vid clip, so she must be fine, is not going to cut it. My being here is the only thing preventing Mrs Cathey reporting Billie as a missing person.' Beat. 'To the police.' Then he added, pleased to have had the thought: 'Billie's discharging psychiatrist isn't happy either. Feels the comms haven't been what was promised.' Dan didn't know that was true, but suspected it was an easy reach to make and definitely worth the punt. He made a future note to reach out again and see if Dr Singh would now be prepared to talk. He'd long ago learned that persistence yielded results. 'So, do I need to alert the police?'

Philippe gave another smile that didn't reach his cold eyes. 'You're very persistent, Mr Downes. So let me prove it another way. But if I reassure you, will you agree to go on your way and not come back? Otherwise,' the smile deepened to show very even, very white teeth, 'it'll be us calling the police on *you*.'

Dan gave a nod of assent and Philippe continued, 'I'm going to ask Ted here to discharge his shotgun when you tell him to. Billie will hear the noise. You'll see her reaction on screen and then you'll know that she is – just as I've already explained – lying by the pool. We have excellent vitamin D pool heaters to boost the beautiful but often weak sunshine.'

Philippe brought up the video of Billie again and passed it to Dan. She was still on the lounger, her long red hair now pulled up in a bun, shades on.

Philippe cleared his throat. 'Are you ready, Mr Downes?'

Dan nodded and Ted cracked the barrel and the clear sound of the shot reverberated through the trees. On cue, Billie sat up, pushed up her sunglasses and squinted into the distance. *What was that?* she clearly mouthed and Dan breathed out, both relieved and disappointed. They weren't lying – this was Billie right now. He had to accept it – she looked healthy, safe and well-treated. He passed the iPad back. 'Thanks – I'll tell her mother she's okay.'

'It's been two months, Mr Downes. She is getting better. She is studying for her degree again and having therapy. We think we can help her. We think,' he paused before standing to one side, pointedly suggesting that it was time for Dan to go, 'she should be allowed to try. She is twenty-four and while I am, of course, concerned that her mother is worried, I think a few weeks is not a very long time for an adult to be able to concentrate on their own health and healing, don't you?'

'Mrs Cathey was given a wrong number.'

'Then let me give you a real one.' Philippe pulled out a black business card devoid of anything except a gold drawing of an oak tree in relief. On the back he wrote a number in the white box. 'That's my direct number. She can call me. But perhaps if she can't trust us, she can trust you.'

Dan started to walk down the beach, then remembered. He turned to find them both staring at him from under the shadows of the trees: faces impassive, eyes and sunglasses unreadable. Lifting his chin, he strode back, proffering the greeting card that Jo Cathey wanted Billie to have. 'Can you pass this on please? Just a note from mother to daughter. She's thoughtfully left it unsealed so you can check the wording if you want.'

Philippe's mouth tightened to a smile that did not reach his eyes. 'We are not a prison, Mr Downes. There's nothing we need to check,' he said, taking it from him.

Back in the boat, Dan watched the shore of Dorcha disappear behind them. Philippe and Ted hadn't come out of the woods – no doubt acutely aware that to be seen escorting Dan off the island while carrying a shotgun might be poor PR.

Andain had only grunted when he saw Dan approach, perhaps disappointed he hadn't been longer.

Dan decided he would report back to Jo Cathey and think about next steps. The reaction to his visit suggested that Arbor did not want intrusions and they obviously wanted to keep their hooks into Billie. But why? Not just for health and healing, that was for sure. In his experience, organizations that had enough money to buy private islands rarely acted philanthropically – and the more they wanted to pretend to do good, the more there was to hide. Tax breaks were the usual reason but this didn't fit. Good PR was the other reason – but, again, this operation was so secretive they obviously didn't want any media exposure. And he was unsure how what happened to Billie could be monetized. Pharmaceutical companies wanted to cure the most prevalent health problems of the day so they could make big money, they didn't usually bother with rare and obscure phenomena.

So, after reassuring Mrs Cathey, Dan decided the next person to speak with must be Dr Singh. He'd treated Billie first, and he might have something interesting to say.

TWENTY-TWO

'Hello, everyone, very exciting to be back after my week away. It's tricky to have to keep leaving you all, but those are the demands of the job,' said Nathalie, as she entered the small observation room adjacent to Billie's bedroom. 'So, how are you all? How is Billie? Last time I was here, she was sleeping badly, and Philippe thought she might leave. But has she now settled?' She already knew the answers to these questions from Philippe, but she liked her team to feel that their feedback was of vital importance.

A South Korean doctor, Dr Bo Yeeun, had jumped up to allow Nathalie to sit in front of the monitor; everyone shuffled around to make space and agreed, yes, they were pleased to see Nathalie back. Yes, Billie seemed to have settled and there had been no more crying in her sleep since last week. The team of five doctors – all handpicked by Nathalie – represented the most senior of the medical staff. Folders of information, alongside coffee cups and bags of crisps, were pushed further along the desk out of Nathalie's way.

'How long has Billie been asleep?' Nathalie took the

leather chair, thanking the doctor who'd vacated it. For a long moment, she stared at the dark glass screen, watching Billie asleep in her bedroom. She watched the rise and fall of her chest, but Billie was otherwise still. To Nathalie, she was mesmerizing. Perhaps she'd been transfixed too long, because Philippe gave a polite cough, breaking the spell. She took her cue and addressed the team. 'Where are we at?'

'She's atypical already. One hundred and twelve minutes – that's just been one sleep cycle, so significantly longer that we would expect,' said Philippe.

'Ah, Billie,' she said, pressing her hands together, 'we just know you are going to be our star pupil. How are the others?'

Bo pointed to their readings on a different screen. 'Nothing to see there yet.'

'We've noticed another feature to Billie's atypical sleep architecture.' Philippe tilted his screen towards Nathalie, pointing at a line on a graph. 'Something seems to happen between the different sleep stages of N3 and REM.'

Nathalie put her glasses on and leaned in. 'So, unintentional dux gregis – if it's going to happen – is in the N3. Deep sleep. Interesting, given it also occurs during full consciousness.' She pointed at a different line on the diagnostic display. 'What's this lacuna?'

'None of us are sure yet. I'll tell you what it isn't though – it's not the onset of REM. Although her theta waves are typical, her cortical frequency is not – it's faster. But: she has no paralysis – in fact the opposite.'

'Is she sleepwalking?' Nathalie shrugged. 'We're aware of the REM disorder. Thank you, Stefana, for your help with that. The significance of the "creepy" voice,' she said to everyone, 'is that we think that the changed architecture of Billie's brain, and the enlarged amygdala, with its structural role in emotional responses, memory formation, decision-making and activating fight-or-flight response, has resulted in increasing the vividity of her dreams. Stefana, do you want to comment here?'

'You've said it perfectly, Nathalie. But yes, we think that the change to Billie's voice might signify a male in her dream – hence the deeper "creepy" intonation.'

'And you suggested that, because of the imperative use of 'home', perhaps that male figure is her father, who we all know died several years ago. Because of Stefana's conclusion, and some strategic planning from Philippe, Celine has been specifically engineering Billie's therapy towards her father and encouraging reflections to suggest that he would want Billie to remain at Arbor. Clever team.'

Stefana returned Nathalie's smile, like a proud pupil.

'She's second cycle now,' Richard said, checking the digital wall clock, 'noting the first minute.'

Nathalie leaned forward and the room fell silent as they watched Billie continue to sleep.

The watch that Billie wore had a sophisticated sensor that could be activated by the team, giving them a constant update on every biomarker in her bloods while she slept, in addition to the huge range of information they gathered on her: heart rate; body temperature; blood pressure; oxygen levels; eyeball movement; brain activity. All this information appeared on several screens in front of them. After studying the readouts for nearly half an hour, they could observe nothing notable.

Philippe finally lifted his pen. 'Stefana, would you do

me a kindness and run and get a glass of water please? I wouldn't ask but I'm supposed to take some antibiotics and I dare not leave at this crucial time.'

'Sure, of course – no problem,' Stefana said.

As she left the observation room, Nathalie caught Philippe's gaze. Imperceptible except to him, she raised her eyebrow a little.

But he didn't react, instead turning his eyes to a different screen – to the one outside in the corridor. The security camera showed the corridor from every angle. Vital for security, the observation room, on the same floor as the bedrooms, was hidden, the doorway concealed by the birch ply panelling.

Philippe watched Billie's readouts without moving, except for the tiny rub of nail against thumb pad as he moved it back and forth, back and forth.

Nathalie glanced at him, studying him briefly with shrewd eyes, before returning her gaze to the information displayed on the screens. Nothing to see. Billie slept on. The readings didn't change.

Unnoticed by everyone but Philippe, Stefana could be seen on the security screen. Walking away, she disappeared out of view and then, a couple of minutes later, returned and walked back down the corridor carrying the water. She came back into the observation room and placed the water next to Philippe. 'Thanks, Stefana,' he acknowledged without looking up.

The minutes ticked on, and Philippe made some more checks.

'She's still in delta,' muttered Nathalie, scraping her hair away from her face. They watched the screens. Then, she pointed at one. 'Look, her slow wave is extended. Significant?'

Philippe didn't say anything. He checked his watch again and reached for the water, but as he touched the glass, eyes glued to the screens, he knocked it over and it fell to the floor and smashed. Philippe shook his head, appearing shocked. 'Oh no! What have I done?'

'What *have* you done, Philippe?' asked Nathalie. She raised an eyebrow, trying to figure out quite what Philippe, who was the least clumsy person she knew, was up to.

'How stupid of me. Look, guys, I can't get up to clean this up mid-moment here, so please can I just ask if you can be really careful—'

'I'll go and get a dustpan,' Stefana said, already up.

Philippe gave her a deep, wide smile. His eyes shone at her. 'You're so kind – typically kind. But really, I would feel so—'

'Honestly, Philippe, I'm already gone. You must concentrate.' And without waiting for an answer, she'd slipped noiselessly from the observation room.

'Generous colleague,' he said, his focus only on the screens and Billie sleeping in her bed in front of him.

Nathalie watched Philippe with a falcon's scrutiny. He didn't return her gaze, just made a note of a measurement.

Suddenly the lines on the screen began to move more rapidly, showing an increase in brain activity. Bo Yeeun spoke. 'She's moving into REM; capillary RBC flow is increasing—'

'But what the fuck is she doing now? That is *not* REM behaviour,' said Nathalie, staring at the monitor showing Billie's bedroom.

Billie, still lying in her bed, was slowly, very slowly, raising her arm.

'But that's not the interesting thing. *This* is the interesting thing,' said Philippe, pointing at a different screen.

TWENTY-THREE

in the woods again.

Billie felt uneasy. It was cold and the low grey light suggested it was dusk. How could it be so late in the day? It must be autumn because she could smell leaf mould and damp earth. Normally, she liked autumn but looking around, everything felt moribund. There was no birdsong, she noticed, not even the movement of insects. The forest wasn't just empty, she understood ... it was dead.

I'm dead too, she thought.

No. Nearly, but not quite yet.

But I am utterly alone. It was as if she could call and scream and shout out, but it would make no difference. Where was her father? He was always with her in the woods. Where was Firkin? Why would they leave her alone in such a place of despair?

She realized she had her leather gauntlet on; flexing her fingers in it gave her comfort. The smell of leather brought her back to happier times. The gauntlet was too big – it was her father's really. He'd bought the leather gloves but, needing only one, gave the other to his keen apprentice falconer. Billie, being left-handed, felt like the spare had been made for her. 'You being right-handed is the sign that we are the perfect match,' she said to him once, putting her small gloved hand in his.

'Yes, Billie. Together we make a pair.'
'You never used to call me Billie.'
'That was the past. This is now.'
'Now? Where are you now?' she asked her empty gloved palm. Father and Firkin. She raised it up, hoping that Firkin would see it. And if Firkin, then her father, too. *Firkin, come to me*, she said, grasping her hand, hoping to hear his bell, *come to me*, and she willed it, really willed Firkin to come to her, hand up, grasping, reaching and hoping – compelling . . .

TWENTY-FOUR

The CCTV screen that Philippe pointed to showed Stefana walking back down the corridor towards the observation room. In one hand she carried the dustpan and brush she'd gone to retrieve to clear up Philippe's broken glass, but her left hand – in perfect synchronicity with Billie's – had started to raise. Although more than fifty metres apart, with a wall between Billie's bedroom and the corridor, they both moved together, a silent unseen communication between them.

Nathalie and the team watched as Billie continued lifting her left hand, arm stretching up, perfectly matched by Stefana.

'They've flocked,' Nathalie said in quiet wonder. 'Finally, five weeks in, just as we'd started to give up hope ... well, well, isn't she feisty? We give her the perfect gang to sync with and she picks on a doctor. What a girl.'

'Just what we hoped for,' said Philippe. 'Dux Gregis time check: three zero seven.'

'Three zero seven, DG,' agreed Bo, noting it down.

'But what about Stefana – this is not the plan?' Richard

said. 'This is *not* the plan,' he repeated, looking at Nathalie. 'Request to wake the patient.'

Nathalie held up a hand to Richard – *wait*, her narrowed eyes fast appraising the range of screens and monitors. 'CT, MRI – tell me what you see.'

'Cortex highly active—' Bo Yeeun answered.

'Which areas?'

'Forty-six, thirty-one A ...'

'You're hesitating.'

'Permission to wake Billie,' repeated Richard. 'We have a duty of care to our colleagues and—'

'Not given – MRI, where are we at?'

'Stefana has her hand straight in the air like Billie. She's stopped walking. Eyes open – obviously brain activity unknown.'

'MRI, where are we at?'

'Look: Billie's left hand is open upwards and is making a grasping action – just like Stefana is doing now.'

'This is not the *plan*,' repeated Richard, face reddening. 'We need to know what the corresponding brain activity is doing. Otherwise, this is virtually pointless.'

'We continue with the reactive dynamic assessment,' answered Nathalie. 'What's happening? Cortex, people?'

Bo spoke: 'Anterior insular – with marked raised blood flow with arcuate fasciculus.'

'Billie is getting off the bed – Stefana has stopped outside Billie's door. Permission to wake the patient,' persisted Richard, his hands rubbing his beard with visible agitation.

'So, she's feeling empathy? – but speech? She's not talking.' Nathalie paused. '*Shit, could they be communicating telepathically?* Thoughts? And Richard, your objections are formally noted so stand the fuck down.'

'Mirror neurons in the Broca found in primates when observing and copying behaviour. Possible?' Bo suggested.

'I like that,' said Nathalie. 'Shall we get Stefana under a scan? See if there's a response? We can see it – *shit*, she's outside the door – but can we *see* it? Thoughts?'

'Too dangerous – unknown what might happen if she receives extrinsic pressures.'

'Actually, we *do* know,' said Richard, 'and if we don't take action then we are in danger of seeing it *again* and we have not planned for *that* at this juncture.'

'You have a point, Richard. But, just because this is so rare to observe – and with respect, we don't know this isn't going to be an anomaly, an outlier – then shouldn't we at least debate what we might see?' said Nathalie. Then adding in a tone of voice that sounded playful but concealed something more icy: 'And with respect, you all signed up knowing the risks. You've all taken a seat at the table for the sizeable rewards – Stefana included – so let's keep that in sight. So keep talking, people.'

'Somatosensory association is also showing elevated levels of activity . . .' said Richard.

'And?'

'Supramarginal gyrus looks red hot.'

'She's still empathizing then—'

'With Stefana? Or more?'

'Billie's getting up!' said Bo.

Nathalie's voice took on a steel edge: 'What about the rest of the group?'

Bo checked the screens. 'Normal. No further sign of DG.'

Stefana had passed the observation door. Billie stood up, gradually putting her arm down – Stefana following the action at the same speed.

'Readings! I want to know what the fuck is going on!'

The doctors hurried to obey, shouting out what they were seeing on their screens.

Nathalie almost smiled, pressing her hands together. 'This is good. Billie should be in REM but I don't know what this is. Her major outputs are mostly congruent, but look at her brain.' She pointed to a different monitor showing the MRI.

As Billie walked to the door, Stefana stood on the other side.

'This could be dangerous,' said Bo. 'Stefana can't be sectator ducis to the patient.'

'Too late. And I prefer the term dux sectator – I took Latin, but most haven't.'

'But it's the more accurate term. "Follower of the dux" is sectator ducis.'

'But it obfuscates. I think it's helpful that the language is clear: dux gregis for the first wave and dux sectator for the second wave.' She waved her hand, dismissing the point. 'It just improves clarity.'

Nathalie exhaled long and hard. 'And she is following Billie now. Dux and damage double done. So, Richard, if you want to intervene now you can, but remember once the connection is made, you waking anyone up isn't going to change it. Once that bond has happened you can't break it. No one can. If Billie wants to dial up Stefana from the other side of the world, she probably can.'

'It's Philippe's fault,' he muttered, rubbing his beard.

'Do you want to wake her?'
'Yes.'
'Philippe?'
'Yes.'
'Okay, let's wake the patient: STAT.'

Philippe nodded and hit two buttons, one with loud bird music and the other raising the lights in Billie's room. Almost immediately she stirred, and her arm dropped down. At the same moment, Stefana's arm dropped and then, after a momentary pause, she too dropped, her body falling to the floor as if a puppeteer had cut her strings.

TWENTY-FIVE

Nathalie shut the conference door behind her and leaned against it; she looked at Philippe sitting waiting for her and grinned. It was three in the morning and neither of them had been to bed yet; with so much to think about she was far from being able to rest. 'So, first things first, Philippe, you are extremely naughty because we had made a plan before I left about how we were going to move her forward and this was not it – but you are very clever, and I do, very much, like the outcome,' she said, grinning and applauding him a little.

Philippe grinned. 'No cleverness about it, but yes, I'm delighted too.'

'I'm *so* delighted, I'm going to treat myself to a mocha.' She selected the button on the machine. 'Now,' she said, sitting down, 'let's cut the BS, shall we? This was no accident, it happened by *your* design. You set up Stefana as an opportunity to be exploited. The outcome *is* super-duper and just what was needed, but walk me through your thinking – which, happy as I am, you should have cleared with me in advance.' She held up a hand to stop him speaking. 'Tell me, we've never done this with the others, so why now?'

'Because the other four never kept us waiting this long.'

'Well, that might be true, but I never fell for the "whoops, silly clumsy me!" routine and nor did Richard, who by the way, will be here,' she said, checking her large, heavy Rolex Submariner, 'in a few minutes, angry that you've now lost him one of his team.'

Philippe pouted. 'Stefana's alive.'

'But off the team permanently. And Richard's perspective will be that a new recruitment will impact on delivery. He had one of the finest young neurologists, and one that didn't fuss about ethics. He'll feel she's not easy to replace.'

'She'll be *very* easy to replace. The money Arbor pays, no one fusses about ethics.'

Philippe was right. It was one of the unarguable facts of life that most people could be brought for a cheque – all that counted was the number of zeroes. 'That might be true, but Richard is going to be here wanting to know why you did what you did without his clearance. He'll have a point.'

'Then let's keep her.'

Nathalie sipped from her cup, looking at Philippe with amused eyes, watching him work it out. 'You've been impetuous but illogical – not like you. She can't be part of the team now, because she's flock and therefore part of the study.'

Philippe rubbed the bridge of his nose. 'I had to do something.' He spoke with deep frustration. 'It's all this concrete. We wrapped them in sleeping units with the density of a bunker when we know that sleep is often when subjects experiment with their new abilities. It's a design fault:

lead-lined, hermetically sealed, and sound resistant. I just saw a way past that by getting Stefana into the hall. Having only one door between them instead of the thick concrete walls enabled Billie to reach her.'

Nathalie laughed a little and sipped her coffee. 'Still naughty though,' she finally said. 'Particularly as I know about your ... little dalliance with Stefana. There's a good chance Richard will, too. The fact you were obviously bored of her and now she's out of the picture is very convenient.'

Philippe pinked and opened his mouth to speak.

She spoke first. 'He might not know – he's not as observant as me. I'm just giving you the head's up because I want this resolved as soon as possible. We'll keep Stefana on site, and give her a different role, one that is blind to new developments. It'll be handy having a dux sectator on site. We've got enough data on the third stage, but we'll badge it as DS corroborative data.

'With regards to Billie, when the others arrive, we'll look at their schedules and adjust accordingly.' She clapped her hands. 'Come on, Philippe, chin up. This is good news. We needed progress and my boss will be pleased, and what pleases Jude, pleases me. *Now* things can change round here.'

TWENTY-SIX

'Dr Singh – *Veer*.'

Dr Veer Singh had just arrived on Warwick ward for the morning shift. He'd hung his coat on the back of his office door, and reluctantly opened it to greet his colleague, staff nurse Nick Lewes. 'Hello, Nick, normally I'd say come in, but—'

Nick stood in the corridor, not listening. He glanced over his shoulder with the agitation of someone waiting for their dealer to open the door. 'I've got to speak to you. *Right now.*'

Veer wanted to say, *Not today, bring me problems any day but not* this *one. Today, I'm shut to weirdness, worries and witchery.* But taking another look, he noticed Nick looked so dreadful, so ashen, he stood to one side and rubbed the circulation back into his own face.

'I don't want anyone else to hear this.' Nick shut the door and seemed to rest against it, either to hold himself up or to stop anyone coming in.

Veer sat behind his desk and felt sick. Today, Veer had very nearly not come to work, but his wife had insisted.

Yesterday, the news had come that both he and his wife had dreaded. Her breast cancer had returned, and worse than ever.

Prisha had insisted they would not despair. Prisha had insisted he get up, shower, shave, and go to work as normal. He'd done it, not wanting to upset her further, deciding to do what she asked, and somehow he would find a way to survive the shift, survive another day on an oversubscribed, underfunded locked psychiatric ward, and not crumble.

But Nick's face as he stood at Veer's office door with a look that suggested someone had died, told him he shouldn't have had such confidence. That he could crumble yet.

Veer felt cold. They'd worked together for many years, but Nick would never push his way into anywhere, let alone his office. Veer knew just what it meant.

'It's happened again.'

At Nick's words, something shifted inside of him – something fundamental and seismic, and his half-digested breakfast toast turned in his stomach. It was as if the world had become a colder, less certain place. *Prisha, and now this.* Veer had always prided himself on being an optimist – he'd always seen the joy in the new life springing from his spider plants, the way the sunlight fell through the windows in the afternoon and the possibility of health in each patient. But since Billie, he'd been losing sleep, every night thinking of what he'd seen – and what it told him about how little he understood human consciousness. Really, what was the point of his job if he knew nothing? When working in chaos, people looked to him for the answers. That meant having surety, confidence – but now he was left with none. Now he was left looking for answers himself, also lost in the chaos – not just in his professional world, but his home life as well.

Suddenly, the tired office that had felt like home after so many years felt oppressive and broken. The wire in the security glass, the cracks in the plaster, the old lino suddenly felt too noticeable. Before, he had such purpose in his life he'd thought he'd never leave, but now it occurred to him that he would. Perhaps he would even give in his notice today. Perhaps he should ignore Prisha and go home to her.

'But Billie's not here now, so ...' Veer said, not wanting to believe it. 'She's gone, so ... whatever that was ... must be over.'

Nick ran his fingers through his hair, eyes wide and haunted. He looked at the door and the window as if he expected Billie to burst through. 'But it's not. It's not over – it's the others. Marjorie Briggs, Raymond and Elsie. They did it again last night.' He started scratching his arm, long deep movements against his bare skin. 'I ... I've been checking on them. Checking the CCTV. The women I check less, obviously, because I need a female staff member. But Chanice, who I'm on nights with this week, had started to ask questions, like why I want to look in on Elsie and Marjorie so much. I said they'd been walking in their sleep and I think she kinda believed me, but ... Raymond, because I can, I've been checking. At night. Just to make sure he's sleeping.

'Everyone had been fine, no funny business at all, but then, last night, I realized it was happening again. Last night I went in just after one a.m. and Raymond's standing there, arm raised. He had his PJs on this time, 'cause I've been hassling him about wearing them at night, saying he might get cold, but really, deep down, I was thinking about this, you know?'

Veer nodded, as if he knew exactly why Nick would want him to wear pyjamas.

'So, he's standing there and then he starts to walk towards me, like some freaky Egyptian mummy in one of the old black-and-white films. I back up sharp – he's a big guy, right? I'm six foot, but he makes me feel small – and then I wonder about the others, Marjorie and Elsie. Now, my life's not worth it if I go in their rooms at night, but I get Chanice and tell her I think they're sleepwalking and I ask her to check. She remembered about finding Elise before and she does check and she finds them both out of bed, arm up, reaching for something like they wanted to pull the stars out of the sky, she said. She calls for me, and of course, I'm right there and I see it. Then, in a couple of minutes, it's all over. Chanice is a little freaked out – because you know how weird it looks like, right? – but it's not that deep for her because it's just two. For her, it's just a weird coincidence even though, get this – they were all doing the same grasping thing with their left hand. I didn't tell her about Raymond, doing the same.' He drew long scratch strokes up his arm and Veer could see he'd drawn blood. Little beads of crimson, as if he'd caught himself on brambles.

'I'm asking for a transfer, looking for jobs – out of the NHS if necessary. I'm history, man. I know they'll likely be gone in a month or two, but I don't like it. What if it's catching?'

Veer wanted to reassure him; it was second nature for him to find words to comfort and soothe. But nothing came to mind. Instead, he registered just how tired he was. Tired and too far from his wife. He'd thought ageing would be gradual – a steady line upwards on a graph. But fatigue rolled over him and he felt the years had caught him in one moment. I'm old, he thought. Every year the ward gets harder. They all said it. They all asked each other, is this the worst the NHS has ever been? How long can we stand it? But we just do, thought Veer. Now, he knew, he didn't want to stand it anymore. He wanted to get out of this crummy office that he now saw with fresh eyes, and go home and be with Prisha. All he wanted to do was to sit in his kitchen and spend time with his wife.

Perhaps he would feign an illness and turn round and go home right *now*. He never had – but he *could*. He could take time to think things through. He looked at the door. He looked at his desk. He looked at the door again. Without thinking too deeply about it, Veer got his jacket from its hook and put it back on. As soon as his arms slid through the sleeves, he felt better. In his pocket, his fingers found his recently used car keys and he wrapped his hand around them and gripped them as if they were a life raft.

Nick watched him and spoke for both of them. 'I'm out of here too, Veer. I like the fruitloops – course I do – but for me it's time for a change. Nice people come through here with all sorts, don't they? But this. I don't like *this . . . this group shit*. She's gone now, but it's like she's still got them in her grip.' He stared at his hands, flexing his fingers. 'I've worked here for a long, long time – same as you. I work for pennies, really, it feels some weeks I'm working just to keep my lights on. And I've seen some right stuff – same as you.' He shook his head. 'But we always go forward – go on. I stay poor, but my work feels purposeful. But this feels different. Anti-human, somehow. I sound crazy, I know. But, for me, crazy or not, *this* is the straw on *this* donkey's back.' He shook his head again. '*This*.'

Anti-human.

Why did this feel like the truth when he wasn't even sure what Nick meant?

Veer shut his eyes briefly against the truth. Squeezing against his temples, he made a decision that should have taken months in only seconds. 'I'm going to retire. I've been thinking of it anyway. My wife, my Prisha, we found out she is sick. She . . .' He shut his eyes briefly against his pain.

If Nick heard him, he didn't react. Instead he continued. 'If I'm not fussy, I'm sure I can find something in a few weeks – and when something else comes up, *bam*, I'll be gone.'

TWENTY-SEVEN

Billie's head felt like it had been split by a flint, but she gritted her teeth and tightened the laces on her trainers anyway. Trying to feel better about going for a run, she inhaled the cool salt tang of the morning air. There was a fresher wind this morning across Dorcha and it brought the distant sound of breaking waves against the shore. From behind the wall of trees, it was rare to hear the Firth, but today it helped ease her head. Since Billie had joined Arbor, Jenna had been quick to establish the routine of an early-morning lap of the island with her and Billie didn't want to let her friend down, even though the pain in her head cleaved her brain.

Getting up felt better than lying in bed anyway. She couldn't go back to sleep because her dreams had been so disturbing. She'd dreamed of ... she wasn't sure

– *blood and feathers, blood and feathers* –

But trying to remember just seemed to make the memory ebb further away. So, she'd put on her running gear, swallowed two paracetamols and told herself it would give her the thinking time she needed – and she had a lot to think about.

Although she still had thoughts about leaving Arbor, Billie had changed her mind about wanting to go home. Yes, she was still irritated at the no-contact rule with her mother (and she hadn't heard from her at all), and yes, she remained suspicious of the depth of their monitoring, but, with Celine's help, she'd started to reframe the institute.

Partly because the therapy provided a space to think about her dad again. It had been a long time since he'd died but the trauma had smashed through her world; when she'd rebuilt the fragments of her life back together following his death she could focus only on her survival. Being here now, with endless therapy, support and a connection to nature, meant she had space to think about him. And it felt good to be able to remember happy times: time spent with just the two of them, in woods and fields, walking and hunting with Firkin. Celine was right: her father wouldn't want her to risk her health and leave Arbor. And how would her mother feel if she returned only to do what Tama did? The razor-sharp threat of Tama loomed close; who wanted to be Tama?

And Celine was kind. 'You're not shallow, Billie,' she'd said with a reassuring pat to the arm, 'just because you've got used to living in a lovely place. You must forgive yourself for making human choices, either here or where you were being looked after before. No one requires you to be pious after what you've been through – you're allowed to enjoy nice things.' And Celine was right; she'd quickly adjusted to a life with a choice of pools, a jacuzzi, private woodlands, serviced room, delicious food, not to mention the opportunity to get a degree with Arbor's debt-free study programme. Leaving all this behind would be hard. Would her mother even want her to?

And now there was Stan. *Stan*. She was sure something was happening between them. Really, she couldn't believe it – *Stan*. But she'd started to see beneath the silly exterior. Peeling back the playful, sometimes annoying, outer layer, revealed a vulnerability. And he seemed so focused, so keen on her. He was always looking at her; always touching her. He made her feel important, and it had started to feel intoxicating. Perhaps it wasn't him so much as the promise of something new and shiny and hopeful after the hideousness of the last two months. But either way, for now, with no better plan, thoughts of leaving had ebbed away on the tide.

She could hear the waves louder now and she rubbed her fingers against her temple, not quite ready for a run, but feeling better for space to think.

Jenna jogged towards Billie. 'Sorry, I've got to go back! I forgot my headphones – I'll just be a minute. Meet you on the path.'

Glad to be on her own, with legs feeling more powerful than her head, she crossed the lawns. Noticing something dark against the green, Billie changed course a little. From a distance, it looked like someone had dropped a sock, but then she saw another – and another. As she got nearer, she could see it was a dead bird. They were all dead birds.

She bent down to examine it. It was a starling. There was no sign of injury, it hadn't been

– *blood and feathers* –

shot. She jogged over to another – the same, blameless of injury. She didn't want to touch it but nudged it gently with her trainer. The wings and the neck held a little – the end of rigor mortis.

They must have been dead for a few hours. But what had

killed them? She jogged up to the path and as she neared the trees, she saw it was not just a few starlings that had perished. Between the trees the ground was littered with bird corpses. Not just starlings either. Blackbirds, several magpies, a blackcap.

She looked up, wanting help. Stan was jogging towards her. *Stan.*

He raised his hand and reached her. 'Philippe wants Jenna to test her sugar levels pre-breakfast so she can't run with you now. I said I'd jog with you if you wanted, but I can see you're too busy killing the local wildlife. I mean, what the fuck, Billie? Did you have to?' His laughter was nervous as he stared about him.

'It's shocking, isn't it? There's so many.'

He bent down and rolled one over. 'No sign of injury.'

It seemed like an echo from her dream. She tried to remember

– blood and feathers –

but couldn't. For a second the memory was close, but then gone. 'I've never seen anything like this, have you?'

'No, definitely not. It's so weird.'

'And they're everywhere, not just under the trees but on the grass too. So, some of them must have been in flight.'

'Look at this one,' he said, pointing to a blackbird, its wings extended. 'This one must've been flying.'

She stood up and stared upwards. 'So strange. Like they'd been pulled from the sky,' Billie said, hand extended, remembering a fragment of her dream:

– come to me –

He grabbed her hand, breaking the moment. The memory had gone.

With a conspiratorial mischievous wink, he pulled her into the woods. 'Come on, we can investigate in the woods before then. Ted will just get all grumpy and chuck them in the incinerator. Now's our chance to have a proper recce first.' His hand felt large and warm, and it felt good – *together we make a team* – to have the comfort of someone close. So, she didn't pull away and instead they walked the circular wood path hand-in-hand, only pulling apart to stop and count the dead animals. They found a dead barn owl, huge and white, a lingering ghost after a departed nightmare. When she cried to see it, Billie let Stan fold her in a hug.

'What has happened here?' she asked, enjoying the solidity of his shoulder. 'Natural gas? A virus? Some sort of bird scarer?' She narrowed her eyes. 'Or *Ted*? I mean,' she checked behind her, 'I like him now, but when I first met him – when I thought he was the chauffeur – I found him intimidating. Do you think ...?'

'I dunno.' Stan shrugged. 'He does a great job with his team looking after the grounds. He loves Dorcha – I just don't think he would want to hurt the wildlife. It makes no sense.' He sighed. 'Billie, can I tell you what's in my heart?' he said, smoothing her hair and lifting her chin. His hand pressed against her back and he looked at her directly, blue eyes focused on her own. The moment expanded. For a moment he didn't say anything, then he reached up and she could feel the trail of his fingertips against her cheek. It felt surprisingly light and she held her breath in response. She hadn't been touched in a long time – now this felt breathtaking. Her mother had hugged her goodbye two months ago, and since then? The people who touched her were long gone. An ex-boyfriend she broke up with ten months ago, Ella and her friends, all gone. She liked it. She missed it. She leaned in. She liked Stan but it was more than that – she wanted to feel alive.

'I want to kiss you. All this sadness ... I want to kiss your tears away.'

'It could get complicated.'

He didn't say anything, but instead leaned in and kissed her. His lips were firm and warm and for a moment, the sensation felt overwhelming.

When he pulled away, his smile lit his whole face. 'It already has,' he said. He kissed her again before pulling away, his face thoughtful, his eyes searching.

'Stan? What are you thinking? You look so serious.'

He sighed and broke away. 'I've got so much on my mind. And I'm not sure how to handle it. I know everyone just thinks I'm the fool – here to entertain. But Ash knows me best. He knows ... secrets I've got – *we've* got.'

'What secrets?'

'This is the problem. I want to tell you – of course I do. Even more now. Truth is, Billie, I was mad about you from the moment I saw you. I still am. But Ash is my best friend and I promised him – *promised* – that I wouldn't tell anyone, not even you. But now we've kissed, I feel like I really want to share with you – but I don't want to wrong my friend. You see?'

'It's a dilemma. But if it helps to know, I'm really very trustworthy.' Billie gave a smile.

'I know that.' He nodded. He checked over his shoulder before leaning in so close, she thought he was going to kiss her again, but instead he whispered in her ear. 'We don't trust Arbor. It's difficult to talk. I'm not even sure there aren't microphones hidden in the trees. Can we walk across the open ground?'

They walked away from the trees to the lawns that spilled out in front of them, leading up to Arbor a good half-mile away. The dead birds were visible, still against the grass, and Billie felt a chill cross her skin. Her heart raced from the moment of his kiss, the talk of secrets, the dead birds and the confirmation she wasn't the only one worried about the amount of surveillance. He glanced over his shoulder and motioned they should sit down.

'We'll just look like we're enjoying the morning sun and we'll see anyone coming from here.'

'What's the issue, Stan? Why are you worried about being overheard?'

He brought his knees up to his face, as if to cover his mouth. 'Maybe nothing. I like it here – don't think that I don't. It's just ...'

In his pause, she said: 'If you don't want to tell me, you don't have to. But if you do tell me, I swear I won't tell anyone.'

'I do trust you, Billie. It's just ... Ash and me have ... We were talking about dux gregis and how we were pissed nothing had happened and ... keep your face neutral, okay? Just in case someone is watching us. We ... Ash and me duxed yesterday. Flocked. *Don't tell anyone.* Definitely don't tell Ash I told you.'

'Oh, wow. *Wow.*'

'Keep your face neutral!'

'Sorry, yes. Okay, that's a lot to take in. Like, why don't you want anyone to know? And why are you worried about microphones in the woods? And won't Ash know you've told me, given that your brains are linked now?'

'It's not like that. I think if he went looking for the information, he'd find it. But we trust each other; respect each other. I know about the microphones in the woods because Tama once told me he saw one near the path. He'd already noticed the little cameras dotted around – have you seen them? – but the microphone out here finished him off. To be honest, that's when he started to talk about leaving – he felt claustrophobic. He said he needed his privacy and freedom. And I'm not cool with it either . . . it pisses me off, but I guess it's kinda why I need a route out. A plan. I don't want to just lurch and splat.' He pulled a sad face. 'I liked Tama, he was chill, but he should've been smarter. That's what Ash and I both think. That's why Ash and I decided to try. We wanted to get a handle on it, get to grips with it, so when we want to leave, we won't crash and burn.'

'What's it like?'

Stan's face moved from strained to a childish look of wonderment. 'Weird. Cool. Not even a bit like anything else. I feel like . . . it's hard to explain, but like he's my best friend now. I felt like that before when we all flocked, but as time went on, and it didn't happen after Tama left, the feeling sort of ebbed away. The memory of it was like those old sepia photographs – not even a bit like the real event. But it's back and I'm stoked. I know him so well – like *proper* understand him, you know?'

'But why don't you tell everyone?'

'Because we're both pissed at Arbor, because we think flocking is a good thing. We don't think we need to be cured, like Philippe says we should be. I also can't stand

Philippe – I think he's slimy and not to be trusted. Ash doesn't agree with me on that. People think I'm joking when I call him our handler, but that is what I think. All those pills we take for' – he flicked his fingers in the air like quote marks – '"brain growth"? They could be anything.'

'You don't trust Arbor?' Billie's mind reeled with everything Stan was saying. She'd thought she was the only one with reservations, doubts. She could barely take it all in.

He shrugged. 'I like Nathalie; I like most of the staff, I'm just not sure. Ash thinks I'm paranoid and that they're right to monitor us. Says we're caged lions and Philippe's really brave dealing with people who could take over his brain.'

'Could we?' Billie asked, surprised.

'Doubt it. Think he'd just crash and burn like we nearly did. The brain rewire seems to fuck people's brains up. But what Ash and I do agree on is that we shouldn't stay here until we're cured. That might be never. And should we be? We sort of think that if everyone could be flocked – look, don't call me a dick, I'm being serious – then perhaps there would be no wars. There wouldn't be any crime, because everyone would just be nicer to each other. Everyone would be united.'

He looked thoughtful, resting his head on his knees, so he gazed only at her. 'It's intimate and interesting and I want to experience it with you.' Then, when she didn't say anything, he reached out and took her hand. 'I feel like I want to try with you – will you? I love Ash, but I don't want to be that close with him if I'm not with you.' He tucked a stray lock of hair behind her ear. 'In case you can't tell, Billie, baby, you're my favourite here.'

She smiled and when he asked what she thought, she said she was thinking about it.

'When you were a kid, did you ever do that paper cups on a string thing?' he asked. 'That could be us – always together with the connection.'

'It's cute, Stan, but I've got to think about it. It's not you, but I now know that I had decided to never try.' She hadn't grasped it until now, but knew she'd unintentionally been holding back. She breathed out, glad to understand herself better.

He sat up. 'You don't want to? Why not? I thought we all wanted it.'

Billie shook her head. 'It's too dangerous. Look what happened to our friends.'

'But they're not the same as us. For us, now we're stage two, now we're at the DG phase, it's not the danger it was. I'm here right now, aren't I? And Ash is fine – he's doing leg day in the gym as we speak. When Tama was here, we achieved it three or four times. It was surprisingly easy. We felt safe and it was pretty cool that we all kinda were happy about it. It chased the nightmares away to feel like what brought us all here is controllable, manageable. And I really like you, and I want to try with you – because . . .' He trailed his fingertips against her jaw-line, moving up to her mouth. 'Because I really like you – *really, really like* you, Billie.'

She shut her eyes briefly, enjoying his touch. 'I'll think about it. Is that *okay*?'

'Sure. As long as you need, baby. But Ash suggested it to me first, and he said that we should keep developing it because it might never just go away, even if we wanted it to. We're changed, and probably for good. He told me that we have to accept it, live with it, harness it. Besides, I like living here because I'm lazy, but I'm ready for a change. Winter can be tough here and – don't tell Philippe – I'm not staying for another one. I want to go back to California, set up a diving school. Maybe even have a few little Stanleys of my own one day – I can't do that stuck in here, flicking my balls.'

'California, huh. I've never been.'

'I was hoping you'd come with me.'

Billie laughed. 'Now I know you're full of it.' She stretched her legs out and lay back looking at the sky. A bird flew overhead and she remembered the dead birds and

– *blood and feathers* –

And her mood tilted.

When Stan spoke, he sounded serious too. 'Not true actually, Billie. I'm thirty and turning the big 3-0 makes me want something else. Something permanent. I've always been nuts about you, and now would I even want to be with someone who didn't have what we have? To be with you feels like I'm understood. In a world of difference, we are the same.'

'Did you rehearse that line?'

He laughed, the moment broken. 'I did. See? You know me so well. Shows you, though, I've been thinking about this because it's important to me.'

Staring at the sky, the warmth on their faces, they both lay there with their own thoughts. Then an impulse came upon her. Maybe it was the talk of California, or the thought of Tama, or the idea of winter coming, but Billie felt the urge for change. 'Okay, let's try,' she said quickly, before she could change her mind. 'How do we do it?'

Stan propped himself up on one arm. 'Really? You sure?'

She nodded.

'Great. I'm sure you'll feel more positive about it once

you get there's nothing to fear. To me it feels like learning to drive – like learning how to use the clutch, or like balancing on a bike. With practice, we can control it, and if we can control it, maybe that's the closest we'll ever get to a cure.' He looked over to the woods. 'Let's go back in there so we can't be seen. We'll whisper so we can't be heard.'

He stood holding his hand out to her and she took it, deciding she liked having someone special. She suspected that Maddy and Ash had a thing going, just kept on the low from everyone. Thinking about it, a thing with Stan could be nice, she decided. It could definitely improve her stay at Arbor. She took his hand and followed him into the woods. They found a space under an oak tree, and after Stan had a look round for microphones, he came back and stood close in front of her. She could smell him: a mixture of hair clay and deodorant. She liked it and felt the thrill of anticipation.

'It just sort of happens by reaching out, finding a connection – I'm not sure that explains it very well, but why don't I lean in and connect with you this way first,' he said. And before she could comment, he leaned in and kissed her very lightly. 'And then we might be able to connect with each other mentally as well as physically.' He kissed her again. After a minute, he finally pulled away. 'Now, that is a lot more enjoyable than any task Philippe or Celine have come up with.' He was smiling this huge, dippy smile at her and she felt herself return it.

'Happy to try again?' he asked. After she nodded, he added: 'I'm going to try and reach you then. I'm going to enjoy the moment and just meet you there – wherever that is.'

He leaned in and they kissed, this time with her returning

it, glad to be— But she didn't finish the thought because she relaxed, enjoying the moment before taking a deep breath and reached out and ...

Instantly. She felt the deep cleave of her earlier headache but without the pain. Instead she felt a terrible tugging, falling sensation accompanied by the feeling that she could mentally push against a membrane; that it could easily yield. She pushed just a fraction harder; felt the barrier give, like testing a bubble's wall and finding she could push through.

But just at the point of breakthrough, she stopped.

'What was that?' Stan asked, pulling away from her, his eyes wide, pupils dilated. He looked wired. 'What happened there?'

'What do you mean?' Billie said, playing for time. Suddenly, it felt important – vital – that he didn't know how close they'd been to the dux. She didn't want anyone to know – not yet, without having time to work out why. 'Why do you ask?'

Stan rubbed his eyes. 'I don't know – maybe nothing? I ...' He sounded unsure. He shook his head, sharper now. 'Did we flock or am I mistaken?'

'I didn't feel anything.'

'Do you want to try again? Or at least the kissing? I'm sure we could do it if we kept trying – and I can't think of a better way to spend time.'

He really doesn't know. I was nearly in his head – nearly in his mind – and he sensed me, but didn't know for sure. It was so strange. He was right: *it was so easy.* Too easy: she wanted a chance to think it over. What if she didn't like what she found? Everyone thinks mean thoughts, does bad things – what if she saw them in Stan, could she still like him?

Glad now she hadn't admitted it, she vowed not to tell anyone that she knew now she could easily flock – not until she'd had a chance to unpack it, logically think things through. It changed everything – she just wanted to be clear how.

The pressure of Stan's hands on her waist made her aware he was looking at her, waiting for an answer. 'Do you think we could try another day? It's all these dead birds – I think it's putting me off. That and this,' she tapped her watch. 'I worry about it even picking up we're kissing, let alone if we dux. Did you worry about that with Ash?'

Stan shook his head. 'I forget I'm even wearing it. But I'm sure it can't pick up what happens in the brain through the wrist.'

Billie pulled at it, bothered by how tight it was. 'Heart rate, blood pressure, no doubt location – and they're just the basic functions from a decade ago. Imagine what the latest Arbor toys can do?'

Stan laughed. 'You're just saying you're never going to get it on with me, because you're worried it will set off sirens.'

She reached up, and smoothed her hand down the back of his head before pulling him in, and kissing him very long and slow. When she finished, she was pleased to see him looking stunned. 'Trust me honey,' she said with a smile, 'if we got it on, it *would* show through the watch.'

He placed his hand on his chest. 'And you trust me honey, you kiss by the book.'

She pulled a face. 'You've ruined it now quoting *Romeo and Juliet*. Now you've made us star-crossed lovers.'

He laughed and grabbed her hand. Holding hands, they continued to walk through the trees, spotting more dead birds as they went. Within half an hour, they'd counted two hundred corpses, but Billie, although she cared deeply about their destruction, couldn't stop thinking about the dux. It had only been for a second, but she had pressed against the edges of Stan's consciousness and could have stepped right in.

Now she'd done it once, could she reach into anyone's mind?

The questions seemed endless.

The possibilities seemed endless.

TWENTY-EIGHT

Philippe stood by the counter in the dining room, sorting through the endless bottles and tubs containing the various pills and powders he used to boost the group's health. Returning from their walk, Billie and Stan had reported the dead birds to Philippe over breakfast, and then both were annoyed by his lack of interest. 'We'll get Ted the gardener to clean them up,' he'd said, barely looking up from his task.

'We're not asking you to clean them up,' Billie said.

'What are you asking then?'

She shook her head, both still overwhelmed at what had happened between her and Stan, and upset at all those dead feathered bodies. 'To care?' she said finally, not meaning it to sound as it did, but feeling it anyway.

Philippe paused from measuring out the supplements they'd all got used to having daily.

'Sorry, Philippe.' She tried a weak smile at Ash, Maddy and Jenna. 'You just had to see it – it was so odd and horrible.'

'Billie, no problem, but please know this.' He gestured at the little plastic cups laid out in front of him. 'Spirulina.

Resveratrol from organic grape skin. DHA- and EPA-rich omega supplements from wild salmon. Pantothenic acid. Ginkgo biloba. Huperzine A. Bacopa monnieri. The list goes on. So, you see, I do care, Billie. I've selected these and everything else, because I probably care *too* much about *you*.'

He looked at her so intensely she instinctively leaned back.

Perhaps Jenna sensed the weirdness of the moment, because she reached across the table and slipped her hand into Billie's, squeezing it briefly. 'All of us, I hope, Philippe.'

Ash grated his chair against the floor, the noise loud and abrupt. 'There's an army base at Dundee – perhaps they flew jets over us last night on the way out to the Atlantic,' he said, changing the subject back. 'I've heard that a sonic boom can kill birds. Perhaps there was one last night and that's what caused it.'

'The concrete walls would protect us from the sound,' agreed Stan, reaching for another cinnamon bun. 'Cool. I'd love to fly fighter jets.' Then catching Billie's look, added: 'But I wouldn't do the boom – poor birds. And Billie's right – it was gross and freaky to see all those dead birds everywhere.' He grabbed her hand under the table and held it.

Philippe poured more coffee and then handed round the supplements to be taken after food, which was always a bit of an ordeal to get through, and then they were excused for the rest of the day. 'Tonight,' he reminded them, 'I'll collect you at ten o'clock for the sleep study.'

They discussed what everyone's plans were for the day. Jenna wanted to work on her collection of poetry by the pond and asked people to consider her not available. Maddy and Ash were heading to the library as they both had essays due; Stan was due to join them but changed his mind, saying he wanted to ask Ted if he could take the boat out. Billie grabbed Stan when Philippe wasn't around and asked him if he could take her out on the boat, too. 'You have to get your section lifted first,' he said, dropping a kiss on her forehead. 'I'm not releasing a classified nutbag on the good folks of Wemyss Bay.' He grinned. 'Seriously, I've been thinking: you should nag Philippe to get it gone. It's a formal process and you'll not get into the States with it hanging over you. Promise me you'll sort it?' He did agree to buy her some stamps, leaving her pleased to have both him and the promise of being able to write to her mum.

The morning's cool sea wind had dropped, leaving a blue sky and a warm summer's day. July had eased into August, and there was real heat to the sun. For the first time since she'd arrived at the institute, Billie realized she would be left completely alone – and it felt great. Billie grabbed a book, changed into her swimming costume and dressing gown and breathed out; she had the day to herself to relax, think everything through. Being by the outdoor pool was easily her favourite thing to do, to the extent she knew the long winter would mean she'd be restless and want to leave. She didn't think he meant it, but the thought of chasing Stan and the sun to California suddenly seemed like the most appealing thing. Stan was right about trying to flock – thrilled now to have jumped the hurdle of fear, she already felt that she could control it. He was right about getting the section lifted, too. The possibility of a future away from here glowed.

Walking out to the pool, she felt happier than she had in a

long time. I can leave. I can rejoin my life. But a darker idea lurked: was it true that she had a great power over others? What did that mean for herself? She lay back and shut her eyes, glad of the chance to think everything through. It was both bewildering and exciting and she'd just started to relax, warm in the sunshine, when a shadow cast over her. She opened her eyes to see Stefana smiling down at her.

Looking very chic in a yellow bandeau top, blue bikini bottoms, a large floppy hat and Chanel-style dark glasses, she clutched a large raffia bag. 'Hey, Billie! Sorry, I didn't wake you there, did I?'

'Oh, hey Stefana.'

Stefana took the lounger immediately next to her despite ten others being free.

Billie felt the crush of deep disappointment.

'How are you. Billie? I hope you don't mind, but I saw on the CCTV you were here on your own and I thought: *perfect*. I haven't seen you for ages and ages, so I grabbed my stuff and thought I'd join you.'

Billie gave her the warmest smile she could. 'It's a lovely idea,' she said, but felt puzzled. Stefana was acting like they were old friends who hadn't seen each other for a long time – but Billie barely knew her. 'Have you got a day off? I don't normally see doctors by the pool.'

Stefana gave a little grin and leaned closer, her voice a conspiratorial whisper. 'We get the day off too, when there's a sleep study. Strictly speaking, I'm not supposed to be up here, but I just saw you on the camera and thought ... I'd love to join you.'

Billie thought about the CCTV that she knew was there, but to think of people watching her, still disquieted her.

'I've been a bit run down,' Stefana continued. 'Apparently, I fainted at work. I don't remember it, but they've told me I've got really low iron. I woke up, tucked up in bed feeling fine, but they insisted on bed rest until my anaemia improves. Anyway, I'm back at the desk now, saw you here,' she said giving another grin, 'and just decided some sun on my face would do me good.'

Billie gave a weak returning smile. 'I'll see you tonight then at the sleep study?'

Stefana shook her head. 'I doubt it; they're easing me back in with desk duties. I'll be doing data analysis. So, I'll be there, but in the study lab instead of watching you sleep.'

Billie's first thought was, Stefana is *creepy*. But then she understood that Stefana was annoyed. She didn't show it – she looked relaxed stretched out in the sun, face tipped to the sky, but she *knew* she was furious. How? Billie had the strangest feeling of déjà vu – or some other feeling of familiarity. Had she met Stefana before she came here? Or did she remind her of someone else? Or—

We're flock

No. Impossible. She would know if she'd duxed with someone. But she also knew that *was* it. How? Why wouldn't I know? Why wouldn't she?

I could just check. I could just take a little peep and see her thoughts. Billie kept her own sunglasses on and pretended to read her novel. If she had just flocked with Stefana accidently, there was no harm in trying deliberately this time.

Billie felt herself instinctively reaching out to her, as Stefana picked up her raffia bag and started to root through it. Just like with Stan, she felt her mind sliding against a membrane, like trying to break through an oily bubble. She forced herself to keep pushing through the feeling of falling, tugging, nausea, and then she was there, in Stefana's mind. Suddenly, she could see through Stefana's eyes, could see inside her bag (book; zip-up pouch; hairband; tissues; phone; purse; sunglasses case; hairbrush).

Billie inhaled and blinked. She could see from both her own viewpoint and Stefana's. Like seeing something but remembering something different at the same time. It felt easy. She pulled her mind away and broke the connection and that was easy too. It was breathtaking – all this time resisting flocking, all this time feeling the fear and worry about what might happen, but Stan was right, she was fine. *It* was fine. The ridiculous ease of it – as easy as walking, as swimming – already felt second nature.

And as for Stefana: yes, they were *flock*. It was like walking into a house she'd been in before. *How*, when she had no memory of it happening, she didn't know – but she knew it was true.

Billie exhaled, determined not to show that anything had happened, but did Stefana know? She looked round, watching Stefana still rooting through her bag. 'What have you lost?' she asked. Despite feeling the fireworks of excitement, bewilderment and incredulity, she worked hard to keep her voice even and natural.

'Just my hairband. I wanted to go swimming. But . . .' She looked up, face blank, sunglasses hiding any thoughts, 'but I feel a bit dizzy maybe? No, not dizzy, just . . .' She shrugged. 'Nothing. It's gone.'

'Your anaemia?

Billie reached again, just to see if she could. Pushing

through the pervious walls of a bubble; noting the tugging feeling in her own brain, but no nausea this time.

Tip your bag out. It's in there.

'Sorry, did you say something?' Stefana asked, looking up.

Billie pulled back out, as easy as pulling her hand out of water. Connection broken.

She shook her head, pointing at the noisy flock of geese as they passed over. 'I think you heard them,' she said. But thinking: *you heard* me.

Stefana turned her bag over and tipped it all out. 'Found it! It was in there all along!' she said, holding it high.

Billie smiled. *Stefana followed my command.* Of course, she might have chosen to tip her own bag out at that exact moment – but *still*. She *heard* me. It occurred to Billie, sunlight sharp on cut glass, just how much power she could have.

Desperate to be on her own to think, Billie decided to swim in the pool. Instinctively, she reached to take her watch off, but she couldn't. It was too tight and she pulled against it now, a new habit developing. Underneath it, her skin would be wrinkled and damp. She dove into the water, the irritation of being forced to wear it, gave her power in her limbs as she kicked through the water. Feeling strong, she did ten laps of crawl.

As she turned on the eleventh, she saw Philippe standing talking to Stefana. Grabbing quick looks as she snatched breaths on the return lap, she saw he looked angry and Stefana was shaking her head.

By the time Billie got to the end, both Philippe and Stefana were walking away.

TWENTY-NINE

in the woods again.

In front of her, in every direction, are rows and rows of dead birds. Pigeons. Magpies. Two barn owns. Endless, endless starlings. Crow upon crow upon crow. Billie feels a rising panic. 'Is Firkin here? Is he dead too?' she asks her father, knowing he is here.

You are not asking the right questions, Wilhelmina.

Something terrible has happened. Her father stands behind her – his voice relaxes her. How could anything be wrong with him right here?

'The birds are dead,' she tells him. 'This is terrible.'

Wilhelmina, it's just an image – not real, do you hear me? Not real – because this is just a dream –

'But Firkin might be dead too?'

Firkin is with me. He is always with me.

She can smell rotten leaf litter, the sodden, dank, green smells of soil and autumn – and the smell is getting stronger and stronger and stronger. She looks around for her father to ask him about it, about why it is getting worse, but he isn't here. The carpet of death just extends in every direction away from her, disappearing outwards through the trees.

She relaxes: Firkin is safe, her father is right. She can hear his bell now up in the trees and knows he watches her.

Can you smell the rot, Wilhelmina? I'm worried you're blinded by the beauty.

Beauty – yes, a shift in focus shows her this. 'But it is beautiful. Can you not see?' The carpet of birds (possibly, perhaps, just sleeping?), chest side up, showing varied and stunning plumage. Breaking through the leaf canopy, sunlight drops golden coins onto the woodland floor, and wildflowers grow sweet, nestled treasure among the tree roots.

No, Billie. Stop it. Stop changing the optics. Look again.

He never tells her off, but he is sharp now. She has never heard him so cross with her. And he's called her Billie again – and he never calls her Billie.

'You never call me—'

He cuts her off. *It's* now *Billie. You've got to listen to me. I do call you Billie in the now. Now – look again.*

Blinking back tears, she notices the wood no longer smells of leaf litter but of blood. Raw flesh, iron-tanged blood. But this is not the smell of a fresh kill from Firkin, a ripped rabbit still warm from life. No, she grasps, gagging horror rising – this is the sweet, sickly smell of flesh long after rigor has set in and left. This is the smell of spoiled flesh rotting.

THE INSTITUTE

It's rotten, Billie, and you need to understand that it's dangerous, so dangerous. I'm worried you—

And blood, dark, inky black blood starts to seep from the bodies, oozing from the carpet of flesh and feathers, then flowing through the leaf litter. It pools now around her ankles, the flowers gone, the forest floor gone, the trees standing in a rising sea of blood, the death-upon-death-upon-death all hidden.

The blood is rising; the blood is rising

He is right: the blood does keep rising. 'Help me, Daddy.'

But he wouldn't answer her, instead just kept saying in his deep voice: *The blood is rising; the blood is rising*

'I know that now,' she shouts. 'But how do I get out?'

But he doesn't answer the question – just keeps repeating: *the blood is rising; the blood is rising.*

Firkin's bell has fallen silent, and she knows they have both gone. Now it's just her screaming: *the blood is rising; the blood is rising.* She can't help it because she is alone and she knows the blood is coming for her.

And it *is* rising.

Fast.

THIRTY

Veer Singh sat at the breakfast table opposite his wife, Prisha. The sun streamed into the kitchen as he drank his tea and shuffled the daily newspaper around, trying to relax his nerves. There was the chatter of Radio 4. He reminded himself with determination that he was right to quit work – it was hard enough waiting for news on whether Prisha would get the new drug or not, without having to deal with the realities of an understaffed mental health ward.

Prisha didn't agree, he knew. She sighed now and started to tidy the kitchen.

'I'll help,' he said, getting up.

'Thank you but no, dear, you'll only get under my feet.'

That phrase again. He wanted to help but she was neat and quick and when he tried to help, she always huffed and he fumbled. She'd just finished another chemo round, but had told him loudly this morning that she had decided to return to her job as a chemist next week. She'd taken to sighing loudly as well when he sat in the kitchen too long. To get out of her way, he did more in the garden – the convolvulus strangled everything – and when that was done, he'd walk to the shops.

But it was quiet at home. Quieter now he didn't think he was ever going back to work. Dreams of writing his memoirs had disappointed in real life – within the first hour, his excitement had waned to boredom and since then, he'd struggled to commit. He'd started to think, perhaps if Prisha's chemo worked, perhaps if she got the new drug Tarquilat, he'd go back to work. It was too much to hope for, but Tarquilat would almost guarantee Prisha her life back and it was within touching distance of approval. Prisha's consultant had given her the nod that if it got licensed for NHS use, she would be first on the prescription list.

It had been a week since his conversation with Nick, following which he'd put on his coat and driven home, ringing in to say he'd been taken very ill. Prisha had her own private views about his not-sick-leave, he could tell. But, if it were possible after thirty-five happy years together, he loved her a little more for not sharing them. Instead, when he'd told her what he'd done, Prisha had replaited her hair and then, very reasonably, had asked him to think for one full week about if he really wanted to resign.

Now, the kitchen tidy, Prisha kissed him then said she was going to her mother's for the day and wouldn't be back until late. Not wanting to sit alone, he got up but dithered, uncertain: what to do now? The cupboards were full of food, he'd hoovered last night; the laundry had been refolded yesterday morning. What should he do with his day? The house was silent in its answer. He almost jumped when his phone beeped.

Without thinking, he picked it up to check his messages. It was from his colleague, psychiatrist Sally Simms.

> Veer, sorry for contacting you when you're off sick (hope flu better btw), but we've had a rather unusual incident of three catatonic patients during the night. If you're able, I'd appreciate a second opinion this morning – ideally before I go off shift.

Feeling genuinely sick now, he pressed the call button. Using a voice he didn't recognize as his own, he asked what had happened and to whom.

Sally answered, sounding shaky. 'It is nothing – well, not nothing – it's just so *odd*. If I'm honest, you're the only person I would report it to, for fear of getting put on the ward myself.' She gave a nervous laugh. 'I've just never seen anything similar – I can only describe it as a group catatonia.'

'Who?'

'Marjorie Briggs, Raymond Tate and Elsie Burham. We did the usual checks and found them in their bedrooms sitting up in bed, completely unresponsive. But the worst thing was they kept repeating over and over again, "The blood is rising; the blood is rising!"'

'"The blood is rising?" Just that?'

'Yes. Only that, over and over and over. But that's not the strangest thing.'

Veer could hear his heartbeat in his chest. *I don't want to know*, he thought, but then thought: *Billie*. 'Tell me.'

'We used our walkie-talkies to be sure, but – remember they were in separate rooms and couldn't hear each other – it was clear they were saying the words at exactly the same time.'

Veer shut his eyes and pressed his hands hard against his eyelids. 'Like a shared night terror?'

'Yes. Exactly that.'

'Did their voices sound like their usual voices?'

'No. How did you guess?'

'Something I read once, maybe. How were their voices different?'

'You couldn't really tell with Raymond, because he's so deep anyway, but both Elsie and Marjorie were both talking in a much lower register than I've ever heard them use.'

Veer said he'd come in and hung up the phone. He pressed his hands against his face. He had known about their previous strange behavioural episodes and had done nothing. Had he used Prisha's illness as an excuse? Had he left them, or even his colleagues, in a state of danger? No wonder poor Nick had had enough. Then another thought occurred to him: what if Billie had experienced the same episode at the same time as the Warwick ward group? This phrase, the blood is rising, was it her saying those words? And did it mean something awful was happening to her?

Veer pressed against his temples and shut his eyes. As tired as he was, the truth was he'd taken the Hippocratic Oath, promising to call on others when their skills were needed. To recognize when there was something he didn't know. Billie was sick and he'd been her physician. Perhaps, if she wasn't under appropriate care now, that meant he was still responsible for her.

He knew what he should do. Time to pull his head out of the sand.

With purpose now – and glad of it – he headed for his study. He forced air into his lungs, overwhelmed by the vortex of anxiety he was experiencing, making himself focus on the small tasks: shutting the door; taking a seat; turning on his computer. But he held his breath as he searched through his deleted emails. When he saw it, he exhaled as if the breath had been held underwater before coming up for air: it was still there.

The journalist's request for contact.

He hit reply and started to type.

THIRTY-ONE

After arriving on the ward and speaking with Dr Sally Simms as she finished her night shift, Veer had taken over, and with delicacy so as not to alarm Marjorie, Raymond or Elsie, had interviewed them, and after making extensive notes, he'd rung Prisha to explain he'd been called in to work. The delight in her voice matched the contentment he'd found in himself: he was Dr Veer Singh and it seemed, whether he liked it or not, Dr Veer Singh needed Warwick ward just as much as Warwick ward needed Dr Veer Singh.

That evening, Dan Downes sat in Veer's office, with staff nurse Nick Lewes. No one queried it when Veer signed Dan onto the ward; it was Veer's ward and he'd checked the roster, picking a time when no one was on duty who had met Dan previously. Now, it was the quiet time after supper before the end of the evening shift, and the staff were settling the patients down for the night. Within the privacy of his office, they could speak freely.

They drank Veer's Earl Grey from chipped, mismatched mugs, but Veer thought, judging by the way Nick looked, it was just as well it hadn't been served in cups and saucers, or the journalist would hear the rattle of their nerves through the porcelain.

Veer pushed his comb-over into place with determination. 'I'm afraid you find us at a difficult time, Dan. It's been tough; the strangeness on the ward has unsettled the staff team. You feel the same, don't you, Nick?'

Nick stretched out his long legs and nodded. 'Too right. The whole situation is just too ... kooky. And since kook is my day job, that's a *lot* of kook.'

Veer steepled his fingers and stared at them. 'I've not had a sick day in twenty years, but the events here meant I had to take a week off. I have not told my colleagues the real reason why – only Nick knows. But I came back today for a purpose.' Around him was the detritus of a life spent in the room: painted pebbles from his kids when they were younger; thank-you cards from grateful patients; a framed photo of Prisha. Behind him, his books lined the shelves, including every diagnostic manual ever issued, with its lists of psychiatric illnesses. This was home, he understood, as much as his kitchen table.

'I don't know you, Dan, but your emails reassure me that I can trust you – or at least that we have common interests. Do we agree to share what we know – but to keep it confidential to us?' After they did, they then spent the next thirty minutes detailing their knowledge and experiences. Veer and Nick watched Dan's videos from the Grand Canyon and the Bhupen Hazarika bridge. They watched them several times. Nick swore and Veer undid the top button of his suddenly too-tight shirt.

'The same as what happened to Billie and her friends,' said Veer finally. 'And she had no memory of the event.' He rubbed the bridge of his nose, dislodging his glasses. 'Like Elsie and the others have no memories of their shared experiences, here on this ward.'

'I wonder if Billie said the same as them – about the blood rising,' said Nick. 'And she's not even close by now, is she?'

'I can confirm she's over four hundred miles away,' said Dan. He looked at his teacup. 'Don't suppose you've got anything stronger, Veer?' He shrugged when Veer said no, not on an NHS ward. 'So, the question is,' continued Dan, 'why does this behaviour start and why does it continue?'

'Because, I believe, Billie has established a connection never documented before. They seem to be having some sort of shared night terror.'

'Nightmares?'

'No, nightmares you remember, but night terrors you don't. They happen at a different part of the sleep cycle and in night terrors, the person isn't dreaming – it's pre-REM sleep. The person's eyes can be open, and they can move, talk, scream – that definitely fits the patten here. We don't know if Billie is doing the same at night as we saw when she was here, but it's not inconceivable. And even if she's not,' continued Veer, 'whatever connection they all established when she was here, it's ongoing for three of our patients.'

'Okay,' said Dan, thinking it through. 'This is interesting, definitely. You've never heard of this sort of thing before?'

'Not shared like this, no. No one truly knows why night terrors exist in adults, but depression and anxiety – which Elsie and the others do suffer from, obviously – are a cause. I've ordered an MRI and then we're going to look at adjusting their medication. But do I think we'll find the root? No. Do I think a change in meds will help? No. I think we are seeing something new here – a shared night-terror experience which started when Billie entered the ward. Billie who of course was only here because of her shared catatonia that led to shared suicides. That's why we'll keep Elsie and the others on the safety of the ward for the foreseeable future.'

Dan nodded slowly. 'I knew nothing of this. This is another layer to the story I've been chasing – the story which Billie is part of. I just thought it was group suicide and that's where it ended.'

After some silent drinking of tea, Veer spoke. 'It explains what neither Billie nor I could. I've met hundreds of suicidal people over the years, and Billie never presented as one of them. She was adamant she never wanted to kill herself – that in itself is not unusual. But I contacted her university and spoke to several staff that knew her a little, and they all said she was engaged, capable and working on target. Her mother confirms that Billie thrived at uni; loved her friends and the lifestyle. No recent relationship break-up. No substance abuse or gambling habits. No debt. No sign of suicidal ideation. So, no. What happened at Gatwick Station was not because of her design, but was the start of her change, I am certain. *Certain*. Not least because all her friends changed instantaneously too. Impossible to have come across a contaminant that, if introduced earlier, caused the same simultaneous reaction. It had to have happened there, and it had to have been an instant reaction.' He pressed his hands together, hunched lower and looked at both Dan and Nick long and hard. 'We don't know the catalyst, but it happened there and observable chronic and acute alteration has occurred. If this is the case, the ramifications of this are huge. *Huge.* Momentous. Have you considered the possibility here of some sort of telepathic control?'

Both Dan and Nick looked at each other. Dan shook his head. 'Telepathy doesn't exist. And it's a subject that has been extensively researched with conclusive results.'

'But isn't that what we've seen?' challenged Veer. 'People in different rooms saying the same thing at the same time?'

'They could have rehearsed it, as a prank,' said Dan.

Nick shook his head. 'They wouldn't do that. Elsie doesn't even like Raymond. Come onto the ward tomorrow and meet them – they'd love a visitor and a game of gin rummy. You'll find they're not the pranking type. A prank wouldn't explain the timings either. Even if you practised it really, really carefully, wouldn't they end up getting out of sync as they were out of earshot of each other? They were timing-*perfect* for nearly ten minutes. I don't think that's possible.'

Dan opened his hands and shrugged in a gesture of, *I don't know what the answer is.*

'If this is some sort of telepathic control, then the implications are colossal,' Veer said.

'How so?' ask Nick, leaning in.

'Because if you can control how someone moves, talks, acts, democracy is over.' A beat passed after Veer had spoken.

'Hang on,' said Dan. 'This is getting away from the subject here. How do we go from group suicides to the collapse of democracy?'

'It seems that Billie can control movement and speech from a great distance – she is four hundred miles away.'

'We don't know for sure she's been part of the "blood is rising" chanting. We're reaching there.'

'True. But we do know they exhibited the same strange behaviour on the ward here. We also know that Elsie and the others did nothing like this until she turned up. And we also know that it hasn't changed because she's left. Perhaps whatever link seems to have been established will never get beyond a shared bad dream. But if Billie is able to influence the patients on our ward, that's a first. If that control was strengthened, it could be dangerous. Imagine if you had the power to control people from such a great distance; you could invade a country without even setting foot in it.'

Dan shook his head, went to speak and then stopped. Then after a beat, tried again. 'This is getting – with respect – ridiculous. When I started this journey, it was only ever about sudden group suicide being denied and covered up. What you're suggesting is something quite different. And we have no proof that Billie is behind what's happening here.'

Veer persisted. 'We can't show you the footage of what happened on this ward, because we deleted it. We were frightened. But Nick, why don't you tell Dan?'

Nick explained in clear detail.

When Dan didn't say anything in response, Veer continued. 'Shared consciousness. Shared thinking. Shared actions. Not nightmares. There has been no documented evidence of complete telepathic responses to this degree. And people have looked. The Victorians were obsessed by it; the Nazis also were desperate to find telepathic ability. If you are an internet warrior, it'll tell you so have the CIA. Consider why?'

'I don't know, because they're wacky?' Dan accepted more tea and when Veer told him to think harder, he bristled a little.

'From what you've shown us tonight, it seems there are two different aspects to this. The first is the videos you've shown me of the incidences in India and America: group suicide. But Billie survived her incident. What if after this survival, this step two, she was able to draw in others — others totally uninvolved in the first incident? And now the connection is made — and I agree, I'm speculating a little here — it at least presents as continuing in this sleep form, regardless of time or distance?

'What we have seen from the patients on this ward is not a shared psychiatric disorder. No, they are displaying a mirroring of thought — no, that is not quite right.' He shook his head, frustrated. 'It's bigger than that. They are showing a subjugation of independent thought and will. They presented as not self-determining — in other words, no longer in charge of their own minds.' He sighed, raising his hands and then bringing them down hard on the table in frustration. 'This is potentially very dangerous. We are seeing something completely new — we must consider the potential ramifications. What if Billie was not a good person? She could gather the world in and command the people at will — or at least those within a four-hundred-mile radius. In heavily populated areas, that's quite the headcount. Tell me this: what need is there for war or democracy or armies or any kind of consensus if you can just bend others to your thinking?'

Dan shook his head. 'This is all a little hyperbolic.'

'And if it's not?' asked Veer. 'I had a look at Arbor and its parent company.'

'NorGline Pharmaceuticals.'

'Exactly. I wonder if they know the potential here? It might explain why they are interested in Billie.'

Dan swore softly under his breath. 'I've been trying to puzzle out the same thing. Their website says they are interested in the brain – and while I could see the correlation, I couldn't understand their motivation. But now I'm wondering ...'

Veer nodded. 'It would explain their reaching out to me, to Billie's mother, the no-expense-spared set-up. It would also explain why they want to shut her off from everyone else. She is their test guinea pig and through her, they could unlock the biggest change in the human race since ... since ...'

'Ever?' offered Dan.

'Ever. Yes, agreed,' nodded Veer.

Dan put his head in hands. 'I can just about believe it all now,' he finally said. 'But it means they'll never let her go. There's never going to be a point when they say, *thank you, Billie, for letting us study you, but we'll let you go home now with your huge power, worth ... well, the biggest sum of money in the world.* And I've been to the island, I've seen the corporate grip. The security detail; the remote location; the slick and smooth determination.' He explained what had happened when he'd tried to visit Billie, and about meeting Jo Cathey afterwards, her relief and acceptance that her daughter was being well cared for. Dan too had been convinced that Billie was fine but now his initial fears flickered back into life.

Veer nodded. 'Yes, I'm worried that she's trapped and she might not even know it yet.'

'And they're not going to give her access to a phone if they won't even give her mother a telephone number without a third party travelling four hundred miles to get it,' said Dan.

'Jo tried the new number as soon as I passed it to her. The man I met, Philippe Bouchard, answered the phone, but told Jo that a visit at the moment was impossible. Jo's tried the number since and she says that it hasn't been answered. She's a little worried, but reassured that I saw Billie happy and well. She's uncertain who to turn to because of Billie's age and the psychiatric treatment order. Billie's not exactly allowed to leave. And there's only her and Billie – no other family to turn to.'

'I will contact the institute; as her last NHS psychiatrist, I regard myself as entitled to an update.'

'And we will share what information we receive?' asked Dan. 'Are we now agreeing to work together, to pool our resources?'

Veer rubbed his chin and cut a glance at Nick. He didn't need Nick's permission, but he received it anyway with a little nod. 'I am going to have to trust you, Dan. I've already shared too much, but only out of safeguarding concerns. I don't think the usual channels can be effective here, that's my thinking. Perhaps I'm acting unprofessionally, but I'm at the end of my career, and to me what matters is that I'm doing the best thing I can for my patients, Billie, Elsie, Raymond and Marjorie. Someone should have oversight of this. Sadly, it seems it is us.'

Dan nodded slowly. 'Veer, I have the highest regard for you, and for Nick. Anything I eventually report, you will have sign-off on it, I can assure you. Nick, all this is done with your agreement?'

'Anything to make it stop. I feel for Elsie and the others. We can't let them go home. Elsie lives alone. I can't see that she would be safe.'

Dan nodded. 'I can see that. I'll do some background digging on Arbor and NorGline – see if I can work out their intentions.'

Veer patted Nick's arm. 'We'll keep the others here safe, until we know it's over. Whatever over looks like.'

THIRTY-TWO

'What's the weather like where you are?' asked Philippe over the Zoom call.

'Blue skies. Hot. Love the States,' answered Nathalie. 'And with you?'

'Cold winds today. Suits me: I'm in no mood for sunshine.'

'Oh Philippe, why not? The video you sent me?'

'Exactly. It's just so typical that there was nothing in the last sleep study, then away from the full spec monitoring, this happens. So irritating. I take it you got a chance to see it then?'

'I have and I appreciate you putting Billie and Stefana's night CCTV side-by-side on screen. It made for compelling watching – although it went on a bit.' She laughed. 'What do you think she meant by "the blood is rising"?'

'I don't know. Stefana still doesn't know she's flock. I asked her if she had any dreams, but she didn't remember anything. Just goes on about Billie all the time though, like a crush or something. She's irritating enough now to make me want to ship her out to you.'

'You're just tired of her because Richard knows about

your little dalliance with her,' laughed Nathalie. 'But yes, send her over here. Could be interesting to see if it breaks the dux selector between them. Just how far will the followers follow? Is there a break point for the dux selectors? Why not make that happen ASAP?'

'Okay I'll get on that. I might get Celine to do a bit of hypnotherapy on Billie and Stefana first. See if she can find out what was meant?'

'I shouldn't bother – it's just a dream and Jude wants it all sped up now. Chasing dream chanting is just more of nothing consequential. And we're all tired of waiting.'

'I feel the same. It's just the research paradox is very uncomfortable, isn't it? I feel like I'm permanently holding my breath.'

'We are walking a very difficult line, but we always knew that would be the case. But it can't be helped. It's like holding a wasp's nest and hoping they don't wake up before you drown them.'

'That's a very perfect simile,' said Philippe with admiration in his voice.

Nathalie laughed. 'My English teacher would be proud of me.' She laughed again. 'She wouldn't be, actually. Quite the opposite. Anyway, one thing I did want to raise with you is the tweaked timeline I've been working through with Jude. He's making some adjustments to the roll-out schedule for OmnieX, bringing the sales as forward as he can – there's huge interest in the dux, and since that's what we are about he wants to put the drug up for sale as soon as possible.'

'Still on an auction basis?'

'Yes, with invites to purchase going to the top – well, what Jude likes to call the point one per cent, but it's not really, is it? It's the top hundred power players in the world. But they won't be told all the details immediately; it'll be a staged and spiralled release of information. Timing is everything – just in case someone didn't approve of OmnieX's impact. But Jude liked the dead birds. Felt the same as us about that. Suggested it was new territory that needs research.'

'He doesn't think it will put people off purchase?'

'He'll look at it and thanks you for the specimens – he just wants us to crack on. But we're waiting for Billie, so we can't.'

'We can't,' agreed Philippe. 'I say, let's hold our nerve. Our plans are progressing. I think the end of August will be when we can finally put the wasp's nest down.'

'Good – no later. I'm bored of the travel and looking forward to getting onto the next stage. And getting richer, of course.'

THIRTY-THREE

'Help—'

Billie stopped floating, putting her feet down, and stood up in the inky dark of the indoor pool. 'Can someone please put the lights on? Somone needs help.' She looked around, alarmed. It was ten thirty at night and they were in a Celine-led group session.

Celine stood by the light switch, concern heavy in her face and voice. 'All okay, Billie? Lights are on now. Darling, who needs help?' Stan, Ash, Maddy and Jenna all stood with her in the pool, blinking in the sudden light. They looked fine – confused, sleepy, but fine.

Billie had grown to love Celine, and not least for her wild and eccentric ideas. This one involved draining and then refilling the indoor pool with a salt solution to resemble the Red Sea and achieve buoyancy. The pressure was off as Celine was clear she did not want them to dux in the pool – 'it could be dangerous in the water' – and that the activity was designed to 'reset and rejuvenate', and be 'a beautiful bonding moment for you all'. They'd had to wait until night-time, so no light leaked in to ruin the blackness. They had been drifting on their backs, heads at the centre of the flower, each body like a separate petal while Celine oversaw their formation as they held hands. But now, Celine looked worried. 'Ash, Jenna, Maddy, Stan, are you all okay? Do you need help?'

They all confirmed they were fine.

'What's the matter, Billie? I think everyone is okay and doesn't need anything?' Celine looked confused; the four others in the session looked at Billie, bewildered.

Feeling the burn of her cheeks but knowing she'd heard a voice – *help* – now she didn't want to say; didn't want to admit that she'd heard a voice when clearly she was the only one to do so. To save her embarrassment, she hedged her bets. 'I ... we were all so silent and I was worried ...'

Celine crouched down by the pool, barefoot, wearing sweatpants and a T-shirt that said: ALL WE NEED IS HUGS! With a cartoon of a koala bear hugging a tree. 'My dear, what are you worried about?'

The moment passed. Billie did not want to tell anyone that in the silent reverie of her floating session, when she felt at her most relaxed, and half asleep, she'd heard – very plainly and clearly – a single word asking for help. Billie gave a small laugh, told them all not to worry, and they settled back down to the session. The lights went off again. Stan had wiggled in between her and Ash, and she was glad. She liked the feel of Stan's hand in hers. His hand was large, and he held her tight; his thumb stroking the back of her hand was comforting.

But Billie remained unsettled. She knew what she'd heard – but it was more than that. The voice felt real, but it was upsetting how charged with emotion it was. There was a clear note of desperation, of fear, in what was a female voice, Billie felt suddenly sure.

With Stan on one side, and Jenna on the other, Billie and the others in the group lay in a circle for nearly an hour, in water held at the same temperature as their bodies. It had become essentially a huge floatation tank in complete darkness – even the outside lights had been turned off to ensure nothing broke the spell. From underwater speakers, womb noises – a heartbeat, intestinal gurgles – played. Celine had said she wanted them to stand together at the end, reborn. Drifting in a dark room listening to heartbeat sounds, the group had moved from giggles to relaxation – until Billie had disturbed them all. But she'd heard it, she was sure of it. She hadn't been asleep, she hadn't made it up. That voice, that need for help – it had *not* been her imagination.

Until hearing voices when no one else had, everything had seemed to be improving: her headaches had stopped, and she hadn't had any bad dreams for over a week. Ella's birthday had just passed, and she'd spent the day very teary, but she had got through it, and after, knew she'd passed a milestone. And now she also had a bright spot in her life: *Stan*. They hung out every day. There was little privacy, but they were able to grab kisses. She loved being wrapped in his arms. He still wanted to flock and had given her a couple of nudges, and she'd given him her commitment that she would, now it was just a question of when. She hadn't told him about Stefana – for some reason she couldn't define, it felt better to keep that to herself – but it had reframed her attitude. After all, it had been easy and no one had got hurt – the horror of the Gatwick Station homogeneus gregis it certainly was not. So why not sit down and practise the dux, as Stan called it? The talk of them going to the States together had intensified and he'd fibbed to Philippe about a reason for needing books on California, and they spent time in the library whispering over the pictures that showed the cities, the coast and the wildlife.

Now she had something new to worry her – to add to her list that suggested she wasn't quite right. She had a pervading and persistent feeling that the answer was in the woods (answer to *what*? What was the question when there were so many?). But she decided she couldn't let it bother her as she went up there every day, and there were no more dead birds, just trees and wildlife and nothing to see or find.

She also couldn't settle all her feelings of paranoia – and, determined to manage her mental health, it continued to rankle that she still hadn't learned the full truth about Callie, but she deliberated that if she saw her again she might just dip into her mind like she had Stefana's. (Could she? Could she do that and find out what the truth was without Callie or anyone knowing? Could she be that audacious?) But these were small niggles, easily dismissed.

What drifted into a concern was how her brain seemed to have become compulsive in a way she hadn't experienced before. Not only did she think about the woods, but she'd started to think almost obsessively of Warwick ward – the feeling that she'd left something behind, forgotten or undone, began to really bother her. It was just like the old itch of a misplaced phone – she'd even shouted at herself, when jogging in the woods (because no one could hear her there), *forget it, it's gone.*

But it didn't work.

She didn't know what was gone. It was irrational and irritating. What had been left at Warwick ward or left undone? It wasn't anything to do with the nice doctor, she knew that, and she'd gone through the nurses, and it wasn't to do with them either. And it couldn't have been anything from her bag physically left behind, because it contained only clothes and magazines her mother had bought for her in the emergency, nothing really hers, nothing expensive or personal – so what was it? She'd tried to ignore the feeling, but it continued to beat; like the movement of blood in an umbilical cord, the thought remained alive, linking her back to the place she had left.

Along with Warwick ward, the only main concern she had was she still wanted to speak with her mother. As time went on, the feeling intensified, not diminished. She wanted to know if she was all right – but it was more than that. She wanted to ask her about her father, just to have a conversation about him, because she had been thinking about him so much and talking to Celine about him. But she wanted to know if her mother had ever been to California, and she wanted to tell her about Stan. And now she'd flocked with Stefana, she could tell her about it as example of it being okay, that there was no further harm done. Billie could have an honest and reassuring conversation about what had happened to her. And when she'd asked Philippe if she could ring her mother, he'd said no.

No.

No negotiation, no enquiry why – just a flat-out *you knew the terms when you signed up*. And that was true. She did. But what she couldn't work out was the why. *Why* did it matter if she called her mother every couple of months?

She lay on her back in the dark, the group losing their grip on each other and becoming floating individuals again. She paddled on her back, enjoying the sensation of the water lapping through her fingers. She returned to how she was before she'd heard the voice. It felt like she was drifting in nothing. The womb sounds continued – heartbeat, gurgling – and Billie found it more relaxing than she'd thought she would. Eventually, Celine commanded them to take each other's hands again which led to giggles, brief shouts of humorous frustration and Stan's quips as they tried to reunite – it was harder than it seemed, and it took Celine some time to cajole them from laughter back into silence.

Whoever was now holding her hand on her left was gripping too hard. Pincer-like. It was a smaller hand and it hurt. *Maddy.* Passionate, fierce Maddy. Billie could tell, in Maddy stewed deep veins of moving, molten lava.

The thought of living here for two years like Maddy chilled her. Maddy's hand pinched too hard again. *I can't stay here for ever, drifting in the dark, drifting in inertia. I could become like Maddy with a cult-like fervour. Maybe I have already*, she thought, *now I'm hearing voices. I need to move forward*, she decided. *My neuroses are getting worse.* Stan started stroking her hand again. *California*, she thought, *away from here,* and smiled in the dark.

I just need to take control, she decided. *Like Stan, I need to be gone before winter. Before being caged in here stops me from being better and actually makes me worse. Even if I don't follow Stan to California, I'll leave at the same time. It'll be easier to leave with someone else – but I'll tell them I'll leave if they don't let me ring my mother. I'll insist.* She just needed to give a reason to which they couldn't say no.

THIRTY-FOUR

'I've been at Arbor for two months now,' said Billie to Philippe the following day. She stood in the yoga studio in front of him as he made notes before the group session that was about to start.

He didn't look up, but answered heartily, 'That's right – and we love having you here!'

'Great, I love being here, too. But Philippe, I'm concerned about my mother. It's the anniversary of my father's death and I really feel like I should be in touch with her. I know we talked about this before, but I need you to hear that for me, it's like a dripping tap, I just can't shut off thinking about her. And perhaps,' she said, pushing through to the end of her rehearsed speech, 'perhaps it's that worry that's getting in the way of our ability to flock. What do you think, could anxiety stand in the way?'

Flicking through some papers, he paused – just briefly, almost imperceptibly – before continuing. But he didn't answer.

This morning, Maddy had joined her on the morning jog with Jenna. Billie asked them both if they'd ever asked to call home since being at the institute. Both said no. Jenna, supportive, said that Billie should do what she felt was right – not to be constricted by behaving in the way that others wanted her to. 'Perhaps they won't even care and will let you call. You won't know until you ask,' she'd added.

'You've never asked to call someone?' Billie had questioned her.

'Nah,' said Jenna. 'Both my parents are dead, so I don't have anyone worrying about me. And it's good for me to be away from other people's crap. To be honest, I don't need it. I'll know I'll get pulled back into my old life and I don't want no dramas. I want to stay here – this is the first place where it suits me to follow the rules. But you do you, and don't let anyone get in the way of that.' She'd squeezed her elbow. 'What have you got to lose?'

'My place here?'

Jenna pulled a face and then shrugged. 'Your call. You choose.'

'And you, Maddy?'

'You should be able to call your mum if you want.' Maddy spoke with a furrowed brow and her usual precision. 'She's your mum and it's your human right to call her.'

Billie felt surprised. She expected Maddy to just talk about Tama again – which she'd noticed was the woman's mantra. 'Really? You think I should just be clear?'

Maddy widened her eyes and tossed her long hair over her shoulder. 'Just as long as I don't have to call *my* mum.'

'You told me you didn't have a mother,' said Jenna.

'She left me in care when I was six months old. Trust me, the things I would say, she wouldn't *want* my call.'

They had given her courage so, despite being ignored

by Philippe now, Billie persisted and repeated her request. Philippe picked up and drank his espresso, as if she hadn't spoken.

He's rude, she thought, irritation making her stumble over her words: 'I'd like to – no, need to – ring her. Please.' Asking his permission made it seem as if Philippe had become a sort of parent. *Or a sort of prison warder.* The thought reframed him and she recognized it was true: he supervised the group, oversaw their food, nutrition and schedules, and now here she was, seeking permission to speak with a loved one. For the first time, Billie felt a flicker of real resentment and the coals of temper glowed.

Philippe sat back in his chair, 'Billie, we've talked about this just last week. We really would rather you didn't call her.' He smiled and held up his hands as if in apology. 'I'm just being clear out of fairness.'

She was not going to be moved. Not this time. She sat down in the chair next to him. 'I have to.'

Philippe smiled again, deep lines forming in the tanned skin by his eyes. 'It's because of the science here – we need you to be grouped with the others and not be open to outside influence. You'll understand,' he said, sweeping his hand around, 'we've spared no expense to curate the very best experience here. We just can't taint your minds at this crucial time. For the record, I am sorry – if it helps to know that.'

'It's not a taint if it keeps me feeling settled. You've told us all before how important it is that we're settled. One call will settle me.'

'At your age – a grown adult – is being in touch with your mother, who truly has no notion of what you've endured, really going to be the settling experience you suggest? Might we examine that idea therapeutically? She has no idea about dux gregis. There's every chance she'll be filled with fear about the whole concept and is going to – tell me if this is wrong – burden you with questions you can't answer on the phone.'

He paused, letting the point sink in. 'Or you ring her. You decide – because the truth is too big to raise, cover and digest over the phone – to not tell her the truth. She's therefore going to continue to think you're suicidal and she'll need reassurance you are not still in that frame of mind. Either way, these are conversations that are not easy, not calming. Instead, you've opened the possibility of future phone calls which naturally means she, like any ageing parent, is only going to want more.

'Tell me, Billie, what will it really solve?'

He was good, it was true. But his smooth style, the neat press of the black T-shirt, his controlled manner – his confidence – felt like sandpaper on open flesh. 'Philippe, do you think I'm being unreasonable? She's on her own, my father is dead – the anniversary of which is this week – I just think it's the right thing to do and hopefully you can settle my mind.'

'It is August, Billie. Your father died in November.'

For a moment she said nothing, stress and shame turning like a hundred washing machines churning in her head. She'd been caught out. The white heat of her anger burned her cheeks. She wanted to bluster, how did he know? Had he done checks on her? But she thought of the running gear hanging in the wardrobe when she arrived, all so to her taste. She thought of the new trainers (two pairs: running and fashion), sliders, wellies, walking boots, in her wardrobe on arrival, all her size, all similar or identical to things she'd either bought or nearly bought herself. Even the bras she had were the exact same ones she'd bought with her mum in M&S. I should have seen it, she thought, feeling cold: *the bras*.

Too personal, too the same, too much of a coincidence.

But should she have seen it? No, she recognized she was in no shape to spot anything as she'd just survived an incident which killed her friends. I couldn't see anything but the horror of the loss of Ella and my friends, she thought.

But now I can see it all.

Of course they had done checks on her. Even mediocre companies checked the online profiles when hiring a new administrator. But this wasn't just checks: they'd sieved her entire online presence. The big things like significant dates and the small things. Yes, why wouldn't a pharmaceutical company with the clout and power of Arbor check out when her dad died?

That was one thing, but go back through her bank records – no, her mum paid for the bras, so her *mother's* bank records – to discern her choice in underwear. It couldn't be legal. So why break the law?

To keep her here.

Nathalie had told her, the first time she met her on the terrace, she could leave when she wanted. Everything was designed to make sure she didn't want to leave. Everything had been selected so she'd find it perfect. She'd been profiled. And that was why they didn't want her to speak with her mum. Anything that might connect her with wanting to leave.

She felt cold – locked in and suddenly small against the mighty. But she let her anger carry her. She stood up. 'I'm going to call my mum, or I'm going to leave. And I can leave. If you stop Stan driving me back to port, I will swim there myself and then call myself an Uber. And my mother will pay for it, and if she won't, I have a hundred people that will. You may be remote, but this is not on the dark side of the moon. I *can* leave. Nathalie said I could. I don't wish to be in any way ungrateful or rude, but nor do I wish to be gaslit. I'm going for a run now and you can discuss it with Nathalie, and whatever you both decide, I will respectfully accept.'

And then, to underline her point, she left the yoga studio just as Maddy was crossing the lawn towards it for the daily group session.

Maddy caught her arm. 'Are you okay? You've gone white. Are they letting you ring your mum?'

'No.' Billie didn't know if she was going to cry or pack. 'I've just had a row with Philippe in the barn. He wouldn't discuss it, so I said I'll leave.'

Maddy shook her head, mouth tight with anger. 'I will too, then. I'll stand with you, Billie. Philippe's outrageous.'

Stan joined them. 'What's got Maddy looking like she's going to kill someone?'

Billie told him and then Stan wrapped her in a big hug. 'Baby,' he whispered in her ear, 'you can count on me.' He dropped a kiss on her forehead. He turned to Ash and Jenna, and told them that she couldn't speak to her mother. They all discussed it with fire and fury, and agreed they'd go on strike and refuse to take part in any more studies, until Billie got to speak with her mum. 'Because we're all orphaned babies,' Stan said, 'means we understand the importance better than anyone.'

With Stan's arm wrapped right around her shoulder, pulling her in, and sensing the unity of her friends, Billie felt safe. Arbor was too much – too invasive, too controlling, but within it were some of the loveliest people she had ever met. Stan gave her a little squeeze and she looked at him as he smiled down at her. *I feel like his girl*, she thought, and she liked it. She had found her people.

THIRTY-FIVE

'This is all your fault, Celine,' Philippe shouted as he slapped the desk. 'I want you to know I hold you unequivocally *one hundred and fifty fucking per cent* responsible for this mess!'

'Tsk, Philippe, at least let her sit down before you lay into her,' said Nathalie. 'Thanks, Celine, for joining us with no notice. I appreciate your speed. Americano with one sugar – just how you like it.' She set Celine's coffee down in front of her on the conference-room table.

Celine blinked, bewildered. 'Just what am I being blamed for, in this rather heavy-handed and confronting way?'

Under an expensive navy blazer (the air con was always too fierce for her), Celine wore a cerise T-shirt that said: KEEP CALM AND PARTY ON. Nathalie suspected the silly slogan was designed to project an air of cosy irreverence as camp counsellor. But Celine was more than the counsellor, she was a professor of psychoanalysis, held a doctorate in psychiatry and sat on the senior leadership team for Arbor.

Nathalie was always particularly nice to her because she suspected that Celine didn't particularly like her. But despite the overtly buoyant exuberance Celine projected, she suspected the counsellor of not particularly liking anyone.

Celine accepted the coffee. 'Is this about my report?'

'No!' snarled Philippe. 'I don't care that Billie got freaked out in the pool! If I had to lie in the dark listening to womb noises, I think I would get freaked out too! This is not about that!'

Nathalie ignored him and instead spoke with a calm voice. 'No, it was clear – you're always very thorough.'

'So, if there's nothing else to add about my report, do you mind if I head off? I've got another session to prepare for and we have got our meeting this afternoon.' She eyed Philippe like he was a large unleashed and angry dog. 'And I'm not in the mood for Philippe's unchecked rudeness. I can come back when he's not – doing *that*.' She waggled her finger at him; he had got up and started pacing up and down the room.

Nathalie smiled. 'Of course. But there is just one thing. Billie has been asking to contact her mother. And now Billie's mother is pressing for contact with her daughter. She sent someone here to find Billie – fortunately Philippe was able to fob her off but he had to give her his number and now she's calling repeatedly. And now Jo Cathey is threatening to visit.' She laughed a little. 'That's all fine, all very manageable, but what's more problematic is that our patient is also pressing for contact. You can see that's a problem?'

Celine frowned. She went to say something, and then stopped abruptly.

'You were about to say,' said Philippe, 'Billie doesn't have a mother. Because your real task for the institute is to search for and select suitable patients, not organize swimming-pool parties and woo-woo bonding exercises. You're the profiler. You're the selector. That's your chief job before being their thought-spy-slash-confidante. It was you who was tasked with looking for students in the universities' bereavement counselling service, of which you are chair. That was the point of you *becoming* chair of the counselling service: so you could find suitable candidates for OmnieX experimentation *who have no parents*. OmnieX in its development was only supposed to be used on young people with *no* family, *no* friends, *no* one who would come looking for them. You have successfully done this several times before, Celine, but you did *not* do it this time.'

Celine looked from Philippe, to Nathalie, back to Philippe. She placed her hands flat upon the table. 'I checked the spreadsheets myself. Billie's parents are dead.'

'Billie's parents were dead, you said, no extended family, no godparents lurking. Clear to drop the OmnieX on her to stimulate the gregis, you said. Correct?'

Celine face had paled but she nodded. She had written a report saying that.

Philippe continued: 'Because, as chair – the very reason you took on that role – you were able to access the charity's data,' he said. 'Your task: select across the nine universities who use the service for students who have been orphaned or have also been in the care system. Select candidates who have no siblings. Select students who have no extended family. In other words, the most important part of who we select for Arbor is who you have said has *no one to fucking come and get them.*'

Celine coloured, her face matching her T-shirt. 'I genuinely didn't know ...' She pressed her hands together. 'If

I've made a mistake, I'm sorry. I'm dealing with lines of data – I don't meet them and interview them for obvious reasons. So ... if you say it's possible that I've made a mistake, then—'

'Yes, I am saying it's possible!' shouted Philippe, thumping the top of the coffee machine. 'I'm saying it's more than fucking possible because, if not, who has been ringing me every fucking day for the last week?'

'Philippe, please,' said Nathalie in the calm voice of a teacher speaking to an out-of-control primary school pupil. 'Not the coffee machine. *Never* the coffee machine.'

'Sorry,' he said, actually stroking the top of it. 'It's been a hard day.' He turned his ire back on Celine. 'You know we hid this problem from you, to save your professional embarrassment? We picked up she had a parent as soon as she entered the health system. But obviously, it was all too late by then, wasn't it? There was a group dosed with OmnieX complete with one still alive. We were forced into shit-pick-up mode – *your shit* – and did a full recce on her mother: bank and employment records, the whole works. She seemed benign. We breathed a sigh of relief that Billie wasn't the daughter of a diplomat or some hot-shot lawyer. Can you imagine the fall-out if she were connected to someone powerful? Fortunately for you, Jo Cathey is a no one and Billie only matters to *one* no one.'

'And an overly conscientious psychiatrist and journalist,' Nathalie said quietly.

Celine blinked, and her eyes started to sheen. She understood just how bad her mistake had been. She must have misread a tick in a column and then didn't read the counsellor's notes carefully enough. She was at the start of the

OmnieX recipient selection process and she'd got sloppy. She had put Billie up for the next OmnieX chem attack. Once she was selected, it was easy for a tail (as usual, Ted) to follow the mark, release the canister (she understood the gas was carried and released in an adapted aerosol can, but she tried not to think about the details, only look at her bank account) and then it was easy to pull the mark to safety. She'd heard that Ted had been barged out of the way at the last moment on the train platform – that they'd nearly lost Billie (this happened more than it should – the logistics of saving someone did not always run to plan because of a thousand different variables). But then she'd been saved by a man on the platform. Celine had been so pleased, because once she'd met Billie at Arbor, she felt that she was a great addition to the institute.

But now they were telling her Billie should never have been here at all.

Billie and her friends shouldn't have been targeted, because somewhere else, there was a student whose tick she'd read on a line of data, who had two dead parents, no siblings, no uncles or aunts, and *that* student, and *that* student's friends, should have been targeted with the OmnieX chem attack, and it should have been *that* student who joined the group at Arbor.

Not Billie.

Perhaps Celine's horror showed because Philippe spoke in a calmer voice even if he still didn't sit down. 'A no one she might be, but her mother still had the nous to send a journalist up here. She knew where the institute was because, despite our instructions to the hospital, she was there when we sent the transfer car *and got in it*. For fuck's sake, Celine, why do you think Callie had to chop her bloody hair off and dye it? You know she's got an infection in her right eye because she's had to switch to contacts as a bloody disguise?'

Celine shook her head, bewildered. 'I don't follow?'

'Callie was in the car with Ted, to collect Billie. Obviously, they did not want a parent to follow them over the Firth to the institute, so they had to make up a lie. They had to pretend Callie was a hire who had come from the Redhill area and Ted said they had to drive Callie back because she was an agency nurse only employed to oversee the travel.'

'Why?'

'We did not want Jo Cathey coming to the institute. She was therefore forced to return home quicker than she would've have preferred, so she wasn't stranded. But then – problemo – Callie was known as an agency nurse, which clearly she isn't, so to save questions, she obligingly, and for a generous bonus, changed her appearance, her name and became Lia instead.'

Celine blinked. 'Callie is Lia? I thought . . .'

Phillipe threw his hands up, exasperated, and looked at Nathalie as if to say, *is it me?* 'Clearly you're oblivious to the nursing team, as well as important data.'

Celine shifted in her chair and ignored the jab. 'It sounds like there is no problem now.'

'So no problem then?'

'Only that *I* had to bluff when Billie spotted her anyway. And *I* had to deal with the reporter who turned up to the island and took a number away for her mother. And now *I* have to put up with the mother calling every day. And it's *me* who has to ignore her. It's also *me* that now has Billie's last psychiatrist enquiring how his ex-patient is getting on. *He* can be fobbed off, because legally *he* transferred her care. But it turns out, Billie's mother does not feel like she's transferred anything! And that's not even the end of my headache! Because it's also *me*,' he slammed the table again, 'who has to deal with Billie asking *me yet again to ring her mother* – despite my rude and savage attempts to deter her. You know I have to give in, don't you? Because she organized a mutiny among fucking everybody *and she's threatened to leave*.'

Celine covered her face. 'Oh, Philippe. Oh, I am so, so sorry. I totally hear you and understand why you are angry. I am so very, *very* sorry.'

'Why do you think that no one turned up to group therapy just now?'

'I don't know ... I just thought you'd given them permission to ... or the time had changed and I was going to ask you ...'

'Philippe, sit down, Celine, pull yourself together,' said Nathalie, pleased that Celine had had enough of a spanking. 'We can sort this – we just need a slight alteration to our strategy. We'll let Billie have a pseudo call with her mother and that will buy some time.'

'But we can't risk them talking,' said Celine carefully, now back to problem-solving. 'We don't want Jo Cathey to know about dux gregis. Any talk about flocking could get out. We don't want Billie giving any hint of unhappiness. It sounds like it's too late to protect our location, but one conversation will lead to another and that's a disaster.'

'Don't worry, we're not taken by surprise. Philippe?'

'The peeps in tech support have already used their AI voice-copy facility,' he said. 'They used the audio from Jo

Cathey's car conversation on the journey up, and when we are ready, they'll set it up so that Billie can effectively feel like she is speaking with her mother. She won't be – she'll be talking to us using the AI program, but that doesn't matter if she *believes* she is.'

Celine clapped her hands together, thrilled the problem had already been solved. 'That's perfect! I love technology. I saw a video of a fish the other day that looked like a dragon. It wasn't a dragon, it was AI, but it was so realistic!'

Philippe pressed for an espresso, and then after it was poured looked at Celine over the top of the cup. 'What I don't get is, you're her therapist. How could you not know she has a mother knocking around the place? I thought all people talked about in therapy was their mothers?'

'Billie talks about her father. Her dead friends. Her fears of dux. The trauma of her lost life. Yes, on a couple of occasions, she has mentioned her mother. But I thought she meant a foster mother – a colloquial term. You can't legislate for new established relationships.'

'We can legislate for sloppy therapists, who listen to podcasts in an earpiece they think can't be seen, instead of listening to Billie.'

Celine flushed and looked at her rings before rubbing at a large opal. 'I should have had more professional curiosity, agreed. But it's not as if I'm practising real therapy – it's only ever been a façade.'

'Well, you have not helped with our *aims* – not one little bit. This research paradox is an impossibly difficult fucking operation: *Billie is dangerous*. She just doesn't know she is – but if she finds out, then we fold. To hold such power – *power that is greater than us* – takes planning, nuance, risk and message management, keeping them *fucking oblivious and away from the outside world*. We are the lion tamers. We are the submariners living with nuke missiles. We are the dictators' wives. We are careful. Delicate. And because we understand the danger we are in, we are always, *always* fucking awake.'

'I'm sorry, Philippe. I get the point. I thought I knew she didn't have a mother and I was too focused on other things to pursue the point. We've been doing this a long time now – I was used to getting this right and I wasn't sharp enough to the reality of getting it wrong. But we are still in control.'

'It's still messy. We still have the mother circling. The psychiatrist is a potential problem. So is the journalist. And Billie now thinks I'm a bitch – which is a problem because she has to trust me: relationships are everything. And of course, once we do this, there's no going back.'

'Because . . .' said Celine slowly, figuring it out, 'once she speaks to the AI fake mother, she can never speak to her actual mother again without risking the relationship with Arbor?'

Philippe shrugged. 'I think you're missing the obvious: what completion looks like.'

Celine sat up straight. 'I'm fully aware of what the project's completion stage looks like.'

Nathalie finished her coffee. 'I've got to go. I've got to go to Chicago. The boss has summoned me for an update.'

'How is Jude?' Celine said, fluffing her hair and recovering a little. 'Does he know about . . . my error?'

Nathalie pushed her chair in and headed for the door. 'I don't worry him about the details. I'm off to find out how long we've got left with Billie. Philippe and I had thought end of August, but after speaking with Jude earlier, I got the sense that completion will be a little quicker than anticipated. I'll be back in two days. Maybe treat the inmates to pizza, obscene amounts of wine and some time off. Most of all, sort the phone call for Billie – tell her ASAP. I'd like everything peachy before the helicopter arrives in,' she checked her Rolex, 'forty minutes.'

THIRTY-SIX

After boycotting the group therapy, they all decided to enjoy the weather and play tennis. As there were five of them, each took a turn to sit out; swapping with Maddy now, it was moments like this, Billie thought, sweat-slicked, sun on her face, collapsing into the courtside chair, she loved Arbor. Their impromptu game was their open defiance against the institute, and they were loving it. Their unity made them feel strong – *look at us*, they said. *We are not going to any circle time, or having any tests done, but instead we are just playing tennis – and there's nothing you can do about it.* It was a fun rebellion.

They stayed out in the sunshine until supper time. Now, the five of them entered the dining room together – Philippe was in there clearly waiting for them, wringing his hands and looking like he'd been kicked by a horse. 'Er, Billie, I'd like to let you know something,' he said.

Jenna grinned, clearly amused, Ash winked, Stan bit his hand to stop himself from laughing, and Maddy, chin raised, gave a tight, controlled smile, triumphant. They purposefully ignored Philippe to point out that Nathalie's helicopter was leaving, but when it was only a pinprick in the sky, they finally had to pretend to hide their silent laughter.

Philippe seemed not to notice and instead just said Billie was to come and find him in the library once she'd finished her dinner. 'You can call your mother and I'm sorry. I was wrong. Both Celine and Nathalie have put me right.' He left, adding as he did so, 'To apologize, I've arranged a special dinner for you.'

Laid out under the hot lamps was a Thai banquet – her favourite. 'He feels terrible,' Ash said, 'and I'm not surprised. He owed you that apology.'

Maddy squeezed her hand. 'I think he's been bollocked. Good. It's typical coercive control. Because none of us have parents, they've never had to deal with this before. But we were going to fight for you as the one person who has.'

Ash used tongs to load his plate with noodles. 'Strange, isn't it, how none of us have parents – except now. We never really talked about it before – too painful, perhaps, or just nothing for us to consider – but what are the statistical odds of that?'

'No idea,' answered Stan, taking the tongs from Ash, 'but I never thought about it because I never thought about it.'

Maddy squealed. She'd opened the drinks fridge and four bottles of wine had been left for them. 'Oh, look! Philippe knows he's been a bad, *bad* boy!'

They all cheered and sat around the table, letting the wine go to their heads. Billie felt jubilant: after dinner she would speak to her mother.

By the time Billie had finished her supper and the wine, it was still before nine. She got up and headed for the library, feeling a little drunk, apprehensive and victorious. In the library, there hadn't previously been a landline phone installed on a side table, but now there was. Philippe was waiting for her; he didn't quite do jazz hands as he said 'Ta-daa!' but he was evidently pleased. He apologized again, checked she knew her mother's number and added, 'Take as long as you like,' before shutting the door.

Now she was alone, she picked up the receiver, desperate to speak to her mum. She rang the number. The phone rang three times and then:

'Hello,' said her mother.

'Hi, Mum! It's Billie!'

'Oh, hello, Billie! How unexpected – but so nice to hear from you. How are you?'

For a moment, Billie was stuck for words. The alcohol, the excitement, the challenge and emotion of the day and now the reality after two months of finally speaking with her mum, meant she felt a tidal wave of feelings.

'I'm sorry I haven't rung. Residents are not supposed to, but they said I could.'

'I remember – they were very clear that was a condition of you staying. But considering all your treatment and expenses are being covered, I thought that was very fair. Don't you?'

'Well, yes ... but I thought you'd be worried.'

'I think I would be more worried if you weren't receiving first-class care.'

'Yes.' Billie bit her lip. Had she misjudged her so much? 'I take your point. I just know that you like me to be in touch.'

'Under normal circumstances, then yes. But what happened to you isn't normal circumstances, is it? I can see it requires a little more ... special attention. Are you getting special attention?'

Billie blinked in surprise. 'Yes ... I suppose I am. The facilities are great, and I've restarted my degree.'

They chatted about that for ten minutes – her mother seemed relieved it was all free, 'how generous of the institute', and they both discussed the essays – perhaps in more detail than Billie would have liked. It felt formal, stilted and a little sterile.

But then her mother started asking small, trivial questions and Billie settled, managing to share with her mother what they did every day, about the food and the activities. Her mother expressed carefully modulated interest in the pool, the food, the yoga. Then it seemed there was nothing else to say. Philippe was right: a phone call didn't feel like the right medium to discuss dux – there was too much distance between them. That meant it wasn't a real conversation – they couldn't talk about what really mattered to Billie.

So, the conversation was safe and reductive, and when her mother brought it to an end, Billie knew she wouldn't be calling the next day. It was okay – her mother was fine, she knew she was fine and really, what could she actually tell her without worrying her?

THIRTY-SEVEN

Dan's mobile rang on his desk. Typing with his right hand, keen to finish his notes so he could go home and get a few hours' sleep before dashing to the airport, he reached for the phone with his left.

His fingers misjudged it and instead of grabbing his mobile, he knocked the Venti takeaway cup; it tipped, and coffee covered his desk. Swearing softly, he jumped up, grabbed the ringing phone from the pooling liquid and hit the green button, simultaneously looking for something – anything – he could mop up his desk with. 'Sorry, can you hold on a sec? I've just spilled my coffee.'

He found a pair of his sweaty socks in his gym bag and, hating himself a little, he used them to mop up the mess. 'Ah – back now. Sorry about that, just been too clumsy. Wrecked my desk and everything on it. You still there?'

'Dan? It's Jo Cathey.'

He gave up with the coffee and the socks and sat down – he'd been waiting for her to call: everything else could wait. 'What's the latest?' They were in almost daily contact now. She was trying to speak with Philippe Bouchard, the institute's director of operations, the same man he'd met on Dorcha. Every day, Bouchard either didn't take her call or fobbed her off. Dan had wanted to call him himself, or suggested returning to the institute, but Jo was reluctant. 'She's twenty-four,' she'd pointed out, 'and she does need to be somewhere. She was very unhappy on Warwick ward – really, she should be at Arbor if that's where she wants to be. I just want to speak to her for a couple of minutes, so I know she's safe and happy, and making a good recovery.'

That conversation had been weeks ago. It was now three months since Jo had left her daughter in the marina near Wemyss Bay and had been driven off in the back of a Mercedes. Three months was the deadline that Jo and Dan had agreed after which action should be taken.

'No news?' he asked her now.

'None. The last three days it's gone to answer machine. I feel that Bouchard is no longer taking my calls.'

Dan didn't want to worry Jo further, but Veer had also been in touch several times, and he had not been given the health report on Billie that he'd been promised either. Together, they'd both decided it was time to escalate. They had to keep Billie safe.

'Jo, let's visit next week. We can go up there, get the police involved if you like.'

'How would that work? She's an adult, she's not missing, and there's no crime.'

'We can let them know we're attending the institute to do a welfare check – and that will give us protection against any issues.'

Jo fell silent and he had to prompt her to see if she was still there. 'I'm here. I think, actually, I might just go up there today. I think I need to be normal about it – not be too heavy weather, if you know what I mean. Just me, just simple. Nothing threatening about a visit from a mum. She'll be fine – you saw her and she was – and then I'll see her and then I don't have to rely on Mr Bouchard or trouble you or anything.'

He tried to dissuade her, even considered breaking the agreement with Veer and telling her the truth of their concerns about Billie's abilities. He only held back because he thought she would definitely be spurred into checking on her daughter if she knew the full situation. 'Jo, I have a flight booked to Germany tonight. I'm covering the escalating events in Berlin, but I could visit with you as soon as I'm back. Please wait until then.'

'Honestly, I'll just go now,' she said with more gentle steel than he'd credited her with. 'Come round for a cup of tea when you get back from Germany if you find yourself in the area. I'll let you know about what I find. It might be interesting!'

'Please, Jo, I beg you to wait for me. I'm . . .'

'Worried about me?'

'Yes. I'm worried that it's . . .' He wanted to say *dangerous*, but of course that would provoke her into action.

'She's my daughter. I'd walk across fire for her. I'm just checking in with her. They probably would be surprised if I didn't.'

She couldn't be dissuaded, and when Dan got off the phone, he stared at the coffee puddle, his coffee-soaked socks and the ruined papers and knew that everything was just such a mess.

THIRTY-EIGHT

Nathalie answered her phone.
'Boss, it's Ted here in security. You're off site.'
'Chicago. Will be back tomorrow. All good?'
'The tracker Callie dropped into Jo Cathey's handbag shows that she's just taken the M6 heading north. Our intel doesn't suggest she has any reason to come up this way – unless—'
'Unless she's coming here to visit her daughter.'
'Exactly. Given that she's been contacting the journalist so often, it's reasonable to assume she's on her way here – probably with him. And if we are her destination, then we should be expecting her, or both of them, to arrive at the Bay in three hours and twenty minutes at around seventeen hundred hours BST.'
'Unhelpful. Can you get Philippe an urgent message? Tell him not to do the AI phone call yet – just in case.'
'It happened yesterday.'
Nathalie hesitated – but only for a moment. 'If she has company, then it's the de-escalation plan. But if she's

alone, then you know what to do. She'll not be missed by anyone other than Billie – and that's not going to matter soon.'

'I'll liaise with Philippe and call you when it's done.'

THIRTY-NINE

Billie received the summons for an emergency drill via her watch. Curious, she met with the others in the reception room. Philippe joined them with his clipboard.

'Room for a little one?' Stan asked, already sinking into the no-gap between her and Jenna on the low, scarlet velvet sofa. He slung his arm along the back, and leaned in close to Billie, his lips grazing her ear. 'I see the ol' nanny means business – she's got her clipboard,' he whispered.

She wished he didn't make her laugh, but she dug him in the ribs to put him right.

'Thanks for coming,' Philippe said. 'It's been brought to my attention that I've made a little error insofar as we've never had an emergency lockdown practice. Every organization has them, offices, schools, department stores, etcetera. It's my mistake and so, to put it right, we'll have a run-through today if that's okay. We are aiming for seventeen hundred hours BST, so I need you all to decide where you're going to be when that happens – start time *is* approximate. You will hear a sound – similar but not the same as the fire alarm. It will ring for two minutes and then stop, but in a real situation it would sound continuously.' He waved his clipboard, and Billie ignored the tickle Stan gave her shoulder to acknowledge Philippe's behaviour.

'I've got a form on here that you'll all need to sign to say that you understand that if the sound is continuous, you will know you are in a real lockdown situation – not a drill. Now the tricky news for you is that you will be locked in for around two hours – but the good news is, for this drill you can chose any location inside the institute. You can be in your room alone, or you can all wait it out together and watch a film in the lounge or library. Or two of you can go to the gym and the rest do some combination of those things. Any questions?'

Stan raised his hand. 'Can Billie come to my room with me?'

'Hey!' She dug him in the ribs again. Maddy narrowed her eyes and he laughed, asking Maddy what the matter was.

Philippe cut through the silliness. 'Has anyone got any *serious* questions?'

'Ouch!' said Stan. 'I have actually. Does it have to happen today?'

'No time like the present,' said Philippe. 'We need to be compliant with company policy. For insurance reasons.'

Stan feigned a horrified expression. 'Does that mean the insurance is invalid right at this very moment?'

Ash sighed, ignored him and addressed a question to Philippe. 'What do you and the rest of the team do in those two hours?'

'Honestly? Just watch you guys on the CCTV. Someone needs eyes on, in case any of you were to have a medical emergency. The rest of the team run a series of tests, computer systems, etcetera. If they finish early, then we will all finish early, but I wouldn't get your hopes up – we've never done this before.' He beamed. 'Anything else?'

'What if we need the toilet?' asked Maddy. 'I need to be able to go to the toilet. You can't stop me. It's my human right.'

'Isn't the human rights lawyer becoming tedious?' Stan murmured into Billie's ear.

'We always support your rights, Maddy – this is about supporting your right to be safe at the institute. If you feel that you will need the loo, then pick a location with an adjacent toilet – there's plenty of choice. Your room obviously; the gym has one; this reception room,' he said, indicating the door behind the oriental screen, 'the library and the dining room both have one. As does the inside pool – so lots of choice. So, everyone, unless you have any other questions, talk about it among yourselves and think about it carefully. Once you've committed, you will not be able to change your mind. If you do, then I need to emphasize that we will have to have a second drill.'

'But what happens if we have an anxiety attack or choke?' asked Maddy.

'Well, obviously, I will come and give first aid. We will just have to have a second drill. But! If we get this right first time, we can organize a treat – something special.'

'How special?' said Stan.

Philippe's smile almost faltered. 'We'll take suggestions.'

'You lock me in a room with Billie for a couple of hours?'

She hit him with a cushion and Maddy told him he was 'inappropriate'.

The group talked among themselves. Billie and Jenna

decided to watch films together ('*The Godfather* one and two please'), and Stan and Ash said they'd hit the gym. Maddy said she wanted to be alone, but feeling a little worried about her – she seemed more and more tense and strung-out – Billie wouldn't accept it, and Maddy finally capitulated and said she'd sit in the library with them.

Philippe checked his watch. 'Okay, everyone, it's nearly four o'clock now, and you have just under an hour to get yourselves sorted. We've laid on a lovely afternoon tea for you so you're not hungry and it's now served in the dining room. Fill up quickly though please – we need to clear away in thirty minutes. A supper will be available when this is all over around seven thirty. Let's go and get ready! Oh, and just one thing.' He held up his hand as they all got up and started to file out. 'I forgot to mention – the privacy blinds will automatically come down and stay in place during the duration of the drill. Obviously, it's to protect you in a real situation – it just means you won't be able to see outside. But really, what does that matter when there's nothing to see?'

FORTY

At just after 5 p.m., Jo Cathey parked in the car park at the small marina near Wemyss Bay and, after a moment of collecting herself, grabbed her handbag and got out. She breathed deeply the salt-tang air and took a minute to watch the rise and fall of the seagulls on the wind. She listened to their cries – seeing large birds in flight always made her think of her husband. She sighed, never wishing more for him to be by her side. Ed had loved birds. He'd been a carpenter, all rough knuckles and unshaven face, and had mostly worked out of his shed, the hawk on its perch keeping him company. He wasn't someone rich in conversation but was always so loving to herself and their only daughter. Nothing had made her happier than watching from the window as little Billie bobbed next to her father, taking the path down to Firkin's house.

She never told him – or Billie for that matter – that the large bird with its thick legs and huge claws unnerved her. It was too clever, with its quick, surgically neat movements and its wild, crazy orange-red eyes. But she kept her thoughts to herself. She always felt the bird was important in some way. Ed never seemed to find people easy, tending to lean towards the obsessive, and she figured a goshawk was more interesting than something like trains. He would have been a granite rock in this situation, but as she watched the birds circle, perhaps after a catch off a boat, she knew she'd just have to check in on Billie for both of them.

Holding her bag tight, she moved towards the small office. The yachts bobbed on the water, lined up against the pontoons. Dan had warned her that the ferry didn't stop at Dorcha, but she'd have to get a private hire. She thought she'd ask at the office to see if someone could taxi her over to the island.

She had nearly made it to the office, when she saw a man carrying two bags of shopping from the car park. She didn't really notice him, her thoughts instead on Billie and what she might find, but he looked up and saw her, lifting one arm so she couldn't miss him. 'Hey, Mrs Cathey, is that you?'

It took a moment to place him. Square jaw, the bluest eyes she'd ever seen, neatly shaved, he was dressed in combat trousers and a dark polo shirt. Then she recognized him: it was the Arbor driver. He seemed different from when she'd last seen him, but she couldn't place why – the dark glasses he'd worn then, perhaps, or the fact he was friendly and smiling. He'd seemed distinctly sullen before, clearly unhappy that she had joined her daughter in the car. He'd barely spoken during the entire drive up from Warwick ward, leaving the good-looking female nurse to do all the heavy lifting with the chat. She'd only really seen the back of his head and he'd seemed reluctant to speak at all. Even when they'd pulled in at the services, he'd stayed in the car when she'd got out and was still sitting there when she came back.

'This is a surprise! I'm right, you're Billie's mum, yes?' he said, acting like he wasn't entirely sure, when for some reason she felt he was. He knew it was her, and for a split second, out of character, she nearly told him that. Instead, she confirmed she was and asked him if they took private boat bookings at the office. She knew she was sorry to have bumped into him, and held her handbag closer to her chest, for although he smiled at her and seemed pleased to see her, the seagulls circling overhead made it feel like they were vultures coming to pick the flesh from her bones. She shook her head at the thought – it wasn't like her to be so grim. She should be pleased to see someone from the institute – it could only make it easier to get to Billie.

'They might, but there may not be someone ready to take you at this time – it's just after five. But my boat's here. Just been shopping.' He picked up his bags. 'I'm always topping up on stores. Follow me over to the boat and I'll give you a lift.'

She didn't want to go with him; for some reason the birds' keening cries and the ridiculous neat timing of seeing him *right here right now* meant she really didn't want to get on that boat. 'It's okay,' she said, holding her bag even tighter. 'If I can't get a private hire tonight, I'll stay at a B&B in town and try again in the morning.'

He looked at her like she was stupid. 'Mrs Cathey, that's my black speedboat, right there. It's so close, I could chuck a stone at it. Come with me and I'll take you now.'

To stall, she blurted: 'I'm here because the number you gave me didn't work.'

He frowned. 'I don't know why that would be. I'm sorry about that. Are you sure you dialled it right?'

'Very sure. Several times.'

'Well, I'm sorry – I'm a little dyslexic so it's possible I inverted a couple of numbers. Come on, let me make it up to you and get you to Arbor now. If you're here, you'll be wanting to see Billie.'

Jo followed him to the sleek black speedboat. He got in first, and held out his hand to help her.

'I can do it, thanks. My dad had a speedboat.'

Jo climbed in. There seemed little choice. *Billie*, she reminded herself, *this will lead me to Billie*. As he turned, he knocked his shopping bags on the seat and they spilled their contents. She helped him collect up the packages and put them back into the bags. He took the dog biscuits and held them, as if precious. 'I've got a terrier called Jack.'

'A Jack Russell?'

He laughed. 'Not very original, I know, but I got him from the shelter. His name was Seyton, apparently named after Macbeth's assistant, but I couldn't be shouting that out in the park. Jack was supposed to be a temporary name while I thought of something else.' He grinned, white, neat teeth showing in a wolfish grin. 'The name stuck. Anyway, come and sit up front with me and we'll be at the island in half an hour. It'll be fast and too noisy to chat, so hang on tight.'

He checked his watch, started up the engine with a huge rumble, and then they were backing out from the jetty and moving out through the open water of the Firth.

Jo kept her face forward and her eyes shut against the wind. The boat bounced and heaved as he took it full speed into the head sea, with the waves coming towards the bow; he hadn't offered her a life jacket and she wondered if he was trying to make her nervous.

But if anyone had told her that the one person she'd met who worked at Arbor would be standing in front of her, waving at her, as soon as she got out of her car, she would have laughed. But she didn't feel like laughing now.

Eventually, they arrived, salt-sprayed and wind-cold. He checked his watch as he dropped the boat back into a low speed and pulled up at a little jetty. Ahead, Jo took in the small beach, the great, intimidating wall of trees, and couldn't believe that her daughter was here, somewhere on this island. She opened her bag and rooted around the debris of her life that she carried with her, finding her hairbrush and powder compact among the melee of tissues, sweets and loose change. She ignored him as she straightened out her appearance; she wasn't a vain woman, but she was representing her daughter. Then, with as much brightness as she could muster, she climbed out of the boat, onto the pontoon, and followed him towards a path that disappeared into the wood.

He chattered so much; Jo couldn't tally this talkative man with the silent chauffeur he had been. She said as much to him, as politely as she could, because it was such an abrupt change, it set fire to her nerves.

He laughed again and dismissed his silence that day as due to having a sore throat and a thumping headache at the time. He checked his watch again and continued up the beach.

She followed after him, the beach disappearing behind them as the dark woods rose up around them. The only sound, apart from the mewing of gulls, was their feet crunching against the path. It was warm away from the water, but she still pulled her jacket around her, and re-hitched her bag. It was feeling heavy now, even though she'd brought only a change of clean underwear and a top. Her plan had only been to check on Billie and then either leave with her or leave her happy at the institute – whatever her daughter wanted. She hoped to find a B&B in Wemyss Bay, or if she were quick, further down the road, lessening the travel burden tomorrow. But she had to keep her options open, she knew that.

'Will you please be able to give me a lift back to the port later, after I've seen Billie?'

'Of course! Unless you stay over tonight – I'm sure you'll be most welcome.'

He strode ahead and it seemed darker under the trees' shadows. It felt wrong, him suggesting that she would be able to stay over. They couldn't even answer her calls when the number was correct, so the idea she'd be a welcome visitor did not ring true. She glanced back over her shoulder, wondering if she should come back with someone else. Dan or a friend, perhaps. But of course, it was too late for that now: she was here.

He swore and put his bags down abruptly. Jo clutched her chest. She was in the middle of nowhere with a six-foot-four man and she felt a chill of vulnerability, with the flash of sudden anger.

'I've just seen my dog!' He pointed into the undergrowth. 'There he goes, did you see him?'

He didn't wait for her to answer that no, she'd not seen a dog, but instead he strode off fast, in the direction in which he'd pointed. 'They've let him out again! Bloody idiots – sorry, not your daughter, she's always great with Jack. Grab the biscuits, will you, we'll need them to get him out of the rabbit holes he's after.'

She paused, looking at the packet of dog biscuits lying so handily on the top of the shopping bag.

'Hurry up, Mrs Cathey! There's a badger sett this way, just off this path.'

She picked up the packet and hurried after him along the path. Just as she nearly caught up, he veered off among the trees, almost running now. 'I see him! Jack! Here, boy!'

They moved deeper into the woods. Even after a few minutes, she couldn't see the path and it seemed like they'd been moving uphill away from Arbor. 'Can you find him?' she called ahead, jumping over a tree root and ducking under a branch.

He didn't answer straightaway, moving so fast, his dark shirt continuing to appear and then disappear behind the trees, leaving her having to speed up to catch him. Branches pulled at her jacket. The sky was lost under the canopy, and it felt cooler away from the sun. It felt miles from anywhere – no sound of human life – and she sharply wanted to be back in her kitchen. She paused, hand on a tree trunk, glancing back behind her – she couldn't see the shopping bags, the path or a sign of anything other than more trees. 'Hello?' she called ahead towards where she'd seen him disappear past some thick shrubbery. 'I think I'm a bit lost?'

No answer.

She picked up her pace, running a little now, afraid of her situation, and the way he made her feel. A twig caught her face and scratched her cheekbone, but she didn't stop, suddenly feeling abandoned.

Then, she turned a corner and found him standing by a tree, looking down into a deep pit. 'Oh!' She clutched her chest, feeling the *wham-wham* of her heart. 'I thought

I'd lost you ... Is there a problem?' she said, clutching her handbag to her chest. 'Is it your dog? Is Jack all right?'

He stared into the deep pit, grave length. 'In there,' he said, pointing in so she had to move closer to see what he was gesturing to. As she peered into the shadows, he made a quick, tight move leaving her sandwiched between him and the ditch.

Jo Cathey was a smart woman – she looked from the ditch to him, understood what was happening and wished she'd done it differently.

And then he pulled a gun from inside his jacket.

She thought he was going to say something, something by way of explanation, but in the end, he just took aim and pulled the trigger, leaving her with her final thought:

Billie.

FORTY-ONE

Dan Downes, glad only two nights in Germany meant carry-on luggage and therefore no baggage claim, jumped in the back of a taxi, then rang Jo Cathey's number. It immediately flipped to voicemail. She'd promised she wouldn't turn her phone off. Perhaps it's just out of juice, he thought, but he still had a bad feeling. A *really* bad feeling. He sighed and tried again and again – instant voicemail.

Big powerful drug company versus Jo Cathey. In every sense of the word, he felt worried. No. That didn't fit, he thought. *I'm scared.*

He thought through his options and made his decision. Knocking on the glass partition, he said after the driver slid it back, 'Look mate, sorry, change of plan. I need to go to an address in Crowthorne. You okay to take me there?'

It would be an hour, but he could expense account it. I'm going to doorstep her, he decided, knowing he would feel better for the trying.

He just hoped he would have a wasted journey, find she

had a technical problem with her phone or ... he couldn't think of another reason.

In just over an hour, Dan rang the doorbell of Jo Cathey's Georgian terrace. He stepped back off the doorstep and looked up at the top-floor windows. The curtains were pulled in both of them as well as in the downstairs ones. He rang again. And then a third time.

Looking through the letterbox, he could see a few leaflets and a handful of letters lying on the hall floor. 'Jo,' he risked calling out. 'Jo, it's Dan. Are you home?'

The darkness answered nothing back.

He thought he'd try the neighbours. He rang the bell next door and heard footsteps almost instantly. The door opened to a teenage boy. 'Hello,' the boy said brightly behind his fringe.

'Hi, my name's Dan and I know Jo Cathey from next door. I wondered if you've seen her in the last couple of days?'

Face scratch. 'You're not from Amazon?'

'No, sorry. I'm just looking for your neighbour, from number fourteen. You haven't seen Jo recently?

The boy blew out a long sigh, clearly uninterested. 'Yeah?'

'She's not home though, and I wondered if you knew when she'd be back.'

'I'll get my mum.'

He left and a woman in her fifties appeared, neat hair, and wiping her hands on a tea towel. 'Hello, yes, you're asking after Jo next door?'

Dan decided it was better to be honest and gave her as

much of the story about how he knew them as he could – that he knew that Billie had been ill and that Jo wanted to check on her; it was always a tightrope to be walked, how much information would be needed to elicit a response. It worked.

'Look, can I be honest too?' she said. 'I'm also worried about her. She came past earlier in the week and told me she needed to check on her daughter, Billie, who was staying at some place in Scotland, but Jo said she wouldn't stay more than one night. She also promised she wouldn't turn her phone off because her cat, Tinsley, is sick and needs some drops. I phoned her and left messages about the meds, but no answer. I had hoped to hear from her by now. I haven't.'

'When did she leave?' he asked, already knowing the answer, but experience had taught him to check even the facts he thought he knew.

'She's been gone two nights. She also said she'd message me if she stayed over even one night.' She scratched her face just as her son had done. 'It's such a long drive – a thousand miles in two days. I said to her, why don't you stay up for a few days, but Jo wouldn't have it. She said she never minded the drive and wouldn't dream of staying up there for any longer than she had to.' Doubt wrinkled her forehead. 'But I'm worried now. Her phone is off. She's very conscientious – I know she wouldn't want to worry me.'

Dan could see concern cloud her eyes. He wished honesty wasn't his policy. 'Yes, I'm a little worried. But thank you for your help. And do you need any help with the medicine? I've always had cats and am very brave about being scratched.'

Her face softened further and she seemed to really see

him. 'Well, aren't you the sweetie. But no, we found the drops in the fridge, and really, we're very fond of that fatty catty Tinsley.' She paused, biting her lip. 'You're worrying me now. You're looking at me like I just gained a cat and lost a dear neighbour.' When he didn't say anything, her face paled. 'Tell her to call me the minute you see her – I'm Amy McCullough.' She pulled her phone from her back pocket and held it up so he could press his against hers to swap the contact. 'The very minute. You know I'll be waiting.'

And I can't just sit and wait, he thought, before thanking his taxi for waiting. He gave his home address and then leaned back against the leather car seat and shut his eyes. I'm going to have to go up there myself. The question is, he thought, was how best to check if Jo and Billie Cathey were safe? Was it time to call the police?

FORTY-TWO

'Thanks for getting out and walking with me,' Nathalie said to Philippe, breathing in the fresh air. 'I forget how nice it is under the trees, and all these constant flights are really screwing with my back.'

'It's good to get out,' agreed Philippe. 'What was the update from Chicago? I gather it's getting a little tense.'

She pointed at the trees. 'There's too many mics here for that kind of chat. Let's get off the path and head over there to that big beech tree.' They walked several metres into the woods, until they were away from the heavy presence of surveillance. Deep in the bowels of the institute, the security room constantly both watched and listened to everything on the island. Nothing happened on Dorcha – whether in the loos, the sauna, even under the swimming pool water – without deep scrutiny. Ted, posing as groundsman and gardener, was really head of security and his team saw it all. Only three places were safe: the boardroom and Nathalie's suite and office. But she also knew the woods had less coverage than the path.

She indicated that Philippe should copy her and face

towards the large tree's trunk. She kept her face turned down, knowing the cameras were up high, and put her fingers to her lips to remind Philippe that the whole conversation should be whispered. Ted and his team were fundamental to the running of Arbor, but much stayed between Nathalie and Philippe.

They shuffled in so close she could smell the damp wood. It had rained overnight, but today had already started with a hot and heavy heat, which would soon become uncomfortable.

'Yes, it is tense, for lots of reasons,' she whispered. 'The interest from private buyers for OmnieX has been so immense, they're going to go to auction for the opportunity to have it.'

'Good news,' he said. 'I'm glad that the results of the individual exposure data hadn't put them off.'

'What do you mean?'

'The findings that the neural plasticity doesn't occur when OmnieX is administered to lone individuals. That a recipient must be in the company of others for homogeneus gregis, and therefore dux, to develop.'

'Why did you think that would matter?' she laughed softly. 'Honestly, Philippe, you're so vain. You think you're the only sociopath in the world – that's very narcissistic of you. Or naïve. Do you honestly think that if the average Joe is content that children mine toxic chemicals for their batteries, and to wear blood diamonds and snort coke produced by violent thugs devasting communities in Brazil, the wealthiest in the world are going to be troubled by a little bystander death, when OmnieX offers them the depth and breadth of power that it does?'

'No need to get pissy, missy,' he grinned. 'I'm glad it's on track. It just makes OmnieX clunky, that's all. People don't like clunk.'

'People like power. Anyway, Jude has sorted it. He's selling the cost of OmnieX in a package with all administration provided. That means that if the group scenario needs to be offered for OmnieX to work, it will be. We've got five case studies where it works in groups and that seems to be enough for the rich and the powerful to be banging on NorGline's door.'

'And are we sticking to our original facilitation plan: get the successful bidders in a room and administer it at the same time? Or should we stick more closely to our current MO and kidnap some randoms and sacrifice them to the greater good?'

'Our greater good,' Nathalie nodded. 'I must admit, as we're getting closer, it makes sense to stick with what we know and don't risk anything not working out in the way we want it to. The figures our potential buyers might be offering are astronomical, Philippe. Simply sensational. And who knows what the eventual price will be when it goes to auction.'

Philippe rubbed his hands together. 'Great news. And you and me, and those on the major investor list from NorGline and Magnus, are still going to get our dose? When the world divides into the true haves and the have nots, I want to make sure I'm have all the way.'

'Yes, Philippe,' she said, smiling, thinking: *not you, Philippe, no. No OmnieX for you, my friend.*

Glad he couldn't read her mind, she changed the subject. 'On other matters, yesterday I agreed with Jude that when Billie flocks just once, we'll complete her.'

'Just once? Does that count if the episode isn't captured by an MRI?'

'It's going to have to. We'll have to include her sleep dux data with Stefana in the reporting, instead.'

'But that's not so sound – it's only passive action.'

'But we've got the data from the others. To be honest, Billie's performance has all started to become a little inconsequential now we've got a list of bidders desperate to get the dose. When we manage the risk of administration, they'll each be able to control everyone around them – maybe more. We're making sure there are no competitors from the same country – that in itself is going to drive the bidding to astronomical heights. The rich and already powerful are at the front of the line for OmnieX – they are keen to pursue more money and more power. And they'll get it. I genuinely think we've seen the last of democracy and wars. We're offering a new world order – for a price. And this new world order will place those who pay in position of Queen Bee. None of this flocking nonsense; it's not some glorious flight motion, but instead, *hive mind*. Hive mind, hive action,' Nathalie lied to Philippe. Instead, she and Jude were now considering something else – something where there was no auction, but the only recipients of OmnieX would be the two of them. But there were pluses and minuses with that plan, and it was still in the mix. What was clear though was Philippe didn't need to know any of that, any more than Celine or the other staff did.

She glanced around again, but could see no mic and no one was near. The good thing about working on the island was the seclusion. Even better was that no one could walk in these woods off the path without being heard. 'To the extent that, if she doesn't flock soon, we can discard her. Jude is right: this project has always had high-risk failure points. The first is securing the deals. All the bidders have signed NDAs. Secondly, the ongoing tension in this project is the research paradox. All the time Billie hasn't been completed but is walking around with the power to take us all down in less than three seconds, means we are vulnerable.'

'Of course,' said Philippe smoothly. 'But, just as with the others, even if she were to choose to flock us, the electric shock is instant. Once that kicks in, she'll be flat on her back and brain dead if that's what we want.'

'Lucky for us, Philippe, that the perils of the job are outstripped by the rewards.'

'Agreed. There are lots of dangerous jobs in the world, but the risk/reward ratio can't be better than this. On that subject, did Jude mention the latest on the stock market?' he whispered.

'Yes. The legal team have been going nuts trying to ensure there are no laws on dux. There aren't. People don't legislate for unforeseen circumstances. But what we do anticipate is that as soon as we announce the development of OmnieX, the world governments that don't have their tyrants already on our bidder's list will try and bring in emergency laws. Three major world governments have already made it very clear that they want to be part of the OmnieX roll-out, so we don't expect traction from everyone. That means all those who've successfully won the auction and have paid their very big bucks to receive it, need to have had the drug before the announcement. We'll announce the development of OmnieX and the NorGline share price will rocket. I suggest you dump your stock immediately. Then, we'll profit twice – both on the share price and the OmnieX sales. Who needs to slave away in the job market once we've had our dose?'

'I'm going to get off this cold rock and buy my own island on the Croatian coast.'

She patted his back. 'I'll come visit you.'

He laughed. 'You won't. I think we'll all want to stay well away from each other in our own kingdoms. Okay, I'm glad my shares are going to do well.' He became serious. 'So, to be completely clear, if she flocks today, then I'll complete her within the hour.'

'Within the minute. Then we'll complete the other four also.'

'All of them?'

'We don't need them lying around being potentially difficult. They can all just go, we were never going to keep them, were we, once we went live to market.' She rubbed her face. 'I'll be relieved. Although we are used to tolerating the research paradox vulnerability, there's just something about Billie I find difficult. It feels like bad fate because she was never supposed to be here. Bloody Celine not wearing her reading glasses, because there was probably someone cute in the room when she was reading the spreadsheet. And I do not enjoy watching Billie become more and more confident. All the time while she's happy, lying by a pool whacked out on the CBD you've been slipping her, then fine. But Billie twitchy makes me twitchy. And I'm all too aware how quickly our lab rats could turn vicious and vengeful.'

'I agree. I did want to lower the CBD in case it was inhibiting her ability to flock, but I daren't.'

'Leave it in place. It's better than the Valium and the

other anti-anxiety meds we trialled previously. As soon as she flocks, Jude wants to set the date for the bidding. The global economic instability is our friend. All the key superpowers – and those with the budgets big enough – are willing to pay to be the key player in the new world order.' She held out her fist for a bump. 'Because it turns out we're the ones who hold the keys.'

Philippe bumped her fist and grinned. 'Is that it, boss?'

'I just wanted to emphasize how quickly I want you to move. We need to pull all the levers now – bring forward the schedule. All the time we are in the development stage, then it's you and me, and the rest of the Arbor team – don't think NorGline will have any links available for scrutiny, if we get suddenly investigated. Arbor will be isolated. Everyone on the board – you, me, Celine, and the others – all burned in any bonfire of vanities.'

She continued: 'Also, thanks to Celine's screw-up, we now have a dead woman in the mix. Someone – like the journalist – might come knocking for her sooner or later, and it would be ideal if we were gone. You to your Croatian island.'

'And you to ... ?'

She laughed and turned away from the tree and headed back to the path. 'I'm not giving you my address either.'

FORTY-THREE

Within four hours of leaving Jo Cathey's house, both Veer and Nick sat on the sofa in Dan's study in Clapham, in his small but perfectly formed terrace house. Dan could tell as they looked around they were impressed: the cleaner had just visited, the dark wood bookshelves gleamed, and even the rubber plant leaves were python-skin glossy. He'd put a pot of Earl Grey in front of Veer and passed Nick a coffee and tried to make small talk as they waited for his school friend Ethan Black to arrive. Veer thanked him and continued to look around with interest. 'Do you live alone?' he asked.

'Just me.'

'No children then? That's a shame,' Veer said, pouring his tea.

'Maybe, but it doesn't feel it. I value being able to go where I want; I like children, but they seem to sponge brain-space, money and freedom from their parents.' *And in the case of Jo Cathey, good sense.* But he didn't say this because, as worried sick as he was about her, there was no point troubling Veer.

Veer chuckled. 'Yes, you are right, they are very absorbent sponges.'

'Tell me about your children?'

Veer's smile touched his eyes, warmth lighting them like lanterns. 'Three – all girls, all chemists, like their mother. We are very excited, my wife and I, because we are soon to become grandparents twice over.' His face grew serious. 'We worry about Prisha's cancer and the timing of it, but we're waiting for this amazing drug to be approved that promises to be a game-changer. We know we need her well with more little sponges on the way.'

They fell silent, each of them in their own thoughts.

Nick eventually said, 'Your school friend's on his way, then? You think he can help us?'

'I think so. I'm glad you both agreed we can talk openly in front of Ethan; I've known him since I was eleven. He doesn't say much, but don't let that put you off. He used to be in the army, and after tours in Iraq and Afghanistan, he now makes serious money doing security stints in the Middle East for wealthy sheiks. He's incredibly capable and he knows what I'm asking, and he's keen for the challenge. He's got another month before he returns to Saudi, and I think he's a little bored. Sounds like him now,' he said, as they heard the doorbell.

At six foot five with arms bigger than Dan's thighs, Ethan filled the door frame and dwarfed Veer as he shook his hand. Thick-necked, but with a quiet reserve of movement, Ethan looked built for trouble but calmly assured. Nick shook his hand and told him that he hoped he was comfortable with 'weird', ''Cause that is what you're gonna hear.'

Ethan quipped back he'd been briefed on the weird, as he accepted a large whisky. 'And that is why I need this.'

Dan started. 'First of all, I want you to know I've been to the police. I couldn't tell them everything without being dismissed as a hoaxer, but I told them enough. I was clear that both Billie and Jo Cathey were missing and passed on the details of their neighbour who would confirm it. I told them that they were potentially locked up in a clinic and gave them Arbor's address. I said when I visited, I received a hostile reception in the presence of a shotgun.'

'Then what?' asked Nick.

'Not much. They filed it and said they'd be in touch with the local police there. I felt,' he said, sighing, 'that I should at least try. What I didn't tell them was what I found on the organization, Arbor – and its parent company.'

'Are you a good researcher, Dan?' asked Veer.

'I know this will surprise you, because I'm such a hip and cool guy' – he cut a wink at Ethan, his old school friend – 'but I actually started in journalism as a forensic accountant on behalf of a broadsheet newspaper. You can chase a lot of information down through the books of organizations. You've just got to know where to look, who to ask – and what and where they try to hide.'

'And what are Arbor trying to hide?'

'Hide, I don't know, but I can give you some facts. You know I already investigated upwards; that Arbor is a subsidiary of NorGline Pharmaceuticals; and in the top five largest pharmaceutical companies in the world, with its head office in Chicago. They developed one of the Covid 19 vaccines and have declared that they are close to developing vaccines against lung and bladder cancer. NorGline, as a company, seems very standard and above board – nothing much to report. They pay their taxes and the history on all their board members – and I've been looking – seems very robust. No scandals; nothing to worry about. The CEO, a Jude Dennison, equally draws a blank – nothing obviously shady.

'Arbor is a subsidiary company, but its arrangements seem less clear. Although the staff on the books are of a very small number, they all have exorbitantly high earnings – earnings vastly inflated above the market rate. But why? What is it that they need to buy from their staff? Another oddity is that they don't seem to have produced anything and have not submitted any intentions for product development, unlike their parent company. The laws obviously vary from country to country, but largely companies must submit declarations of clinical trials – but to date, Arbor have submitted zilch. Each of the sites, high cost, zero output – doesn't that make you wonder why? The company information does much to highlight they pursue the best expertise in the market, but it smells a bit, do you agree?'

'You think Arbor is focused on obtaining this power Billie seems to have?' asked Veer. 'The power to mind-control others?'

Somewhere outside, a moped roared up the road, but none of the four turned their head. They just leaned further in to hear Dan's answer. 'Let's revisit that *exact* point in a sec. Remember, Veer, you said that whatever had happened to Billie – the catalyst, you said – happened on the train station. So last week, I interviewed the man who saved Billie. His name is Will Becker – he was the one who grabbed Billie, saving her from walking off the platform. He was on his commute home when it happened and remembers the whole incident very, very clearly. Interestingly, he told me something I didn't know. He said there was another man there at the time who was instrumental in saving her life, but he'd left before he could be interviewed by the police. Where did he go? And why didn't he hang around?'

'Shock?' offered Veer. 'He'd seen several people die in front of him.'

'Or didn't want to get caught up with police statements?' said Ethan.

'I think there's a darker reason. Let me show you the CCTV.' He encouraged them to sit in front of his computer.

'How did you get this footage?' asked Veer.

'It's not been easy. I wish I could have got it sooner. But let's just say, cash talks.' He opened the file. 'This guy is Will Becker,' he said, pointing at the footage of the busy train station. 'This one over here, in the beanie hat, he's our mystery man that helps Becker save Billie. I want you to watch him. What's interesting is what he does first. Look, here he is positioning himself right in the centre of Billie's group – this guy, to the right of Mystery Man, is Billie's friend, who of course will be sadly dead in less than two minutes after this moment. His name is Gez Fields and he is the first to walk off the platform – Gez actually turns to look at him as Mystery Man arrives on the scene.'

'I'm not surprised,' said Nick. 'He shoves his way into the group. Strange, even aggressive behaviour.'

'Agreed, and Gez obviously feels it because he tries to step away, but Mystery Man just steps into the space created – see? But watch what Mystery Man does next – wait, his hand goes into his rucksack. Billie's friends are in the way, but you can see – *there*. See it? Let me rewind it again. Watch what he takes out of his bag. *There*. Did you catch it?'

'An aerosol can?' asked Ethan.

'Good spot. Does he depress it? There's no way of telling but if he does, he does *not* want to inhale what's in it – because look at how fast he now darts right over there to the edge of the platform – pushes them out of his way – and *then* look what happens to Billie's group. See that stillness that comes over them? How they all become motionless?'

Veer's mouth dropped open and he gave a soft gasp. 'I did not see this bit of the footage before.'

'You've seen it already?'

'When Billie was admitted to the ward. We put in a request and British Rail let me view it. But they just showed them becoming still, then walking off the platform ... not this, not the set-up. I should have been shown *this*.'

'They would've had to know what they were looking for,' said Dan. 'To be fair, one of the first things Billie told me was the truth. She said that her and her friends had been spiked. They were. Watch again.'

They all leaned forward, transfixed.

'*Shit*. So *sudden*, all of them together – it's just so ...' Ethan paused. 'So weird, like you said, Nick. They're just like—'

'Zombies,' said Nick flatly. 'Like Elsie, Marjorie and Raymond.'

Veer placed a hand against his chest. 'Billie also told me that she was spiked, but it didn't seem logical – all together at the same time. We did a routine tox screen, but it showed nothing.'

'But this wasn't a usual substance,' Dan placed a reassuring hand on his arm. 'And what else could you have done?' He pointed back at the screen. 'Watch the old lady there – I think she stops Mystery Man from acting quicker. See how her wheeled shopping trolley turns, and her shopping spills over the platform. Here, where she turns her head, I think she's asking Mystery Man to help pick it up. I think he ignores her, but because she moves into his path blocking him, he does now bend down to pick up the cans. But look at the angle of his head: he's not looking at the shopping as he picks it up, instead he's staring in the direction of Billie's friends. Then, as he hands the shopping back – look – this mother with a pushchair makes him pause as she cuts off his path to the edge of the platform. He's delayed again from getting to Billie, do you see? But Will isn't, so he intervenes and then Mystery Man makes it over and assists Will. From the moment where I first see his aerosol being removed from his rucksack to when Will Becker grabs Billie is forty-six seconds.'

They all blinked, staring at the screen. 'Watch the counter as I speed up now – you can see several people come and assist after the group has jumped and Billie has been saved. Watch: Billie is forced to sit on the platform and the woman with the scarf helps tie her to the post. Mystery Man is still visible – see, he hangs back here. Then from the left, you can see the Transport police walk onto the platform, and then he turns, pulls up his hood and walks off in the opposite direction. He's gone in under four minutes of Billie's attempt on her life.'

'But waits,' Veer said, carefully, 'until he knows she's safe.'

Dan nodded. 'Exactly. And where do they take someone who tries to kill themselves?'

'The nearest psychiatric hospital,' said Veer, shaking his head a little. 'It was easy for them.'

'So who is he?' asked Ethan. 'You got any details on Mystery Man?'

'I've got a still from the video that I've enlarged, which is the best view of his face. I'll open it.' A grainy close-up of a man wearing a beanie hat and sunglasses appeared. 'Veer, do you recognize him?'

Veer leaned in and examined him. 'If I'm meant to ...' He shook his head. 'But I don't, I'm sorry.'

'Let me make it bigger. I'm going to take a punt here, because I *have* met this man. This was the security guy who acted like a rottweiler on Dorcha. Not Philippe Bouchard, who you've spoken to on the phone – who is, by the way, a liar.'

'Bouchard? Please don't tell me he's not medically trained.'

'When I met him on Dorcha he told me he was the director of operations. He told you he was a nurse?'

'Correct. But possible to be both.'

'He's not a director of operations – he's a shareholding company director on the board of Arbor, a professor in biomedical engineering, with a long, interesting career in pharmaceuticals, *and* comes from one of the most wealthy families in Switzerland.'

Veer shook his head in disbelief. 'But why say he's a nurse if he's a medical professor?'

'Not sure. I think to make him seem more benign, give him closer contact with the patients in a non-threatening way, perhaps. But back to *Professor* Bouchard's equally dubious colleague. Now you've only spoken with Bouchard on the phone, but you did meet one colleague of his from Arbor, so is there any chance—'

'Ha! Yes! Mystery Man!' Veer hit the desk. 'I know him, I'm sure it is him. Can you zoom in any more? I didn't recognize him because he was memorable for his striking blue eyes, and there he wears sunglasses. But yes, I can see now ... yes! Mystery Man is definitely the chauffeur that took Billie from Warwick to Arbor,' said Veer, leaning even closer. 'I only met him very briefly because the woman, the nurse, did the handover. He was very unfriendly and only spoke with me because he didn't want to take Jo Cathey in the car to the institute. He asked me to intervene and persuade Jo to stay and let Billie travel alone, but I refused. I thought it was a good idea that she went with her mother.'

'So,' said Dan, 'what's the guy who works for Arbor, carries a shotgun for Arbor, helps save Billie and then turns up at the psych ward to escort Billie to Arbor, doing with an aerosol can, just where and when Billie's friends lose their minds?'

For a moment, no one said anything, but they just looked at each other. Veer spoke first. 'We should have foreseen this. Not only did they find her and want to study her, but they caused it in the first place. They did it to her. They released a neurotoxin to alter Billie's brain and then made sure they retained her. Their guinea pig. I can see from the CCTV they only wanted one – her friends were just collateral damage. They are murderers. Then, once they'd butchered her life and her brain, they simply sent an invite she couldn't refuse timed carefully with a toothy legal letter to the trust. Then, guinea pig secured, they sent the same guy to pick her up and drive her to their lab.' He covered his face. 'And I let them.'

'No, Veer, you—'

'Yes, yes!' He shook Dan's reassuring hand from his arm. 'I could've insisted she remain on Warwick. I shouldn't have listened to the legal department and should have protested to the board.'

'But she had the right to transfer her treatment to a private clinic. The hospital – your bosses – respected that right.'

'Murderers! Those young people. You have to tell the police more or I will never be able to live with myself. Jo and Billie must both be in terrible, *terrible* danger. These people are acting with a reckless ruthlessness and are dangerous.'

'Veer, I told them what I could. I just left out the telepathy idea. They have had the train platform CCTV footage since it happened. And – if it helps – I did say the man on the platform worked for the institute and we believe that group of people were poisoned. But the bodies are gone now, their funerals have passed – the possibility of toxicology analysis is long gone.'

Veer kept his face covered.

'Maybe we need another drink,' Ethan suggested and he and Dan went to make more tea.

When they returned, Veer had composed himself. 'Dan, Nick and I have been talking. Could Billie have been pre-selected? Profiled, even?'

Dan passed Ethan another beer. 'I also thought that. Mystery Man got off the same train as Billie so he could have been following her, waiting for a suitable opportunity to drug her – he works for a pharmaceutical company after all. Then, out comes the aerosol at the right moment, which could be by a bridge, a railway line, a canyon ...'

'You think he's connected – not just to Billie, but he and Arbor are connected to all the videos you showed me?' Veer asked.

'Yes.'

'And we're not going to wait for the police to get her and Jo, are we?' said Veer. 'We must go ourselves.'

'They're murderers,' said Nick. 'We go up there, we don't come back.'

Veer wrung his hands. 'We'd be monsters to just leave them there. I know what it means to face these people – we've seen the level of their ambition.'

'What do you think it's all for, Veer? What is their ambition?' asked Dan. He wanted Veer to change the subject – he planned on returning to Dorcha with Ethan, which was why he was here, but they didn't see Veer as part of that trip.

Veer sighed. 'I've thought about this. Arbor's research relates to the chemical in the aerosol can. This was my fear. It's not a medicine, but weapon development. A biological weapon. I said it before: who needs democracy when the voters will do as you say? Who needs consent when you have the power over everyone? The power available to one person if everyone else loses their free will, is ...'

He stopped, and no one wanted to finish the sentence. 'Endless,' he said in dull tones. 'Endless definitive power.'

Everyone sat in silence, staring at the floor. Eventually, Ethan finished his whisky and then said: 'So this is a superhero origin story? How Billie got her powers?'

They all looked at Ethan, but no one smiled.

FORTY-FOUR

Now *that*, Billie thought, is a beautiful bird. She paused mid-calf stretch to watch a sparrowhawk soar across the blue, cloudless sky. It settled in a tree just on the periphery of the woods and gave its plaintive single-note cry. She kept it in sight as she continued her warm-up. Just as she noticed it, the bird seemed to notice her. It turned its head towards her – no, not it, she. Billie knew the bird with its yellow-orangey eyes was female, because of many hours spent birdwatching with her father as a child. She'd always liked sparrowhawks, probably because her father did. 'What Daddy likes, Billie likes', she remembered her mother saying.

Finished warming up, she bent to retie a loose lace, but the hawk cried again as if to recall Billie to attention. It's watching me, she thought, noticing that even as it resettled itself on the branch with its mighty legs, it turned itself, great striped chest, to face her.

Billie put her AirPods in – now hers for so long, if she'd been given back her old ones, no doubt packaged up from uni and returned to her mother, they would feel unfamiliar.

But there were things she owned that she wanted back – her favourite earrings, her dad's watch, her old teddy – things that Arbor couldn't replace with a bottomless bank account.

She found her jogging playlist on her watch and turned the music up loud, hawk forgotten. As much as she appreciated the sighting, she wanted to get going: she had chosen to jog on her own as she had things she wanted to think about. Stan. America. But most of all, the voice she heard. The plaintive *help*, that she knew she heard in that moment of silence in the pool. It continued to play on her mind. It was so clear, she wanted to – away from the surveillance of Arbor – reflect and perhaps, even try and reconnect.

A woman, she knew that.

She started running but as soon as she did, she stopped abruptly. Two pigeons flew close to her – right across her path, so close their wing feathers almost brushed her face – then alighted in the tree, the branch below the sparrowhawk. It couldn't be possible. Pigeons would never sit below and so near a raptor.

Stranger still, all three birds faced Billie. They are all looking at me, she thought.

She remembered as a teenager sitting at the breakfast table and seeing a sparrowhawk drop onto a pigeon on their lawn. Distressed, she grabbed a broom and ran outside to square up to the huge bird. It stood on the struggling pigeon, grey wings pathetically half-beating against the ground. That hawk had stared Billie down, even stopping her mid-stride as she ran circling the broom over her head and shouting at it loudly to leave the pigeon alone. Bold and brave, it fronted Billie out until she was only metres from her – it wanted its earned meal.

Why would the hawk sit amongst two pigeons and miss the opportunity of an easy kill and instead be more interested in her?

Curious enough to change the direction of her run, thinking of the birds she'd found dead, Billie decided to get a little closer. Sure, they'd move away if she got too close, but perhaps she'd save one of the pigeons from its own stupidity.

She crossed the lawn directly, heading towards the periphery of the woods. Glancing down to change a track, when she looked up, she half expected to find the birds had moved, but saw that not only were they still there, but had been joined by several crows, with yet more crows circling and landing in the trees.

She almost stopped. She felt the brush of raised goosebumps on her arms, despite the heat, because she could now see some small sparrows sitting noiselessly next to the hawk. It would take less than a second for the larger bird to drop onto the tiny birds, but still they sat, apparently unperturbed. Because they were all looking at her.

She blinked. And –

– *Alive.*

All windows were open and she saw everything – herself, standing on the lawn, from many different angles. She saw the top of her head from above. She saw Arbor as if looking from a plane – but nearer. She saw the birds sitting on the tree in front of her. She saw it all. She understood it all. She was the birds now.

Then she heard the voice again. Quiet, but clear:

Help me.

THE INSTITUTE

Then the birds all took off as if in response to a gunshot.

The windows in her brain shut down at once – all that was left was her looking at the hawk, now with a pigeon gripped in its mouth and claw, fixing its yellowy-orange eye on Billie for a long time, before finally taking flight with the pigeon and leaving her alone on the lawn.

FORTY-FIVE

'Do you still think it was right to leave Veer and Nick behind, and keep the rescue to just you and me, bud?' Dan asked Ethan. He sat next to his friend in Ethan's beloved VW Transporter; the idea of a mission with him, who was the most capable man he knew, felt just the right mix of anticipation, adventure and fear.

Ethan checked his mirrors, indicated right and carefully checking again, steered his van onto the motorway. He glanced in his rear-view before answering. 'The short answer is I've packed bullet-proof jackets and I'm not strapping Veer into one of those.'

'Really? Is that true?'

'They've already waved a gun around. These people are not playing.'

Dan was silent for a few minutes. 'I'm glad I know you, Ethan.'

Ethan laughed. 'It's not standard workwear for most people, I get it. And yes, it's great they offered to come along too, but Veer has his sick wife and too many years on him for this. Nick's great, but I noticed his hand has a tremor – and the way Veer watches it makes me think it's new. This trip could send him over the edge.'

For a few miles, they just stared at the road ahead. Ethan took a swig of his travel coffee without taking his eyes off the road; a light drizzle started against the windscreen, triggering the wipers. 'You sure you don't want to swap this madness for a fishing trip at Loch Lomond? I think we're in for a tough time if we go poking into Magnus Inc slash NorGline's business. We could just leave it to the police, particularly as I think there's a good chance Jo is already dead.'

'You really think that?'

'She's missing, so it's definitely a possibility.'

Dan watched the road, thinking. Finally, he said: 'If the police were even a little bit interested,' he made a small gap between his thumb and finger, 'even a *little*, I'd say let's go fishing. But they weren't. They were pretty much yawning when I spoke to them. Jo's neighbour still hasn't heard from her; that barely raised more than "we'll look into it". I worry too, with Magnus slash NorGline money, it would be very easy to make some under-the-table payments and then everyone's looking the wrong way. If that's true, we need to look the right way. Plus, it's not like we're going to bust in, just take a quick look around and see if we can get some good photos, possible evidence of the Catheys' difficulties – or freedoms.'

'Risky though. If it wasn't you, I'd turn this down.'

'If it wasn't you, I wouldn't go. Truth is, if it were a case of both being dead, then we could theoretically wait for the police to figure it out. But I'm scared for Billie – scared what a clinic like that could do to someone with a brain like hers.'

'I think with a brain like hers, perhaps the clinic should be scared of her.'

'I hope you're right.'

'Do you fancy this girl?'

Dan kept his eyes shut. 'Don't be ridiculous.'

Ethan laughed and hit the steering wheel with his palm. 'Yes, you do! That's why we're driving halfway up the country to see her!'

Dan pressed his fingers against his forehead. 'No, you've misunderstood me. I feel too responsible for letting Jo go alone. I told her not to – but, I don't know, I should have done something to stop her.'

'You told me you couldn't go by her timescales because you had to catch a plane for work.'

'Correct.'

'You know, Dan, maybe it's time to let go of your saviour complex before it gets you killed. Jo Cathey is a grown woman making decisions about where and when she wants to see her adult daughter. Billie chose to leave an NHS ward, deciding it was better to be locked up on a private ward instead – and can you blame her? I'm not sure at what point you take on responsibility for those decisions without making yourself a massive chauvinist A-hole.'

Dan pressed his lips together and kept his eyes on the motorway. Ethan was always the provocateur. At school, he'd been the smartest in a class rich in talent and liked nothing more than poking someone in the tender spot and watching them catch the fire.

'Easy, tiger,' Ethan said, 'sorry if I've pissed you off there. I'm just letting you off your own metaphorical hook, so you don't feel to blame when you're not. I'm trying to be a good mate – that's all.'

But time and the army must have rounded him off because the old Ethan would've never apologized, thought Dan. 'I'm just worried about them. Too much of my working life is about seeing the little guy pitched against the big guy, and time and time again, it never ends well for the little guy. And my research makes me think that we've underestimated the big guy. You might want to go home when I tell you.'

'Oh, yeah? You think this soldier isn't up to the fight?'

They all fell silent again.

'So, even though Arbor is bigger than just a building on Dorcha, even though it has the might of NorGline, which has the might of Magnus Inc., behind it, you're still okay to proceed? Shotgun-wielding bad man included.'

'I wouldn't be ex-British Army, mate, if I couldn't face a gun. Besides, I was brought up to believe in David and Goliath.' He slapped his friend on the thigh. 'Let's stick to our plan then. We have on our side that they won't be expecting us. And after our recce, we'll go back and make ourselves a nuisance with the police if we need to.'

Dan glanced over his shoulder into the back of the van. Two kayaks sat on racks ready to drift across the Firth at night. It was a good plan – get in, try and get some information about Arbor or Jo and Billie's welfare, before getting out again. But what would they find? Billie still lying on a sunbed? Jo sitting with her enjoying afternoon tea, being entertained as a treasured guest? Would they consider him just an irritant coming to ruin their peace? 'Ethan, I was thinking about what Veer said – about what you said too.'

'Which bit?'

'What he said just before he left. About how if Billie has this power that he thinks she has, then they can't hold her against her will – no prison could hold someone who could just get the guards to unlock the cell. That the person with the greatest power on the earth doesn't need rescuing.'

'That might be true.'

'In which case, we're wasting our time.'

'Only if she's content where she is,' said Ethan. 'Perhaps Billie chooses to stay, because firstly she doesn't know what power she has, or secondly, she doesn't understand she's sleeping in a nest of vipers. Or thirdly, perhaps the patients mirroring Billie was just a sort of pointless nothing – a weird thing but not a powerful thing. But she will comprehend the situation, and if it is a powerful thing, then she'll try to leave. They're not going to let her just take over their minds so they can throw open the front door and let their carefully created asset go home with Mummy. She's worth a lot of money.'

'But how would they do that? How would they protect themselves from her abilities?'

'How am I supposed to know? I've only just found out about this. But they've had months, maybe years, to prepare. If they're as big an operation as you think they are, they've got a system that works. They'll know what they're doing. I know enough about army ops to know that forewarned is *always* forearmed.'

FORTY-SIX

It was nearly the end of August now, Billie thought, noticing the brown and copper amongst the trees. She carried her towel out to her favourite sun lounger and peeled off her dressing gown. She'd eaten light at breakfast, as they had a free day, and Billie was looking forward to beating her swimming Personal Best. She'd started to rely on physical exercise more and more. She'd always enjoyed swimming and running, but here at the institute, with such great facilities and too much time on her hands, she now spent much of her abundant spare time exercising. It was working too: she was getting stronger. Se flexed her forearm and patted her bicep. *Powerful*, she thought and smiled, amused that for the first time in her life, she did feel strong.

It was sunny today and already warm. There's nowhere lovelier than Scotland in summer, she thought for the millionth time. But as she slipped off her sliders, she shivered at the contact of bare feet against cool porcelain tiles, and with it, thought again that when it got colder, she would leave the institute. Maybe she would follow Stan to California for a long winter holiday, maybe she'd return to her mum's, perhaps she'd do something else entirely; but she wouldn't stay here. There was no real need to now she had nothing to fear – she would never be Tama.

She had the confidence now – dux gregis might even help her, but now she'd learned to control it, it could never hurt her. The birds episode had been upsetting, strange, and the voice asking for help continued to play on her mind. Unsure of what it meant, but not willing to discuss it with anyone, Billie had decided there was nothing she could actively do. Perhaps she did just need to practise the dux more. Stan was keen and she promised to try again with him as soon as they were alone. Perhaps, the best thing for her to do, was to accept this was part of her life now. Celine was right – it'd happened and this was just who she was now. Acceptance was easier than fighting the reality.

With powerful legs, she stood by the side of the pool, arms raised in the dive pose. Then launched. Mid-air the voice cut through her – help me – and as she slid into the water, she heard – save me –

Frightened, Billie flailed underwater. Huge bubbles of oxygen rose and for a moment the surprise meant that she couldn't orientate herself. Then she saw the surface and emerged in a rush of bubbles and noise. The voice again – after the pool therapy session, then yesterday jogging and now *this*. It was becoming more frequent. And clearer too, with more panic, more anguish than before. Who was she? Billie pressed her hand to her mouth, frightened herself now. This was something real, something important, and it was *not* going away.

With watchful eyes, she glanced about, wondering if it was obvious what had happened. She knew there were cameras around Arbor, had seen them on day one in the bushes, but she didn't want anyone to know about this. Yesterday, she'd jogged immediately back to her room, but it was so early, she didn't think anyone would have caught her reaction to whatever it was. She didn't think she could explain it – didn't want to explain it.

Deciding to swim to conceal her fear, Billie started a faltering breaststroke. Her heart was no longer in swimming, but if she got out now, it might raise suspicion. Thoughts like bullets in her mind, she just needed time. Who was she? What was she? A ghost? A real person? Was this a trick created to provoke a response? On the return lap, she saw someone through her blurry goggles. They were standing on the edge of the pool, hands on hips. Feeling resentful at being disturbed, she stopped, pushed them up. It was Maddy. Billie sighed inwardly – she could see storm clouds in her friend's eyes, and her hands were now balled into fists. She needed time on her own, but clearly Maddy wasn't going to allow that. 'You okay, Mads?'

'Sorry to interrupt.' Maddy's foot tapped, agitated; mouth drawn tight. 'I wanted your opinion on something when you had a minute.'

Billie stayed in the pool, reluctant to engage with her more than necessary – she needed to think about the voice she'd heard. 'Catch up after my swim? I've just started and wanted to do fifty lengths.'

Maddy had skipped breakfast, which was unusual enough, but now she was here, foot twitching, eyes wild, and seemed too full of agitation to take a suggestion. 'I just need you, Billie. I'm losing my mind.'

You and me both. Perhaps she was hearing voices too.

Either way, Maddy had been very supportive over her wanting to call her mother, so she heaved herself out, wrapped herself in a towel and asked Maddy if she was okay.

Maddy pressed her hands against her face and sat down on the edge of a lounger. Billie worked out that this was going to take a while. 'It's Ash.'

Billie sighed. In that moment, she understood she didn't want to be the only person hearing voices – she really wanted Maddy to say that she'd heard the frightened woman. 'Ash? Is he okay?' Billie pulled the towel tighter against her.

'We had a thing. I thought it was more than a thing,' Maddy looked out from behind her hands, tears in her eyes, 'but now I see it wasn't much at all to him. I feel so angry,' she continued, jaw tight, the muscles in her face tight, even her hands were still clenched into tight claws. 'I thought it was going to go somewhere, that it could be more than just a passing fling.'

Billie, stunned, didn't know what to say. 'Are you sure that he's not keen? You're a lovely person – I bet it's just a misunderstanding.'

Maddy's eyes showed all the white. 'He's said it's not going to happen again!' She made an animalistic growl through bared teeth. 'I just cannot believe it!' Her eyes then narrowed to slits and she glanced around as if looking for someone. 'It's because of that fucking nurse, Lia, I'm convinced of it. He's got a thing going with her now and he's dropped me.'

'Whoa! I don't think you need to worry about that. I always thought Lia' – *Callie*, she thought, still convinced – 'was seeing Ted?'

Maddy looked at her then – really looked at her as if she

was seeing her for the first time. She didn't say anything for a moment, but became still, the agitation muted, her gaze analytical. Then the moment was gone, and she shook her head, hair falling forward, and she was hidden again. 'No. You're wrong. It *is* Lia. I can see the way Ash looks at her.' She started tapping her foot. 'She was flirting with him only this week with the fitting of the MRI cap, and then later when we were getting ready for that rebirthing pool session, she practically licked his biceps while we were waiting to get in the water.' She punched her hand as she added: '*It was disgusting and embarrassing!*'

Billie held up her own hands, which she noticed were going white. She suffered with Raynaud's syndrome, and she would soon have no feeling in her fingertips. She either needed to get back in the pool and swim, or get dressed. What she really wanted to do was lie in a hot bath and *think* about the voice she'd heard and what it meant.

Maddy mumbled a response and stood up, pacing around. 'It's just so overwhelming. What can I say to her when she's staff?' Then she muttered: 'She's such a dirty slut though. Somone should tell her. I might, I just might.'

Billie realized this was more than just a chat. She looked around for help. 'Come and sit back down. I'm sure we can talk this through.' She held her hand out to her. 'Please – I agree there's something about Lia that's like she's been drinking sour milk, but whenever I think of something like that, it's important to balance the thought, like, Lia must be caring because she became a nurse.'

'Well, that's fucking naïve,' Maddy answered with a look that suggested she now wanted to kill Billie, but she did sit back opposite her friend.

She took Maddy's hands and met her gaze. 'I'm going to say I believe you, because there's nothing worse than not being believed, I know that. And maybe Lia is the problem, but I don't care about her, and I do care about *you*. You know that I was hospitalized as a teenager after the stress of my dad's death and how I was left paranoid. No, don't pull away, I've told you I have no reason to doubt you. I won't bore you again with it, but what I am saying is: *I know*. I bet you're not sleeping?'

Maddy dragged her sad gaze back to meet Billie's and shook her head. Billie could see the shadows like smudged charcoal under her eyes and cheekbones. 'I slept late because I swear I was still awake at four.'

'Being tired will make you feel worse. Are you eating okay?'

Again, another shake of the head. 'I just feel sick.'

'And that's the anxiety but you've got to try. Philippe will want to help; he'll fix you things like bagels which are easy to eat.'

Maddy pulled away, looking pained. 'I just can't face anything.'

'You need to try.' Her voice was clear; an imperative. 'You also need to counter the negative thoughts. They will drag you down. You need to talk this through with someone who can help give you balance. What about Celine and Ash together? That way, if you're not understanding something, or he's not listening, Celine can help. You'll have the support and you won't be on your own with it. That's the most important thing – when I got ill, it happened because I stopped talking to people. My dad was the person who I did talk to, so when he died, I had nowhere to go with my thoughts.'

Maddy got up, taking the warmth of her hands. She kept shaking her head, hair falling over her face. 'You're right, but I just can't talk to Celine anymore. I've been here too long, I know it. It's just ... *two years* ...' She trailed off.

'It gets too much?'

She pressed her small hands against her face again. 'Tama, Tama,' she said, shaking her head once more. 'I think of him and I know I just can't die.' She shut her eyes. 'Better trapped in here than out there dead.' Then she abruptly got up. 'I'm going to go now. But thank you for listening to me. You're a good person and I'm glad I got the chance to know you.'

Billie watched her go and gave up on her swim. Perhaps if Maddy had stayed, she would have tried to help her with flocking so she could leave too, but there was something so combustible about her, Billie wasn't sure the trust was there. With the voice in her head, she rearranged her towel, cold now. She stared at the sky; the bleak grey cloud crossed the sun.

Feet soft against the patio, Billie went to get a quick shower to warm up, before going to find Celine or Philippe.

FORTY-SEVEN

Outside her room, Billie found Stan leaning against her door. 'Billie! Good! I wondered if I could have a word?'

She shivered. She was dripping too onto the sisal runner. 'Weren't you going out on the speedboat this morning?'

'I changed my mind. I told Ted I had a headache. I really need to talk to you.'

'You decided not to go out on the speedboat? Wow, are you okay, Stan?'

He shook his head, impatient. 'I'm fine, I just decided that it was more important for me to speak to you. There's something on my mind and it's important.'

'About Maddy?'

Stan frowned and shook his head. 'Maddy? No. *No.* Well, sort of – it's difficult to ... and not here ...'

The air con was always fresh in the corridor and, standing wet in her swimsuit with only her dressing gown on top, her teeth started to chatter, but was it possible that he'd heard Frightened Woman, too? 'It's not because you've heard anything ... odd, is it?'

He blinked, puzzled. 'No, it's not that.'

Disappointed, she gave a sad smile. 'Sorry, Stan, I've got to get on then. Maddy's struggling ... she needs some help and I've got to find Celine or Philippe. Have you seen them?'

He frowned again. 'Sorry, no. But I've got to talk to you and it can't really wait. It's important,' he repeated.

'We will talk, it's just I'm freezing cold, and I've got to quickly change because I need to get help for Maddy. I think I've got to do that before anything else.' She touched his arm. 'Sorry. She's been a good friend to me, I feel I owe it to her to help if she needs it.'

Stan sighed. 'Okay, bad moment. I'll go and see if I can find them while you get changed. Then, meet you by the trees?' He glanced around, agitated. 'I really need to ...' He mouthed the next phrase: *talk to you about something. But not here.*

She paused briefly, staring at Stan taking the stairs two at a time, before letting herself into her room. He seemed agitated – plus Maddy. Plus her.

She had a bad feeling about today.

FORTY-EIGHT

Billie jumped into the shower and was out within five minutes. She dressed quickly for warmth and just as she reached the door, heard an abrupt knock. No one knocked on each other's doors in Arbor; privacy was respected, and it was assumed if you were in your room, you wished to be undisturbed. She opened it and found Philippe standing there, looking annoyed. 'Billie, we were expecting you.'

'Expecting me where?'

'You're due in a group exercise in the observation lab on minus two.'

'Today is a free day – nothing scheduled.'

'Why does everyone think that?' He rolled his eyes in unbridled frustration.

Billie tapped her watch to find her schedule. 'Because nothing's listed – oh. It is. That's odd. Sorry, it was blank this morning – definitely – the rest of us discussed it at breakfast.'

'Well, this is what happens when I take just a few hours off for myself. The daily listing is wrong; I hear at breakfast the cinnamon rolls were doughy and now I've had to go rounding everyone up.' He seemed to see her for the first time. 'Your hair is wet.'

'I was swimming. Look, I was about to come and find you. I'm worried about Maddy. She seems cross and, well, a little too anxious.'

'I've found her and she's up at the lab waiting to start. She's stressed, she's told me. I'll have a proper talk to her after the group analysis. She can get like this, I know. Look, why don't you dry your hair or you'll get cold. If you give it a quick blast, I'll wait outside so I can take you down in the lift. Okay?'

Billie agreed, glad Maddy was under supervision. Within ten minutes they were in the now-familiar large lab. Staff were fitting Ash, Jenna and Stan into caps, which they were already complaining about.

'Where's Maddy now?' asked Philippe with obvious frustration. One of the nurses told him that she had left to go to the library. 'The library!' he said, throwing his arms up. 'This is ridiculous. Like herding cats!' He turned to everyone else. 'No one else leaves this room. This exercise takes thirty minutes tops. If you need a wee or a drink, well, hold it, I just do not care,' he said, slamming out of the lab.

As soon as he left, Stan gave a small miaow.

Billie caught one of doctors tipping a small wink at Stan in reply and a few others didn't hide their chuckles. Too worried about Maddy now to be amused, she looked to Ash. 'Did she seem okay to you?'

He shrugged. 'I didn't see her; I've just got here. There was no listing for this; I was on a run.'

'Stan, did you see her?'

'I went up to the woods, remember?' said Stan. 'But

got called straight back for this waste of time,' he said, humour gone.

'Oh, okay . . .' She saw the flush to his cheeks, but couldn't read his eyes behind his long fringe, longer now as it had been pushed down by the cap. Had she agreed to meet him there? 'Sorry,' she said, meaning it, but distracted by concern for Maddy.

They sat, quietly chatting, tension in the air. A nurse fitted Billie's cap, a different one to the usual, as it had a strap that came under the chin, and covered most of her head. 'It's a bit tight,' she said, not liking to complain, but it hurt across the back of the neck and pinched under the chin.

'Told you,' the others said to the nurses, but the nurses assured them it was for better connectivity. Afterwards, they stood around checking their watches. Billie was glad Lia was nowhere to be seen.

'Guys,' said a doctor, 'we're just going to see what's going on here – maybe they're next door in the study lab. Sorry to keep you sitting around in the caps. Is everyone comfortable if we just duck out and see if we can locate the others? They seem to be taking a while and we've messaged both without answer.'

Ash, always reasonable, nodded. 'Sure, whatever it takes.'

Alone, they sat waiting. Just as Billie started to deliberate taking off her cap and going to find her, Maddy suddenly slammed into the lab.

'You're here!' Maddy shouted, pointing an accusatory finger at Ash. Jaw squared, curly hair a Medusa's mass, fists balled, she stood strong, a wronged warrior queen. 'I've been looking for *you*,' she said, voice low, eyes narrowed, and took a step towards him. '*You've* not been the nice guy *you* make yourself out to be, *have* you, Ashley?'

Ash sighed deeply and stood up, not even faintly ridiculous in the cap, so used were they all to wearing them. 'Maddy, you've got it all wrong and for the good of everyone, you really need to start listening to the—'

'Facts? Would they be your facts, or her facts? Because my facts are that you told me that you and me were the real deal, and then I've seen you and her up against a tree out in the woods—'

'Maddy,' Jenna intervened, standing up, her movements also inhibited by the wires of her cap, but she was closest to Ash. 'This can't be a good—'

'Fuck you too, Jenna, for taking his side.' Maddy started to throw spears of accusations at him, in fast succession: that he was ignoring her, dodging contact with her and 'playing' her 'for a fool'.

Ash held up his palms. 'Calm *down*, Maddy,' he said to the salvo of words. 'We can talk about it.'

Maddy, red-faced, jaw defiant: 'I will not calm down. You can shut the fuck up if you think you can tell me what to do!'

Billie could see that her face had changed from red to white. It was a sign, she had read somewhere, that someone was about to attack. Wanting to be free to go over, Billie started to pull at the buckle under her chin. Jenna, also thinking the same and being nearer, stood up between Maddy and Ash. From behind Jenna, he continued to plead with her to calm down.

'Maddy, don't you think that we could just all talk about this?' Billie asked, becoming frustrated with the impossibility of the clasp (how *was* this thing buckled?). 'Just give me a minute to get this thing off and then we can go for a walk and talk it through.'

She ignored her and instead pushed Jenna, hard. 'Don't you defend him!' she shouted at her.

'Hey!' said Stan, also getting up to intervene. 'You need to chill the fuck out, *now*.'

'He's been banging that bitch, Lia,' she said without looking anywhere but at Ash. 'And I'm just supposed to look the other way? I won't be anyone's doormat, but definitely not his!' She went to push him, and then land a punch, but Jenna blocked her blows, echoing Stan's words to chill out.

Billie, giving up on the buckle, tried pulling at the rubbery strap – it gave half an inch, but not enough to pull over her chin. Instead, flapping her hands, she tried to see where she could unhook the wires. The nurses always did this; she never touched the machinery. 'Maddy! Don't do anything you'll regret!'

Maddy swung another punch, this one connecting with Jenna's jaw. Jenna mumbled an expletive as her head snapped back. Then she pushed Maddy hard in return. Jenna, much taller than Maddy, flung her easily to the floor. 'Just back off! I don't care about your beef with Ash, but don't you *dare* punch me.'

Maddy adjusted her balance and ran at Jenna, arm lifted before she connected another punch, harder this time against Jenna's chin, forcefully snapping her head back.

Ash stood between them, telling Maddy that she got it wrong. Stan swore at his cap, and then pulled a penknife from his pocket and, undoing the scissors, cut the strap from under his chin. Then, simultaneously yelling at Maddy, he tried to grab her shoulder, but she ducked swiftly, knocking away his penknife.

She grabbed it first and pulled out the largest of the knives from the pen knife holder.

'Hey,' shouted Stan, making a grab for it. 'That belongs to Ted. It belongs on the boat. And he will literally kill you for taking it. Give it back, I'm supposed to return it today.'

Furious, screaming, Maddy kicked Stan in the balls, and silent, he folded like a penknife himself.

Billie screamed, understanding now that Maddy was completely mad and dangerous. She found where the wires jacked into the machine and tugged on them, but they didn't pull free. Crying with frustration, she tried to unscrew one, half watching as she fumbled at it and half watching Maddy.

Then Jenna made a lunge for the knife. Maddy took a neat side-step out of the way, before almost pirouetting completely out of reach. She then lunged back towards Jenna, knife low and tight. Her movement was quick, full of anger and intent. The blade pushed forward into Jenna's stomach. Billie saw Maddy's eyes widen and then, as if in answer, when the knife slid in (so quick! so quick!) Jenna's seemed to answer by widening too – at the pain and the shock of the stab.

Jenna's hands floundered like trapped birds' wings – then found the knife wound, but never took her eyes from Maddy's own. The blood began to spill, oozing from between her fingers, dripping from her wrists – and then when she removed her hands to look at them, in bewilderment first at Maddy and then at her blood-soaked palms, the blood poured, and she dropped.

After she hit the floor, there was not a sound. No one

moved. Even Maddy, still holding her blood-stained knife, breathing heavily, froze. Everyone stared, braced for more violence. She looked at each of them. Finally, after a long moment, she said: 'You shouldn't fuck with me.'

Maddy stared at the knife as if it were a confusing friend that had betrayed her and then with a disdainful shake of her head, she threw it from her where it hit the far wall before clattering to the floor. She too then also sank slowly to the floor and sat cross-legged, staring at Jenna.

Ash dropped to his knees, straining to reach Jenna because he too was still attached to a machine, covered the bleeding wound, and shouted for help.

Stan started to swear loudly, floundered, still holding his crotch and stumbled to a stand, repeating Ash's requests for help. When no one arrived, he went over to the observation glass and started to bang it. 'Where have they gone?' he yelled. 'Help us! Help us!'

Ash unzipped his hoodie and held it against Jenna's wound. 'Where's Philippe? Is he in the study lab? If we don't get help soon, Jenna's going to bleed out.'

Stan didn't answer but ran to try the door, swiping his watch against the panel. 'We're still locked in! They don't understand!' He started banging on the observation glass again, shouting for help.

Her friends – her friends were dying again.

She had a brief memory, her cherished last memory of Ella popping a chip into her mouth as she plaited her hair on the train. With it came the memory of the old pain at the base of her head, where the man on the platform had grabbed her plait and saved her life.

She thought of a memory of her father telling her to see

the rot and that it was dangerous. *Blood*. She knew then she had been dreaming of it. Cold and dark, she saw her memory as it rose around her.

And then Billie felt it. Like testing the edge of a bubble and it yielding; like a tugging deep inside her – running up her spine to her brain, a feeling of nausea rising on the return wave. Then it was like light on water. Bright, clear: she was Stan. She was Maddy. She was Jenna. She was Ash, and she made it all stop.

Just stop.

And they all stopped.

And ...

Nobody moved.

And she had them ...

And it was easy, so easy to hold them.

Maddy used the knife to cut her own cap strap, then Ash and Jenna's, then Billie's straps and then the five of them, released, walked to the observation window and in one smooth movement of choreography that would have looked planned but was not, they all lifted their right legs and kicked at it together, raising a crack from the impact. They steadied and then lifting their legs again (even bleeding Jenna, *sit down, Jenna, you are bleeding*, and she sat down) and –

And within them, she could see something: something amongst her friends. But then – relief – they were safe because Philippe and five blue-uniformed nurses rushed in to help them, swarming around Jenna.

– Wilhelmina, it's just an image – not real, do you hear me? Not real –

And the memory was warm breath on cold glass, steam … and then gone.

And feeling they were now safe, she let them go.

Billie would have doubted what had just happened was true but when the moment passed, every person in the room became one of two groups, those flocked – Stan, Ash, Jenna and Maddy, who blinked, released, as they refocused unknowing and a little bemused, unsure of what had just happened – and those who'd witnessed the flock, the medical staff who'd seen it all, who as if in a flock themselves, turned owl-like to look at her.

FORTY-NINE

'Please, someone – Philippe, Richard, anyone,' said Billie, 'help Jenna. Help her! She's been stabbed.' Billie pointed at Jenna slumped on the floor, Ash holding his hoodie to her stomach, to stop the oozing blood.

Philippe didn't move towards Jenna, but instead touched his watch. 'Safe word?' he muttered.

Stan, Ash, Maddy and even Jenna all looked up. 'Acorn,' they all answered.

'Acorn?' Billie offered after, unsure. Everyone looked at her as if waiting for her to say something else.

Philippe looked at her. And for a moment she saw – *truly saw* – him. His eyes, empty of emotion yet scrutinizing, looked at her with a scalpel's cruelty: cold, cutting steel. She remembered Jenna, the first time she met her, suggesting they were guinea pigs, and thought: Philippe seems like how research scientists must look at a lab animal before they splice and cut and inject.

Can you smell the rot, Wilhelmina? I'm worried you're blinded by the—

But the thought went unfinished, because he pressed a

button on his watch and everywhere within her an electric fire sang in reply. Electric shock blazed: heat and fire and pain. Abrupt white inferno everywhere – *everywhere*. Every nerve frozen with heat. *White. White. Whi—*

Then nothing.

Billie fell to the floor.

For a moment there was silence, then both Maddy and Jenna got up, looked at each other with a grin and shook hands.

Ash threw down the bloody hoodie he'd been holding, wiped his hands on his trousers once, looked at the mess and yelled: 'Can someone get me a cloth or something? This fake blood stuff is gross.'

Only Stan went to Billie lying on the floor. 'Is she okay?'

'She'll be fine,' answered Philippe, getting to his knees and producing a stethoscope to listen to Billie's heart.

'It wasn't too much voltage?'

'Stan,' he said with exaggerated patience, 'Billie's watch is a sophisticated piece of kit. It automatically adjusts the voltage according to if she's in water, or even if she has dry or sweaty skin. Ambient humidity and temperature, her temperature, everything, all adjusts the level of shock she is given. She's out, but she'll be round in a few minutes, which is why we need to move fast. So, move back, you are,' he said, turning impatiently to beckon over the nurse pushing a medical trolley towards him, 'in our way.'

The nurse handed Philippe a cuff and portable machine, and Stan, waved out of the way a second time, shuffled back as Philippe wordlessly took Billie's blood pressure. 'Okay,' he said to the nurse, 'you're free to fit the cannula. And be quick – I don't want to have to shock her again. I'd rather her be alive than dead at this point.'

The nurse swabbed the area and then removed the cannula from its packaging, before sliding the needle into the back of Billie's hand and taping it in place. She then produced a bag and passed it to Philippe to check. 'Propofol. Good,' he said, 'that'll keep her out for a hundred years.' He passed it back and the nurse hung the bag up and attached the other end to the cannula.

He checked it and then added: 'Let's get an airway in now.'

She passed him a packet which he opened and removed the plastic supraglottic device. He lifted Billie's chin and carefully inserted it through her mouth. 'Are we getting a trolley in here any time—? Oh, you're here, great. Let's move her out of here and into the study lab next door and get her on oxygen,' he said as two staff pushed in a trolley. 'Stan, *will* you now get out of the *way*!' snapped Philippe as the trolley was paused mid-push because he was still sitting near Billie.

Philippe stood back, and everyone watched as Billie was lifted, laid flat, and then pushed out of the lab.

'Job done,' breathed Philippe. 'Job *done.*'

FIFTY

Dan and Ethan had pulled up at a secluded spot just outside of Portencross. It was dusk and they both stood on the bluff, hats on, hoods up, wind behind them. They were lucky: it was dry and the winds were offshore. Dan breathed deeply: it smelt of salt and ozone and freedom.

They wouldn't waste any time once the sun had dropped below the horizon. Waiting for the light to fade brought not just excitement but uncoiled a sense of entrapment that had been sleeping in Dan. Perhaps he was in need of change in his life, he decided; perhaps it was time to do something that was different, or be different, or go and live somewhere different. He wasn't sure, but it was something to think about, winds of change and all that.

They could see Dorcha, a low whale hump rising out of the waters in the distance. 'There's more than one Arbor site,' said Dan into the wind.

'How many?' said Ethan.

'Not sure. But I have found an Arbor in the same countries where there've been reports of the group incidents caught on camera. NorGline have a head office in Chicago, but they also have an Arbor Institute a few miles out in Illinois. Easy enough, if you've got a private plane, to poison someone in the Grand Canyon and fly them out to Illinois. No passport needed, just an internal flight.'

'You're thinking of the Grand Canyon videos. Interesting. Where else are they?'

'There's an Arbor Institute tucked in the countryside just outside of Hyderabad, India.'

'Why on earth would they tuck an Arbor out there?'

'India's become a huge site for pharmaceutical companies. Hyderabad's economy is heavily underpinned by pharmaceuticals and now the nineteen-thousand-acre Pharma City is there. It's essentially an industrial park for different pharma companies, attracting nearly ten billion dollars' worth of investment. So, doesn't that seem the perfect place for NorGline to have a discreet pharma base?'

Ethan gave a low whistle.

'They have another in Switzerland.'

'Why Switzerland?'

'There are over a thousand industry operators in Switzerland, including two of the big boys. NorGline comes in only as fifth, but interestingly, something's going on, because their share price is increasing at a steady rate, which suggests that people are getting wind of something. Pharmaceuticals and the chemicals industry is Switzerland's leading exporter, generating about fifty per cent of total annual exports and seven per cent of GDP. With that level of activity, again, a sensible place to site an Arbor without anyone wondering why.'

Ethan stared at the water; it was darkening as the sun dropped. 'You were right about this being big.'

'But you're still in?'

'With you, Dan, I could never be out. What else have you found?'

'Not much, except the presence of these sites proves they've probably been trialling this for years. As Veer says, there's been documented interest in telepathy since time began.'

They both stood silently, listening to the crying of the seagulls, waiting for dusk.

'In my experience,' Ethan said finally, 'people – particularly the rich – are very comfortable in taking what they need from people. Consider illegal organ harvesting – people are tricked, trafficked, I've even heard of eyeballs being stolen out of the heads of kids for the cornea trade. And it's not just the criminal gangs – there's criminality at worst, bad ethics at best, involved in industry too. What about the incidences of drug companies operating trials in African countries in the past – there've been cases of them having to make payouts for a number of reasons.'

They returned to silence, watching the landscape become darker and darker. Away from any town, there was no light other than the moon obscured by cloud. The land became as black as the sea, as black as the night sky, save the white lights from some of the houses on Great Cumbrae in the distance.

Then they enacted their plan. 'These first, even if it means we can't zip our drysuits all the way to the top.' Ethan handed Dan a black vest with Velcro at the sides and shoulders. 'Ballistic and stab proof. We don't take them off until we're back on mainland.'

Dan strapped it on, feeling like he was sealing himself

into a coffin. Then pulling on black drysuits, Dan and Ethan climbed into their kayaks, before dipping their oars into the sea. The seabirds had finally given up their mewling, so the only other sound was the lapping of water against their hulls.

They didn't speak for the entire journey; Ethan led the way using GPS and Dan followed in his wake. It was peaceful listening to the repetitive sound of paddling, and eventually Dorcha loomed blacker against the ink sky. Nearing, they slowed their paddle movements to minimize sound. Nerves were undetectable; it felt good to be on the move, to be doing something tangible. If Arbor had something to hide, they stood a chance of finding it.

Approaching the edge of the island, Ethan first, then Dan following, they climbed out of their kayaks and dropped into the water. They walked the kayaks in for the last few metres, and then both took a grip on each of them and walked them up the short beach. Ethan paused, Dan knowing he was looking for laser tripwires or similar. Then they were both up and across the beach as noiselessly as possible. They'd decided against trying to sink the kayaks in case they needed to leave the island quickly. Instead, they got under the cover of the trees and, using camouflage sheets, covered them and then added any woodland debris they could scrabble together in the dark.

Satisfied, they headed off to the spot Ethan had identified as the best place to set up their hide. It took only a couple of minutes to get to – the wooded ring that encircled the island was dense but they needed to have sight of the institute, yet also to be off the path.

As Ethan strung the snare wire between the trees around

what would be their overnight camp, before twisting foil and alarms into the string, Dan cut pieces of shrubs and used them to cover their hide.

Finished, they each climbed into sleeping bags and thought about what the next day would bring. The plan was that Ethan's watch was set to vibrate before sun-up. Then they would spend the day watching through their binoculars for signs of anything they could take to the police as evidence of wrongdoing.

They were ready. If Jo or Billie needed them – they'd have all the help they wanted.

FIFTY-ONE

Nathalie stood next to Philippe in the study laboratory on minus 2. The study lab was vast and the main hive of activity for the doctors at Arbor. It was broken plan – split into sections for lab, group and desk work. At one end stood a kitchenette with the vital lab equipment of a coffee machine and dishwasher, which sometimes had fifty mugs in it at the end of a day. Then banks of desks and computers, photocopiers, a noticeboard and rows of lockers formed an office environment. There was plenty of adjacent space for breakout planning, with a conference table, plasma screens and, nearest to the door, the most sizeable area was for scientific study: work benches and a line of stools under specialist lighting, shelving filled with a vast array of scientific equipment – microscopes, burners, magnetic stirrers, imaging equipment and sinks.

Although Billie had visited the observation lab next door many times, she had never been in here – until now.

She lay on a hospital bed, unconscious. Discarded now, she was no longer of interest to the medical teams who moved around the large room with a frenetic but purposeful energy. Their focus had shifted to more important things. With less than twenty-four hours until departure, there was much to do. Besides, there was little point in checking Billie. She lay under a duvet of heavy sedation, a general anaesthetic used in surgery; they could have removed her legs and she wouldn't have stirred. She had little monitoring now – there was not much to see other than her heart rate, oxygen levels, blood pressure and the other vitals. The pillows were oversized and almost buried her; an oxygen mask covered her face and the air-filled mattress wheezed softly; she could lie like Sleeping Beauty for a hundred years. If she hadn't been number five, she might have done. If she had entered this state at the beginning of OmnieX's development, like Luca in Switzerland or Cassidy in Chicago, she would have been kept like this potentially for years. But Billie was number five. Five had been the number decided upon as a secure enough, yet realistic and manageable, sample – given the risks – to reassure bidders that OmnieX was safe. So, the medical staff knew the project had been completed and was about to go to market, and Billie was surplus to requirements.

'When do you want to complete Billie?' asked Philippe. 'Still today?'

'Yes. The others need to go too. My final job will be to go to each site and oversee the completion of the five. All loose ends must be tidied.'

'You're going to oversee it personally?'

'Jude thinks it's better that we don't take anyone's word that it's done.'

'Want me to increase the dose now? She'll fade away within an hour or two.'

'Yes.' Nathalie watched as Philippe pressed a few buttons on the syringe driver and increased the dose.

'Done,' he said.

Nathalie only nodded. She looked at Billie and then tidied her covers so they almost completely obscured her. 'Go on now,' she said to her. 'You go and join your mother. Thank you for your service.'

She turned, breathing a sigh of relief, and then went to stand in the middle of the room before clapping her hands. 'Your attention, please. Billie is completing, everyone – I repeat, Billie is completing now. Ted will pop in in a couple of hours and he'll tidy this all up – you leave this,' she said, gesturing in the direction of Billie lying in bed, 'to him and only to him, please.'

She paused for emphasis – she didn't need any kickback or misplaced empathy, not this close to the end. She continued: 'Your focus, team, is to make sure everything else is tidied and finished as we leave tomorrow. But we'll take a break first. I'd like us all to meet now in the conference room for a little celebration of what we've achieved! We all deserve a moment to celebrate how well we've done! Clever us! I look forward to seeing you there in ten minutes.'

FIFTY-TWO

Nathalie rearranged the champagne glasses that the housekeeping staff had left out for the celebration. She set them in neat rows on the white tablecloth that now covered the conference room table. Philippe, the only other person present, watched her, amused. 'You're a control freak, Nathalie.'

'I used to work in housekeeping for a hotel when I was nineteen. There are certain ways of doing—' Her phone cut her off and she answered it.

'Ted? I've got both topside and medical teams turning up in about one minute, so, you've got twenty seconds.'

'We've got a code three. The journalist plus one other.'

She mouthed *code* and held up three fingers to Philippe and his eyes widened briefly. 'Irritating – particularly today of all days – but not unanticipated.'

'Do you want me to dispose?'

'Please.'

'Consider it done.'

'What are they doing?'

'Just sitting in the woods watching us. Bit of reconnaissance, I thought. I've been watching them since they arrived, just before daybreak. But I didn't want to act because of your plans today, we agreed ...'

'No call until after twelve thirty. Fair,' she acknowledged. 'That all went to plan, by the way. Billie will be completed in an hour or two. I'll need you in there to clear up. But obviously, now you've got to prioritize this clean-up operation first. Any challenges, do you think?'

'None. I've got this covered.'

'Do you think this was a rescue party?'

'If it was, it sounds like they're too late.'

She laughed. 'Ted, you're so dry! Anyway, whatever it is, the only party is here. I'd say pop by, but you've got some heavy lifting. Good work, by the way. You're appreciated,' but she didn't wait for him to respond before terminating the call, because the guests were arriving.

FIFTY-THREE

'Congratulations, team!' Nathalie rose to clap all of those seated around the conference room table. Richard Williams, Bo Yeeun and the rest of the medical team, including Callie, which totalled nearly thirty people, all crammed in, leaving some with standing room only. Celine, Philippe and Jenna all had seats and sat on Nathalie's left, and on her right sat Stan, Maddy and Ash. 'It's great to have you all here to celebrate what has transpired in the last hour!'

The table was assembled for a celebration: white linen marked the difference. Champagne flutes now stood in Nathalie's neat rows next to trays of enticing canapes, and three magnums sat imperiously in ice buckets.

Although everyone smiled, Philippe noticed that it was only the medical team that brought the joy and enthusiasm; in contrast the topside team of actors gave only polite, careful smiles. It was not what he expected: perhaps they were tired. To lift their mood, he said: 'We know it's only lunchtime, but we thought we'd have a little party as it's such a incredible moment. Topside team, this is for your brilliance – you've been amazing!' Again, more restrained nods and civil thanks to his applause. Philippe cut a questioning glance at Nathalie.

If she noticed, she didn't show it. Instead, she continued. 'Agreed, Philippe. Jenna, Stan, Maddy, Ash: your work is done! You must be so relieved. What a sustained, relentless effort it must have been to stay in role, constantly immersed for months, hiding that you are talented doctors, and instead pretending to be the damaged post-dux you portrayed. But you've succeeded. You are all fantastic undercover agents, wonderful actors, and we finally now have what we needed: Billie has finally, willingly flocked. She's shown us the dux gregis and even better – thanks to the well-designed caps from Philippe that made them impossible to remove – we have the data. Philippe, would you be so kind?'

Philippe started handing out champagne flutes. 'Drink deeply. No expense spared. I think we all need the afternoon off – wow, that was quite the drama – and we've got more bottles if we need.'

'I always think that magnums are the only real vehicle for champagne,' laughed Nathalie, helping to ensure everyone got a glass. 'Don't you? And what is it we are drinking?'

Philippe popped the cork. 'We've got Louis Roederer Cristal Brut 2008, which is excellent,' he said, opening a second bottle and passing it to Richard. 'Do the honours, won't you, Richard? There's lots of us, but plenty to go round.'

Richard had been transformed from his former uptight self to someone as rowdy as his colleagues. They hugged, fist-bumped, shook hands and congratulated themselves. Giggling, Celine kissed every one of them on the cheek. If any of them noticed the actors sitting mute at the table, they didn't show it.

Nathalie continued as the toast was organized. 'Arbor has now, across all its sites, got our fabulous five needed for the next stage of the OmnieX roll-out. Five sets of results, plus the wealth of other data, means we are unofficially market-ready. Jude and the team in Chicago have got a number of parties salivating at the thought of us going live to auction, so we know there's great hunger for what we've developed. So, today we're not just celebrating Billie, but the final stage, in what has been a labour of love for over a decade. A prodigious moment indeed. So now we will all have a drink – everyone has one, yes? Good – then I'd like you to raise your glass.'

'What are we drinking to?' asked Richard. 'Billie?'

They all turned at her name to look at the huge plasma screen showing a close-up of Billie sleeping. As soon as the flocking had occurred, Philippe had shocked her through her watch, before giving the sedative. She couldn't wake from it unless they chose it. And they weren't going to choose it. There were no plans to let Billie ever wake up now.

She had completed her role.

Nathalie shook her head. 'We thank Billie for her service, but I had a different idea of who we should toast.'

'To us?' shouted Bo. 'For all our fabulous work?'

Nathalie laughed. 'Of course, Bo, you are all remarkable, but I think the original toast is the best toast. How about I ask you to raise your glasses to ... *good health!*'

'Our good health!' said Celine.

They all cheered and drank their champagne, before settling back down to hear from their boss again.

Nathalie continued. 'I think it's important to recognize how far we've come, what a goal we've achieved. Bio-agility:

biological solutions with multiple applications. What many pharma companies now covet, we've now created. The power to create or the power to destroy. Let's go back a few years, to remember our journey to this point. Post Covid, the world looked to us, pharmaceutical companies, to keep them safe. And that's our job. We take it seriously.'

'We are heroes!' chipped in a laughing Richard, lifting his glass again and drinking deeply.

Nathalie clapped her hands in delight. 'Yes! Yes! Agreed, Richard. Philippe, would you do the honours? They have finished their glasses.' Philippe obliged and noticed that the actors' glasses still remained untouched.

'Post Covid, it didn't take long for the world to return to old fears. But whether viral or nuclear or AI or diminishing resources or birthrates or global warming, ultimately fears of the populace continue to centre around *lack of control*.' She emphasized the words. 'Lack of control leads to chaos – and chaos is dangerous.

'So how do we, as scientists, contribute to negating societal and global chaos? How do we help provide control? Well, we – you, me, us – at Arbor have dared to look further into the abyss. And in it, we've found a game-changer. And with it, we are shaping our world for the better. Gone is the need for propaganda. Gone is the need for armies. Data is no longer king. Ideas of dealing with the masses have distracted our competitors – instead our focus has been on the micro: the few. By providing clear control to the few, we provide calm and clarity. So, no more chaos and let's drink up to celebrate! Eat the food, let's celebrate and enjoy our day of success!'

Nathalie took her seat and relished the buzz of the

moment. Now they could offer the ability to control all the people, everywhere. There wasn't a war she and the successful bidders couldn't stop. Not a war they couldn't start. Not a war she couldn't win. She would offer the ability to control the money markets. The voting. The population decrease – increase, whatever. A favoured few would be in control and she would be one of them. And ultra rich with it.

Bo, Richard and the other medical staff all roared their cheers, downing the champagne and passing round the bottles. Another cork was popped, and they reached in over the seated, silent actors, to grab the canapes. Nathalie and Philippe circulated. Then she moved to Stan, who sat staring at his hands. 'Stan, you were sensational! You all were – all utterly credible, believable and just so exciting to watch. I'm so pleased that Philippe and his AI had the brainwave – forgive the pun – to add to your storyline to include romance. I think it was intrinsic to keeping Billie here, and of course, it gave us a secondary option in case the drama didn't work tonight.'

'Thanks. Glad it's done,' he said, finally taking a heavy drink.

Celine rubbed his shoulder and dropped a kiss on the top of his head as she passed, but he didn't even look up.

Philippe raised an eyebrow at Nathalie, before turning to Maddy. 'You did a great job, Maddy. I'm pleased that our plan A worked. Well done.'

Maddy looked sombre. 'The stage knife was tricky. I nearly forgot to lock the blade out when I threw it against the wall – imagine if it hit the wall and it concertinaed in again. It would have given the game away that it was a fake knife.'

He nearly told her not to look so grim, but decided not

to acknowledge it. Instead, he tried with Jenna. 'You burst the fake blood pouch at just the right moment – it did look really authentic.'

'Thanks. It wasn't hard.'

They all looked miserable – miserable and lifeless. He'd known them for a couple of years, having recruited them from Arbor's network. They were all doctors, all quite brilliant and ambitious, and certainly were not like this before. He tried again: 'The AI prediction of a fear slash danger event provoking her reaction was simply perfect.'

Nathalie reached forward and gripped the nearest hands of Jenna and Maddy. 'And now you are fulfilling your brief as the wonderful staff of Arbor that you are. Now you'll head back to Chicago to continue the work.'

'And Billie,' asked Stan carefully, 'will she will stay here on Dorcha?'

'We can't fly her out,' Nathalie said, equally carefully.

'But you're shutting this branch.'

'Billie has already been dealt with.'

Nobody said anything, their gazes small and guarded. Maddy continued to rub her nail repeatedly over her thumb pad. Stan shut his eyes and squeezed his fingers against his temples. Jenna chewed her lip, gaze fixed and blank. Ash rubbed his fist into his palm, staring as it made a circular, recurring motion.

'I was worried she hit her head, when she hit the ground like she did,' Jenna said finally.

Nathalie paused, smiled, and continued. 'It happened as we rehearsed it.'

'I didn't care about her then,' said Ash. 'But it felt too brutal.'

Nathalie's smile deepened to her eyes. 'But let's not move from the science. As you know, a typical brain's oligodendrocytes not only detect electrical signals from nerve fibres, but also respond by increasing their energy intake. This energy required for the brain's complex network of signals far exceeded what we expected to see. When Billie flocked with you all – I don't know how else to describe it – you all lit up. It was very much like a beacon being answered by another beacon. It was phenomenal. The best we've ever seen. We know as dux sectators you won't have any abilities to flock others as you've not been exposed to OmnieX, but like Stefana, you'll be valued members of the med team back in the States.' When no one showed any interest, Nathalie felt herself continuing just so she didn't have to acknowledge the silence. 'What's really exciting is that we've not seen this level of power before, which means we've either not measured it correctly with other post-OmnieX patients, or—'

'Or Billie's special?' asked Stan with a tilt to his head and a sincere look in his eye.

Ash, Jenna and Maddy all nodded and said together, 'Yes, Billie is special.'

Philippe cut another glance at Nathalie; this time, she held his gaze just long enough to know that she agreed. They were *creepy*.

'But why knock her out so quick?' asked Ash. 'I mean, wouldn't a gentler dose of the electric shock be better? It could've killed her.'

'You know the plan was to disable her instantaneously. It was clean, effective and allowed protection of all medical staff. You understand the research paradox of handling something so powerful that it's dangerous, and this is what the disabling shock gave us, the ability to research her. Remember, if she accessed your memory banks, then she'll know your real role here. Not friend, not fellow flock, but a paid imposter here to manipulate her actions. So, we milked the venom from the mamba with care. Anyway, these are all moot points now. Billie is done. Past tense. Are we clear?' Brightening instantly, Philippe smiled like a proud father. 'Good. Drink your champagne – there's much to celebrate. The plan tomorrow is we leave for Chicago.'

Nathalie checked her watch, and stood to address the crowded room. The medical staff quietened to listen. 'It's lunchtime. If you haven't been sated by the canapes, feel free to grab the trays and take them with you. The same for the unfinished wine – you've got the afternoon off, just don't get so pissed that you forget to pack and complete your reports.' She closed the lid of her laptop and addressed the actors at the table. 'Topside team: if you wouldn't mind staying two minutes more, I wanted to just add one more thing.'

After the medical staff, led by Celine and Richard, all filed noisily out, clearly going to extend the party, Nathalie smiled. 'Jenna, Stan, Ash and Maddy, I've got some exciting final news. Arbor is so happy with you that you'll find your bank accounts have experienced a rather generous bonus. Tonight, you'll be credited with an additional two hundred thousand pounds.'

They all cheered, glad of the money.

Maddy and the others thanked Nathalie for the bonus. She watched them leave, happy again and refocused, patting each other on the back as they went to find a place to celebrate.

Philippe waited for them to leave and when he was sure everyone had gone, he asked, 'An unscheduled bonus! I didn't know that was on the cards?'

'Nor did I until I said it.'

'A nice idea though – rather broke the strange atmosphere. Weren't they odd? All that worrying about Billie. They were never bothered about her before – they were only interested in their careers. The contrast was like night and day. And Ash too, he used to be such a cold heart, he made me look caring – but now!'

Nathalie felt an unusual wave of tiredness herself and got up to go. 'It's going to be challenging.'

'You think it's an issue?' asked Philippe, tidying the glasses onto the sideboard where some nameless cleaner would remove them.

'Love is always an issue.'

'Love?'

'Did you see the way they looked when talking about her? Did you see Maddy's intensity? She was clearly working hard not to contribute to the discussion – she kept her hand over her mouth the entire time she was here. None of them wanted to eat or drink. And my, how Ash glowed.'

'The bonus brought them back.'

Nathalie picked up her notebook and headed for door, only to pause as she left. 'You've never been in love before, have you, my little sociopathic friend?'

Philippe laughed, the old joke between them still amusing. 'Maybe I'm not built that way, but I've heard all the best pop songs, so I think I'm reasonably well appraised.'

'It's not all hearts and flowers. The thing about love is . . .' She sighed and checked her watch. 'Love is hard to control.

When we ran the AI programs this didn't come up as a possibility. We humans didn't see this possibility either, which means we didn't plan for it. If they've seen it at the other development sites, they didn't tell me or we didn't pick it up. Anyway, this will have to wait. I've just been messaged – got to take a call from the Chicago Arbor. Cassidy is raising some markers. I really don't want to have to fly out earlier than tomorrow.' She shut her eyes briefly. 'Really, I just need the time to think. And sleep. All this jetting around to Switzerland, India, Algeria, Scotland, the States – I'm exhausted. I haven't had a day off in three years.' She pulled herself together. 'Nearly there.'

'Nearly there,' agreed Philippe before following her out the door.

FIFTY-FOUR

Ethan heard him before he saw him. It was the crack of a broken stick at the same time as one of the foils on the tripwire he'd installed around their hide turned and winked its warning in the sunlight. He reached over and placed his hand over Dan's mouth to stop him speaking, before motioning to alert him to the danger that someone was outside their makeshift tent.

The man's voice sounded clear and easy: 'Gents, I come hands up – I'm not here for trouble, but if you can step outside and talk about this, that would work for me.'

Dan looked at Ethan and mouthed: *'Ted.* Shotgun man.'

His boots were just visible below the sheet they'd used. The boots were well-maintained; Ethan decided he would bet a year's salary that whoever was outside used to be a military man. But either way, they were caught. Dan raised an eyebrow and Ethan shrugged: they had no choice.

'I've got my hands up,' Ted repeated. 'Dorcha is private property, but I think you know that. But I'm keen to resolve this with as little fuss as possible. Come out so we can talk.'

Dan sighed, annoyed to be discovered. They had

long-range photographic lenses pointed at the institute and longed to catch some action. Then, finally, two minutes ago, they had seen four young people walk out together, cross the lawn and sit. However, the game was up. Perhaps they had been distracted, perhaps their whispered conversation ('Billie isn't with them'; 'I recognize one of them – he sat next to Billie by the pool last time I was here'; 'is her absence significant?') had led him to them.

Ethan had his Sheffield Fairbairn Sykes British Commando dagger tucked in his waistband under his coat – long and lean, it was his favourite. He was sure he wouldn't need it, but he liked to keep old friends close. He sighed, and called out, 'Are you alone or with company?'

'Just me,' the man called. 'My dog's close, though, if you like a Jack Russell.'

'We don't want to face the shotgun,' Ethan called out.

'My hands are in the air. I'll keep them there.'

They both stepped out of the hide. Wanting to keep him amiable, Ethan greeted him warmly. 'Hey, how are you doing? Sorry if we're trespassing.'

With his gloved hands still in the air, Ted looked coldly amused. 'You know you are. I've met Dan Downes, investigative journalist, already.'

Ethan looked at the two staring at each other like dogs getting ready to fight. He attempted to break the mood: 'What's your dog's name?'

'Fred – after the Flintstone. You haven't seen him around, have you? In the bushes, back there, somewhere? I'm worried he's stuck in a hole.' He gave a smile that didn't reach his cold blue eyes.

But what Dan missed, Ethan caught. The classic, ask a

question that gets someone else looking around – looking anywhere but at the person asking the interrogative. Ethan instinctively reached behind him, hand closing on his dagger.

But Ted also moved. For a second, it was a confusing image: he seemed to grow another arm as a third one moved beneath the jacket and appeared holding a pistol. Three arms. One not real. His real arm had been concealed under his jacket, no doubt holding the gun the whole time. The open-handed arm, a fake to feign surrender. The real hand pulled the trigger.

The bullet didn't even sound that loud to Dan as it punched him in the chest. His knees went first and then he hit the ground, a breathless slam that moved everything ninety degrees to the right. He thought: *Billie—*

Ethan's knife was already in his hand as he stepped forward. As the second bullet hit him in the neck, he stabbed at Ted, the long, elegant knife making an uppercut to the groundsman's throat. Ted moved, but it still sliced across the right side of his neck. Dropping the gun, his hands went to the wound, and like a third tree in storm, fell just after Ethan with a bang to the woodland floor.

FIFTY-FIVE

Jenna, Stan, Ash and Maddy, all without having to discuss anything, walked as far as they could from Arbor without looking suspicious and flopped on the lawn. They lay in the sun for ten minutes; the sun was at its apex and it felt warm. Nobody said anything until they heard a couple of cracks coming from the woods and the birds rose in protest.

They looked, but didn't comment. They were used to Ted and his team killing animals, although they were always told it was simply target practice. But the flock rising broke the spell of silence.

Ash spoke first. 'We've got to talk,' he said, stretching out on the grass to look casual. He propped up his chin with one hand, so it covered his mouth. 'We know there's no mics out on the lawns, but I suggest we keep our mouths covered when we talk.'

'Agreed,' Jenna, Stan and Maddy confirmed at the same time. Maddy unwound her hair. She tilted her head forward, so her mouth was concealed by the curtain of loose hair. 'I'm going to make a daisy chain,' she said, as she started to pick daisies. Jenna lay on her back watching the occasional cloud drift, and Stan slumped like Ash, his sunglasses on and cap pulled down.

'I want to tell you something – it's a little weird, I guess,' Ash said carefully, 'but I think it needs to be said.' He hesitated again. 'It's ... strange – hard to describe.'

'If it helps, I know what you're going to say. It's about Billie, what they did to her and how I feel now,' said Jenna, voice low. She spoke around the fingers now at her mouth, as if she were chewing a nail. 'I know, because I feel the same.'

Stan swore under his breath. Then whispered, 'Me too, me too.'

'I didn't notice it at first,' Ash continued. 'When Billie hit the floor, I was glad it was finally over. We'd all worked so hard for it, right? All the storyboard planning meetings, making adjustments to our dialogue, even improvising – like when Billie refused to go to group therapy because she wanted to speak with her mum, so we all went with it and played tennis instead. We'd stayed in character so long, it felt great to be finally released. To just be me. But I got cleaned up, she got taken away, then it was just the four of us. And, man, I felt straightaway that it was like a missing tooth – a gaping hole. And at first, it was just missing her ...' He sighed, glancing over to Arbor. 'It's only been a couple of hours, but this feeling – it's something else. Is this what you guys feel?'

Jenna nodded. 'And it creeps and creeps and creeps. Fast, too. And loud now. Like a sound being turned up until it's blaring and—'

'It's all I can hear,' interrupted Stan. 'Wow. Thought it was just me.'

'I know how weird this sounds – but the nearest I can get to it, is that I feel that . . .' Ash waited until they each looked at him square in the eye. 'I miss Billie. Like I want her back. And it's bad, like not being with her makes me feel like a little kid again and I can't see my mum in a busy shopping centre. At first, I didn't notice – but now . . . *now* the missing is like a scream in my head. Find her. Find her *now*.'

Maddy had been pressing her nail to cut into the slim, slight daisy stalk, but looked up sharply at Ash as he described the scream in his head. Her eyes watchful. 'And me,' she confirmed.

'So, what are we going to do?' said Stan. He stared at Arbor and remembered walking Billie down to it on that first day she arrived. He knew then that she would never leave that building once she went in – she would die in there. The plan was always to force the dux gregis, measure it and then 'complete' her once the data had been collated. None of them was under any illusions what 'completing' looked like. He couldn't believe now that he hadn't cared. She'd been a means to an end – his first job on Project OmnieX. She was nothing more than a delivery job; a parcel to drop off. A lab animal.

A path to gold.

Stan had trained to be a doctor and worked out fast that it was very far from a get-rich-quick scheme. So, when he'd seen the ad for NorGline he'd applied and worked two straight years on standard pharmaceuticals in Chicago. His pay in pharma finally hit the spot. He was starting to feel wealthy and he liked it, but then after a while . . . it wasn't *quite* enough. His then-boss had suggested he meet Professor Bouchard. He'd heard of him, knew he wasn't well-liked, but still attended the informal interview for an unspecified 'project' anyway. He then completed six months of profiling: they scrutinized his socials; made him take personality tests; had flown him out to the Scottish base to see if he could live there a year. He'd even been contacted by an ex-girlfriend, who was still sweet enough on him to let him know that some guy in a bar had asked so many questions about him, she thought he was signing up to the CIA. He rode it out, got offered the role and hadn't looked back.

But now he felt the burn of shame: he'd betrayed Billie. 'They're talking about her in the past tense. Do you think she's dead yet?'

'No,' they all said in unison.

'I feel that too. But she won't have long. Philippe told me ages ago that they just turn up the anaesthetic,' said Stan.

'They moved her from the obs lab to the study lab on minus two,' said Maddy, slicing another cut into a daisy.

'Are you saying that we go there and save her in some way?' asked Jenna.

'We've got to go in there anyway, to file our reports,' Maddy said.

'What do you all want to do?' asked Ash.

Jenna looked at him with large eyes. The last hour had been confronting: who was she? What did she want? She was on the verge of having more money than she'd ever had – enough to set her up for life. If she did nothing, she'd bank enough in the next twenty-four hours that, on return to Chicago, she could buy her dream of a 5,000-square-foot luxury waterfront condo, and develop her passion for art. 'They'll know if we help her,' she answered, thinking of Billie, already knowing she would now never buy that flat.

'Not if we make a hole in the IV feed. We just need something sharp and small that wouldn't be noticed,' said Maddy, threading another daisy through. 'Like a thumbtack on the noticeboard in the lab. If the tubing was then positioned so the slack was coiled under the covers, it'd drain out without anyone noticing. If she's not under sedation, she'll stand a chance.'

'How long do you think it'll take for her to come round?' asked Jenna.

'She's on a heavy dose of Propofol. But,' she checked her watch, 'she hasn't been under for very long, only around one hour fifteen. She's fit and strong and if we make sure she doesn't get any more, it won't take long – around thirty minutes, maybe less.'

'The syringe driver has an alarm,' said Stan.

'And it's nothing to turn it off,' Maddy replied.

Ash examined Maddy with careful eyes. 'You've been thinking this through.'

'I'd like to say,' she said, linking both ends of the daisy chain together, 'yes, since the moment she hit the floor. But really, it took seeing the champagne to know what a truly heinous, horrible witch I'd become, to betray someone I love. I'd rather be poor again.'

Ash got up, mind already made up. There was no time like the present. 'We won't just be poor – I think they'll kill us.'

Maddy put the flower garland round his neck. 'Not if Billie kills them first.'

FIFTY-SIX

Chicago Post
5 September 20—

SEARCH FOR MISSING WOMAN CALLED OFF

No sign of Cassidy Clarke after tragedy group drowning fleeing bear attack

The Wisconsin Department of Natural Resources has confirmed that it has finally closed investigations into a woman missing at Devil's Lake State Park. This follows their investigations into student Cassidy Clarke, 23, and the mystery drowning of her boyfriend, Ryan Wolfe, 26, and friends, Bob Lindon, 26, and Laine King, 23. DNR officials said first responders were first called to the scene on Tuesday 26 June and grizzly bear scat and a damaged campsite consistent with a bear attack were found, alongside traces of Miss Clarke's blood. Ryan, Bob and Laine were all found drowned, suspected of entering the water to escape the bear. High levels of alcohol were found in their system.

The park was reopened the following day, with an extensive search for Cassidy lasting two weeks, with ongoing investigations until yesterday. DNR official Rich Sullivan made the announcement yesterday, saying: 'Troopers and locals have been relentless in their attempts to find Miss Cassidy Clarke. Sadly, however, even after the use of sonar equipment and dogs, we have been unable to locate her. This seems to be a tragic outcome for all those involved. Although we may never know what happened to Cassidy, it's suspected she either entered the water or the woods to flee the attack.'

The National Park Service representative issued a statement reminding the public that attacks by bears in the area are 'extremely rare.' The *Post* understands that an inquest is due to be announced. The families are yet to comment.

FIFTY-SEVEN

Dan came to, knowing that he'd only blacked out for a second. He'd hit his head as he fell, but the shock of seeing that third arm, the gun and the attack on Ethan kicked in and he sat up, eyes wide, adrenaline pumping.

Ethan lay at his feet and, in front of him, Ted lay on the ground. Dan sprang up and grabbed the gun that Ted had dropped. Then he knelt next to Ethan. His friend was already dead. Blood was everywhere, sinking into the earth. It stank of iron. Blood covered the right side of Ethan's body. Part of his neck was missing, smashed out and leaving a large wound. It was meaty and frightening. No one could ever survive that. Death must have been instant.

Dan stared at the open eyes of his friend. Nothing was processing properly – he couldn't believe it, it all felt so surreal. He'd known Ethan since they were at school together. He'd been his best friend then and, despite their busy lives keeping them apart, they were best friends still. Dan placed his palm gently against Ethan's face and moved it down so his eyelids closed. Ethan had saved his life – not just with the bulletproof vest, but by taking out Ted, who would have followed up on him with a head shot. Dan's chest ached as though he'd been hit with a hammer and it felt like he had a broken rib. But he was alive.

But Ethan was dead. His throat ached with grief as he grappled with the reality: *Ethan is dead.* Dan shoved his hand between his teeth to stop himself from crying out. He had to move quickly – whatever he was going to do, he needed to do it fast. Arbor weren't just dangerous: they were lunatics.

He checked Ted next. As he walked over, Ted opened his eyes. Covered in blood from his own much smaller neck wound, he looked terrible. 'Help me,' Ted said in a gravelly voice.

'And do what? Take you to the institute? I bet there's a dozen guys who'll have gun sights fixed on me before I get within a hundred metres of the place.'

The blood was still oozing through Ted's fingers – it needed stopping. Dan grabbed a long-sleeved T-shirt from the tent and wound both sleeves to wind round his neck to stem the flow. Red blossomed against white. Dan doubted even stitches would save him.

'You have a gun – you can use me as collateral. My watch,' Ted said as he tried to hold up his wrist, 'will give you security clearance wherever you want to go.' He reached into his pocket and held out his keys. 'My quad is just on the beach. I left it there so you wouldn't hear it. You could drive us down.'

Dan took the key. Ted was a dead man walking, and he definitely wasn't going to do anything he suggested – in fact, he bet the smartest thing was to do the exact opposite. He pulled his phone out. 'I'm going to call the police.'

'They won't come.' Ted rasped. 'Arbor has paid them off.'

'You can't pay off everyone.'

'The call will be downgraded.'

'I don't believe you.' Dan dialled 999.

As the operator spoke and Dan started to answer, 'Hello, I'm calling from Dorcha Island, my name is Dan Downes—'

Ted continued to talk. 'You'll be put on silent and then the operator will claim you dropped the call.'

'Hello caller, I can't hear you.'

'I'm Dan Downes, calling from Dorcha Island. Can you hear me?'

'Caller, I can't hear you.'

Ted continued, 'You'll be coded as a network glitch or a dropped call, and they'll follow up with a call to the island later to tick the box.'

'Caller, this call has been dropped or there is a network glitch. Please call back.'

'But I can hear you? Please – my name is Dan Downes, I'm calling from Dorcha Island and—'

Ted: 'They won't come and they'll tell you they will—'

'Caller, we will follow up with a welfare visit.'

Ted: '—conduct a welfare visit. Then they'll contact Nathalie.'

Dan hung up and looked at Ted with narrow eyes. 'You people . . . how much did you pay?'

'Everyone has a number that they'll agree to. Take me back to Arbor and we'll find out what your number is. Trust me: this will all seem much better soon. You'll be rich enough to forget you ever knew this place's name. And as for Billie, you're too late. There's no one to save now but yourself.'

Dan took a few seconds to think his options through – but

never once did he entertain listening to Ted. He left him and strode back up the path to the small beach where he'd first arrived on Dorcha. Parked there was Ted's quad. He jumped on and started the engine, then drove it back to where the camp was and, without speaking to Ted, dragged him to the bike. After a moment's hesitation, he propped Ted up, then retrieved the gun. He wanted it both for evidence and in case Ted tried anything.

'Hold on,' was all he said.

Ted gripped him round the waist with one hand, the other still pressed against his neck. 'Good choice', he said in a gravelly voice.

Perhaps Ted had shut his eyes, because he didn't say anything until they stopped where Dan and Ethan had hidden the kayaks. Half-unconscious, he gave a brief protest when he became aware that Dan hadn't driven him back to Arbor.

First pulling the life jacket onto Ted, Dan then used Ted's bootlaces to tie his hands behind his back. Then he dragged him into Ethan's kayak. If Ted protested, Dan didn't hear him. He doubted that he would be alive by the time he got him back to the mainland. But either way, he intended to drop his body – dead or alive – on the floor of the police station. With the gun. This man had murdered his friend. He would get Ethan justice. He would ensure that Billie and Jo Cathey got help – or justice. But either way, he wasn't going to take direction from Ted or sit here and wait for the police to not arrive.

Dan leashed Ethan's kayak to his and pushed off into the Firth. He'd come at night, but now it was daylight. As he fixed his sights upon the coast, he remembered that Ethan's Transporter was parked at a point he couldn't quite be sure of and the keys were still in Ethan's pocket. He hadn't thought it through properly in his panic. But ahead was Wemyss Bay.

That would be his destination.

FIFTY-EIGHT

Stan, Ash, Jenna and Maddy stopped off at the kitchen and grabbed cakes from the larder. Then making their way back to the conference room, they found what they were hoping for – another magnum stashed in the wine fridge. Grabbing it, they headed to the busy study lab on minus 2. 'Hey, everyone,' shouted Ash, 'we have brought the party! Time to celebrate! Who's for cake or a top-up?' Everyone cheered, already bored by the mundane work of packing up and wondering when the promised afternoon off would materialize. Maddy paused by the noticeboard. 'Want me to take down the notices?' she offered to everybody and nobody. She didn't wait for an answer as she started unpinning them.

Stan started to cut pieces of cake and Ash topped up the alcohol. Maddy and Jenna wandered over to Billie in the corner. They stood tightly together, with Maddy first turning off the syringe driver alarm as Jenna grabbed the UV tube and pushed it under the covers. Then Jenna leaned across the bed, as if to speak to Billie, concealing Maddy. Maddy's hands snaked under the sheet and found the tube, before pressing three neat holes into the plastic, using the noticeboard's push pin. She felt the liquid escape immediately and knew it would pool under the covers.

Stan and Ash were doing a great job – something one of them said resulted in a loud cheer. Whether the staff were high on champagne, the thought of now being ultra rich or leaving Dorcha wasn't clear, but spirits soared. Maddy and Jenna joined the group and, after cutting a wink to each other, made sure they gave the loudest cheer of them all.

Phase 5: fledgling

FIFTY-NINE

in the woods again.

The sun is bright through the trees. She can hear the call of a robin, its rolling, pretty song just above her. Ah, it is summer, she thinks, and then understands: *August. This is now.* She can see patches of blue sky above her and feels a deep contentment, as the sun throws shards of golden light down through the green leaves, onto the forest floor, onto the shiny crimson blood.

Crimson blood! How did she not see? She screams. She's standing in blood. It's now at her waist. *The blood is rising* (still rising – where *has* she been?).

'The blood rises higher because you did nothing, Wilhelmina,' says her father. He sounds cross – worse: there is a searing heat of anger in his voice. 'You've been looking the wrong way.' She can't see him, can only see Firkin has settled on the branch of a large oak opposite, and is looking at her with his clever orange-red eyes, presenting his striped broad chest. If he is close, her father must be close.

'Help me, Daddy!' she cries. 'It's rising! I'm going to drown and . . .'

'I cannot help you.' His voice is coming from Firkin. 'You are in one world and I am in the next. You must get out of the woods that surround you. That which circles you, keeps you prisoner.'

The blood is easing steadily higher.

'Daddy, I don't know how to get out.' Her feet are stuck deep and she cannot move. She lifts her hands up. 'Release me, send someone to help me!'

Firkin, with her father's voice, speaks again. 'You have everything you need to save yourself. Use it.'

The blood is at chest level now. The robin's song has been replaced by a constant, panicked *tic; tic; tic; tic; tic; tic*. The warning sounds on and on and now she can smell the blood. It's a tang of iron, of meat.

'Where's it coming from?'

'Everyone. Everyone lost to the power of the few. It's a tragedy. So much death. Stop them, Wilhelmina.'

She is angry now. Her father won't save her. 'Stop them? I don't even know who they are! Firkin, help me!'

tic; tic; tic; tic; tic; tic

Then huge relief floods her as Firkin cocks his head, fixes her with his orange-red eye and unsettles, finally lifting his wings, and swoops magnificently, silently, down low to her. In her mind's eye, she thought she

THE INSTITUTE

would take his feet, and he would lift her free of the blood that was now at her shoulders. But instead, he lands on her wrist, huge claws digging in. Then he bites against her wrist, deep, searing, ripping bites that tear into her flesh and bone.

'No, Firkin, that hurts, stop hurting me—'

He rips at her tissue, peeling back skin, veins; the pain is electrifying.

tic; tic; tic; tic; tic; tic (not a robin now but seconds on a clock. 'Time is ticking on,' agrees her father. '*Wake up*, Wilhelmina.').

'Stop, Firkin, that hurts!'

But he rips on and on and on and on and around her fall a thousand black Arbor watches, like overripe fruit falling heavily from the trees, followed by a thousand plastic door cards, like autumn leaves falling in a heavy wind, all raining down on her and Firkin, all dropping lost into the sea of blood, which is still rising, now up to her neck—

'*Wake up*, Wilhelmina,' he shouts, and then again: 'The clock is *ticking*! Wake now or die!'

She inhales, lifting her chin out of the blood.

I'm—

SIXTY

—awake.

Billie heard: 'I found another stash of champagne – six bottles!' followed by shouts and cheers from a crowd of people. Billie didn't open her eyes – she felt too tired, but she also felt too scared. Nothing felt right in her body. She felt cold, achy – and her wrist burned. *Burned. Stop, Firkin, that hurts!* Why? She couldn't remember what happened to her wrist, in fact she couldn't remember anything.

Everything around her also felt wrong. It sounded like she was at a party, but it smelt like she was in a hospital.

I'm in Arbor, she realized.

Through her shut eyelids, she could tell it was light. She listened to the unfamiliar noises: conversations, bottles popping and the clink of glasses. Someone walked past in soft-soled shoes; I am not in my room, she thought. She decided to wait – not to open her eyes and ask for help because ... because ... it didn't feel safe. She had a dream of blood and feathers and the feeling of fear remained. Every thought was leaden, like feet stuck in deep mud (and rising blood). It occurred to her that she'd been drugged. She was so tired. She listened to the sound of her breathing, bothered by the pain in her wrist and—

Jenna. Maddy stabbed Jenna.

Then what?

Then she flocked them. Took control. Saved Jenna from further attacks. She could hear Jenna now. Yes, yes – and Maddy. They were in this room now. How much time had passed because, confusingly, they were laughing and cheering together. Feeling sharper now, Billie wanted to look – wanted to see why they were laughing and joking together. Had they made up? Would they help her? Did she pass out after she helped Jenna? She lay – just not sure, just not sure and tired too – thinking, remembering, mind like mush. It had been easy to pull them in – effortless, in fact. But she had seen something in them – some commonality, something they knew but she didn't, but there was no time. It had all happened so quickly; everything had been focused on saving Jenna. Everything had been driven by fear – and the desire to save. And she'd only been in their heads for perhaps not even two minutes . . . but there had been something there. Like a secret. Something they all knew – but she didn't.

She could hear the whisper from a nearby machine, like air slowly being released from a balloon. The beeping from another. Why was she in a hospital bed? Why had she been asleep immediately after Maddy stabbed Jenn—

Philippe. His cold eyes. Him pressing his watch.

The fire in her wrist.

The shock of the memory nearly forced her eyes open, but she worked hard not to move. She had been electrocuted – now she was in no doubt – and that meant she was in danger.

But nothing made any sense. It felt a struggle to think clearly, but she had to try, she told herself, for her dad. Strange thought, she acknowledged, but dismissed it. She tried to focus. Why would Philippe attack her when she'd been helping Jenna? She listened to the laughter, confused that she could be in a bed, yet somehow there was a party going on nearby. Where in Arbor was she? She couldn't think of anywhere where that would fit. There were so many nice places to have a party here. Really, the terrace by the pool would be the best place for a – *focus*, she reminded herself.

It felt important.

She couldn't remember. She couldn't think where she was. She didn't understand why Philippe would hurt her when she had been the one protecting Jenna.

The conversation remained in a far corner. She heard a man shout something excited and upbeat – Richard, the doctor. She'd never heard him sound happy before. A round of applause. Another cheer. What were they celebrating? And Jenna now, saying something loud and everyone laughing. Why was she even at a party after being stabbed? Or had so much time passed?

I could flock with someone. Instantly, she understood this was the safest way of finding out why she was in this strange situation. The thought of flocking them again wakened her further and glittered like a bright eye in the dark. She would see the secret that they held. She would understand everything and she knew from Stefana, they wouldn't even know afterwards. Yes, she decided. She would wait and listen but first she would have a little nap because she was so tired ...

Some memory of time being important *tic; tic; tic; tic; tic* and a memory of a panicked robin intruded, its message sharp and jabbing, like metal between molars.

Okay, I'll do it now, she thought, changing her mind. *Before I sleep.*

She heard Jenna's laugh above the bubbles of chatter. Without waiting, she reached out to Jenna ...

It felt natural. It felt easy to pull on those threads left in Jenna's mind. The feeling of a push on a bubble's wall; the dragging feeling; rising sickness and then she'd reached Jenna.

She opened up and allowed herself to see. She stood – Jenna now – holding a glass of champagne. It was a shock – Jenna was mid-swig and the bubbles moving down her throat – and the reality of standing at a party in a room talking to Stan and a doctor she recognized, in a huge laboratory she had never been in – was disorienting. So much information all at once. Seeing a bed thirty metres away, with someone lying in it hooked up to machines, knowing it was herself, was a shock. And she understood in an instant the many secrets they'd all shared without her and why.

And that was the worst shock of all.

SIXTY-ONE

Arbor Institute, Chicago branch

'We have a brain pulse!' The doctor hit the silent alarm that contacted the rest of the team. Two other doctors ran into the observation room, taking seats at the desk next to Dr Haley Bykofsky.

Haley did not raise her eyes from the screen. 'This is *huge*. We are picking up a neurological pulse – grade seven. Cassidy is surging.'

'Are you sure?' asked one of her team, as he took a seat at the desk. He leaned close to the monitors, eyes narrowing as he attempted to analyse the complex data on screen. They'd been too relaxed, taking an extended break. Cassidy was long past tests and was now just waiting for Nathalie to visit so she could complete. Since she'd been fitted with the blocking plate, there had been nothing to see for a long time. Perhaps they'd become complacent. 'The most we've seen is a three, since we fitted the brain plate, so—'

Another of the team interjected. 'Now there's no

grade – it's topped out. It's unreadable. There is no scale. Repeat: now there is no scale.'

'Shit,' Haley muttered under her breath, finally looking up at the patient prone on the hospital bed, behind the glass wall. Cassidy Clarke lay as if asleep – but she was not asleep, simply secured. Her vocal cords had been severed, so she couldn't speak, and her intravenous cocktail included a muscle relaxant so there was no danger of injury from her trying to escape her wrist and ankle bonds. A white scar ran across the length of her shaved head, following the brain surgery last year. 'Can we get Nathalie on a call? Is she in Scotland or India? She knows we've seen some elevated markers and said to tell her if it happened again.'

'Scotland. I'll reach her there,' someone offered and then left the room.

Haley raised her voice. 'Who or what is Cassidy communicating with?'

'Waiting ... no, not anyone here in the lab. But—'

'Talk to me – what's the but?'

'She *is* communicating. Her readings are red hot. The same as before – but more, much more. But I can't see – no, wait, yes I can. Confirm, patient is communicating but not – double checking their readings ... give me a sec ... Sorry, no. Just ... no.'

'Just *no*?' asked Haley. 'I can't use that. Has she circumvented the plate and who is she communicating with, exactly? Same question, but I need a different answer. Is she flocking with someone? You?'

Deadpan return. 'Not me, no.'

'And do you think she's flocking with her dead boyfriend and the rest of her now worm-food flock, who were not bear-scare, but OmnieX-aired by that nasty little cunt, Ted Thatcher-the-flock-catcher?'

'No. No, I don't.'

Haley threw her pen against the glass observation wall and it bounced off. 'Then who the fuck do you think she is reaching? What are we getting? Why are we seeing this now? Ideas! Anyone?' Pause. 'For fuck's sake – *anyone?*'

A junior member of the team, Dr Louis, keen for recognition, broke the silence: 'She's like a sonar – before we fitted the blocking plate, she could dux with anyone. But what if the plate in her brain is still working – we're still protected, so that seems logical – but she has now some redeveloped communication ability? The question is, if Cassidy is reaching someone and it's outside the bands of control we've witnessed, is there anyone else capable of receiving a signal from her? Someone else who would have the ability to receive a limited communication?'

'Say more – explain what you mean?'

'It's simple, we know all brains have the ability for huge plasticity in the creation of new neural pathways following brain injury – Cassidy has a brain injury in the form of the blocking plate we put in. But what if we're seeing something different to DG, something that she's developed through neural regeneration of some sort? And we're seeing the results of this now?' he continued, glad to finally have a voice and be heard. 'If Cassidy could communicate with someone far away, where would she choose to go? Maybe anyone, anywhere, but we can't monitor that, so for now, we should disregard that idea and stick to what we might be able to detect and monitor. Let's stick with the logic. Who might she choose or be able to reach?'

Haley picked up another pen, rattling it against her teeth. 'Cassidy was selected partly because she has no family. Any ideas on who else we should look at then? Other possibilities who Cassidy might reach?'

'What about others that have been exposed to OmnieX?'

Haley stopped rattling and turned in her swivel chair to face him: 'Like in India and Switzerland, do you mean?'

'Exactly,' Louis said. 'The other Arbor sites – the other OmnieX test subjects.'

Haley tilted her head, questioning. 'You mean, you're considering those in the different *countries*?'

'Yes. She's off the scale – so why not? We're unable to measure it, so we can hypothesize beyond what we thought possible. Scotland has Billie Cathey. Switzerland has Luca Blasi, Algeria has Hamid Amara and—'

'Savita Das in India. I do know. I fucking work here too,' Haley finished for him. She pen-tapped her teeth again, thinking. 'You think that's possible?'

'We don't know it's not.' Louis sat even straighter in his chair, pleased to have come up with a hypothesis. Even if it wasn't correct, he'd now be seen as someone who gave answers. 'Also easy to check: you could just reach out to the medical teams at those sites and see if any of them had any interesting activity.'

'The fabulous five are also about two minutes from being completed, but interesting and worth a shot.' Haley gave a quick nod. She pointed at Louis first as she addressed the three other doctors in the room. 'See this, you lot? *This* is someone who answers a fucking question. *This* is someone with fucking ideas. Ideas that might be stupid, but better that than your offer of *dead doll eyes and dumb fuck silence*!' She pointed at Louis. 'Do as he suggests and email all the medical teams in the other sites. Be specific – I want it in writing and then I want you to call them too. Tell them that Cassidy is showing powerful DG, or something close to it, and it's possible it could be with Luca, Hamid, Savita or Billie. Or fucking all of them, who knows. She might be raising an army of the near-dead. Tell them to look at their brain activity in close – and I mean *fucking close* – detail, quote me on that. Say it. Repeat that now.'

'They are to look at the OmnieX patients' brain activity in close—'

'No!'

The doctor flinched as if she was going to hit him, but she just hit the desk with her pen instead. 'Again. *Fucking close*, dammit. I'm not just cussing to make my mama cry – you need to emphasize the importance of the imperative. Do it again!'

'They are to look at the OmnieX patients' brain activity in fucking close detail.'

'Yes. *Exactly*. If any of them even so much as look like they're thinking while taking a shit, I want to know the exact time it happened. We are still measuring the not-dux-dux, so we'll let them know the exact time it stops. In fact, ask them to send us a file on those subjects, and we'll also look at their actions here too. But not Bouchard – he's such a mega-cunt, he'll claim the ideas as his own. So, as Nathalie is in Scotland, go directly to her. Got that?'

He nodded and started to draft the email. With it sent, he then left the room to make the calls.

One of the team spoke up: 'Stats update: Cassidy's BP is one ninety over one ten and rising. We have hypertensive crisis and heart is tachy at one sixty – and rising. We are going to lose this patient.'

'Shit, shit – do we intervene?' Haley placed her hands over her eyes and for once wished Nathalie was here to make the decision. Anything she decided would be wrong. Lose the patient or intervene and affect the whatever-the-fuck-it-was. She relented. 'Give the sodium nitroprusside. We keep the patient.'

'We've been told she can complete now. That the pursuit of goal one is paramount.'

'I get it, but ...' She covered her face briefly. 'When we don't know who Cassidy is communicating with, I'd rather wait. For all I know, it could be the entire Chicago state area and tonight, I'm going out to my car to find a thousand zombified Illinoisans carrying pitchforks and sickles, waiting to cut my throat.'

She leaned her forehead on the cold observation glass, watching as the team administered the intravenous drugs. Cassidy had been with them a long time now; given what they'd done to her, Haley conceded a sickle across her own throat would be fair treatment.

SIXTY-TWO

Billie breathed, focused and determined to keep smiling as Jenna – *be Jenna, don't just inhabit her, convince others that Jenna is still in charge of Jenna* – when really, she wanted to cry. Surrounded by everyone drinking champagne, everyone who she thought had either suffered the same as her or was here to help her, but instead only seemed delighted that she was dying, felt suffocating and disturbing and painful.

She had been tricked – so terribly and completely tricked. From the moment her mother had shown her the details on the website, to the moment she stood here now as Jenna, everything had all been a carefully constructed lie.

Overwhelmed, she needed to escape. 'Loo break,' she muttered, and with a shaking Jenna hand put down the wine glass and stumbled out of the main door, realizing as Jenna, she knew where the loos were. In there, she locked herself in one cubicle, put down the toilet seat and sat Jenna down.

There was so much to take in – not least now that she could walk around as someone else. No one had noticed, no one had reacted. She'd simply gone into Jenna's mind and body with extraordinary ease. And now she knew what Jenna knew. Everything from where the toilets were, to her favourite primary school teacher, how she felt about mushrooms and who her first kiss was with. Billie understood it all. She was both of them – distinct and separate, yet together. She felt her real body lying on the bed and yet she was here in the loo, looking at Jenna's feet, wiggling her toes, marvelling at the size of them compared to her own. It was strange and weird and brilliant and scary.

There was too much to take in and—

tic; tic; tic; tic; tic; tic; a memory of a panicked robin for some reason reminded her there was not much time.

How much time? She needed to understand and decide what to do, but Jenna wasn't sure.

Billie covered Jenna's face with Jenna's hands. How could she betray her? How could she be so wrong? She was Jenna who *worked* for Arbor, who was *not* her friend, who *lied.* Lied like *they all had to her.* That was the secret she'd almost seen when she'd flocked them to save Jenna. She'd nearly seen it then – although there'd been no time as she thought Maddy was trying to kill her – but she saw it now.

Shock burned away to confusion. But now Jenna loved her. Jenna had also risked everything with the others to save her.

Then Stan. *Stan. Oh, how I had really started to like you.* She knew he'd only been playing a role – his feelings for her just a storyboard. Or was that true? Jenna thought there might be something more.

And what now? She needed to get out of Arbor, off Dorcha and home – fast. Her emotions churned: heartbreak;

disappointment; anger – even joy and gratitude that Stan, Ash, Jenna and Maddy had all broken their contracts to save her. That's why they were even in the room drinking champagne – they were there to watch over her while she came round. They even expected her to flock with them again.

It was too much to process now – she had to shut this down emotionally, deal with the now, deal with getting away safely, then she could think about all that she had learned.

It was painful to have been tricked. Painful to have been the only one. Jenna was being paid a lot of money, she discovered.

Gosh, that much?

Yes, that much.

All of them?

Yes, all of them. But they were giving that up – risking everything – for her now.

Billie shook her head, disappointed, shamed, angry. Betrayed. Confused. Grateful.

And there was no Tama either, she learned. Tama wasn't real – never had been. He'd been made up, a work of fiction, a script for Maddy to spout, not a person who'd stayed at Arbor. Never someone who had been their friend and left, only to flock again. More lies, designed to deceive. Designed to manage Billie by keeping her afraid, paranoid and locked in.

Then she understood that Arbor had poisoned her and Ella and Fin and Vena and Gez and Leo: allowed them to jump to their terrible deaths. Being flocked wasn't some strange accident of nature; they were actively involved in an illegal drugs trial, something called OmnieX. They were responsible for her friends' deaths, for saving her, and now she was being used to help them develop a weapon that they'd sell off to the highest bidder, giving them the power to bend everyone to their will. They had designed it all. All for money. Huge tides of unchecked, inestimable money – but still only money.

Billie couldn't breathe. The bright, bright fire engulfed Jenna's lungs, her blood, her intestines, but she felt it as if it were her own. As Jenna, she collapsed to the floor, unable to completely mute the guttural cry of anguish but desperately not daring to let the sound go.

She covered Jenna's mouth with both hands, forcing herself to breathe deeply and slowly. Eventually, she found herself feeling calmer. She needed to think – and to be clever. The key was to be able to get out alive. She looked at Jenna's wrist – she also had a black watch. Could it deliver an electric shock also, or was that just hers? There was no way of knowing, but Billie decided to remove both. She just needed scissors – which would be back in the kitchenette of the large room she'd left. She needed to move fast – in case someone realized that she'd flocked Jenna.

She stood up and let herself out, pausing briefly to catch herself in the mirror. Jenna looked back at her. She lifted her chin – no one would know. *Feel powerful, Billie*, she told herself, *because you are.*

Phase 6: adult

SIXTY-THREE

Dan was in pain. His chest hurt, his shoulders hurt, his hands hurt from the force of paddling the Firth. His chest seared like fire where he'd been shot, and though the jacket was bulky, he didn't dare remove it, imagining the Arbor speedboat filled with faceless security catching him and taking pot shots. He also dreaded running into the ferry and hoped for a boat or cruiser, but didn't see either. On his side, the current went his way and there was an onshore wind – without it, given the dragging weight of the second kayak behind him, Dan didn't think he would have made it this far back to shore.

But he powered on, Wemyss Bay getting closer and closer.

He kept paddling, towing Ted behind him. Ted would face justice – this thought was what had helped over the journey. Eventually, they got close enough to the small beach next to the ferry terminal. Dan clambered out, into the cold sea, exhausted. Knee deep, he untethered Ted's kayak and, with him still inside, dragged it up the stony beach. The other started to drift away, and it felt like a metaphor for losing Ethan.

Ted had bled through his neck binding. Dan opened one of the man's eyes and the fixed stare suggested he was dead.

The carpark was up on his left and already busy with vehicles. He could call out for help but he didn't want to scare anyone. His knees were covered in Ethan's blood and it was smeared over his hands and up his arms. He took out his phone and rang 999 again. This time he didn't even bother giving his name. 'I need an ambulance and police to the beach in Wemyss Bay, adjacent to the ferry pier and carpark. I have a dead body. I'm injured and unarmed, but there is a gun in a kayak on the beach. It is a murder weapon. When you arrive, I will report one murder …' he thought of Jo's unanswered phone and Billie's absence on the lawn, then added: 'and two suspected murders. I have hurt no one – I am a survivor of the Arbor Institute.' Then he had the satisfaction of hanging up on them. 'Bet you don't drop that call,' he muttered, before collapsing onto the beach. He lay on his back and waited for the police. He stared at the sky; a gull soared low overhead, perhaps curious. To see it lift on the wind made him cry again.

It made him cry because it was safe and free.

SIXTY-FOUR

Billie, as Jenna, returned to the party. Staying focused, she went to the kitchen and knew, from Jenna's memories, where the scissors were kept. She found them in the drawer, slid them up her sleeve and then nipped back out to the loos. If she was seen, she would have to deal with that. The priority had to be to protect herself, but it was helpful to know that she was safe as Jenna. But when she tried to cut the strap, it was clear that it had some integral strength that meant it couldn't be cut through. She needed to think again.

She needed something else – glass, rubber, plastic – something she could slide under the watch to block any electric current. Jenna had seen rubber mats in the lab, used to rest beakers and flasks on, to prevent slippage. That material would be perfect but testing the looseness of Jenna's strap, whilst she saw she could fit it under this watch, Billie knew that her own watch was too tight. There would be no way she could angle anything other than something wafer-thin between the watch and her skin. It had always bothered her how tight her watch was – and of course now she understood why: to make sure the shock could be conducted.

Come on, Billie, *think*. Then it came to her: an image of a falling black Arbor door card, and she knew that was perfect. She knew it was in her bedside drawer. But how to get it? Did Jenna have access to her room? Just like thinking through something in her own brain, Billie could think a question and if Jenna knew the answer, then she would understand it. Jenna did not have security clearance to her room. Who did? All medical staff – all nurses, all doctors. So who to flock and send? It would be easier to flock everyone in the room, but there were about thirty people, and Billie wasn't sure she could do it. If she tried and failed, she would be in danger – she had to protect herself from another shock first, before trying anything big.

As Jenna, she returned to the laboratory. She saw the nurse who insisted she was Lia but Billie was convinced was Callie. Jenna knew she was Callie. She had lied, just as she'd thought. Yes, she would flock *her*.

She focused on her as she laughed and joked with Richard. The strange tugging sensation, the breaking of a bubble wall, the sickness, and then she was there in Callie.

Billie kept Callie's smiled fixed as she adjusted. She could see Richard had a piece of spinach in his teeth that Callie had never intended telling him about. His breath stank and he was clearly very pleased, mid-conversation about some story that he found really amusing. Billie was glad she could just pause and maintain Jenna as well. She found she could almost pull out of Jenna's mind and allow Jenna to be Jenna. She debated letting her go, but she knew she needed the practice of holding more than one person – if she were to get off Dorcha alive.

Callie was vile – Billie felt amazed that anyone could be

so different. Callie was a mean, materialistic psychopath all wrapped up in the misdirection of pretty packaging. Even being in her head felt unpleasant – like having a bitter bad taste in one's mouth.

She'd called herself Lia to cover the lie about ... her mother. So that was a lie too – they didn't want her mum to see the island ... because if they had they would have killed her. Killed her! Billie believed it – they had killed her friends and would have been willing to kill her mother too. And there was something else there ... another memory linked to killing her mother. Then she found it – her, Callie, in bed, with Ted. And Ted telling her what he had done that day. She heard Ted telling her about killing her mum. Laughing about how he tricked her and left her in a ditch. And Callie had just yawned and asked him to top up her wine.

White, white, *white* anger boiled. There was sadness there too – great grief she knew would roll over her as a tsunami later – but for now, to feel Callie's uninterested emotions, to hear Callie's memory of Ted's voice with his coldness at shooting her lovely mum, meant for now she felt only rage and fury.

Billie wanted to cry – yell out – *something*. But she reminded herself she needed to move fast. Her lovely mother would not want her to crumble now. Her mum would not want her grief for her to make Billie vulnerable. Now she had to take action. She would have to – as painful and impossible as it was – take action later.

Forcing herself to refocus, she felt sick. Pain twisted in her sternum. She inhaled and finding strength from somewhere, she understood she had three in the flock now – herself, Jenna and Callie. No – *wait* – there were more – not actively open, but she knew she had connected, duxed, with other people ... Stefana? No – Stefana was gone. Dead? Callie and Jenna didn't know but it felt like that to Billie, felt like she had died. Before it had felt as if there was a familiarity between them, like a shared memory, but now it felt not just gone, but non-existent. Cold. The link she felt now was with three others not here. No ... they were not actively flocking with her now, but it was more like strings between them, some lines of connection, like what remains when you no longer see someone you love. But also not that – something stronger, more tangible, like an umbilical cord of mental connection.

She allowed herself to reach out to flock again and felt the bubble wall, the sickness, the tugging sensation and then, to her surprise, she found herself back on Warwick ward, looking out through the eyes of Marjorie Briggs, Raymond Tate and Elsie Burham. She instantly ingested their names as well as the names of their children, their fears, their faiths ... She knew so much about them yet to her they were strangers. Billie didn't know why she had flocked with them, but understood she had at one stage, and she hadn't left them properly. She wondered if she could use them in some way to help – their thinking was unclear ... but Elsie was drawing. She made her write *Billie needs help at Arbor* and give the paper to a nurse. She hoped that would be enough. She doubted that elderly psychiatric patients could do much to help her, and it was too distracting, too dangerous to be there when she needed to be here, so she let them go, closed those windows in her mind. She felt she could do that cleanly – she felt it work.

And they went. The connection broken.

Feeling clearer, she said as Callie to Richard, 'Got to go run an errand. Be back in a mo,' and left before he could ask.

She knew how to get to her room from the lab, because Callie knew. Moving quickly, in case anyone saw her, she took the lift up a level, to the bedroom area, and then along the corridor. She held Callie's watch against the door pad and the door to her room opened. Straightaway, she found in her bedside cabinet the Arbor door keycard she'd been given on her arrival by Jenna. She tucked it in Callie's pocket and was back out and back down to the party in the lab in under five minutes.

Then Billie enacted the next stage of her plan. She got Jenna to stand on a chair, bang a spoon against a bottle and start a long congratulations-to-everyone speech. Everyone turned to look and joined in with noisy appreciation. It was surprisingly easy to allow Jenna to be Jenna and carry out the instruction, while getting Callie to go over to her own body lying in bed and insert the card she'd snapped in two in the lift, pushing one piece under the watch, then forcing another in behind it, to protect her wrist. She did it. Now Billie was safe and protected from another shock. Now she was free to be Billie, she knew the next bit might not be possible. If she were to leave the island without being shot or restrained, she needed to be able to hold as many as

– Help me –

Who *was* that? It was as if everything else had been quieted for this voice. It was the Frightened Woman again. But it was clearer now. She had an American voice. Her name was Cassidy.

Billie felt cold. Hot. Cold. And then heard it again. She took a breath and allowed herself to listen. To relax. To receive. This was someone like her – she let herself be . . .

> white, clinical surfaces. A small room. Throat hurts. Can't speak. I'm Cassidy. I am trapped in Arbor. Help me.
> bound to a hospital bed – restraints round my body. Head, against the pillow, shaved. Skull hurts – it's been cut. I'm in the lab in Arbor. Come and find me, Billie.
> They've fitted an implant in my brain which stops me flocking with others – I can't reach any others, only you. They've limited me – I can reach only you. Reach only you. Only you. You.
> Help me.

And then she was gone and Billie was back. Billie knew Cassidy wasn't in this Arbor. Jenna and Callie both knew there were other OmnieX test subjects in different labs. Cassidy was in America. How little they both had cared for what NorGline was doing to people in the pursuit of money.

She needed to get out fast. She needed to get everyone into the flock so they couldn't stop her. Not knowing if it was possible, but knowing that it needed to be done if she were to be able to get away from Dorcha without being restrained or shot, she had to try.

Once I'm free, I'll help you, Cassidy, she thought, hoping she heard.

As Callie, she looked at the assembled group. She decided to start with Ash, Stan and Maddy, because she figured she'd done that before and it might be easier. She started with Stan, because – even though she hated herself for caring – she wanted to know if he cared about her or if it had all been a storyboarded lie.

The bubble wall: tugging; sickness; and she was there as Stan, looking up at Jenna. She found he did care – more than she'd understood; found his shame and his desire to help her even at the expense of himself. In him, she found love. Not the talk of going to California with her – that had all been a lie – but later, much later. And unlike with the others, his desire to help her had started before she'd flocked them – when he caught her outside her room after she'd been swimming, he'd been trying to warn her of the plan about to happen. He'd been willing to risk his life to help her – he had secretly copied the speedboat key on the day he said he'd get her stamps and she stayed by the pool. He'd planned on taking the speedboat and trying to escape with her. Hoping to save her from the trick that was about to happen, he'd been desperate to meet her in the woods – but instead Philippe turned up at her room and delivered her to the lab. But Stan had wanted to try and in that kindness, she felt relieved, comforted, grateful. In him, she'd had a real friend.

In Ash and Maddy, she found much the same. They had pretended to be her friends, lied to her for months, but in the end had discovered real comradeship – and again, she was surprised to find, love.

She'd been so invested in how they really felt about her, she didn't notice how easy it was to hold them all. Like the villagers in Minecraft, she could move them around, but if she needed to, it was like leaving them on idle mode, where they passively continued with what they wanted to do. Bo had wandered over to the group, for example, and picked up a glass of wine. It was like his free will was still active, still running, but easily overridable. It made it incredibly easy.

Billie, like rounding up sheep and putting them in a pen, collected each member of staff, one by one. She didn't bother examining them – they were all the same. Materialistic to the point of sociopathy.

Within minutes, she had them all. It had been so effortless!

Then, the door opened and Philippe strode in.

As she sat up in bed, Philippe looked over with wide-eyed horror and reached for his watch. Within a second, Philippe started pressing his watch.

He's trying to electrocute me, she thought.

'Billie!' he said, pointing at her. 'Richard, Bo, get her.'

Billie swung her legs out of bed.

Still pressing his watch, he screamed: 'Don't just sit there – she's awake! Adjust the syringe driver now!' Then, when they didn't move, 'This is not a party!'

Billie slid out of bed, her bare feet touched the floor. The feeling of solidity was what she needed. She thought again of her mother. And with it, she retrieved another memory from Callie – Ted had told her that when he produced the gun, he had thought: *she knows she's going to die.* And he almost admired her – admired her for figuring it out and not running. 'So many run, even when they know there's no point. I don't get it.'

The knowledge made Billie sway and she had to reach out to the bed to steady herself. But seeing Philippe gave her the strength she needed.

Philippe reached for his watch and tried again, muttering, 'This is not fucking working.'

'Billie knows you killed her mum,' said Callie to Philippe. 'Ted fired the gun.'

Philippe, still fiddling with his watch, looked up at Callie. 'How did you—'

'She found out from me,' Callie said.

Then everyone in the room spoke in unison: 'And Billie told us.'

Philippe's jaw dropped. He looked back at everybody. Then, he looked at Billie. 'Have you flocked them all?' Philippe asked.

'Yes,' everyone said together. 'And you're next.'

Philippe scrabbled back in alarm, turning and running towards the door.

But then Billie just reached out and took him. Then she was in his head and it felt revolting. This was the man who didn't care who he hurt. He was vile. Billie marvelled at the diversity of the human. A dog was a dog really, just as a cat was a cat. Yes, there was variance, but in the gap between one dog and another, not much. Not like this. He smiled like a human, talked like one, but there was no recognizable humanity in this man's mind. There was no shared humanity between them. That in itself was shocking: she'd eaten with Philippe, joked with him, argued with him, laughed with him, been directed by him, helped by him – and all the time, a crocodile smile was hiding a rotten heart.

What – who – she really needed now, was Nathalie.

Philippe took out his walkie-talkie. 'Nathalie, you really need to come to the study lab,' said Billie through Philippe's mouth. 'It's amazing, you'll want to see this – but hurry.'

Then they all waited, like guests at a surprise party, eyes riveted to the door, until the star turned up.

Wanting to greet her properly, Billie forced herself to get up, feeling shaky from grief, the drugs in her system, but combated by adrenaline and cortisol. But she let the anger for her mother fuel her. And also the anger for all the lies – for the sheer, blatant, cold greed. And for Ella and Fin and Vena and Gez and Leo. She found a clean glass, tipped in a couple of inches of champagne, and stepped neatly behind some nurses. As if they were penguins wanting to keep her warm, she shuffled them to close the gap in front of her, to obscure her from sight.

Then, within minutes, Nathalie came into the lab. She looked furious. 'Thank you Philippe, I was just on my way down. I've been on a call to Chicago. They've been emailing you, Richard and Bo, to alert you to changes in Cassidy. They say they've had no response from either of you, and now I can see why.'

'We wanted you here, to make a toast,' Philippe said, smiling just as Billie made him.

'Have you heard me, Philippe? We've got a massive situation in Chicago.'

'Yes! And we are here to celebrate! Raise your glasses, everyone!'

Nathalie pinked, forked fingers through messy loose curls, her jaw set. 'Have you lost your mind? Are you all pissed?'

'We are raising our glasses in celebration.'

'Celebrating *what*?' Nathalie blanched.

Billie, stepping out of the crowd, was glad to see Nathalie's eyes widen in terror at the sight of her. 'To justice, Nathalie.'

'To justice!' said everyone in unison.

'Are you ...' Nathalie cast around. 'Are you all ... '

'Yes,' said everyone.

'I've been waiting for you,' said Billie.

'Welcome!' said Philippe, Callie, Bo, Richard, Stan – everyone, smiling and speaking in perfect unison, glasses raised high: 'To the flock.'

And then Billie took Nathalie too.

SIXTY-FIVE

In the end, Veer had decided on Gatwick Airport police station. It wasn't his nearest police station, but he figured they would be the most likely to believe him given they'd dealt with the deaths at the platform. He couldn't call it suicide, not now, and he told them that as he went in and presented himself at the front desk, the old-fashioned way, and said he wanted to report a series of crimes.

He'd talked it over with Prisha, finally telling her everything. She hadn't believed him, even when he'd shown her the note that Elsie had written: *Billie needs help at Arbor.*

'And the nurse then gave this to you?' Prisha asked.

'Yes. She remembered Billie and passed it on to me. She hadn't understood it, but she was wise enough to share it with me. And look at this.' Then he'd shown her the second, saved footage of the activity of Elsie and co on the ward at night.

'Legally, I don't think you should be showing me this,' she'd said as he'd pressed play. But by the end of it, she insisted he go to the police and had started to pack his lunch.

'Stay there until they do something – insist on it. Make yourself a nuisance, Veer,' she'd said, handing him two rounds of cheese sandwiches, a flask of tea and an apple. She'd also made him take an extra sweater – 'Because it'll take so long. They won't believe you, then you'll have to work hard to *make* them believe you, then they'll have to fact-check everything, which will take time, and then – and *only then* – they *might* believe you. And if you get that far, they'll make you say it all again.'

She was right of course. He now sat on a plastic chair in an interview room; he'd eaten the sandwiches an hour ago. The tea had been drunk two hours ago. Not cold but needing the warmth, he'd even put on his extra jumper.

But now they had listened to him – not immediately, he'd had to be determined, but it helped being an NHS psychiatrist. It'd helped that the constable had passed him on to the sergeant who had been on duty the night the students stepped off the platform. It'd helped that there were doubts about the behaviour of the students yet to be publicly expressed in the inquest booked for February.

In the end, although he'd come to report his full concerns, he didn't want to be kicked out. He decided to stick to the simple facts.

He'd come because he was desperately worried about Ethan and Dan. He'd wanted to go with them, to keep an eye on them as much as anything – but they'd dismissed him. Probably because he was old.

And he had such a bad feeling. Such a terrible feeling.

He'd woken in the night out of dreams he couldn't remember of blood and feathers, and with a surety that Jo Cathey was dead. He'd rung Dan, but Dan hadn't answered, instead messaging back saying that he couldn't talk right now. He was either in danger or didn't want to be told to turn home.

Veer decided that perhaps he had to balance what he knew and what he thought he knew. He didn't know what Billie could and couldn't do – and didn't even know her as a person, which would have helped to understand the choices that she might make. He did know that everyone who went to Arbor stopped being in touch once they got there.

He took his handkerchief out and dabbed his eyes; he did it quickly, he didn't want the sergeant to come in and think he was crying. It was just the older he got, the more his eyes watered.

The door opened and the sergeant came in with someone he hadn't yet met.

'Okay, Dr Singh, if you're still willing,' he said, introducing himself and a detective colleague, 'then we'd be grateful if you could give a statement. There's been some reported activity up in the area you've been talking about. We'll hear what you know and then we'll take it from there.'

Phase 7: flocked

SIXTY-SIX

Cassidy—

Yes ...

I'm coming to save you—

Thank you. Don't be long – I think I'm dying. There's others too – now. They did it to other people. Fitted something in my brain so I can't reach anyone – but you, I could get you because you're different. You've got dux too, but no brain implant.

Billie nodded. She knew. Because she was last, they never planned on keeping her alive – not like the others, kept alive for the just-in-case. So no blocking plate for her.

Now she had Nathalie too, she knew everything. She would take the plane back to America, and take the Arbor labs. Save Cassidy. Then she would take the plane to the other Arbor locations and seek out justice to those who deserved it. She couldn't see the other duxes yet, but with Cassidy, she could sense them, like figures stepping out of the mist.

They need your help.

Yes, I know where they are. I will help them. Hold on. We won't be long now, and I'm bringing help—

Billie smiled as she, Nathalie and Philippe stood on the lawn. Inside Arbor, they were wrapping up the institute. As soon as Nathalie, Philippe and Billie were in the air, Stan agreed that he would call the police. Until then, there would be a lot of sitting on the floor for everyone. Stan was in charge. He'd taken her to one side and placed his hand against her cheek. 'For the record,' he'd said, 'in another time and place, we would have done better, because I would be better. I wish I could go back.'

'I know you wanted to save me.'

He'd pressed his lips together. 'I've been a bad person. I'm sorry.' Then, because she was still in his head, he only had to think it: *and baby, you do kiss by the book.*

And she thought back: *back at you, Romeo.*

She thought again of them all: Stan, Ash, Jenna and Maddy. She forgave them. She'd give them the opportunity to run, but they all agreed they wanted to do the right thing. For you Billie. We love you Billie.

As for the medical staff, they would face justice. All bright, talented people who'd been tempted by the shiny dollar. Really, their fate was no better than hers – but they didn't know the true extent of Nathalie's plans; not even Philippe knew. But she knew it now; now she knew everything. She almost pitied them, but she'd saved them – better to go to prison than die.

Nathalie and Philippe could face American justice – but first she would use them to save those who needed saving.

She climbed up into the helicopter after Philippe and

Nathalie. Nathalie gave the pilot instructions to return to the jet.

'An extra unscheduled trip so soon?' he asked, visibly surprised.

Billie made Nathalie smile and say: 'No rest for the wicked.'

Billie turned back to take one last look at the institute. The sparrowhawk, pigeons, sparrows and magpies had gathered again, perhaps to watch her leave. She thought of Firkin and her father, the image of them suddenly so clear. Then for reasons she didn't fully understand, she murmured, 'I'm safe now.'

And then as if in answer, in one unified, single co-ordinated movement, the flock took off, breaking apart in different directions, no longer united, leaving just the sparrowhawk and its amber eye to watch over Arbor.

EPILOGUE

Two weeks after his visit to the police station, Veer turned on the TV in the kitchen, selecting his favourite gardening programme, before he went out into the hall to collect the Sunday papers. He wouldn't get a delivery soon; the newsagent said he was stopping the paper rounds. Apparently, not enough people wanted their papers delivered, so it was no longer financially viable. Everything was changing, Veer thought, and it seemed to him it was never, ever, for the better.

He carried them through, reading glasses on, slippers shuffling against the carpet. 'Tea, Prisha?' he called up the stairs as he passed. He didn't hear an answer, but she'd just got in the shower. He put a teabag in her favourite mug. She'd be a while yet, washing and drying her hair. She valued taking her time now, she said, but maybe they both just valued what they had now. She was getting better. She'd been put onto the new, much hoped for, medicine – Tarquilat – and they were having an amazing effect. The doctor had told them at the last check-up, but she'd known before then, she was better. He got the tablet box out of the cupboard and set it next to her mug.

Then he saw the name in the top right of the packet. He'd been distracted recently, hadn't had his eyes open. But they were open now. Prisha's new medicine was made by NorGline. He sighed, cross with himself for not noticing. But what would he have done if he did? They still wanted the medicine – needed it. They were desperate for it. But the fact it was made by NorGline felt profound. Everyone demanded advances: but what advances were the right ones? And how much did everyone really understand about the reality of testing and production?

He stared at the tablet box feeling old again. He felt like he understood a little about something he didn't want to understand.

Then, his attention was caught by the TV. The gardening programme had disappeared, replaced by a newsreader. A red banner ran the newsfeed message along the bottom of the screen:

Breaking News: we have halted all programming to report on the latest world developments.

He put her tablets down, already forgotten. It was the look on the familiar TV presenter's face – one of shock, awe and something else he couldn't quite place.

Unblinking, he watched the images and listened to the reports from America.

He shook his head a little, trying to take it in, trying to make sense of what the presenter was saying. But it was impossible. He rubbed his face. It was unthinkable. Unattainable.

Disbelief. That's what the newsreader's expression said, and he felt the same now.

'Prisha?' he called out, prompted by duty but restrained from calling a second time as he wanted to hear every word.

Without taking his eyes off the screen, his hand flapped around like a bird's broken wing trying to locate the remote control. He needed to turn it up.

He stood silently, watching the streams of army personnel attend a docked submarine, before the coverage switched to another submarine at another dock, then another at another. The newscaster discussed the different American submarines, each with Trident nuclear capability. Then ten minutes in, another banner:

Further breaking news. India is joining America in disarming its nuclear weapons.

The images were shaky, shot from above. But it was clear that this was a huge airfield with large warehouses teeming with army activity.

'It's spreading,' he murmured to himself, shaking his head, not believing it. 'She's spreading or ... the idea is, or ... Prisha! *Prisha!*' Come and see this! Billie's okay! She must be – she's done it!' He threw back his head and laughed and laughed and laughed.

And then he cried. Standing in his slippers, his shoulders heaving, he cried so hard from the wonder and relief and the surprise of it all, he had to remove his glasses before they slid off.

He grabbed his phone and texted Dan, asking him to call. They spoke often. The police had arrested Dan on the beach, in what sounded like a dramatic moment with the police gun squad. Because Dan wasn't there, it wasn't clear how Dorcha had been taken, but an officer had told Dan, who had told Veer, that it had been even more dramatic with police boats and a helicopter. He'd been in a cell but Veer's police report and a call from the island had all almost coincided and Dan had been de-arrested. As soon as he got back from Scotland, they met with Nick. Veer had wept to learn about Ethan's murder. Every night now, he'd gripped Prisha even closer.

Without taking his gaze from the news, he drew up a kitchen chair right in front of the television, so he could watch the world events unfold. It occurred to him that it might not stop with this – and he imagined briefly, deviously, what other possibilities might happen.

Finally, he could hear his wife, voice cross from his noise and then her feet on the stair.

Breaking news: the UK has joined America and India in its immediate and complete nuclear disarmament.

He dabbed his face with his handkerchief: oh, how he'd been wrong. So wonderfully and incredibly wrong. 'You'd lost your hope, Veer,' he told himself, laughing again and dabbing his eyes. But he could see now.

Change was coming.

ACKNOWLEDGEMENTS

I have been fortunate that this is the fourth time I've been published, and before reading this, a moment with a cup of tea saw me reading back through my previous acknowledgements. What struck me is the people I owed then, I still do now. Writing is a fearful thing – so many questions, so many unknown answers – and it has been the same band of people who have carried me on the sometimes bumpy road of writing. Always a joint first is the wonderful team of my agent Stephanie Glencross and my editor Katherine Armstrong. They are both so many things: wise, experienced and kind. Writers need the company of these talents, none more so than me. Stephanie: thank you, thank you, thank you. Katherine: thank you, thank you, thank you. A special thank you to the rest of wonderful team at Simon & Schuster: Louise Davies for all her patience and perception; Jessica Barratt for support; Paul Gooney for the beautiful cover; John Sugar; Olivia Allen, Nicholas Hayne, Rich Hawton, Maddie Allan and the sales teams; Alice Twomey and the audio team; Karin Seifried and the production team. Thanks to Susan Opie and Gabby Nemeth

ACKNOWLEDGEMENTS

for insightful editorial; also to Camille Burns and the wonderful team at DHA.

In the time I've been published, I've worked at the same school teaching English. To be in a building with over a thousand teenagers is the perfect counterpoint to the introversion that is writing. I would like to acknowledge all the lovely people I work with. To name them would be too lengthy, but teachers are truly amongst the best people I know.

My husband, Bradley – I so, and perhaps increasingly so, appreciate your support. My children, Cooper and Casper, together with my husband the three suns in my world. My mother: enduring light. Grateful thanks to my sister, Juliet Hunter, and Jo Furniss for early reads and illuminating feedback. Mara and Jack for lightbulb moments. Warmth from wonderful friends: Dorrie, Roxy, Kate, Hannah, Hannah, Emma, Claire, Sanna, James, Tanya, Lucy and Lexi. A glowing literal thank you to God – opportunity is everything. x

The SISTER HOOD

Vox meets *The Handmaid's Tale* in this feminist reimagining of *1984*

In Oceania, whoever you are, Big Brother is always watching you and trust is a luxury that no one has. Julia is the seemingly perfect example of what women in Oceania should be: dutiful, useful, subservient, meek. But Julia hides a secret. A secret that would lead to her death if it is discovered.

For Julia is part of the underground movement called The Sisterhood, whose main goal is to find members of The Brotherhood, the anti-Party vigilante group, and help them to overthrow Big Brother. Only then can everyone be truly free.

'Frightening and timely ... the book everyone should read this year' Christina Dalcher

AVAILABLE IN PAPERBACK, EBOOK AND AUDIO

SIMON & SCHUSTER